A PLUME BOOK

MISS ME WHEN I'M GONE

PHILIP STEPHENS's poetry collection, *The Determined Days*, was a finalist for the PEN Center USA West Literary Award. His work has appeared in *The Oxford American*, *Southwest Review*, and *Bomb*, among other publications, as well as in *Da Capo Best Music Writing 2004*. He lives with his wife and sons in Kansas City, Missouri.

"Lost and living by their wits, Philip Stephens's wise and foolish people drift along the hardscrabble edges of America, some trying to escape the past, some to reclaim it. *Miss Me When I'm Gone* mixes the barbed language of Denis Johnson with the eternal verities of roots music. This is a rich and beautiful debut."

—Stewart O'Nan

"Philip Stephens is an uncommon writer: Lyrical, frank, gothic by turns, his prose draws us into uncharted worlds and minds. He transforms small-town Missouri into a mythical landscape peopled by lonely misfits of Faulknerian proportions. *Miss Me When I'm Gone* is a novel you will never forget."

—Claire Messud

"*Miss Me When I'm Gone* is a lavishly written, vividly imagined, and wholly compelling work of fiction. Philip Stephens has an unfailing ear for the rhythms (and subtle treacheries) of human speech, which gives this book its unusual immediacy and power, as if the reader is eavesdropping on the life-or-death conversations of travelers on a train. I was spellbound. Often, in fact, I was in awe."

Acclaim for *The Determined Days: Poems*

"Stephens has a realist fiction writer's flair for scene, speech, and character, and the incidents in his poems are as all-too-humanly true as those in a good John O'Hara short story . . . An excellent first collection."

—*Booklist*

"Read as a whole—as they should be—the cumulative effect of this truly accomplished collection is powerful, disturbing, and authoritative. I am filled with admiration for Mr. Stephens's work."

—Anthony Hecht

"A poet for the people, an accessible writer whose work fuses the beauty of Robert Frost with the conviction of Walt Whitman."

—*Kansas City Star*

Miss Me
When I'm Gone

Philip Stephens

ⓟ
A PLUME BOOK

PLUME
Published by Penguin Group

Penguin Group (USA) Inc., 375 Hudson Street, New York, New York 10014, U.S.A •
Penguin Group (Canada), 90 Eglinton Avenue East, Suite 700, Toronto, Ontario, Canada
M4P 2Y3 (a division of Pearson Penguin Canada Inc.) • Penguin Books Ltd., 80 Strand,
London WC2R 0RL, England • Penguin Ireland, 25 St. Stephen's Green, Dublin 2, Ireland
(a division of Penguin Books Ltd.) • Penguin Group (Australia), 250 Camberwell Road,
Camberwell, Victoria 3124, Australia (a division of Pearson Australia Group Pty. Ltd.) •
Penguin Books India Pvt. Ltd., 11 Community Centre, Panchsheel Park, New Delhi – 110 017,
India • Penguin Books (NZ), 67 Apollo Drive, Rosedale, North Shore 0632, New Zealand
(a division of Pearson New Zealand Ltd.) • Penguin Books (South Africa) (Pty.) Ltd.,
24 Sturdee Avenue, Rosebank, Johannesburg 2196, South Africa

Penguin Books Ltd., Registered Offices: 80 Strand, London WC2R 0RL, England

First published by Plume, a member of Penguin Group (USA) Inc.

First Printing, February 2011

10   9   8   7   6   5   4   3   2   1

Ⓟ REGISTERED TRADEMARK—MARCA REGISTRADA

LIBRARY OF CONGRESS CATALOGING-IN-PUBLICATION DATA

Stephens, Philip, 1966-
   Miss me when I'm gone / Philip Stephens.
      p.   cm.
   "A Plume book."
   ISBN 978-0-452-29678-7
   1. Folk singers—Fiction.   2. Missouri—Fiction.   3. Domestic fiction.   I. Title.
   PS3569.T4518M57   2011
   811'.6—dc22   2010027739

Printed in the United States of America
Set in Granjon

For My Travelers:
Jennie Lynn Hanna
Walker Lee Stephens
Garrett Lewis Stephens

In Memory:
James Wesley Cunningham, 1874–1967
Hilgar Lee Cunningham, 1906–1987
James Edward "Bud" Garrett, 1913–1981

Only what is entirely lost demands to be endlessly named:
There is a mania to call the lost thing until it returns.

—Günter Grass

For there is hope of a tree, if it be cut down, that it will
sprout again, and that the tender branch thereof will not
cease. Though the root thereof wax old in the earth, and
the stock thereof die in the ground; Yet through the scent
of water it will bud, and bring forth boughs like a plant.

—Job 14:7–9

Sometimes parts of an old tune will suddenly come back
to you many years after you heard it played. In those
circumstances, you have no choice but to make up your
own name.

—Art Galbraith, Missouri fiddler

Miss Me When I'm Gone

The hog-eyed man returned to her. He arrived months after Ruth Harper tried to drag a bale of straw to her garden, but the straw was rain soaked, the twine rotten, and when she stopped to catch her breath, what she took to be a passing cloud threw a shadow at her feet, and the day went black.

At dusk she came to—thirsty, sunburnt—and got to her feet. Her head throbbed. Beyond the clothesline, redbuds had broken into blossom. "'For the fashion of this world,'" she said, "'passeth away,'" a sentiment her late husband had held from the pulpit but one Ruth now twisted into a curse. She kicked twice at the bale and limped to the house. Headaches crippled her after that, but her senses grew so acute that by the time petals fled from dogwoods along the bluff, she heard on the wind the voices of the dead in Dooley Cemetery. They said they knew her long-suppressed desires, which Ruth admitted she herself could not recall. Grape leaves hissed on the arbors north of the house, vines her husband had planted to try to make his fortune, selling communion grape juice to dry denominations— Nazarene, Holy Roller, and Baptist. Come the first humid days of summer, samaras broke from silver-maple branches and skittered across the road, and she asked the trees *why*. They said the winged seeds were scared for her life on the edge of a bluff overlooking a river whose current had been stifled for as long as they could remember. Ruth drew the shades in the back room and took to bed.

When at last the Dog Star rose before dawn, the hog-eyed man reappeared. Jorge, her hired hand, set two tomatoes from the garden on the kitchen counter, but when she turned to thank him, he was gone, and the hog-eyed man stood outside the wire gate facing the woods at the east edge of the yard. At first she took him for her youngest, Cyrus, returned from California. On the cabinet door beside the icebox, she'd taped a newspaper review of Cyrus's only album, which had arrived at her doorstep one day via book-rate mail, and beside it a Polaroid of him and Saro together on a rack-lit stage. Cyrus had tucked the fiddle to his chin, the bow a blur. Saro had lifted the guitar to the side as if tugging it from a stranger. An Electro-Voice microphone rose between them, and they leaned toward it, so close together it looked as though one had come to still waters to drink, the other no more than a reflection destined to vanish.

But the man outside wore a brown wool suit, matching derby, and mourning-dove-colored spats. His cordovan St. Louis flats were run over at the heels. A drummer, maybe, peddling Bibles or pots or vacuum cleaners with mail-order attachments. The days of drummers were long past, though, and the back of his neck was pink, his shoulders thick enough to haul away cotton bales with ease.

Ruth knew him well. He'd first come years ago, but she had spurned him, so he turned to her daughter. As Ruth recalled, he threw Saro from the bluff. More than sixty feet through limbs and off ledges to the shore of that dammed-up river she fell, and the hog-eyed man, along with the other hog-eyed men hidden behind black walnut and oak, had snickered.

Ruth stepped over the dozing dogs on the porch and down the

walk until she was within arm's reach of him. His flats were scuffed. Old-gold and royal blue thread had frayed at his jacket cuffs, and the fabric at the elbows was shiny. "What do you want with me?" she said.

With his cleft hand he tipped his derby. His face was covered with coarse hairs; an outcropping of skull shaded his blood-black eyes. He wiggled his snout and commenced a jig, singing:

> *Sally's in the garden, siftin', siftin',*
> *Sally's in the garden, siftin' sand.*
> *Sally's in the garden, siftin', siftin',*
> *Sally's upstairs with a hog-eyed man.*

"You'll not have me," Ruth said.

The hog-eyed man sighed. "Nothing's more tiresome than a re-luctant woman."

"I ain't reluctant. I refuse you."

"I see," he said. "But remember? If you refuse me, Ruth, you refuse music. And if you refuse music, then you refuse the one last grace that, for now, might save you from your fate."

"Spare me," Ruth said.

"Precisely my point."

"I know what you're about."

"Is that so. Perhaps we might discuss my nature over a glass of ice tea, then."

"That'll be the day."

"That'll be the day," he mimicked. "Shall I finish that quaint little bromide for you, or just let it hang in the air between us?"

He plucked a honeysuckle blossom from the fence, popped it into his mouth, and swallowed. "So be it," he said, staring Ruth back up the walk and into the house, where she locked the door.

That day, as he grazed the honeysuckle vines clean, she raised the window shades and carted bedding to the pastry table in the middle of her kitchen; there, from its tin top, she kept her vigil.

❧

Fall came and Indian summer followed, but the hog-eyed man stayed put at the gate until, one night, as rain thrummed on the roof, he toed the gravel as if to demarcate a boundary, then plucked his watch from his vest pocket and pinched it by the chain, catching what light was cast from the porch.

Ruth lay curled on the pastry table, watching. "Go on," she said. The gravel crunched as he shifted his weight. More and more hog-eyed men were crashing through the tall grass. She could not keep them back, and she could not keep on keeping watch.

Thumbtacked beneath the rotary phone on the wall was her elder son's realty card, though what good would Isaac's office number, or his mobile, as he called it, do her now? She pulled free the Polaroid of Cyrus and Saro—evidence of a reality she might have known—and carried it down the hall to the bathroom. They had given her the photo for Mother's Day, along with a Panasonic tape deck and a cassette recording of that performance passed to them by a university musicologist attempting a study of Ozark song. Ruth had hidden the photograph and player from Ott in the back of her stocking drawer, but after he was dead, she listened to the songs so often that the coating of rust on the tape began to shed, the blended voices of her youngest children distorting until one day the tape snapped and fed itself into the machine.

The rain let up. Clouds began to break. "I'll take care of you," she said to the darkness. From the medicine cabinet she took down prescriptions doctors had given her for years and screwed open the bottles, lining them on the edge of the sink. Behind her, the shower curtain stirred, plastic rings clicking on the rod. The shade of the hog-eyed man appeared in the cabinet mirror. He stepped over the lip of the tub and pressed his face to hers, resting one hand on her shoulder, the other on her hip. He smelled of mildew and fallen leaves. His blood-black eyes reflected what moonlight filtered through the window. He grinned, and his gums shone.

"Perhaps now it's time to make us some tea," he said.

"All I've Got Is Done and Gone"

Cyrus Harper blamed unseasonable rain and rough winds for his foul disposition, his drinking binge, and his incessant ache for a girl, though his attitudes and appetites were pretty much the same as on any other evening. He was not in one of the North Beach bars where he sang regularly, however, but was seated at a new club south of Market Street in a city he had come to deplore in spite of its charming triumvirate of streetcars, streetpeople, and fog.

He could have placed blame elsewhere: three years without a new song; no paying work as a heavy equipment operator in the East Bay; news yesterday from his publicist informing him the independent label that had produced his album five years ago had gone belly-up; even the phone call late this afternoon from his brother, Isaac, who berated him for not owning an answering machine like the rest of the developed free world. Their mother was in intensive care. She was near to death. Isaac had been calling for days.

"I'll leave tonight," Cyrus had said.

So he had packed a nylon bag with the basics, locked his second-floor walk-up on the edge of the Western Addition, and hurried downstairs to abandon the dregs of his checking account and a forwarding address with his landlord, Mr. Viswanathan, who, being better at bigotry than anyone Cyrus had ever known, began another rant about the new Vietnamese family next door. By the time Cyrus managed a graceless departure, arguing that everyone had to live somewhere, he was late to the club and allowed to play, as opener of the opener, just half his set. What did it matter? The sound was bad. A smattering of people sat at the tables; few applauded; none had come to see him.

Now the club was crowded. People shouted to the stage, nodding with the beat as if they agreed with nothing in particular. Three girls gyrated just below Brat Splat—as Cyrus had taken to calling the headliner—his D-45 slung so low he could hardly reach the strings, and rarely did, thank God for small favors. The band backing the Brat was responsible for the racket, which the music rags had referred to as folk/rock/hip-hop/fusion. If this was folk music, let the folk rot. Cyrus gestured to the waitress and she brought another bourbon.

He lifted his glass to a young woman four tables away, but she averted her eyes, so he drank alone and worried over the news from his brother. The last time Isaac had called, he'd asked Cyrus to photograph a plat of government property up for auction—an attempt to expand into West Coast development. Cyrus had mailed the film home but heard no more. Home. Where his father had philandered, his mother had lost sight of what was real, and his sister had vanished. Cyrus still searched the clubs where he sang, hoping Saro might show after spying a handbill or calendar of events, but tonight, as on many other nights, the faces grew indistinguishable, all glossy eyes and immaculate hair and mouths contorted in conversation. The man seated at his table might have been taken for a neophyte trucker back home, though, what with his long sideburns, windbreaker, and flannel shirt, but his pristine black work boots blocking the aisle gave him away.

"Nice boots," Cyrus shouted over the noise.

The young man shifted in his chair.

"I said—" Cyrus's cheeks were numb. He thought he might fall over. "Nice boots."

"Thanks." The young man kept his eyes on the stage.

"Buy those yourself?"

"Of course."

"Thought maybe your mama bought them for you."

The young man turned to Cyrus. "Funny."

"Funny? I'll tell you funny. Those boots are work boots. W-O-R-K. Folks do actual work in boots like those."

"Didn't I see you onstage?"

"I work."

"And I'm just trying to watch the show."

"Easier to watch than listen to, ain't it?"

In the most recent issue of *Spin*, the Brat had called himself a poet, a voice of the folk. He said his music was what people in this great global climate desired.

"Know what that kid up there says? Says he's never listened to Woody Guthrie." Cyrus himself didn't care much for Woody Guthrie. "Never," he said.

"Woody Guthrie sucks."

Cyrus lunged across the table, and the young man toppled, grabbing hold of Cyrus's throat on the way down. People turned, clutching their drinks, as Cyrus swung, grazing maybe a jaw, then rose—but not of his own volition. He tried to fight off the bouncer behind him. Faces of onlookers blurred, and one man lifted his glass—a toast!—before Cyrus was tossed through the double doors and skidded face first outside. The concrete was damp. Feet stopped in consideration of him, then moved on.

He pushed back through the doors but the bouncer, grinning, grabbed him by the shirtfront. The club was quiet as the Brat twinked his strings—*bink-bink, bomp-bomp*. "Thanks. Thanks a lot." Flipping his hair off his shoulder, he mumbled something about the plight of people who ride the bus. "Like, sometimes, they have to stand in the rain."

"I brought a guitar," Cyrus said to the bouncer. "If you don't mind."

"I used to ride the bus," the Brat told the crowd, his lip ring scratching against the mike. "I'd get wet. Well, like, I got wet only when it was, you know, raining." The crowd cheered. *Bink-bink, bomp-bomp.*

Cyrus tensed for a roundhouse, but the bouncer simply poked him in the chest with his finger, spinning him enough off balance that he led with his chin into, then out of, the double doors, which opened and closed like hands brushing themselves clean.

"Cool," the Brat said, and he began to rock.

Facedown again, Cyrus made it to one knee, but the street faded out and he drifted against someone. He could smell lilac perfume and cigarette smoke. A voice squawked—"I'm sure"—and Cyrus was shoved against the wheel of a car, where he sat cross-legged until a guitar case shot out the club doors and slid to the curb. Cyrus crawled to it, picked it up, and, with what dignity he could muster, staggered across the street.

He wandered a few blocks, stopping at a storefront window proffering wigs and lingerie. Locks and Lace, the place was called. Yellow block letters arced across the glass: WHAT YOU CONCEAL GIVES HIM A THRILL. Below that: ANY SHAPE. ANY SIZE. WE DO ALTERATIONS. Backlit and lined in tiers, heads of white styrofoam squatted like mushrooms, a few adorned with yellow, black, or aubergine tresses. Above the rows loomed a headless torso in a crotchless teddy. When Cyrus examined his bloodstained teeth, his eardrum crackled.

Winds off the Pacific bore the smell of cut earth and rotting fish, and he could not understand why the odor troubled his mind, until a memory from his boyhood along the lake came back to him. His father, the Reverend Arthur "Ott" Harper, was preaching revivals or lost in his grapes or vanished up to the house beside County Road W, where a sheet printed with red and yellow giraffes sometimes flapped on a line, signaling to the Reverend Ott, noted philanderer and man of God, that Mrs. Delphi Reaves's husband was away. Cyrus pushed a toy truck through mounds of dirt. Saro was scolding a tangle-haired doll against the silver maple in the yard. On winds shimmying the dogwoods along the bluff, the stink of something dead rose—a deer, maybe, run by dogs to crack open on the lakeshore below. A shadow passed. Another. When finally Saro told Cyrus to look, he saw buzzards—fifteen or more, swirling over the house. Some flew so low that if he had been older, taller, he could have touched their wings. He ran to the screened-in porch, where his mother lifted him into the swing beside her. The birds were after him, he said. Nonsense, she said, they ate dead things. She worked an arm around his chest, then, meaning to comfort him, sang a hymn of apocalyptic visions. A blue vein in her temple pulsed. Her eyes tracked the circling buzzards. Dancing across the yard, Saro tossed the doll skyward—an offering the birds did not accept. Cyrus called to her, but she did not seem to hear, and Ruth Harper kept wailing. She would not loosen her grip.

As he leaned his shoulder against the storefront glass, Cyrus felt her hold on him and heard the tune in his head, so he took the guitar from its case, wasting a few notes on the people hurrying by. He could not find the words. Finally, a couple too young for the bars stopped and stared, and Cyrus quit playing. The girl asked how come he was bleeding. He dabbed his temple with his palm and said a man had tried to steal his guitar.

"Wow," the girl said. "That sucks." The boy crossed his arms.

"Yeah," Cyrus said.

"You gonna sing something?"

Cyrus hated busking—the random coming and going of stran-gers, the tiresome sucking up. Mostly he despised the songs peo-ple requested, Top-40 pop and country that had calcified in their minds. "Something you want to hear?" he said, but there was noth-ing in particular she could think of, so he sang "Lost Lover Blues," tossing in loose-jointed yodels for kicks, then "Little Maggie with a Dram Glass in Her Hand," scuffing his boots on the walk for percussion, then "Old Joe Clark," barking guttural laughter on the chorus. His flatpicked riffs reverberated off the storefronts. Other people gathered. They looked like gawkers at a highway accident.

When Cyrus finished the songs he toed open the case. On the velveteen lining was a black cat's likeness: white whiskers, sharp teeth, wide yellow eyes. "Folks," he shouted, but when he raised his arm in greeting, the crowd seemed to tilt, and his pick hand throbbed. "Folks, my name's Cyrus Harper and this here's Kitty, and I'm sad to say poor Kitty's starving tonight. But you all look like gentle enough folks and kind enough folks and generous enough folks to see to it Kitty don't go hungry."

A few watchers shifted from foot to foot.

"Now, Kitty does snack on silver, but what she craves is that lush green cabbage. Oh, it's fine and foldable green leaf that keeps a cat healthy and wise, but let me tell you folks, it's only gonna go bad sitting there in your steamy little pockets."

A quarter whacked against the case lid and dropped in. The gawkers laughed. Two boys in back high-fived. "Easy now. Kitty ain't got no dental insurance." Cyrus strummed a couple of chords. "Dickheads," he muttered.

He sang for two hours, shilling the few CDs and tapes from his jacket pocket and working the crowd with contrived folksy banter and old blue jokes that made the girls roll their eyes and the boys rock back on their heels. He did ancient hill stuff and country blues and a few of his own, but he played loud, and sang in a voice both nasal and plaintive enough that he passed as a curious relic. Some people even threw down money. It wasn't such a bad night.

When his voice cracked at the end of a song, a young woman asked if he needed a drink. He turned and found her leaning against the wig-shop window, wearing a polka-dot dress and a leather aviator jacket. She shook her long black hair off her shoulder and held out a pint bottle.

"Enjoying the view?"

"You wish."

Cyrus took a pull of bourbon. "Maybe."

"Maybe," she said. "You gonna sing something we know?"

"You know 'A Man at the Close of Day'?"

"Is that what you are right about then?"

Cyrus passed back the bottle. "Oh, I'm something right about then."

"I bet," she said.

They drank between songs. In the midst of conversation she turned his cheek to the storefront light to admire the swelling. She said she had been in the Army, stationed in Germany, but had friends in Los Angeles. She hailed from Oklahoma, was an eighth Osage, and did know some of the songs he sang. She did not necessarily like them, but she knew them. When the crowd dwindled, Cyrus packed the evening's proceeds—a good fifty dollars—into the case compartment with his check from the club and stowed the guitar. She suggested a liquor store and a stretch of beach, where they ended up clinched atop the cold sand. After Cyrus worked his hand up her thigh, she recommended a motel.

She left the light off and flipped on the TV without sound: footage of a soldier mobbed in Somalia followed by the President holding forth from the Oval Office; then came a grim talking head and a teaser of a house crumbling down a slope. Hills in the East Bay had broken apart. Cyrus set the guitar case on the dresser. "Why don't you leave that in the car?" she said.

"It stays with me," Cyrus said. "It's my sister's."

She shook her head, then stepped out for ice. Cyrus opened a beer. When she returned, she dropped her jacket in a chair by the window, slipped off her shoes, and sat on the edge of the bed. "Fires in L.A.," she said, scratching at her shin with her heel. "Santa Anas. I love this state, don't you? It's so wild. So unpredictable."

It occurred to Cyrus she was talking too fast. He wondered if maybe she was crazy. "You're a dancer," he said.

"I don't know if I'd call it that. How'd you know?"

"Your feet."

"Oh. Yeah. They're fucked. You know, singers love dancers. Puppeteers with puppets. It's a control issue."

"So I've heard."

"Yeah?"

"Old girlfriend back home."

"Where's that?"

"Apogee Springs, it used to be called. Missouri. Utility company dammed the river, railroad come through to the north; place pulled up, renamed itself Apogee. We lived out where folks tried to take their cure. Soaking troughs, ruined cabins. Stairs going nowhere."

"Ghosty," the girl said. "You ever see a ghost?"

Cyrus glanced back at the TV. Two women in a gleaming white kitchen were demonstrating the grease-cutting merits of a dish soap. "My mother used to see a hog-eyed man."

"A what?"

"Man chasing skirt's one way to put it. Hog-eye's what he goes for under the skirt."

"Classy."

"It's in a song. Hog-eyed man's a roustabout. My mother saw a guy with a pig's face."

Liquor was loosening his jaw, beer greasing his joints. He longed to rest his head against a cold window and shut up. "Music," he said. "It's just waves of sound. Disturbance through a medium. Given the proper medium, you can see the waves float on by."

"So you ever see you a hog-eyed man?"

Television light spasmed over her girlish dress. Beach sand laced her ankles. He wondered how old she really was. Why she had picked him. "You see what things you're ready to," he said.

After Saro had disappeared, Ott had taken him and Isaac hunting. They were after turkey, he said. A lie. Snow had started in, angling hard and grainy against them as they climbed above Saline Creek into a limestone glade. Wind stirred the surrounding cedars, and out wandered a pointer—a pile of bones, an ancient dog. Its jaw hung loose, like it had been shot off, and the dog was bleeding. Ott whistled it up, but when it was a shadow's length away, he raised his twelve-gauge and blew off its head. "Know what that was?" he said. Cyrus thought to say, *That was a dog*, but he looked to Isaac, who was chewing at his bottom lip, staring out beyond the mess Ott had made. "That was mercy," Ott said, then he picked up the smoking shell and recited a psalm: "'For as the heaven is high above the earth, so great is his mercy toward them that fear him.'" Often he spouted scripture that seemed apropos of nothing, though Cyrus came to find that most of the quotes claimed man had no control over his fate. If God was paying attention, He had control. If not, who knew? The longer Saro was gone, the more Cyrus would look for her, taking her guitar into the woods and playing it so that she might hear. Once, out by the falls, a dog stepped from a tangle of gooseberry. It didn't have a head, yet it stood there as if listening. Then it turned back in the brush like it had never been there at all.

"Hog-eyed man?" Cyrus said to the girl. "No. No. Old-timers used to tell stories about headless animals. Things like that. They made up scary stuff so the world didn't seem so scary. You can hear it in their songs."

"Hey, if you're a singer, how come you ended up here?"

"It's where I work."

"Get work in L.A. Sing there. Don't you want to be famous?"

"You don't get famous singing like I sing."

"You make much money?"

"Enough."

"How much is that?" she said. "I don't think enough is ever enough." She vanished into the bathroom and came out working at her nose with her knuckles. "What're you doing?" she said.

Cyrus fixed on the screen where, again, the house was falling. "Watching Berkeley collapse."

"Not a bad way to spend a night." Setting his beer on the TV, she dragged him by the arm to the mattress, then pushed her tongue into his mouth. A jagged pain ran the length of him. "Too rough?" she said, wriggling from her dress. "Poor baby." Blue light flickered over her small breasts and her leopard-print underwear. A shiver of regret passed through him, and he pulled away. "C'mon," she said. "Let's go."

❧

When he had toured to promote his album, the nightmares had started, and he'd come to dread the close of day. Nightmares, night sweats, sometimes a grating three-day-long insomnia that led back into nightmares. Alone in his motel room he would strain to recover scenes that might grant him some semblance of peace, fixing often on a favorite that came to him now, unbidden, as he lay with his back to the girl and listened to her slow breathing: himself and Saro making a second appearance in Springfield, Missouri, on a long-running television barn dance soon to be pulled from the air for a national game show. Wide eyed under flashing lights, Cyrus flinched at the overtly enthusiastic fanfare induced by APPLAUSE signs. An aging ex-chart-topper called Rollie introduced them. He wore a rhinestone Nudie suit and hailed their music as "the old country fashion." Cyrus could still call back the taste of shine powder, a waxed studio floor of mismatched checkered tiles, chin rest slipping on his slick neck, and red foam microphone covers as bulbous as a clown's nose.

Afterward, an old gaffer in overalls stepped toward them past a crowd of music stands and broke-down staging. Cradling a boom like a rifle, he thumbed ambeer from his chin and thanked them, then stared at the still-lit stage and shook his head. "They go to fix what ain't never got broke," he said. "Pedal steel. Karo-syrup violins. I tell you, flying cowboys and flaming drum kits is next." Over south of Eminence, though, he said, some young scholar sort from the university was gathering songs, Ozarkian remnants, to make a movie of it all. "I'd go if I could get away," the gaffer said. "I'm just saying."

The setting where this rumored gleaner of relics labored was itself an anachronism, a banked and long-gabled tobacco barn with a chert-stone foundation and silvery oak planks built on soil so poor it might yield just leaf-enough for a family. Cyrus and Saro stood by a general store down the hill from it, watching rusted trucks and squared-off sixties-model Chevies and Fords climb the knob and park helter-skelter as far up the slope as their retreads could find purchase.

Cases in hand, they slipped up scree to a gaping door and were greeted by a woman in a lawn chair, her immaculate beehive netted in place with a lilac polyester scarf. "Queer night," she said, meaning most Thursday evenings folks picked and sawed in a round down in the store. But the scholar had hauled in equipment. She lit a Parliament with a blue-tip match, blowing smoke at the bronze light deepening over the hills. "Mind the cords now. They're thick as stobs."

The stage was a low loft illuminated by a rack of lights. Near the back of the barn, bearded graduate students manned a sixteen-millimeter camera with a zoom, two reel-to-reels, and mixing boards. Players and onlookers perched on rickety tiers, stable rails, tumped-over troughs, tractor fenders. A Depression-era microphone stood beneath a rafter where rows of abandoned tobacco leaves hung like stalactites.

As soon as Cyrus and Saro found seats on a bale near the recording equipment, a man knelt in front of them. His black beard failed to veil his youth. Ink stained the breast pocket of his shirt. Dust coated his high-tops. He took their names, address, phone number. Could they write him a set list? Depending on how much he could use he might follow up on what he called the provenance of their renderings. He handed them a photocopied page and a fountain pen—a release for them to sign.

Ancient locals, longtime couples, haggard autoharpists, thick-fisted fiddlers, frailers, and flat-pickers took turns at the mike. Some sang unaccompanied. Saro scratched down titles and passed them to the man at the board. They just had the two speakers, he said, and the mike. "Stand to it so folks think you got stitched at the waist. It'll pick up what all. I'll mail you a tape."

Their turn came. Chaff speckled the puncheon floors. Kernels crackled under their bootheels. As they took their place on the loft beneath the hanging tobacco, a fragrance of rose oil and sweet hay drifted down to Cyrus. The microphone glimmered, its finish distorting their visages, which wove and split in the front grille as they began to perform: "Seventeen Come Sunday," "Oh, Who Will Shoe My Foot?" "Pig Ankle Blues," "Two Crows," "Future Blues," "Old Bangum"—*dilly-um-down-dilly-down-dilly*. When the man at the mixing board called for one more they chose "When the Ransomed Get Home," their voices melding until his voice was hers and her voice was his, and his voice was more than it had ever been, more than it would ever be, the hewn planks of barn rolling the song back into them, filling him until he knew he was whole.

Or so he believed. He once could lull himself to sleep and stave off nightmares by rehashing that distant scene. Drinks could smother bad dreams too, or girls could, or drinks and girls, but sometimes now the nightmares came in spite of his best efforts, and even conscious recollection failed to deter his mind's unconscious wanderings. He might float down dim halls lined with stacks of *Broadman Hymnals*. There would be a sound of water dripping and the reek of mildewed paper, and searching for a safe room, he would climb stairs, stepping into the galvanized sheet-metal baptistery of his father's church, where green water lapped at the wine-colored robes of a faceless man. Music always drifted in and out of these pictures, and Cyrus would try to catch words from a blues progression or the weak signals of an AM station or a choir in a loft where the alto of one pendulous-bosomed Baptist wavered, singing *The son in darkness hides, and shut his glories be*. Light would shimmer off rising water, darkness flash-burn to an intensely white sky. Often in the dreams there were glintings. He could not tell if they were teeth, or knives.

Recently he'd begun to take these for the early manifestations of alcohol withdrawal that, according to books in the library on Green Street, were caused by fluctuations in serotonin levels and treatable with benzodiazepines. Cyrus didn't suffer from all of the symptoms, though. No pink elephants, no rats on the rafters, no spiders crawling his arms.

Well. This time he woke to shrill voices from the other side of the wall. A sour reek of alcohol was leaching from his body, which embarrassed him, because, if he remembered right, a girl lay beside him. He could not recall her name. He was not certain he'd asked it. Reaching across the mattress he found the sheets were cold.

Someone knocked at the motel door, and Cyrus slid from bed,

wrapping the blanket around him as he went. Through the curtains he saw an old woman bent over a canvas cart of towels and spray bottles, and he gestured for her to come back later. At the edge of the lot, his rusted Oldsmobile took up two spaces. Beyond that, scraps of fog drifted over battleship-colored water.

Stepping around a pizza box, he turned off the muted television and steadied himself on a chairback. The guitar case lay open on the dresser. He closed his eyes and swallowed back a rising wave of nausea, then forced himself to look. The guitar was there, the cash still in the compartment, along with the club check, picks, strings, and a miniature replica of the instrument carved out of walnut by a deaf-mute boy back home. The girl had left a note in fat script on the motel stationery:

You're one crazy sleeper. I had to go to the floor. Who you fighting anyway? And who's Kate? I took a ten. Hope it doesn't put you out. Thanks.

Cyrus clamped a hand to his forehead. "Christ," he said. One look at some gnarled feet and he was dreaming up lost innocence. The girl should have rolled him. He found a three-quarters-empty fifth atop the Yellow Pages on the nightstand, dropped a few watery cubes into a cup and poured a bourbon, then headed to the bathroom.

Beyond the sliding-glass window above the toilet was a hillside of ragged bungalows. He had no clear notion of where he was—the end of a continent, the start of an ocean. He had come west to look for Saro. She had completed his voice—a clear harmony to his reedy melody—and often he thought that if he could just find her, she might lead him back to a place where songs would come to him again.

Cyrus raised his cup to the mirror. Bloodshot eyes, abraded forehead, swollen jaw. He'd seen worse. His brown hair was starting to gray, and his flesh had begun to sag on his bony frame. "'He fleeth also as a shadow,'" Cyrus said, a Bible verse his father had been fond of. Then he retched into the basin. "'And continueth not.'" A tic convulsed his right eyelid. He drank, concentrating on the burn in his throat and the ice drifting in the amber liquid.

Margaret Bowman went by many names, or no name at all, but she did not flatter herself to think anyone cared. Though fine boned enough to be mistaken for pretty in a dim barroom, she had borne two children—one still alive—and had begun to lose her narrow waist, which she accented with a braided carnival whip. Her auburn hair had grown out black at the roots, her face was sun-wrinkled with dark circles under green eyes, and a ragged scar ran from her right earlobe to the flare of her nostril—a mistake, the slice made too high by a left-handed boyfriend. A steady rain had soaked her through, but she just kept moving into the darkness along a new strip of four-lane at the edge of the Ozark Plateau. Crossing a concrete bridge, she glanced back at a set of headlights, then hurried off the roadside down through thistle and foxtail, stooping to gather her begonia-print dress; it was her favorite. She shifted her duffel and turned toward the bridge. Underneath the northbound lanes, a faint light shone.

She wanted nothing of hitchhikers or hobos, their delusions and drunkenness, their clumsy advances. And if teenagers were camping there, fishing for bullheads or hidden out for a night of Swisher Sweets and Daddy's beer, she wanted none of that either. She patted the holstered .38 in her duffel and crept toward the underbelly of bridge where it closed in on the broken earth. A wide shallow trench had been dug there; red and gray chert stones as big as bread loaves surrounded it. At one end bulging garbage bags had been heaped, and at the other a human form in a gray hooded sweatshirt sat cross-legged, hunched over some small work. A Coleman lantern beside the figure's knee cast greenish light. When Margaret slipped on loose gravel, the figure looked up at her.

"Why, you're nothing but a boy," she said.

He began to rock, worrying the objects in his hands.

Against the half wall of stones a purple bike leaned, its front basket overflowing with beer cans. Plastic dinosaurs and their precise wooden replicas dangled from the handlebars by lengths of orange yarn, and a miniature license plate—RANDY and MISSOURI: THE SHOW-ME STATE—was wired to the fender.

"I used to have a boy," she said. "I won't hurt you. If you're worried. I ain't here to hurt you."

A semi passed overhead, then a car.

"What you fretting over?"

With his flattened nose, his goggle eyes, his skin stretched tight over fragile bones, he was himself a lizard pulled from limestone depths, but in one hand was a barlow knife, its blade curved like a scythe, and in the other a chunk of root that had begun to sprout the head of some prehistoric creature.

"That's real good," Margaret said. "Making something from nothing." She climbed over the low wall and set her duffel beside the bike. "Randy," she said, taking a seat beside him. "My name's Rachel. Your dinosaurs look real good. Real professional. Wish I had a talent. You could sell them, if you found somebody likes dinosaurs like you do."

The boy watched her askance. Dirt was crusted around his mouth.

"It's OK," she said, but he turned the knife over and kept watching. "What you got in these bags?" She poked one with her forefinger, and he jumped up, hissing, his lips drawn back from his teeth. Watching the knife, she got to her feet. "Sorry. Didn't mean to make you mad. That must be a lot of work. Must take days to gather that many cans. How much you get for a bag of one of these, anyway? C'mon. Nobody's gonna hurt you." She reached out, and he leaned toward her long enough to let her touch his chin, but when she grabbed for the knife, he scooted away, kicking the lantern over so hard it went out.

He shrieked, and his small feet stomped at the dirt. Margaret snatched a garbage bag and her duffel and clattered down along the creek bank, where she could hear only rain falling and water flowing, a sound she tracked until the gravel gave way underfoot. She cut through a stand of willows, climbing a wooded rise to a clearing where a white house stood. The rain stopped, and when the moon broke through the clouds, she made out a dirt lane and rows of grapevines ahead of her. To the north a window glowed in the tin-roofed addition to a barn. Margaret skulked to where the edge of its light lay across the grass.

At a table a dark-skinned man swabbed a plate clean with a scrap of tortilla, then he stood, unbuttoned his shirt, and folded it over the chair. From a washbasin on an oilstove he splashed his face, scrubbing his neck with a cloth. His hair was gray at the temples, his muscles sinewy. He lifted a towel from a rack and held it over his eyes.

Clutching the cans to quiet them, Margaret crept out between the vines. Most of the remaining bunches were slick and rotten, and when finally she found a firm one and tore it loose, the wires of the arbor caterwauled. Two dogs scrambled from the porch of the house and sprinted down the narrow road until Margaret loosed a high-pitched cry. One of them yowled as if to answer; the other sniffed the air. A barn door was flung open and the man peered at the darkness. Margaret wailed again. The man backed from the doorway and the dogs circled each other.

"*No es nada,*" he called. "*Es un gato.*" He slapped his knees. The dogs whined, but when he whistled, they went to him reluctantly. He glanced at the house. The windows were dark. "*Un gato grande,*" he said, and he shut the door.

❧

She made camp on dry needles in a cedar stand and dozed until morning when an engine sputtered nearby. White cattle grazed among the hardwoods, and a steer chomping a clump of goosegrass stared at her. "Git," she said, and the creature stumbled into thick brush just as a rickety Case tractor passed not ten feet away, an old woman at the wheel, a gentleman's straw hat shading her neck from the late-morning light.

When the tractor had disappeared over the next hill, Margaret checked a state map. The four-lane from last night was not on it, but a lake was, a dragon-shaped vestige of river that went on for miles. She gathered her things and angled northward, looking for a town called Apogee. There, she figured, she could trade the cans for a little cash, enough to get her down the road to Independence and retrieve her daughter from ex-in-laws, guardians unfit for custody. After all, the man they had raised had ditched Margaret in Florida only to turn up a month later in Missouri, where he overdosed in a truck stop shooting gallery. Madeline was in Independence now. She was seven years old. Timmy would have been nine. There was nothing left for her to do but take Madeline back.

Up from a low-water bridge, she crossed a gravel road and came to a limestone flat speckled with prickly pear. Springwater rushed from a crumbled escarpment into a tank linked by rusted pipes to concrete troughs, their brims overrun with roiling water.

Margaret wandered the flat, stooping to slice away fruit, which she peeled and ate. In a stand of sycamore uphill a patched boiler and more pipes were ringed by a ruin of chert stones—a pump house of sorts.

She undressed, scrounged a bar of soap from her duffel, and climbed into a trough, clenching her teeth to keep from howling at the cold. When she was clean, she lay naked on the warm limestone. Two buzzards circled overhead, and she spread her arms to them, dozing until she heard men's voices below the ridge and the sound of wood clapping against wood. She dressed quickly. The sun had closed in on the horizon. She had wasted a day.

Bags on her back, she slid down to a lane overrun with sassafras and climbed to where oaks had been dozed in heaps and pine frames stood atop foundations. The beginnings, maybe, of matchstick condos. A crew of shirtless men unloaded particleboard from a truck, then milled about smoking and talking. When the light deepened they departed, leaving her to wander the lane until it dead-ended at a fire ring and a rusted Plymouth Fury on cinder blocks. Nearby, a hole had been dug as if someone had tried to bury something but thought better of it, and from over the lip of the flat where she had slept, falling water cut a slate-blue pool that narrowed as it flowed into the woods. The air was damp with mist, but a chill seemed to rise from the earth itself.

Margaret opened the driver-side door and recoiled from the stink of mold and rot just as a mouse scurried past her from under the bench seat. Yellow toadstools grew on floor mats, the dash slick with fungus. She wet a T-shirt in the spring and scrubbed at the gut of the car, ripping out carpet and abandoned nests. She found a snakeskin coiled on the steering column, a squirrel skull gnawed through at the crown, and an empty pack of Black Jack chewing gum in the glove box.

When the car was clean, the light gone, she stuffed her duffel in the backseat, the cans in front, and banking a low fire, stabbed her last potato and buried it in the coals. Wind filled the woods with night noises. If she was where she thought she was, she had a good two hundred miles to go. Maybe two weeks of walking back roads, a half day by car, but Margaret did not steal cars, and she did not hitch. After serving four years of a ten-year sentence, she had skipped out on parole. It was better to lay low, better to go unnoticed.

The fire burned to an angry red eye. She plucked out the spud, eating it like an apple, but when something thrashed in the brush above the falls, she tossed it away and fetched her flashlight. Picking up a stone, she played the beam along the far side of the creek until the boy appeared. His silence was an accusation. "Git," she said. He rubbed his sleeve at his nose. "I said," she said, but she knew why he'd come. "No. They're mine now." She hurled the stone, striking him in the chest, but the boy did not flinch. Before she could fling another he vanished, as if the woods had inhaled him after a long exhalation.

The Oldsmobile gave out east of Ogallala, Nebraska, the transmission hemorrhaging a spoor of oil down the interstate and onto the shoulder, so Cyrus hauled his guitar and bag to a neon-lit steak house, where he bought enough drinks to strike up a conversation with a trucker who took him as far as Omaha. From there he caught a reefer to a skating rink south of Jefferson City, and in the full flush of morning started walking. The air lay close, the leaves turning at this, the third week of October. The bag's strap dug into his shoulder and the guitar was heavy. Why had he bothered with the old flog box anyway? A 1943 Martin D-28 worth more money than he'd ever had; it belonged to Saro, not Cyrus, and before her, their father, but now here he was, plunking his way toward the end of the century with it. Sometimes onstage he could hear the two of them judging his fretwork. Fine. Cyrus had wanted to play the fiddle.

Ever since he was five, he'd wanted this. The Wakoda County fair had sponsored an old-time fiddlers' contest at the edge of the grounds. Rain dripped through rents in the canvas tent, spattering on aluminum bleachers and soaking straw bales stacked for the overflow, of which there was none. A few sullen teenagers played, pimple-cheeked boys with thick brows and baby fat bulging over chin rests, but the contest belonged to the old men. They pecked at the microphones and squawked out titles: "Sitting by the Yellow

Gal," "The Unfortunate Dog," "Jennie Put the Kettle On." Some danced rickety jigs as they played, their white shirts and dark pants flapping, but it was the almost human squall of the fiddles that drew Cyrus. Ghosts were caught in the spruce and maple boxes. And they were calling.

He tugged his mother's sleeve. "I want to do that," he said.

Only hymns were allowed in the house. No TV. A radio for the weather. His mother sang while fixing supper, and sometimes his father listened as if he didn't trust her to employ the sacred words.

"No, you don't," she said.

Saro had slipped away, and when Ruth realized it, she searched the muddy grounds and mildewed tents, with Cyrus and Isaac running to keep up. They found Saro in a lawn chair under a camper awning, where an obese woman was playing a Montgomery Ward guitar with a purple tassel swinging from its neck. Peering over the top of her wire-rimmed bifocals, she sang like a kettle whistle through her few teeth how there was one thing that grieved her and weighed on her mind, and that was leaving her darling, pretty Saro behind. Ruth dragged Saro away. The old woman called out, "Bye-bye, little Sary," then cackled.

Two years passed. Cyrus and Saro hid in the attic, where they could barely hear their parents arguing. Their brother was always out somewhere, bucking bales, cutting wood, cleaning bricks—any task for pay, any place to escape, any job he could stack before him and say, *This is mine, this is done*. But Cyrus and Saro were too young to get anywhere, so they banished themselves among discard. Skeletons of D-conned mice lay scattered. There was a busted ladder-back rocker, a rabbit hutch, a Grafonola, a nine-tube Philco cabinet stereo with Bakelite dials, and, under bolts of dusty cloth, two cases—one fiddle, one guitar. They each took up an instrument. One rib of the fiddle had been weakly glued to the body. The Martin's back bore scars from a belt buckle.

In the guitar case Saro found a folded playbill that fell in two when she opened it:

Ott Harper and the Stomp Mountain Boys
Tebo's Skate Palace, Texarkana, Ark., 8 pm June 3
Miss Ruthie Garland opens for the boys

A centered photograph showed their father standing before a group of other young men in matching Western-style suits, the guitar strapped to his shoulder. In a smaller, star-shaped photo their mother sang into a microphone, the fiddle cradled to her chest.

It took years to piece together the story. As a child, Ruthie Garland had heard her father sing and play fiddle. He gathered songs and 78s on jobless and drunken wanderings—Columbia label, Victor, Okeh, Edison, Bluebird, Bullet, Brunswick. When he died she took the fiddle and the records. He owed her. She had a knack for making up songs, so signed with the SoCo label, which harvested white singers from down to Texas up and over to southern Missouri and West Tennessee. She was their one girl. The label traveled the South and Southwest, playing records from a loudspeaker and peddling them to stores, radio stations, passersby. In trailers a few select musicians were carted along. Ott Harper was one; so was Ruth. They played roller rinks, bowling alleys, honky-tonks. Western swing and rockabilly, more billy than rock. Three years of the road and they married. Ott Harper was a lady charmer who'd gotten religion. It was better than taking to drink. But the music became forbidden, instruments latched in their cases, records stacked beside the stereo cabinet they had bought with money from the shows. Vanity. All of it.

Cyrus and Saro discovered the records, mostly 78s, and spread them across the floor. Weird titles. Weird names. Mumford Bean, Jasper Bisbee, Bascom Lunsford, Luke Highnight, Jug Blowers,

Corn Dodgers, Skillet Lickers, Grinnell Giggers, Georgia Crackers, Blind Joe Mangrum, Blind Sammie, Blind Blake, Blind this, Blind that.

There were newer records too: 33⅓s put out by Folkways, one album by Buddy Holly and the Crickets, and some red and green vinyl 45s—Ott Harper and the Stomp Mountain Boys and Ruthie Garland. Cyrus plugged the cabinet into the overhead fixture and Saro put on the discs. The speakers crackled, but out came their parents' voices. Ott sang tunes called "Kicking the Bedpost," "Hot Rocking Chair," and "Waiting on the Tears." The label said they were his, but they were Ruth's. SoCo's president thought it improper for a woman to take songwriting credits. Ruth did country covers—"Look What Thoughts Will Do" and "Faded Love"—but she sang them too high and too fast, and when she came to a verse that swore she still remembered her love, which had faded, a prankster in the background howled in mock grief.

Cyrus and Saro took the instruments down to the kitchen, where their mother was washing dishes. Ruth stared, toweling off her hands. Cyrus held out the fiddle. "I want to play this," he said. Saro did the same with the guitar.

"No, you don't," Ruth said, but she tuned the strings. "If your father asks, I didn't touch them. Now, take those to the barn. They're not to make a sound in this house, you hear?"

That night Ott and Ruth fought. Next morning at breakfast Ott announced that if Cyrus and Saro could figure out how to play the instruments, they could keep them. Isaac shook his head, wiped his mouth, and excused himself. "Pretty cruel, Pop," he said, pushing back from the table. Cyrus and Saro had no notion of what Isaac might mean until they tried to meet their father's challenge. They listened to the records for clues, but the musicians seemed to beckon from dark rooms down long, narrow hallways, and when the two children wrapped their hands around the unwieldy necks they choked out unpleasant sounds that echoed in the barn loft. Isaac wondered aloud at the worth of their efforts. He told them there were better ways to play their old man.

A pragmatist, Isaac appreciated the ease of 8-track tapes. He took pleasure from the chattel that mooed up the pop charts. When their father had him sing at church, Isaac ordered from Sunday school materials a cassette of syrupy instrumentals that he patched into the sanctuary's sound system. He gripped the microphone like a telethon host. In college he majored in hotel management, and when he returned to Apogee with an MBA, he was rarely seen but often heard of, selling lake lots, dividing up rocky hills, and profiting in ways their father would not admit he envied.

But Cyrus kept at the fiddle. One afternoon on the flat where the ruined baths of Apogee Springs lay, he was scratching out what he could of "Dry and Dusty" when an old man stepped from the trees, a twenty-gauge under his arm, and demanded that Cyrus hand over the fiddle because he was scaring the squirrels. "Ah, give me the thing," the old man said. "I ain't a-gonna hurt you." He traded Cyrus the fiddle for the gun and began to play.

Throughout the night she startled at every rustle and branch creak, fearing he would return, but woke late and alone with the pistol clenched to her chest. Yellow hickory leaves overhead dimmed the late-morning sun. The day would pass before her work was complete. She couldn't haul two bags into town, not with any haste, and not without drawing looks, so she stowed the duffel with the pistol under the dashboard, then threw the cans over her shoulder, lugging them up the lane to an empty highway. This she crossed, sidestepping up a berm of cedar to dead track, then headed westward into a slough of overpass quick stops and fast-food joints. She cut through a Wal-Mart parking lot and followed a business loop to a grocery store. The tile was waxed. The air smelled of apples. Two checkout clerks at their registers were jabbering—a girl with shoulder-length hair clipped back by a barrette and a woman trying to disguise her age behind thick base and pink cat glasses.

"Don't you worry," the old woman said, picking at a piece of tape on the register. "You'll get you some boy. Boy'd be a fool not to ask you."

"It's this weekend," the girl said. "I mean, this weekend."

"You'll get you one. I just know you will."

Margaret rattled the cans on her shoulder. "I'd like to get the money for these," she said.

The girl patted her barrette and frowned at the old woman.

"We don't take cans," the woman said. "Bottles neither."

"Why not?"

"Just don't."

"That's not much of an answer."

"Well, it's the one I got for you, honey." The old woman adjusted her frames with both hands. "But I'll tell you this one thing. They stink. And the bugs get in them. You can't have bugs in a superstore, now, can you? Bugs'd get all in the food, and people wouldn't come for groceries, would they?" She emphasized the word *people*, as if to exclude present company.

"They wouldn't," the girl said. "That's right."

"Another thing is—"

"Fine," Margaret said. "I understand."

"No. You asked, and I'm a-gonna tell you. Other thing is, just where do you think we'd keep a bunch of dirty old cans around here?"

"I don't expect that's my concern."

"Well. I wouldn't think so." The old woman went back to picking tape and talking at the girl. Margaret stared, waiting them out.

"Besides," the woman finally said, "only person I know collects cans is that old Randy Ellston. Bless his heart. You know that boy?" she said to the girl.

"I seen him around," the girl said.

"Sure. Everybody sees him. He ain't never been right. They say he burned his parents' house down, and them in it." The old woman shook her head as if he had shamed her personally.

Margaret set down the bag. "Where's he sell them?"

"Down to Coffer's Resort, out on the Graver. Tight as Dick's hatband, old Coffer is. Got the first penny he ever made sewed up in his mattress."

"Where's this Coffer?" Margaret said.

"Graver Arm. Just like I told you."

"Mind if I leave these here? I need to get me a few things."

"You can set them outside. Like I said—"

"Right," Margaret said, dragging the cans out the door. "The bugs get in them."

When she came back and turned down the produce aisle, she could still hear the cashiers jabbering.

"How old you think she is?"

"Old enough to know better. That's a doozy of a scar."

From the bins Margaret grabbed two russets and a small white onion. She lifted her hem and slipped them into a pocket sewn inside her dress, then snatched a bag of hard rolls just as a young woman in a tie-dyed shirt and long skirt hurried past—a hippie wannabe, more than twenty years too late for all that peace and love. Her bangs were long and straight, her feet sandaled and dirty. She clutched federal-issue coupons but pocketed them to examine a spray can of cheese. A sign overhead said PLEASE. GOVERNMENT FOOD COUPONS CANNOT BE USED TO PURCHASE PROCESSED CHEESE FOOD, CHEEZ WHIZ, OR LIKE PRODUCTS.

"What're you staring at?" she said to Margaret.

"They won't let you get that."

"So?"

"So I thought I'd save you the trouble. They ain't the sweetest ladies up front."

"They're nice to me. I know them."

"Good for you," Margaret said.

The woman considered the canned cheese in her hand. "Not one decent job around here. Sell T-shirts. Work outlet malls off the dam." She looked back at Margaret. "Just who do you think you are, telling me what's what?"

"Billie," Margaret said.

"What?"

"You asked who I think I am. I think I'm Billie."

"That's a man's name."

"I get by with it."

The woman brandished the bright can like a stone. "Well, listen here, Billie. Mind your own beeswax."

They were everywhere, idiots not smart enough or industrious enough or sly enough to make their way. Margaret had been one herself—too poor to keep up her looks, too frayed by time to note the wasted days. Now here was one threatening her with processed cheese food. It was enough to make you laugh to keep from crying. "I'll keep that in mind," she said, but the woman was already stomping her way down the aisle. Margaret tore open a box of butter and stuck a stick under the hem of her dress.

At the checkout, the old woman eyed the rolls from over the top of her glasses. "That all?"

One register away the hippie started shouting. "What do you mean?"

"That ain't an approved purchase."

"C'mon, Alice," the old woman said. "We weren't born yesterday."

Margaret tucked the rolls under her arm. "How'd you say you get to this Coffer's?"

The old woman pushed up her glasses and sniffed. "You follow the signs. Honey."

❧

Queen Anne's lace had grown thick in the ditches along County Road Z, but the blooms were gray and tight, like the nests of impossibly small birds. Following red and white arrows to Coffer's Resort, she plucked the dry flowers and rubbed them between her palms, dumping loose seeds in the breast pocket of her dress. Though she was not one for flowers or other nonsense men gave women, she had gotten a few flowers in her day. Very few.

Taking in shade along a fencerow, she sprinkled seeds on four buttered rolls. The bread was warm, greasy; the seeds tasted of licorice. When she had eaten her fill, she moved on until she spotted a sign in the distance, its red and white paint peeling from the plywood: COFFER'S RESORT: CABINS, GUIDES, RENTALS, ICE, GAS, BAIT. She slipped into the woods to watch an old man ambling past a line of clapboard fishing cabins. He dumped conduit in a trench by a boathouse ramp, hitched up his britches, then stepped to a stone retaining wall at the edge of the lake. A catwalk led to a long dock, a length of which had sunk into green water.

The old man took a cigarette from his shirt pocket and lit it. Margaret headed down the slope toward him. When she said hello, he jumped, teetering on the lip of the wall.

"Sorry to scare you."

He blew smoke so the breeze carried it. "I don't scare easy." Small waves lapped at the rocks. She heard him swallow. "You're too easy on the eye to scare me." He flicked away his cigarette and it hissed in the water.

"Nice place you got here," Margaret said. "Quiet."

"Going to hell is what it is. Got to put in this new septic system, order of the county. I can't afford it. Used to be you pumped straight into the lake. Nowadays nobody needs a fishing guide, what with those electronic thingamajigs. Ain't no fish anyway. Nothing but cigarette boats and jet skis tearing up water and knocking down docks. I sell them their gas when they get this far upchannel. I don't complain."

Margaret set down the bag. "I have some cans."

"Reason it's so damn quiet is my wife's up to Barnett to play hearts with her sister. No one here but me. Naw, pretty little thing like you? You don't scare me."

"Someone in town said you buy cans."

He toed the bag. "I'd buy what all you got to sell."

A jay squawked in the trees behind her, and she flinched. Why

be nervous? Just another old coot. She squatted to untie the bag.
Beggar-lice stuck in clumps to the hem of her dress.

"Let me help you with that," he said, but Margaret pulled away,
and he stepped back, grinning. "What's your name anyway?"

"Call me Delilah."

"Like Sampson and Delilah?" He lifted his cap. "I ain't got no
hair to speak of. Maybe I got nothing to worry about?"

"Your name Sampson?"

"Friends call me Coffey. You do the same." He nodded to the
bag. "This boy comes, sells me his cans. Where all'd you get these
anyway?"

"Around."

"You don't really seem suited to that line of work."

If looking was eating he'd have pushed back from the table by
now. All the way from Florida she had met his kind: his eyes a
faded blue; his face, arms, and neck as brown as a polished bar top;
his round torso, bared, would be the milky gray of a colorless fish.
With his kind, there was always a price.

The jay squawked again, swooping down to the lake before it
rose against the blue. Margaret tried to follow it, but it was gone.
"How much for the cans?" she said.

"Three dollars, I guess."

"What?"

"That's what I give that boy. He's charity, though. He ain't right
in the head. But I'd be happy to give you three."

Margaret wished she hadn't left the gun in the duffel. "You got
anything you need doing around here?"

"Well. Summers I hire the girls to wear bikinis and pump gas.
Coffey's Compadres, I call them. My wife don't care for it. Brings in
business, you ask me. But you look a little old for that sort of thing.
Anyway, ain't no boats out now."

"You say your wife's gone?"

He nodded, scanning the empty hills across the lake.

"You say you'll buy what all I'm selling?"

"We got most everything we need. My wife does the shopping."

"Maybe I'm too old," Margaret said. "Maybe you miss my drift."

He stepped back and examined her. He clicked his tongue. "I ain't so slow," he said.

The lobby he led her into smelled of fried fish and stale cigarette smoke. "You can leave the cans there," Coffey said, pointing at the stoop. Two vinyl-covered chairs and a low table strewn with faded *Field & Stream*s sat beneath the window. On either side of a mounted largemouth bass were group photos of high-school-age girls in bikinis, sunglasses, and bare feet, all posed around the Coffer's Resort sign. Compadres. More than fifteen summers of shrinking swimsuits and shifting hairstyles. Stuck in a few frames were Polaroids of anglers hefting stringers of dead fish, but one image drew a long look from Margaret. Among a cluster of framed portraits of blue-eyed children posed with teddy bears, blocks, and balls was a taped-up photo of men in camouflage, each clutching a rifle.

"What's with these guys?" she said.

Coffey stepped behind the oaken counter that split the room. "Wakoda County militia. I'm a captain. We aim to set this country straight." He took out his wallet and laid down three dollars. "Here's for the cans."

"I'll need more than three for what you want, Coffey. Seventy-eight with the cans."

"You say you what?"

"Seventy-eight," Margaret said, quieter this time. There was nothing wrong with his hearing.

He ran his finger along his cheek. "Steep for someone just shows up on your doorstep."

"You thinking you'll get a better offer?" she said.

"I just ain't got that kind of cash on my person."

She nodded to the gray steel register on the counter. "What's that doing there?"

He shook his head. "I used to drink some. My wife hides the key to keep me from the cash."

"Oh? You don't drink?"

"Well. I might keep a bottle hid out in the boathouse."

"I bet you know all the good hiding places. I bet you know where she'd keep a key, and you're not telling." She watched the wallet in his trembling hand. Folding the ones into her breast pocket, she shrugged. "Those your grandchildren on the wall there?"

"Yeah, yeah, they are. My boy's kids. Steve and Shirley. We call her Shirl-girl. She sure used to be a funny thing. They're all grown now. I don't know where the time goes."

"You have to pay up front, Coffey."

He scratched his neck, thinking over an explanation for the hearts-playing wife. Finally, he reached under the counter and came up with a silvery key pinched like a minnow between his thumb and forefinger. "It just come to me," he said.

In back a curtained doorway divided a kitchen from the bedroom. Above the bedstead a gun rack was screwed to the wall, and from its felt-lined hooks hung a Franchi twenty-gauge, an over-and-under, a breakaway double-barrel, and some sort of automatic weapon. A real NRAer, this guy. Margaret bet a pistol lay in the nightstand drawer, but she couldn't very well check with him standing there slack-jawed.

"You need to freshen up or something?" she said.

"Naw. If you do, bathroom's just down the hall there." He unlaced his muddy work boots, arranging them at the foot of the bed, then off came his hat, shirt, and britches; these he stacked on a low piano stool beside the boots. A thatch of white hair blazed from the center of his chest. Margaret pulled down the shade, but the room was still not dark enough to hide him. She thought on her best move, then turned back the covers. As he crawled onto the sagging mattress, she nodded to his boxers. "We can't do business that way, Coffey."

"That sort of business is more your business, wouldn't you say?"

Margaret sighed. She undid the whip around her waist.

"That sure is a funny-looking belt," Coffey said.

"That's because it ain't a belt. It's a whip."

A fearful look crossed his face. "I ain't into that sort of thing."

Margaret pulled her dress over her head and laid it atop his ti-died clothes. "You're in luck. I ain't either."

"You got something stuck on your dogtooth," he said. "Top right. Your right. Looks like a seed."

She ran her thumbnail along the canine, then bared her teeth at him.

"Naw. Still there."

"Maybe I *had* better freshen up." She bent to gather her dress, concealing his clothes and boots beneath it, and draped it over her arms. "Down the hall?"

"Just there on the left. Don't be too long now."

Out of Coffey's sight, she dressed, then turned on the bathroom faucet, shut the door, and headed for the lobby. The key glinted on the counter. She worked it into the register and took a handful of dead presidents—three Grants, six Jacksons, a few Lincolns and Washingtons—all there was. "Hey," Coffey called. But with his britches and boots in hand, Margaret was sprinting past the cabins for the woods.

❧

She could splurge on a hot meal, rest up, get gone. At the town square, she steered clear of the courthouse and walked toward railroad tracks until she came across The Squeezebox, a two-story brick building from which mustard-brown paint had begun to peel like shagbark. A George Jones tune and the smell of frying meat drifted out a door propped open with a cast-iron boot. The windows were painted black, the stoop a mosaic of white and burgundy tiles arranged to say FOSTER'S PHARM 1925.

In back, two men shot eight ball under a fluorescent lamp. A few patrons in booths at the edge of the room regarded her, but they went back to their conversations when Margaret took a stool at the bar. The jukebox began "There Goes My Everything."

"When you gonna get some new country songs?" a pan-faced man at the end of the counter said.

"What do you mean 'new country'?" the bartender said.

Another man tipped up the bill of his Dekalb feed cap. "He means the peppy stuff."

"I'll get some of that new country just as soon as I get the TV fixed."

"Aw, Red," Pan-Face said. "That TV ain't ever worked. I mean, how many times can a man listen to 'It Wasn't God Who Made Honky Tonk Angels'?"

"That is a classic country tune."

"Yeah, to you. You wasn't even born yet. Know what those old tunes remind me of? Remind me I'm old."

"You *are* old," Red said. He toweled off his hands, then turned to Margaret. "What can I get you, darling?"

She ordered a beer, two cheeseburgers with everything, and fries.

Red set an open can on a napkin in front of her. "Big night, huh?"

In the mirror behind him, Margaret saw the dark circles under her eyes. She hung her head, sipped foam off the rim, then set the drink back onto its damp ring. Too often now when she sat still, Timmy's face in death would come to her—she rarely remembered him any other way—so to distract herself she tried to compose letters to Madeline in her head, straining to focus on what good things she wanted for the two of them. Each letter started the same, like a prayer, but unlike prayers to God, whom Margaret had witnessed neither hide nor hair of, these gave her some small hope: *Dear Maddie, I will get to you and make good.*

At the end of the bar the men were watching her. She stared them down until they went back to studying their beers. *I have come to believe a mama makes things right for her daughter. For some I expect that is easy, but it is hard traveling now. I should have known. This is big country, and by the time you get to where you're headed you are not the same. That is all for the good.*

One thing people always tell you about miles is that good things come and bad things get left behind—like maybe you can shed the bad with your steps. If that's so, then the reason is that now each step gets me closer to you.

A man straddled the stool beside Margaret. He set a straw cowboy hat, brim up, on the counter, and the bartender gave him a shot of tequila and a longneck beer. In the mirror, Margaret recognized him from the night before last—the laborer in the shed. His pressed work shirt was too big for his stick-whistle frame.

What can I say to you now? Lately I wonder how many teeth you've lost, and if the new ones come in straight. If they are straight and square, you have my teeth, which are not much trouble. Your father had rotten teeth. He had a sweet tooth and a tooth or two for other things that were no good. I got a touch of bad tooth myself, but I keep it filed down.

I think a lot on how I love you. Blood greed is what some of love is— the strong part. Greed, like hunger, is not bad. It just is. And the only way to get you back is—

"Hey there, Beano," Pan-Face said. "You gonna put away some to-kill-ya tonight? Eh, señor? Put on a little fiesta?"

The laborer muttered something in Spanish about bedding the pan-faced man's mother.

Margaret whispered to him, and he cupped his hand to his ear.

"I said, *Creo que te deben molestar terriblemente.*"

He shrugged. "*Creen que no comprendo. Si supieran, temerían por sus vidas.*" He lifted his foot from the bar rail and pulled from his bootleg a cheap hunting knife, a plastic compass embedded in the tip of the handle.

"You speak English, then."

"A useless language," he whispered. "It will be dead soon. Even *you* speak my language."

"What do you mean even me?"

He threw back his tequila and backed it with beer, then gestured to the bartender: a round for him and Margaret. "You know what I mean. Little white flower."

"You think I'm too stupid to know your language?"

The bartender brought her order in a plastic basket. "He bothering you? If he's bothering you, we'll get him out of here."

"He's fine," she said, but the bartender had stepped down the catwalk to the other men, all three leaning toward each other as if making plans.

Hand over his mouth, the laborer whispered, "People here do not speak my language. You must be from somewhere else. Texas. California. Where the water tastes like wine." He chuckled. "Yes. A California girl."

"I'm gonna eat now."

"It is, as so many people here are happy to remind you, a free country."

The bartender returned with the drinks. "Let me warn you," he said. "He gets drunk and goes bothering our women."

"You own some of the women here, do you?"

"He gets in their faces. Talks shit nobody understands. That's all I mean."

The laborer grinned. One bicuspid was silver.

"I'm just trying to eat," she said.

The bartender tapped his fists together. "Okeydokey."

"Hey, Beano," Pan-Face called. "When you headed back to Chee-hoo-ah-hoo-ah land? Got the crops all in?"

The laborer lifted his beer. "*Chinga tu madre,*" he said.

"You want me to tell him what that means?" Margaret whispered. "Or would you just rather I say you speak pretty good English?"

"Please, no. It is best I play the fool."

Margaret smiled to herself. "Where is it you got to get back to?"

"I send them money. They have no other use for me."

"Where you send it?"

"You would not know the place."

"Try me," she said, and started in on her second beer.

He said he was a Mixe Indian. A *pelagato*. A nobody. Even he did not speak his own language. He told her the name of a village below empty mountains that gathered down lightning each night. A nearby river had washed away the fields. Nothing grew there.

"Never heard of it," Margaret said.

"You are not as smart as you think."

"And I don't think I like your attitude."

"That is because we have not made proper introductions. My name is Jorge. Your name is?"

"Eve. If it's any of your business."

"Tell me, Eve. How did you get that scar on your face?"

"You ask a lot of questions for someone I don't know from Adam."

"Adam. Eve. Hah. But I am only making conversation."

Fatigue washed over her; she wanted to lie down. "All right. I had this crush on a boy in elementary school. Gilford Elementary. Out in California. You were right. A California girl. It was fourth grade, and this boy, this Jeremy Harrison—had a head shaped like Ireland, and a chin covered with red freckles—went down a slide face first. He dared me to follow. There was a piece of metal or screw or something sticking out along the side. I caught my face. It never healed right."

"That is not even a passable lie."

"Ain't a lie."

"Those are the most words you give so far. When people lie they give too many words. They think the more they say the more they will be believed. My daughters told long stories when they were small. A child's game. No. A knife did that to you." He put his hand to her face. She flinched, but he shushed her, running his index finger from her nose to her ear. "A very sharp knife. Look." He untucked his shirt. A curved ridge ran from his lowest rib to his belt. He took her hand and made her touch it. "See?" he said.

She pulled away. When she had spied him through his window, she hadn't noticed the scar.

"With my own knife she would have had my heart. Men think of women as lambs. But they are wolves."

"Men ain't any better."

Jorge tucked in his shirt. "But no one thinks of men as lambs."

"Why'd she need to kill you?"

"Another woman, of course. What did you do so bad he needed to kill you?"

Margaret put her hand over the scar.

"Even in the dark I see you hide things. You have not told me how you learned to speak my language."

Margaret was too weary to hold her liquor. Still covering the scar, she leaned against the bar to steady herself. "I took Spanish in school. My stepbrother used to sneak into my room at night. He took liberties, and to block him out I'd conjugate verbs in my head. I got an A in every Spanish class I took." She flashed Jorge a smile. "*Amo, amas, ama.*"

"You read that somewhere," Jorge said. "A tell-all book. Or a novel."

"I used as few words as I could."

"A scar tells a story. Like when you turn down the corner of a page. You know where you have been. Then you can go back to the story."

"Who'd want to?" Margaret said.

"A fool forgets where he has been. When you forget the past, you fear what is to come." Jorge tried tugging her hand from her face, but she pulled away. He tried again, but she shoved him to the floor.

People looked up from their drinks. "Goddammit," the bartender said.

Margaret slapped down two fives and slipped out to the walk. Running south past empty storefronts, she crossed a side street and ended up at the railroad tracks. A boarded-up depot hulked in the west, its loading dock crumbling to the ballast. Off east a half-moon hung in darkness and, below it, along the edge of the streetlight's reach, a man came stumbling toward her over the odd spacing of the ties. He carried a guitar case and a bag, and she took him for some tin-eared troubadour out of his gourd on weed or drink and filled to the gills with troubles. Without once looking back to see what might be gaining on her—the laborer, the troubadour, the past, the truth—she put her head down and cut through a stand of trash trees to the highway. Margaret came from California, Arkansas, Texas, Oklahoma, any place far from where she was at the time. She had cut her face on a slide. Thrown a rod in Morgan City. Grown up in a three-story, yellow-brick house in Illinois, where she had been a prodigy on piano until stricken with a rare degenerative disease. No one questioned her; no one cared.

When a truck crested the rise behind her, she stepped to the ditch to let it pass, but it stopped. The laborer leaned out the window. "Do you live around here?"

"I'm headed to my uncle's."

The truck bucked beside her, the bumper swaying from baling wire. "Oh?"

"I'm visiting. His wife left him. I'm just lending a hand. With his chicken farm."

"Chicken farm. I can smell my way to a chicken farm, Eve. Let me take you."

"I know how to walk."

His silver tooth glinted. "You could get there sooner if you rode."

Margaret slowed down, as if to prove she was in no hurry.

"You do not need to be afraid, Eve. Ride in back. Tap the roof when you want to stop."

What choice did she have? The road was empty, with open fields on either side. She climbed over the tailgate, but when oak limbs canopied overhead and the road turned to gravel, she beat on the roof of the cab. Dust glowed red in the taillights' glare, and the bed fishtailed. He was going too fast for her to jump.

Past the vineyards he steered into a driveway, the truck rattling over ruts, then braked hard as he pulled into the barn. She crouched in the bed, but he stayed put, whistling to a song on the radio. She smelled hay, burnt oil, manure. Back in the darkness were a tractor and a bulldozer. When the song finished, Jorge killed the engine. "Now, Eve," he said, stepping from the cab. "Where is it you need to go? Tell me the truth."

Margaret scrambled over the side, but her feet found a loose stack of lumber and sheet metal and she fell, turning her ankle. Pain shot through her hand.

"Be careful, Eve," Jorge said. He reached, and Margaret saw the knife sticking from his boot.

She hobbled out the barn door into the vines, but there the dogs found her. "Come," Jorge said. "She is frightened of me." He laughed. "I am nothing to fear, yes?" And the barn doors clattered shut.

After a long, blind slog, she came limping past the falls down to the cul-de-sac. Greenish light shone in the car, and she asked who was there. A bright globe rose, revealing blood on her dress and a gash across her palm, then bobbed along the stream as she fetched her own light and cut the beam low through the trees. Randy lifted his lantern toward the car, then back to her.

"That's right," Margaret said. "My things. My place. Now git." She stooped as if to fetch a rock, but he bolted to the edge of the falls and vanished. Leaves fell on other leaves. Branches clacked. "You leave me be," she said.

In the car she found a small dinosaur carved out of cedar. Her own boy dead, and here was this other trailing her like a spirit. She took the carving in her good hand and rubbed it against her cheek. A creature sanded smooth. The wood still warm.

Nearing Apogee, Cyrus saw fence lines of Osage orange and combines stalled like schooners on distant ridges. He counted bottle caps in chert gravel. Kicked beer cans. Noted edible but vile-tasting flora in the ditches: henbit, dock, goatsbeard. It was the same as always. It was too close to home.

Ott Harper had moved his family to the edge of a bluff to keep them united and the world at bay. But there they disintegrated, and one early summer afternoon Ruth pushed Saro from the edge. Cyrus was the only witness, and though he had tried to stop his mother he still blamed himself. The authorities stayed out of it: a family matter. Ruth was not in her right mind. Ott could not stop grieving. Saro almost died, but she mended quickly, nursing a slight limp. She would hardly speak to her mother and began to fret over matters she would not mention. An offhand remark of hers one morning had stuck with Cyrus, if only because soon after, she vanished.

Their version of "There'll Come a Time" had been playing on the tape deck one morning as Cyrus drove them to school, and she'd noted three of his clunkers, which irritated him. The sun was up, but hoarfrost was thick on milkweed pods in the ditches. Saro had the rearview mirror twisted toward her, lipstick at the ready. She'd been wearing heavy makeup at school, wiping it off before she got home; the previous summer, she had worked at Coffer's Resort, pumping gas for boats at the dock in a bikini. Men asked her out, and she sneaked over her bedroom sill at night to meet them. These shenanigans interfered with the music, and she picked at Cyrus—he was flat or sharp, he played too fast or too slow, the lyric was stupid, they should just chuck the whole song.

"Pull in," she said, pointing with the tube at a cattle grate. "Pull in, pull in."

"We're late."

"The Ottmobile," she said. Half hidden in a stand of oaks was their father's Plymouth Fury. Before leaving the house, he'd scraped a patch of frost from the back window.

Saro grabbed at the wheel, but Cyrus blocked her. "I don't like to see that."

"If he's gonna make you miserable, you might as well have a little fun at his expense."

She had a point; she always did. Cyrus drove over the grate into the oaks. The Reaves's farmhouse stood back in a clearing. On the wash line in the side yard Delphi had pinned the sheet printed with red and yellow giraffes, the signal of her husband's absence. Given the frost, and the time of day, it was a little conspicuous.

Saro stared at scrub cedars along the rim of the clearing. "I'm gonna get out of here," she said. "I'm gonna go to San Francisco."

"What?"

"Leave my heart there. Like the song says. Better there than here, you know?"

"City of free love," Cyrus said.

"No such thing." Saro unsheathed a knife from her purse. It was long and double edged.

"My God."

"What?"

"Where in the hell did you get that?"

"Willie Gilmore."

The Gilmores were longhairs populating rotting fishing cabins on Dead Horse Cove, more bog than cove. Five Gilmore boys, including Willie—Wally, Wexler, Wyler, and Wade Jr.—and the matriarch, Fanny, who'd lost her husband to prison after he'd shot off her ear, though the joke around town was that Wade had shot Fanny in the fanny. Willie was the youngest, and while the other boys had proven to be bar brawlers, petty thieves, and vandals of public and private property, in and out of county jails and emergency rooms, Willie seemed the exception. He kept his yellow locks groomed in a Prince Valiant cut, some precursor to the mullet. He pressed his oxfords and polished his loafers and had been admitted into the National Honor Society and Spanish Club, as well as the Air Force Academy in Colorado Springs, where he would be headed in the fall. He wanted out of Wakoda County as bad as any of them.

But a Gilmore was a Gilmore. Under his oxfords he wore sleeveless concert T-shirts. He got odd jobs doing masonry work, and with the money bought a Bondoed Trans Am and deer rifles with scopes he kept hidden in the trunk. He liked drinking, driving fast, weed, cocaine. When he liked a thing, he liked it good, and meant to have it for himself. Some girls said he could turn mean, but then who couldn't?

"His idea of a gift?"

Saro was turning the knife in her hands. "He won't miss it."

"What do you need it for?"

"Willie's all right."

"Yeah. Most snakes *are* harmless."

"You don't know everything about people, Cyrus. Anyway, there's more pretty boys than one."

"*Girls.*"

"I know the song."

"So what's with the knife?"

"Let's you and me let a little air out of the Ottmobile."

Cyrus got the truck in gear.

"You're the one hates him."

"Put it away."

She polished the blade on her skirt. "Give me Pop's keys, then."

"Why?"

"Hand them over, you old prude. And keep an eye on the house."

Saro fetched the jack and tire iron from the Plymouth's trunk, then set to work. Once she'd loaded the right rear tire and spare of the Fury into the bed, she got back into the cab.

"You're crazy. You know that?"

"In this family? How could you ever tell?"

As Cyrus drove into town, Saro got quiet, watching frost-shrouded oaks pass by. She had changed the subject on him, and he feared her moods too much to press her.

"California's a long way to go."

"Ain't far enough."

Whatever she had meant, she was right. With one phone call, Cyrus was on his way back. But when he came to a point where the road should have narrowed to two lanes, new four-lane ran between meager reaches of corn, fresh cuts divided the old hills, and where a gray plank barn had stood off a side road was a beige warehouse with a candy-striped roof. OUTER REACHES RANCH, the sign said. WHERE DREAMS BECOME REALITY. Lights flashed along the eaves, illuminating a length of painted thigh, greenbacks tucked into a garter. Cyrus counted nine pickup trucks scattered across the gravel lot. Unless the place peddled in nightmares, Cyrus doubted he'd find his dreams there. Still, he could use a drink.

The narrow lobby was furnished with a pine bench and a Lions Club gum ball machine. Music pulsed from behind a metal door, and when he shouldered it open, a few men at round tables turned to consider him before deciding he lacked qualities as interesting as what haunted the T-shaped runway and stage. At each tip a naked woman danced. Cyrus ordered a bourbon at the bar.

"We're a juice bar," the bartender said.

"What?"

"We got Cokes. We got club soda, tonic water, OJ, cranberry. We got V8, or something like it. We got grapefruit juice too."

"OK. I'll take a little bourbon if you can spare it."

"Bud, it ain't that hard to figure out. We don't serve liquor."

"That's no way to run a bar," Cyrus said.

"Hey, you order you a juice, you get you a good look." The bartender pointed to the stage. Dark blue walls of corrugated steel were spattered with fluorescent red and yellow paint—a slovenly galaxy of stars. Purple light emanated from crevices in the floor. Pink neon spiraled on beams overhead. The women wore nothing but silver knee-high boots. The flat-chested ones were relegated to the sides, moving like their feet had been glued down, but the big-breasted one got to spin around a chrome pole at center stage. She had been poorly augmented, and her breasts rode high, as if they were trying to climb over her shoulders. She turned and shook her hind end at the men.

Cyrus looked back at the bartender.

"You get full frontal nudity here, bud. You can't serve alcohol and have full frontal nudity. You come here, you get to see what all these girls got."

"I know what girls got," Cyrus said. "These ones different somehow?"

Hands on his hips, the bartender shook his head with theatrical disdain at the catwalk.

"Fine. How much for a cranberry juice?"

"Five dollars."

"God in heaven." Cyrus reached for his things, but a hand clamped onto his shoulder.

"Hey, hey, man. Problem?"

A stringy fellow grinned down at Cyrus. His teeth were the color of ashes, and a ragged yellow Fu Manchu drooped over his mouth. He had a lazy eye.

"I normally take juice with breakfast," Cyrus said, and he headed for the door.

Outside beyond the lot lay a familiar vista, hills blue with haze and, up a distant rise, a farmhouse crumbling in on itself. He paused long enough to figure how many miles remained, then cleared the last row of pickup trucks just as the skinny man called for him to wait up.

"Look," Cyrus said, turning around. A crude tattoo of a reptile serpentined from under the man's sleeve. "Look. I ain't hunting trouble."

"Hey, I ain't either. You passing through? You want you a little something? I can get you something if you want it." His left eye gazed off to the edge of the lot.

Whatever the man had to offer, Cyrus didn't think he wanted it.

"I can score for you."

"I was just looking for a drink."

"Man, I can get you some bud, some crank. No, wait." He wiped his hands twice on the thighs of his jeans, which looked as though they had gone awhile without washing. "Well, I got something. My buddy Hiley and me started this business? We'll make a ton of money. I got movies too. I got this barber's chair? You can sit in that and get wasted and watch movies. I used to cut hair. There ain't no money in it. Maybe I can get you one of those girls in there." The man leaned against a pickup. Fidgeting his leg, he scanned the four-lane.

"I don't have a lot of cash," Cyrus said.

"I take credit. You can owe me. Hey, my name's Gerald." From behind the truck seat he rummaged up a fifth of Southern Comfort.

"I got a bottle," he said. "We can take it inside. I can take it. I'm in the business of making people happy. That's it. The happy-people business."

"I thought you couldn't drink in there."

"You think anybody'd be in there if they couldn't drink? You think guys'd go just for titties? Titties are nothing. You can see those when you got half a mind to. You sneak a bottle, buy mixer. That's how it works." Grinning, Gerald undid the top button of his jeans and forced the bottle down his pants. Up the hill the farmhouse had melded into shadows.

"OK. One drink."

Gerald slapped his thigh. "Great. That's great. Hey, hey, is that guitar yours?"

"No. Not really."

"Why you carry it for, then?"

"Why? Hard to say."

"You're fucking with me, ain't you? That's OK. Everybody fucks with me." Gerald walked backward toward the Ranch. "I used to play 'Gimme Three Steps.'" Humming, he slapped his belly for accompaniment. "You know that song?"

❧

Cyrus sat at the bar, trying to shut out Gerald, who'd done nothing but chatter since they'd come back inside. One eye fixed on Cyrus, the other leering toward the stage, Gerald talked a litany of cop shows, which seemed to have given him an expertise in police procedure. He described X-rated movies in detail and outlined the demise of neighborhood barbers caused by quick-cut joints in malls. Now the subject was the manufacture of methamphetamine, a business Gerald had started with his buddy Hiley, whom Gerald characterized as the smartest man since Albert Einstein.

"You got to know chemistry," Gerald said. "I didn't even take chemistry in high school, but Hiley? Hiley knows. What he says you got to do is knock off an oxygen molecule."

Cyrus poked at the ice in his drink. He did not much care for Southern Comfort. "Knock it off what?"

"Oh, hey, I don't know. Off pseudoephed, maybe."

California papers described big operations overseen by bikers and Mexican cartels with a grip on ephedrine shipments, as well as mom-and-pop setups run—if you could call it that—by down-and-outs like Gerald who'd found cold medicine an easy resource. So this was the coming thing in Missouri. Cyrus had read that meth made people paranoid. Or made them think they were invincible. Or smart, even if they were stupid. He caught Gerald's reflection in the bar mirror. He was flexing his biceps, his good eye watching the reptilian tattoo wriggle.

For Cyrus, alcohol had proven a sufficient vice. He appreciated how liquor punished him the next day for excesses the night before—a shot of carelessness followed by a dose of guilt-ridden pain. The Baptist in him needed that. "How do you get enough pseudoephed?" he said. "You buy in bulk?"

"Oh, hey, hey. You know about meth? We send out high school kids to buy at drugstores and Casey's and things. They want it, they go get it. That was Hiley's idea. He calls it 'creating the market.'"

Onstage, an emcee touted a sister duo. Blue lights pulsing through a fog of cigarette smoke gave the women an unsettling pallor, as if they were made of marble, but they labored to entwine like mating snakes. They did not look at all like sisters.

A bristly geezer elbowed Cyrus. "They do get into it, huh?" he said.

"Sure," Cyrus said.

"Good God almighty, they do."

"We got a perfect place to cook it," Gerald said. "Hiley found it.

Ain't even a real road in or nothing. One of those old resort houses by the lake? It's got a room off the kitchen for flammables. Hiley says that's important. One wrong move and—*boom*—he says. We're going to get stuff to cold-cook too. Ammonia, starter fluid. We got a ton of batteries. Hiley knows all about it. He's smart."

Only one resort house had remained inhabitable. "That's Loman Kirby's place," Cyrus said.

Out on the limestone flats of Apogee Springs, the shotgun-toting fiddler had taught Cyrus by ear his first tune, "Ragtime Annie," as the waters passed them by.

"Ain't nobody's place. Nobody's lived there for years."

A retired TWA mechanic, Loman had returned home from Long Beach with his wife, Pearl, to purchase the one intact house of Apogee Springs. As a boy he had envied the visitors to the resort houses until he came to despise them, even patrons sick with polio and TB—after all, they were still wealthy. His love for the meek and his longing to pass down the old music had drawn him to Cyrus, and Cyrus, in turn, had been drawn to Loman, and his place. His door was open come all hours. He gave Cyrus beer in Dixie cups and chain-smoked Pall Malls, letting the ash grow so long it seemed to defy gravity. He was leather faced, hangdog; Pearl had recently died.

The house was high ceilinged and two storied, meant for the wealthiest patrons of the springs. It commanded a view of the lake and, before that, the river, though cedars and jack oaks had encroached on the knob. An ornate player piano sat across from the fireplace, along with a pile of boxed and brittle rolls, holdovers from the resort days. The rest of the instruments were Loman's—fiddles, guitars, tenor guitars, mandolins, banjos, ukuleles, and banjo ukes, and a nine-string Gibson of Loman's own concoction—and he made Cyrus take up each in turn, "the better to larn a chune," as he put it: "Rabbit in the Grass," "Blackberry Blossom," "Money Musk."

From under his horn-rimmed glasses he'd peer at Cyrus, then say, "Nope," and whistle the offending part. "Try 'er again."

He taught Cyrus to harmonize to old standards, such as "The Coo-Coo Bird," "Poor Ellen Smith," "The Train That Carried the Girl from Town"—tales of stifled desire, tragic murder, supernatural forces, noble outlaws, and trains that carted one's baby, or the dead, away. Sometimes Loman cried to hear the old songs; sometimes he slapped his knee, especially when Cyrus did bawdy tunes like "Long Peggin' Awl," "I Saw Her Snatch," and "She Keeps Her Boody Clean."

Once at supper, when his mother asked what he'd learned that day, Cyrus sang to the tune of "Turkey in the Straw":

> *I got a girl in Kansas City.*
> *She's got a gum ball on her titty.*
> *She can sing, and she can dance,*
> *And she's got a mustache in her pants.*

Thus, at age seven, Cyrus learned the taste of Ivory soap, and was forbidden thereafter to visit Loman Kirby—a prohibition that, in time, drew Saro as well to what the old man had to teach.

Sometime after Cyrus went to California, Loman had to give up the house. A few years later, Ruth wrote to say he had died in a wheelchair in a rented room in Olean, Missouri. Cyrus regretted he'd never told the old man good-bye.

"There a piano in that house?" he said to Gerald.

"We couldn't even move it. Hiley starts it up sometimes. Goes by itself. He runs it with the pornos. Freaks the kids out when they're fucked up. Hiley gets a kick out of it."

The first time Loman had run the rolls—"Ophelia Rag," "American Beauty," "The One I Love"—Cyrus had been frightened by the keys moving of their own accord.

"Sounds like a riot," he said.

"Hey, hey, it's weird. There was all kinds of things up in the house and out in this trailer? We pawned them. Got us start-up money that way. We even sold the trailer for scrap."

❧

"Bring those," Loman had said one afternoon, pointing a cigarette at Cyrus's fiddle and Saro's guitar. They followed him to the pad-locked trailer behind the house. Inside were funeral parlor chairs and microphones in stands. A snake's nest of black cords covered the floor. There were two 4-tracks, reel-to-reels, and a TV in pieces. On the coffee table a bottle of Dickel accompanied a ceramic island castaway leaning against a palm tree, the surrounding ocean choked with cigarette butts. Saro stared at a large black guitar hung on the wall.

"L-5," Loman said. "Like Miss Mama Maybelle used to play. I won it in a poker game. That Carter scratch I taught you? That's what she played it on. A belly crack makes it buzz some. Happens in archtops. I'll fix her one of these days. Go ahead, play it."

Saro slung the strap over her shoulder and began to pick "Oh, Take Me Back."

"Suits you," Loman said. "That Mama Maybelle, she did not take no crap."

Saro examined the guitar. "I like mine better."

"Maybe when old Cyrus gets meat on his bones, he can play it. You two sit down there. I want you to run through a few so you can hear yourselves."

The first song they recorded was "Fly Around My Pretty Little Miss," one of Saro's favorites, a romp of wandering verses. There were many titles, many versions. "How Old Are You My Pretty Little Miss," "Fly Around My Blue-Eyed Gal," "Seventeen Come Sunday." You could not know which rendition came first because

the song was ever changing. Its nature suited Saro, her unpredictable moods and passing fancies.

Over the years they laid down tracks on the reel-to-reels and
transferred them to cassettes. Sometimes Loman sang with them,
his voice sanded down with age, liquor, and smoke. "Ain't nothing
sweeter than sibling harmonies," he'd say. "They heal what ails you.
Bolicks, Delmores, Monroes, Louvins, even those Everlys. They
sang sweet, but most of them just couldn't get along. You bear that
in mind. Beauty's got its price."

Cyrus had kept a few tapes but lost them during one of his many
moves in San Francisco. "You say there's stuff in that house still?"
he said to Gerald.

"Was. Old junk and electronics, tapes. Hiley said it was shit. We
dumped most of it in the ditch out back."

"Hiley a real connoisseur of music, is he?"

"Those tapes, man. Weird. Hiley thought they were hilarious."

"I'll be," Cyrus said. "I didn't know a little puckered asshole
could have a sense of humor."

"What?" Gerald said.

Cyrus slipped off the stool. "You heard me."

Gerald was still flexing his biceps. "Hey, man. You can't talk that
way about Hiley."

"That's where you're wrong," Cyrus said, but he exited before
Gerald could prove otherwise.

Along the shoulder of the four-lane, bagworms had spun their
webs amid the dry moonlit leaves of oak branches. Cyrus took bar
matches from his pocket and struck one, holding it to a web that
went up in flames—an old chore to keep the trees from dying, but
a futile gesture then, and now, for who would take note of it? He
went along the fencerow, setting gauzy nests afire and watching
the embers in the trees. Sparks arced, fading before they hit the
ground.

Then lighted billboards appeared, advertisements for caverns, Nazarene churches, cabin rentals. One said ABORTION IS MURDER. Another, REVELATION 9:6. Some had been around in one form or another for as long as Cyrus could remember, but there were new signs for motels, marinas, and lakeside condos. Tourist traps had multiplied, development creeping to this arm of the lake. There were billboards of airbrushed girls with greased lips and teased hair too, silhouettes of women reclining in martini glasses, a goggle-eyed hillbilly ogling fishnet-stockinged legs: HILLBILLY HEAVEN, it said, WHERE YOU COME FIRST. Then came a realty sign, and Cyrus saw his brother's grinning face: ISAAC HARPER IS SELLING WAKODA COUNTY. Isaac had put on weight.

Cyrus walked on. Ahead was a new overpass. APOGEE. The population had shrunk to a thousand—eight hundred less than he recalled. Fast-food restaurants glowed in concert with self-serve stations and mini-marts, lighting up the place like an accident. So confounding was the landscape he had to trace dead track into town—rusted rails, torn-up ties, Chinese elm and sarvis breaking through granite ballast—before he could find County Road W, its blacktop miles finally bleeding into gravel that petered out at the bluff. The house was dark. As Cyrus stood studying the chalky clapboards, a snagger down on the lake started his boat, the flatulent racket fading up the channel. Cyrus pushed open the gate and two dogs scrambled off the porch, one growling low, the other howling. "Hush," he said, and they did. One stretched as if taking a long bow. He did not know what to call them. He had been gone longer than a dog's life.

A lake breeze stirred the porch swing, setting the chains to squawking, while the dogs settled by the kitchen door. Through the panes Cyrus made out the pastry table, quilts tangled atop it, a dishrag hanging from a drawer handle. He tried the knob, and the door opened, but the pump of a shotgun crunched in the yard behind him. "Who is there?"

He closed the door. "Cyrus Harper. Who're you?"

An angular shadow shifted in the darkness. "Jorge," it said.

"I'm Ruth Harper's son, Jorge."

The gun barrel glinted in moonlight. "Prove it. Please."

"I'd feel more comfortable proving it if you'd put that thing away."

"The safety is on."

"It goes off easy too," Cyrus said. "But OK. You work twenty-five acres of grapes. Another hundred or so's mostly oak. There's a seventy-three Ford pickup in the barn, I expect, a Case tractor, and a Cat bulldozer that's a bitch to start. There used to be a garden where a smokehouse burned down. Maybe still is. Isaac pays five dollars an hour for you to work and keep up the place. He pays your bus fare from Mexico to Kansas City and back. Maybe he pays extra for you to be a security guard too."

"I thought you were someone else," Jorge said.

"You get much company this time of night?"

"Some woman. That is all."

"What woman?" Cyrus said, but Jorge's footfalls faded across the grass.

The past was never past. It was a song of wandering verses, each lyric hooked to the next until it made little sense, and the best way to end it was to cease singing before all meaning was lost. Sense might be made one verse at a time, though. His brother had called, expecting him not to show, but here he was, come home to his mother; here he was, hoping for his sister. And the slat-wood swing was stirring as if someone had been seated there only moments ago. Cyrus stood very still, watching it move of its own accord.

Mama, you say if folk will take a thing from you, then they must need what they take more than you, but Mama? Gone. Gone Papa. Gone Roger, gone silver horn he blew into my ear so I could hear, he said, a lick or two, but all I heard I felt was like a shade-spring eddy stirred up cold, then gone. Gone up in smoke our eggshell house what topped the knob where we looked down on Dooley's rows of headstones set for folks so deep in sleep if when they wake, the good book says, the stars fall gone. Gone cans. Gone bag of cans. But here, a can, and here, more and more cans to trade for coins I give for Wal-Marts dinosaurs. I know. The dinosaurs have gone to stone, but for the avians I try to catch before they're lost in sky. Old Knobhead? Here. To pinch out coins for cans. And here the girl not now a girl but was. She keeps my coins safe down below the ground. I bring her flowers. I bring her wood I carve. What can she tell? I saw but cannot say what came of her. And now this other woman comes who must need cans more than I need. I'm sorry, but I watched her bathe down at the springs and rise in sun what made her skin persimmon-shine. She threw a rock to hurt where my heart kicks like it wants loose, but Mama? Gone. And I am here, and here my heart hurts kicking. Here.

"You Never Can Tell"

C yrus sat up from the welcome mat, roused by the insistent din of rain on the porch roof. Last night he had balked at the darkened door of his childhood home; now clouds scudded over hardwoods across the lake, borne on a gust that chilled him, and the dogs lifted their heads from between their paws. "You got names?" he said, and they thumped their tails on the porch floor as he gathered his bag and guitar, took a deep breath, and stepped into the kitchen. Quilts were crumpled on the pastry table, doors flung open as if someone had gone looking for something. His old room was as it had been, as were Saro's and Isaac's, and his father's clothes still hung in a bedroom closet. But in the narrow bathroom his mother's pills were scattered on the floor, the shower curtain torn from six of its rings, and in the tub was an old Polaroid photo, the image washed away by the slow drip of the faucet.

He filled three large bottles with small moons, bright capsules, and variegated pastel tablets he could not begin to name, and shut them in the mirrored medicine cabinet. The swelling in his jaw had subsided, but fatigue drew out his mother's features—black-walnut eyes, graying hair, high cheekbones—and it came to his mind he was the age that she'd first come unhinged.

He showered, shaved, dressed. Stepping into the dim hall, he saw, in silhouette, a thick-necked man in a rancher's hat leaning against the counter. "Ought to lock your door," the man said. "Never know what might walk in."

"So what has?"

"If you'd drag your yellow ass out here, you'd find out, wouldn't you?"

The voice was slow, measured, a little too familiar.

"Darby?"

"Yeah?"

"You had you a growing spurt," Cyrus said.

The skinny, freckle-faced rabble-rouser who'd been accomplished in the art of getting anyone but himself in trouble was now broad-shouldered and packed into an ill-fitting sheriff's uniform. Though he still had his red hair and fair skin, his jowls had sagged into a scowl. Cyrus stepped forward and pumped his old friend's hand.

"Somebody went and whacked you with a stick," Darby said.

"Yeah. Ugly stick."

An embarrassed silence settled. Darby inspected his boot soles, then admitted he'd come out to check on things. "Your hired guy's pretty much a pain in my ass."

Cyrus nodded to himself. "Not my hire."

"Well. Your guy found your mom. I'll give him that. Awful sorry about her. I should have said that for starters."

"Do you know how she's doing?"

"You don't know?"

"I just got in."

"Well, ain't the pills, in case you jumped to conclusions from what all got sowed across the bathroom floor. Stroke or something. Like got your pop."

Darby Carlton knew more of Cyrus's story than anyone in San Francisco ever had, but with all the time that'd passed between them they might as well have been strangers.

"Last I heard, you were a cop in Kansas City."

"Last we heard of you wasn't shit. Figured you'd jumped off the Golden Gate."

Cyrus nodded. "Ain't the fall I'd mind."

"Old Uncle Grunt," Darby said. "There he is, up from the grave."

"Right. So what's with the outfit?"

Darby pulled a packet of Red Man from his pocket, shreds of leaf dropping to the floor. "You are looking at the sheriff."

"Lord. They elected you?"

Darby packed chaw into his cheek. "There always will be a majority of fools," he said. "Wasn't my plan, you know. I jacked up my knee in Kansas City chasing some fucker over a privacy fence. I missed a ledge; he didn't. Cocksucker just stood there laughing. I can't hardly walk some days, and it hurts like hell when it's cold. They give me a job pushing paper, so I come back and run for sheriff. 'Local Boy Fights Big-City Crime.' Folks ate it up. I never did let on how I got crippled, though. Might make a difference, might not. Never know. Anyway, I got more paperwork than ever, and weirdness here beats what all I saw in the city. People with money or sense—and there's damned few of those—moved. Now we got freaks, pedophiles, commandos. And, Christ, the teenagers ain't what we were. Punks with nothing better to do than fuck up what's already fucked. They ain't got no guidance, no parents. You wouldn't believe how weird it got."

"I might," Cyrus said.

"Yeah, well. If anybody would, you would. We would."

"What's Jackie think of this? About being back?"

"You ain't married, are you?"

Marriage was commitment; commitment, denial. "I haven't managed it yet," Cyrus said.

"Let me tell you, high school sweethearts don't end up so sweet. Speaking of, Cate O'Connor's back."

That girl in the motel had dragged Cate into his mind already: straight back, thin arms, black hair pulled taut in sunlight. Now she was here. "I thought she was dancing in New York."

Darby shrugged. "The more things change, the more they get back to being the same. I saw the guitar there. Still playing, I guess. I read that article last I was here."

On the cabinet behind Cyrus was a torn strip of Scotch tape and, beside it, a scrap of newsprint, a review of his album from a San Francisco weekly:

> The songs of Cyrus Harper are dreamscapes where people stuck in dismal lives stay stuck, where misfortune strikes, and supernatural forms appear. Characters haunted by their past keep turning to face what plagues them, though what they confront are their own graves, which they see have not been kept clean. The songs are tinny and gritty, as if cobbled from Child ballads, country blues, and mail-order instruments. Mostly, they are grim. It is a wonder this singer-songwriter can get out of bed in the morning.

Cyrus did not recall sending it.

"I sound like a cheerful sort, don't I?" he said.

"When I'd see your mom, and she was clearheaded, she talked you up. Said she wished she could have heard you both singing on that album, though. I always did intend to buy it."

"Wouldn't be your sort of thing, if I remember right."

"You might. You might not. You had your nose tacked to the sun pretty good back then."

"Uh-huh," Cyrus said. Saturday nights, he would help Darby cart his old man from a bar or off the street or out of a field where his car had rolled to a stop. They would take him home, a dervish of whip-poor-wills in the woods, crushed leaves underfoot, and the wooly fool slurring he would kill them all even after they had propped him on the couch. "What do you mean when she was clear-headed?"

"Same old stuff. You know. Hog-eyed man and all."

"Yeah," Cyrus said. "How come the bathroom got left such a mess, Darb?"

"We ain't a cleaning business, Cyrus. And I expect old Isaac's too busy moving and shaking, what with the plans he's got. Got half the county stirred up with stuff he's building."

"We don't talk."

"I don't blame you."

"You don't suppose Cate might have been out here looking for me, do you?"

"No," Darby said. "No, I don't see why that'd be."

"I don't either."

"What're you asking for, then?"

"Jorge greeted me funny this morning. Thought I was some woman."

"I doubt he meant Cate."

Cyrus studied the quilts on the table. He lifted the corner of one and set it back.

"What?" Darby said.

"Nothing."

Darby looked off down the hall, then at Cyrus. He checked his watch. "Uh-huh. Well. Look, I got to get gone, but tell me something. You making much money? If you're staying awhile, I can hook you up singing."

"I got cash," Cyrus said. "I'll be all right."

"I know a place. I think you'd like it. I think you'd like it a lot."

"I don't expect I know the right songs."

"Why don't I swing by around six? You go on ahead and bring that guitar."

"This place serve drinks? I ended up somewhere last night just sold juice."

"Took a peek at our wild side of life, huh? What'd you think?"

"I think a bar ought to serve drinks."

"We'll set you up. Promise. But I do got to go push some paper." Darby rested his hand on the doorknob. "Do me a favor," he said, pointing at his knee.

"I won't tell a soul," Cyrus said.

He paced. He checked the icebox: milk, butter, eggs. He rummaged through kitchen cabinets. Not a drop in the house; never had been. But in a drawer crowded with warranties, coins, dried-up ballpoints, and old grocery receipts was an Instamatic print that stopped his search. He and Saro stood in front of Ott's church doors. He was ten maybe—kindling-thin and squinting into the sun. His mother's fiddle was tucked beneath his arm. Saro held the guitar in front of her. She was caught somewhere between womanly elegance and adolescent awkwardness. Windblown leaves blurred their feet.

Those years ago Ott Harper had conspired to weaken the cor- rupting influence of Loman Kirby, arguing that if their musical in- clinations were so profound they could use them, then, for the glory of God. He cited the parable of the lord who gave unto one servant five talents; and to another, two; and to another, one. The servants with five and two traded with those accordingly blessed. The ser- vant with one hid his in the ground. He that had received five gained five more; he that had received two, two more. He that bur- ied his one had it snatched away by his lord. "'For unto every one that hath shall be given,'" Ott said, "'and he shall have abundance. But from him that hath not shall be taken away even that which he hath.'" Cyrus had no idea what their father was talking about.

Ott Harper had made them study the lyrics in *The Broadman*

Hymnal, Primitive Baptist Hymn Book, and *The Harmonia Sacra*—or Hominy Soaker, as it was called, a coverless text with crumbling pages. Ruth taught them tunes and fingerings but refused to touch the instruments, as if she feared them. Saro played guitar and harmonized. Cyrus sang melody and accompanied on the fiddle. An unspoken resolution was made: Sacred music was allowed; profane was not; and as long as Cyrus and Saro acted as God's musical disciples, Ott Harper feigned ignorance of the visits they paid to Loman Kirby.

They performed on alternating Sundays at the Baptist Church of New Light and Free Grace, the Reverend Ott Harper officiating. They were dragged to select revivals Ott preached—not to stained-glass-and-brick sanctuaries in towns, where women wore slick polyester dresses and lipstick, but to squat tar-paper churches with low ceilings and water-stained walls and, always, one oily-looking print of Christ staring doe-eyed at the heavens, roadside churches that stank of mildew and the candle-wax-and-paper smell of the elderly and infirm, who could barely manage a cough at the end of a song, let alone an amen.

Ott meant to turn his children away from the music he and Ruth had abandoned, to increase dominion over his family and prove to the people of Apogee and beyond what a strong, holy, and upright man he was. None of that came to pass.

When Saro turned sixteen, Loman Kirby recorded them in the trailer behind his house, and they sent out tapes and got jobs singing in VFW halls. They won contests at fairs. They busked at carnivals. They performed at contests, weddings, and funerals of old-timers. They played twice on TV in Springfield, though Ott forbade them to go and hid the truck keys. The first time, they hitched. The next time, they hot-wired. Isaac admired their ingenuity and salesmanship. Cyrus said they weren't selling a thing. "Everything's for sale," Isaac said. But Cyrus liked things to seem pure. Call it folk, roots, traditional, Americana—to Cyrus it was the old way or no way, though he knew well enough that the men who'd cut 78s in the 1920s and '30s hadn't bothered with ideals. They'd wanted to make their mark, and money, and they'd do what all to get attention. Hokey outfits, hick shtick. One old fiddler used to dress in an Indian costume. Cyrus would not admit to falsity in the music; Saro, however, harbored no misgivings.

Saro the theatrical; Cyrus the taciturn. She played second to his fiddling, and they'd share a microphone on rickety stages under sun or stars or canvas or asbestos-coated gymnasium ceilings. Often when Cyrus looked out at the uplifted faces, he wanted to climb down and let Saro do the show. He could hardly swallow, let alone sing. But when she'd touch his arm and say, "Ready?" together they'd go. Sliding the ribs of the fiddle over his heart, Cyrus would chicken-scratch the strings, and when he'd rare back and dig into a solo, Saro would lean to the mike and shout, "Did you ever see anything like that?" Before the gathered could answer, she would yell, "That's my brother!"

They fled into a past full of dead singers, poorly reproduced songs, words and melodies passed down through the centuries like gossip. In the rising dust and trampled grass and cricket-ragged shadows they brought their voices together, though Saro preferred fast tunes, nonsense verses, and wandering lyrics that could settle into most any melody, while Cyrus took pleasure in slow ballads and parlor songs, all lost love and sorry demise. He longed for story, ordered worlds, moral lessons.

When Saro needed a break, Cyrus would stand alone to play some song she liked—"Fruit Jar Rag" or "Cripple Creek," maybe—just as fast as he could. Then, when Saro stepped to the mike, she'd spread her arms as if to hug every last person in the audience. "Neighbors and friends," she'd say, "before we got to singing in front of you all, my bashful brother coaxed me into this foolery. He

needed someone to play second, but I was reluctant. You understand. Such a sweet voice and a fit fiddler to boot, don't you think?"
She soaked up applause while Cyrus studied his feet. "Oh, thank
you. Now, he likes the old slow ballads. But you don't hear many of
those these days. It's a shame you don't, but you don't. So I'm gonna
do this for him while he gets his breath." She'd sing "The Un-
quiet Grave" or "After the Ball" or the one they called "The Jealous
Lover." Her voice was sunlight through ice, and it suited tunes
of botched love, misdeeds, and murder in which a boy might ask
his girl to take a walk, only to plunge a knife into her breast. "I
buried her so lovely beneath the willow tree," Saro would sing,
"where nothing but whip-poor-wills would keep her company." In
the front row little girls looked up to Saro with wide eyes and open
mouths, but at the edge of the tent loitered high school boys in letter
jackets—potential hecklers, quick with a *yee-haw* or a *soo-wee*. Saro
kept them quiet. Her figure caught their eye; her voice calmed
them.

Cyrus set the photograph on the counter and pulled the guitar
from its case on the kitchen floor, then he picked a riff:

> *Sally's in the garden, siftin', siftin',*
> *Sally's in the garden, siftin'—*

A draft stirred the curtains. Down the hall, beyond his parents'
bedroom window, rain began to angle across the ruined garden. He
was killing time. He needed to go see his mother. "Goddamn flog
box," he said, and he closed the guitar in its case and stepped outside,
the dogs tailing him all the way to the hired man's quarters. But the
truck was gone from the barn, so Cyrus wandered the arbors, drops
popping on the yellow leaves, then he cut across the road and crashed
through underbrush all the way to the flats where the cold springs
flowed. Minnows flashed over shifting silt as Cyrus followed the

limestone bank to the bluff overlooking the falls. Down in the cul-
de-sac, the Plymouth his father had abandoned still festered on
blocks. Beside it was a blackened fire ring and a hole as long as a
grave. The senseless labors of teenagers, no doubt. Punks, Darby
had said. Turning back to the house, Cyrus thought on how he had
wasted his share of time at the falls as well, playing the guitar, singing the old songs, watching for the faintest movement in the woods
around him.

He reached the porch just as some foreign make of swollen station wagon parked at the gate. Slouched over the steering wheel,
Isaac made a call on a mobile phone, then stepped into the rain,
shoulders hunched as if he might melt. He had thickened, his gut
weighing down his belt, but his face and hands were tanned: the
manifestation of amorphous deals with commissioners, county
execs, bankers, and builders, all matched up to tee times and sealed
over heavy four-star meals. He wore a white oxford, burgundy tie,
gray suit pants—an inoffensive enough uniform. At the stoop he
swept his hands toward the lake. Prophet and promised land. From
backhoes in the East Bay, Cyrus had witnessed developers, foremen,
and architects doing the same damn thing.

"Surveying, chief?"

Isaac pushed open the screen door. "What're you doing here?"

"Your exact words were that I needed to get my sorry ass
home."

"I didn't see a car."

Cyrus picked a few burrs from his shirtsleeve and flicked them
away. "You did not."

"What happened to your face?"

"Girls were so taken with a recent performance of mine they
rushed the stage."

Isaac shook water off his tasseled wing tips. "Quite the life you
got, my friend." He kept his gaze to the porch floor, hands in his
pockets, jaw tensed as if he might soak a blow.

Cyrus thought maybe he should feel sorry for his brother. It was possible that Isaac envied the way he had forced change, however meager, into his life by leaving the county. Isaac had stayed tied to home and tried to alter the very lay of the land around him. They'd both attempted to transform what came before them, but to what end?

"I'm kidding," Cyrus said.

"I know. I do still have some sense of humor."

"How's Mom?"

"Why don't we go inside?" Isaac said, blowing on his hands. "It's freezing."

Cyrus followed his brother across the threshold, glancing back to see the porch swing stirring, then he shut the door behind them. "Darby Carlton told me Mom had a stroke."

Isaac plucked a wooden spoon from a crock on the counter. "Carlton. He's more trouble than he was years ago, thanks to that uniform, and he don't know shit from Shinola." Isaac pointed the spoon at his head. "Aneurysms. Bleeds. Doctors say they've been there awhile. But don't go thinking they account for past behavior. They ain't been there that long."

From childhood on, Ruthie Aileen Garland had been called "sensitive" by her family in east Oklahoma, "touched" by citizens in her hometown, and "crazy" in more distant and less discreet circles. As a girl she sang beside creek banks, words dropping to her from the sky. She could recount conversations with long-dead relatives who she said paid her visits, and she would sketch their visages in detail. She spoke with inhabitants of songs she picked up from her father, women named Oma and Barbery and Polly. She forecasted weather by listening to trees. She could predict when her father would return, begging forgiveness, from his latest binge. She could tell when his drinking would start again, which piece of furniture he would break, which family member he would throttle. After he was dead and she was touring, she would spot him on street corners, hiding his face behind his hat, and creep toward him, talking low, as if to calm a bird trapped in a house. This behavior spooked the other musicians, including Ott, no end. Nevertheless, she was pretty and smart, and Ott figured with God's help he could control her. When he stopped the music, the visions stopped, and she became the model preacher's wife.

Sometime after the instruments were hauled from the attic, though, the visions came back. A hog-eyed man. The resident of a blue dance tune, a gussied-up roustabout, sniffing around for a piece of tail. He tapped at the windows for Ruth. He cornered her in the old smokehouse where Ott kept his tools, and threatened her with a wrench, but she locked him inside and burned the shed to the ground. "You hear him in there?" she said to Cyrus, but he heard only wood hissing in the flames.

Doctors and pills did no good, and Ott Harper no longer pretended to have control. He sneaked off with women, mostly with Delphi Reaves up the road. He raged from the pulpit, and church attendance declined. He spent hours with his grapes, pruning runners, mowing grass, chasing birds. There he had dominion.

Cyrus started folding the quilts on the pastry table. "She still in intensive care?"

"No, she's stable. They got her on some solid foods, even."

"So I can go see her?"

"You'll do what you want." Isaac toed the case on the floor. "Always have. Music making you much money these days?"

The girl Cyrus had picked up had asked the same. So had Darby. Cyrus didn't care for the question; it signified advice, a deal, or a trick. "I get by," he said.

"We got things going on I need you to hear." Leaning on the pastry table, Isaac straightened his tie. His hair was stiff, immaculate. Behind him, rain made crooked paths down the window. "In the will Mom and Pop put together—"

"Mom ain't dead."

"No. But the will calls for us to take certain responsibilities."

Cyrus stacked a folded quilt onto another. "What's this bedding for?"

"Mom slept there to track her hobgoblin. He was out at the end of the walk."

"Hard to imagine her just laid out on the table like that."

"You don't know," Isaac said. "You know *why* you don't know? You can't face it. Why don't you use some of that imagination folks talk about? Some days I'd peek my head in the door, and she'd say, 'Don't let the hog-eyed man in.' What do you do with that, exactly? If you'd just checked in for half a second, Cyrus, you'd have half a notion of what was going on."

"I lived with that hog-eyed man all through high school. While you were out studying how to peddle lakeside."

"You never saw no hog-eyed man."

Cyrus didn't care to argue over whose lot was worse. Still, he would not be bullied. "I saw more than I cared to. Saro. Mom. You'd have done the same if you'd seen."

"I've seen things lately, no thanks to you, and Mom ain't—" Isaac took a deep breath. He set his hands flat on the table. "I'm sorry. It's hard. It's hard to come back; I know it is. But Mom ain't gonna be what she was, healthwise, so we're gonna have to think on this will. The equipment, for what it's worth, and the land goes to us, but if we want to sell the property, or develop it, we both have to sign off. So—"

"Ah, there we go. Develop. Profit. Your inner Pop's showing, man."

"Look. There's things afoot I've got no control over, and it would benefit us to take advantage of them while we can. Or else we lose. I guarantee you, we won't get this chance again."

Rain blew against the window, blurring bare dogwoods and dark cedars beyond the glass.

"I got nothing to lose," Cyrus said.

"Everybody's got something, Cyrus. Soon enough we'll have a pile of hospital bills. Listen, I've gone and bought property either side of here, past the springs, past Dead Horse. I'm putting up condos by the falls. Years back, a state bill went through allocating monies for road improvements. It made the new four-lane around Apogee; there's plans to run another perpendicular to the spring road. That'll jack up land values, and when we talk lakeside property, the land's worth even more. What I'm thinking is make this acreage a resort. I got investors to back me up on this. Four-lanes suck people in. There's room for golf, tennis courts. It's a way to keep the place in the family. We can call it maybe Arbor Villa Resorts or something. After Pop's grapes."

"Save your vision," Cyrus said. "I won't sign a thing."

"Why not?"

"Well, Pop'd say from the pulpit how it's easier for a camel to pass through a needle's eye than it is for a rich man to enter the kingdom of heaven. And I for one am just itching for heaven."

"Cut the crap, Cyrus."

"Right. You married Episcopalian. Then my next reason is the world does not need any more condos. Or golf. Last reason? Mom ain't dead."

"If she was?"

"Listen to you."

"I don't mean it like that. It's just she's seeing her hobgoblins. Doctors say she'll be in a wheelchair, and this house can't handle wheelchairs. The doors ain't wide enough."

"You measured the doors."

"You need to grow up and face this," Isaac said.

"Yeah, grow up, plant a little zoysia. Get all the other grown-ups to drive their Range Rovers in here from Kansas City and St. Louis and whack little white balls at the sky."

"Land Rover," Isaac said. "I drive a Land Rover."

Cyrus rubbed his eyes with the heels of his hands and laughed. Then the kitchen door swung open. Darby's windbreaker was soaked. "Am I interrupting?"

"I was just leaving," Isaac said, and he slammed the door behind him.

"What's eating him?",

"That'd be me," Cyrus said.

Darby set a grocery sack on the counter and pulled from it a case of beer and a bottle of rye. "I thought we'd have us a few."

Cyrus considered the offerings. "That ain't gonna be enough," he said.

∽

While Darby talked over the rain thrumming on the roof, Cyrus drank greasy rye from a jelly-jar glass and chased it with beer. Blue light pooled atop the pastry table, the shade of Saturday evenings in winter, when the house smelled of cooked carrots and onions and windows steamed over and the rooms filled with homely music: his mother stepping from sink to stove, his sister chatting at dolls, his brother fussing with an Erector set, and his father flipping parchment pages of a King James. Then the light was gone. There may never have been such light. Or such music.

"I can't see a thing in here," Darby said. "You wanna hit that switch?"

"What?"

"Never mind. We ought to shake a leg anyway."

Cyrus gathered up the bottle and beers.

"Your guitar," Darby said.

The case seemed to float on the dim floor. "Right," Cyrus said.

They rode in a '79 Grand Prix with cracks in the burgundy vinyl seats and belts that squeaked. When he was running for office, Darby had sold the Accord he and Jackie had bought new—nobody would elect a sheriff who drove a Jap car. He seemed embarrassed by this; Cyrus told him he no longer even owned a car.

"That land's worth something, I bet," Darby said.

Cyrus clutched the rye bottle between his knees. "What?"

A pistol bulged against Darby's windbreaker as he slid a beer into his cup holder. "I mean, I expect you could draw golfers, but I ain't so sure you could get that putting-green grass to grow, not in those rocks."

"It'll grow," Cyrus said. "Those oaks Pop tore out with the dozer did. The grapes grew."

"Your pop'd spin in his grave if a golf course got put in."

"'Let them have dominion,' is what he'd say. Over fish and fowl and cattle and all the earth. That's the one verse he'd quote that gives power to man. People drag it out when they want things. Strip malls. Condos. Grapes. Christ."

"'In all labor there is profit,'" Ott had told his family, trimming the proverb to suit him. Come August, they'd slice bunches from vines, plopping Concords into five-gallon buckets. In the leaves waited snakes, wasp nests, spiders. Hornets swarmed the fruit. You could cut the tip off a finger and not know until you saw blood on the leaves. Breath was hard to come by; sweat was easy. In late winter, they'd prune the wind-whipped rows—two runners to a vine, five spurs a runner, three buds a spur. From a crow's-eye view they must have resembled notes on a withered stave. In time, Ott admitted it was hardly worth the effort. So much for labor's profit.

"Your brother's got dominion, that's for sure," Darby said. "He's snatched land from the dead, the near to it, and every poor boy who can't fix his debts. He's taking over—and he's got every right to, but he's pissing people off."

"You've gotten into it with him, I gather?"

"Commission meeting or two. I don't got the deputies to cover this county, and your brother wants to build, build, and build some more. We ain't got a tax base to keep roads up, or hire new law. If he builds all he wants and what all the commission wants him to build—shit, they're all contractors anyway—I'll have to call in the National Guard just to issue speeding tickets. I tell you, you left, I left; old Isaac sticks with it and makes a mint. I liked him a hell of a lot better when he was just another fat-ass with a frumpy wife."

"Beverly," Cyrus said. "I don't remember her much."

"Trust me," Darby said. Heading south, they crossed a new expanse of bridge. The last of the sun split through clouds, rays of light spreading over the lake in a gaudy print of Christ ascending. "Or maybe you should trust him. Hell, I bet he could make you a mint too."

"If I didn't know better, I'd say he wants Mom in the ground so he can break ground," Cyrus said. "All I want's a new song, or a better line of work."

They climbed between a scattering of new flat-roofed condos and prefab motels. There were no garish tourist traps like Cyrus had known over by the dam—no waterslides, go-karts, or mini-golf with giant fiberglass hillbillies at the entrances beckoning suckers. And there were no opries here either—competent musicians with saccharine harmonies and, always, a banjo-playing rube with a patched hat and a blacked-out tooth.

Cyrus knew well how to play the backwoods fool. After he and his sister had started performing in public, Saro devised some corn-pone comedy by adapting lines from records or ad-libbing whole-sale. Though a reluctant actor, he mimicked the opry goons, stepping offstage long enough to put on a battered felt hat and red suspenders, then shuffling back, hands in pockets and bottom lip stuck so far out an owl could have perched on it.

"Why, it's Uncle Grunt, ladies and gentlemen. Grunt N. Barrett."

Grunt N. Barrett was a moist-lipped, cross-eyed, country-fried curmudgeon Saro had named, a teller of tall tales and bad jokes.

"Why the long face, Uncle Grunt?"

"Aw, I been down to the courthouse all day. Hard times in front of that ole judge, but it ain't my fault. That Widow Ruby went and got crosswise with me."

"Uncle Grunt, Widow Ruby is sweet as taffy. She even wears little yellow flowers in that straw hat of hers, ladies and gentlemen. Besides, Uncle Grunt, you and Widow Ruby were an item awhile back. Ain't that right?"

"That biddy's tongue wags like the south end of a goose. She's got a crooked walk to boot."

"Uncle Grunt, Widow Ruby has a wooden leg. Don't make fun."

"I ain't. There I was minding my own business, driving my Jack and Jenny down Washington Street. And you know what that ole Widow Ruby done? She went and stepped right out in front of me."

"You ran over the widow Ruby."

"Didn't hurt her none. Just smashed up that ole leg of hers. But she is so conniving she took me to court. Said I ran over her with malicious intent. 'Weren't no such thing,' I said to the judge. 'It were a wagon is what it was,' and he saw the truth and threw the whole case out."

"Is that right, Uncle Grunt?"

"That is right. That ole Widow Ruby?"

"Yes?"

"She didn't have a leg to stand on."

When Loman caught wind of the act, he told them to quit it. He'd played an opry or two—he'd worn high-water pants and big shoes and played fiddle between his legs. As years passed Cyrus understood what Loman had left unsaid. A song was a culmination of experience, of celebration, suffering, or stoicism, and it should be presented as such. Music was as complicated as life, and so, Loman might have said, don't make a fool of music because music can make a fool of you. Saro may have come to understand that even before Cyrus.

"Speaking of," Cyrus said to Darby, "where you taking me?"

Grinning, his old friend turned onto an asphalt drive marked by a neon sign—BO's—then wended through a stand of hickory to a newly striped lot. Red leaves littered the pavement. "Here. Is where I'm taking you."

The windowless building was a good four stories high, its roofline rising above the treetops. Covered with sky blue corrugated metal, it might have passed as a warehouse for dainty things, but for the lighted marquee—COMING NEXT WEEKEND: PORN STAR AND PLAYTHING PERSEPHONE PLENTY. Someone had outdone himself in the alliteration department.

"I ain't taking my clothes off for nobody," Cyrus said.

"Well, that's a shame. I bet your scrawny ass in a spotlight shines like a little old lily."

"They won't listen to me in a place like this."

Darby stepped from the car. "When's that stopped you?"

Cyrus followed the sheriff into a chrome-trimmed lobby split by blue velveteen ropes that led to swinging doors and escalators and more doors. White marble floors reflected a sparkling chandelier, a dispiriting contrast to the gloom of the sunken theater they entered. Amber strips of light glowed below a long bar. Library lamps illuminated cloth-draped tables. A large man materialized on a catwalk perpendicular to the stage. "We ain't open, boys."

"Hello, Rudy," Darby said.

"Ah. Sheriff."

"Bo-Peep around?"

The bouncer nodded to a mirrored panel over the catwalk before sinking back into the dark. Darby offered Cyrus a stool.

"Rudy," a voice whined. "You can't keep letting your friends in early." An adolescent-looking waif leaned over the rail. "Oh," he said. He held up one finger and was gone.

"What was that?" Cyrus said.

"That—was your new boss."

The walls whirred and footsteps echoed; the place seemed a warren of hallways and lifts. Then Bo appeared stage left with the fluttery air of a dancer, though he looked too short to dance and wore platform shoes to compensate for his slight stature. Stepping behind the illuminated bar, he forced a smile. A black jacket draped his burgundy shirt, which was unbuttoned enough to reveal a thin gold chain, and his face was so pale that with his sparse mustache and gelled hair he resembled a villain in a silent film.

"Bet you thought disco was dead, didn't you, Cyrus?" Darby said.

"I did."

"Strange things still haunt these parts."

"It would seem so."

"Sheriff," Bo said, sanding his hands together, "what can I get you?"

Cyrus expected a round of juice. Darby ordered up bourbons. "This here's a friend of mine, Bo. Cyrus Harper? Bo Murphy Selinger. Bo? Cyrus is looking for work."

Bo set two filled shot glasses on the bar—good liquor Cyrus could not afford. "I have bartenders, Sheriff, and he doesn't look stout enough to bounce. No offense."

"Cyrus here's a singer."

Bo shuddered theatrically. Cyrus threw back the shot.

"Got an album. Been out on the West Coast."

"So now he's back," Bo said, pouring Cyrus another. "And I'm supposed to be impressed. I've never heard of him."

Cyrus pushed away the glass. "I ain't heard of you either."

"This looks a lot like liquor, Bo," Darby said. "Smells like it too. By God, it tastes like liquor. You know, Bo, county ordinance states there's to be no serving of liquor in an establishment where there's naked women."

"You see any naked women here? Sheriff?"

"If I don't see them, they don't exist?"

Bo shrugged.

"That's a philosophical conundrum, Bo. I don't see the sun out tonight either, but I trust it's up there somewhere." Darby turned to Cyrus. "Bo's a smart one. He had himself the first juice bar in this county."

"It's a cabaret, Sheriff. For gentlemen."

"Bo come down here from—where'd you come from, Bo?"

Bo rolled his eyes. "Chicago."

"Big city boy, Bo is, so it's hard to get one by him. Carpetbagged his way down and found a hole in our laws. He's the envy of all the clubs. For now."

"I need tits, Sheriff."

Darby shook his head mournfully at the glass in his hand.

"All right. What kind of music is it?"

"Folk music, I guess you'd call it."

"Not really," Cyrus said. "It's just old American—"

"I run a business," Bo said. "Not a hootenanny."

"Funny business is what I hear," Darby said. "Like what all goes on in those shower-baths upstairs? And out in the parking lot? That's what I hear in town."

Bo said nothing.

"Bo?" Darby said.

"He'll piss off the house girls. They got to have good music to do floor work."

"It is good music," Darby said. "Don't you say otherwise. You just tell the girls to take a seat in the customers' laps and listen to some fine old American music. Call it a break. Call it halftime. Call it what you want. You're an imaginative fella."

"There's no contact out on the floor, Sheriff," Bo said.

"There ain't supposed to be contact anywhere."

Bo shook his head at Cyrus. "Oh, they are really, really gonna like you."

"He's brought his guitar," Darby said.

"Let me at least set things up with the sound guy."

"Tomorrow night, then? Cyrus?"

No time was meant to sing for men who wanted to watch women humping chrome poles. Cyrus said tomorrow night would be dandy.

Bo sighed. "Nine sharp. When you get in, talk with the sound guy. His name's Newbern."

"That's the spirit," Darby said.

෴

The bridge hummed, the lake below blacker than the sky. Cyrus fished for the bottle at his feet. "Mind saying what that's about?"

"It's an arrangement."

"You just held something over that kid's head."

Darby worked a wad of tobacco around in his mouth. "That kid, as you call him, is a swindler. He's got enough on me to nail me to the wall, but I got enough on him too. What we got us is a symbiotic relationship. He's the dirty old bull, and I'm the little bird pecking bugs off his back. Or vice versa."

"What do you mean 'got enough'?"

"He just knows how shit works. He come down here, blown on a bad wind, a choreographer, for Christ's sake. Started putting on what he called 'tasteful, cabaret-type shows,' but no one would come, or stay. He wouldn't stand for girls doing the bump and grind. It lacked artistic and aesthetic value, he said. Shit. He still puts together shows, but the girls improvise to pull in cash. Shows keep getting weirder. Makes you wonder what's up in his twisted little skull. I used to think he was swishy, but he's got the pick of almost any girl, near as I can tell."

"You know a good bit about him," Cyrus said.

Lights from the new fast-food joints on the edge of Apogee glowed into the vast blackness. Darby spat in his beer can. "I do my job."

"What's this arrangement?"

"Like my old man, a body, when it wants to drink, will drink. So guys sneak it in or have at it in the parking lot. A few places got a real bar next door. Fellas get a snootful, then stagger over and get an eyeful. Bo could do that if he wouldn't put his time into costumes. Costumes. Christ. He makes the girls buy from him because he says they got no taste. Bo argued to the commission early on that his dances were performance art. Hell, what's the commission care? So he gets his way around the laws. But when his shows started to change, I tried to crack down, which didn't work. Now the arrangement we got—and, yeah, I got it with others—is so long as they keep the drunks off the road, I look the other way. His girls do what they want, and he gets all the business he can handle. Buses come down from the cities, college towns, all that shit."

"Looking the other way has a price, I guess," Cyrus said.

"What I take fixes what I don't have the budget for. So far, I got toilets for the jail. New plumbing."

"Fitting. So how come nobody gets caught?"

"You think commissioners—bunch of hairy-knuckled contractors—don't enjoy a drink and a show? Besides, anybody goes in a place like this ain't gonna complain about the setup. Anybody that complains sure as hell ain't gonna find out what the setup is."

"They'll complain when I get onstage."

"Dylan sang in a strip club in Colorado," Darby said. "You told me that."

"I told you he *said* that. Besides, I'm not Dylan."

"Never had a bris, huh?"

"Not that I can tell."

Across Saline Creek, a hooded figure on the shoulder guided a bicycle against traffic. As the car whipped past, Cyrus glimpsed a pale face and bird-claw hands. "Good God," he said. "Was that Randy Ellston? I figured that boy'd be dead by now."

"He ain't no boy anymore, remember? He's our age."

"Yeah," Cyrus said. "I know. I'd take Saro's guitar out to the woods and he'd pop up out of nowhere and set his hands on the belly of the box—listening, maybe. Or trying to stop me. I gave him a ride from school once when some punks were throwing snowballs at him. His folks' drive wasn't clear, so he had me drop him off at Dooley."

"Dooley? What for?"

"I don't know. Maybe he likes flowers and headstones. Anyway, next time I see him he gives me a guitar about as long as my thumb. Walnut. He kept that knife awful sharp, I guess. I still carry it in the case like it's a good luck charm. You can see how well it's worked."

"He burned his folks' house down, them and his brother in it."

"On purpose?"

"Folks talk, and he don't, and they was one weird bunch. Remember how they'd come to football games to watch Roger play his trumpet? Mr. Ellston in that frayed polyester, pant legs to his shins. Mrs. Ellston, a yard wide and not a tooth in her head. God, that woman was fat."

"Where's he live?"

"He takes to caves come winter, and he's caked in mud till spring. I've tried to scrub him down, get him a meal, but he's a slippery fella."

"Kids still rough him up?"

"He steers pretty clear," Darby said. "You see him out looking for cans, or carving dinosaurs. I saw him once on this mud bluff cutting roots off a big old cottonwood struck by lightning. God knows what he was up to."

"A carved branch from a tree of fire," Cyrus said, "brings your loving heart's desire."

"What?"

"Old wives' tale. Wood struck by lightning gets you what you want."

Darby turned off the four-lane, taking back roads into coves, the changed leaves still thick overhead. Cyrus was lost until they reached Dooley, where Darby had to brake for a rusted Galaxie idling kitty-wampus in the road. "Shit," he said. Before Cyrus could ask what, Darby was yanking a man feet first from the Ford. "Don't just sit there," he yelled. "C'mon, give me a hand."

The old man had a paunch and a full head of white hair, and he moaned as Cyrus approached.

"Get his keys, will you?" Darby said.

The Galaxie floorboard was upholstered with crushed cigarette cartons and beer cans. On the radio, a call-in listener was explaining how aliens had implanted a mind-control chip in the back of his knee. The procedure had left a scar. By the time Cyrus killed the engine, Darby was dragging the old man across the gravel.

"Jesus, Darb." Cyrus stooped, picking up the drunk by the shoulders. "Go easy on the guy."

"The guy?" Darby said. "The guy's what's left of Mack Reaves."

Cyrus stopped, but Darby walked on, stretching Mack out until Cyrus toppled.

"Am I gonna have to drag two drunks around tonight?"

Cyrus brushed himself off. "You've had enough practice." As soon as he spoke, he wished he hadn't. Darby crammed Mack into the back of his Grand Prix. Pinch-lipped, he threw the car in gear and drove in silence past Dooley.

"I didn't mean that like it sounded," Cyrus said.

"Forget it."

"I got too many old times coming back at once."

"Old times are past and gone," Darby said.

Cyrus thought otherwise—the past lay like land on the far side of a bridge you crossed over many times, until the bridge collapsed and you could not tell which side you were on.

Darby adjusted his grip on the steering wheel. "Mack's gone more to shit since Delphi died."

"I used to wish she was dead all the time," Cyrus said. "What got around to killing her?"

"Cancer. She was only—what?—fifty-some-odd? But, God, remember? Even when we were teenagers she was hot."

Mack Reaves began to snore. Old men in town called him Silver Star Mack, just not to his face. He'd come back from World War II, a nineteen-year-old with a Purple Heart and a Silver Star and not word one to say about what he'd done. He took a room in a boardinghouse by the railroad tracks, split wood, swept the floor at Dunstan's Drugs. He handed out trays of balls at the pool hall, sold buckets of slaughterhouse blood for bait. A black dog took up with him, and kids gave Mack nickels to make it play dead. He squirreled away enough cash to buy land, clear it, and cover it with cattle. Then he went wild at the bars.

A good ten years had passed since D-Day when he met Delphi Sikeston at the Nightingale Club across the dam. Underage and tipsy, she sang almost on key with the jukebox, running her hands through a tangle of almond-colored hair and letting her deep-set brown eyes linger on the loudest men. Mack stepped to the jukebox and played "The Wild Side of Life." Delphi demanded a dime from Mack and punched in "It Wasn't God Who Made Honky Tonk Angels" and didn't speak to him the rest of the night. For three years he chased her until she gave in. He was decorated, well set. He drank too much, though, and his cattle dealings kept him away from home.

Just once, Mack Reaves came to the Harper house. Stetson in hand, he paced along the fence. Ruth was setting a bowl of green beans and new potatoes on the table, and she told Ott to invite Mr. Reaves in for supper. But Ott spread his paper napkin across his lap and said that if Mr. Reaves were so inclined he'd be at the door by now. Ruth wiped off her hands and called to Mack—did he need to see the preacher? Mack appreciated the hospitality, he said, but he did not need to see no so-called preacher. He would like to express a thing or two to Ott Harper, though.

Before Ott was halfway down the walk, Mack had bloodied his mouth and dumped him under the silver maple. "Set foot in my house again, you son of a bitch," he said, getting in his truck, "I will kill you."

Ott slept on the couch for months after that. Later, he took to the barn with Delphi in bad weather, and to the back field in good.

They could not blame their father, Saro said, given their mother's mind. They could not blame their mother for despising their father either. And no one could blame Mack Reaves.

"I guess you think it's understandable about my pop and her," Cyrus said to Darby.

"Ain't much between the sexes I'd call understandable."

Cyrus waggled the rye bottle. Empty. "Where you going with him?"

"Put him in a cell until he dries out. He don't drive more than twenty-odd miles an hour, and he sticks to back roads. Kids are more trouble than Mack. He just sleeps in his car."

The dogs shot out the gate as soon as Darby pulled to the road's end. A wedge of lake below the bluff shone in moonlight. "I go see Mom tomorrow."

"Well, be back in time for your show. I'll come on out for it."

"You've heard me before when it was me and Saro; that was as good as it got." Cyrus stepped from the car and opened the back door. Mack was asleep, a firm grip on the handle of the guitar case, and when Cyrus tried to pry his hand loose, the old man shot him a wrathful look. "Let go, Mack," Cyrus said, and he did.

In the kitchen he left off the light and strapped on Saro's guitar and stood at the tin-sheet table as if it were an altar. From fragments of old songs, he worked up a melody, downstroking with his thumb so the thick strings droned low and mournful. Lines he mulled over had been passed to him from 78s and Loman, even his mother, who in rare and rebellious moments said to hell with her husband and false piety and no-show saviors and sang what she pleased. Cyrus wanted his own melodies and narratives, yet he grabbed at floating lyrics swapped by wanderers long dead: *Baby, let your hair roll down, please, baby, let your hair roll down, let your hair roll down, let your bangs, please, when I see that girl of mine, she comes from the South, she's so sweet the honeybees go boil them cabbage down, boys, bake that hoecake brown, craziest song I ever heard is in the pines, in the pines, where the sun never shines, I'm gonna shiver in a cabin on a mountain so high where the wild birds and turtledoves can hear my sad cry.*

He laid down nothing more than a nostalgic claim on a time when old songs were new: notes rising on a harsh wind, keys shifting like shadows, a tonic note as ominous as footfalls in an attic room. Quavers, falsettos, fifths, thirds, harmonies, trills, and double-stops from centuries ago hinted to him of some lost place where tunes were dippered cold from a bucket and passed from singer to singer until the dipper was dry and the bucket hauled away.

He swept beer cans to the floor and climbed atop the pastry table. Fighting to stay awake, he watched the moonlit gate at the end of the walk.

༄

First light struck him where he lay spread-eagle in the middle of a kitchen that, when he slid over the table side, seemed to slip out from under him. He gripped the faucet and fixed on the drain catch, scrubbed so often chrome had flaked from the brass. He was fine. Warm sunlight beat through the window. A wren bitched in the eaves. Just another day the Lord had made.

Still, his heart whomped a little too insistently in his head, so Cyrus searched the medicine cabinet. Nothing but pills bottled off the floor, humbug deals prescribed by doctors to drag his mother down. "Forget it," he told the mirror, but when the tic started up in his right eyelid, he pocketed the largest bottle.

After a shower, he fixed coffee and a fried-egg sandwich but couldn't muster an appetite, so he fed his breakfast to the dogs on his way to the barn. "How about I call you Bill?" he said to the yellow dog, and to the black one, "You be Earl." The dogs snuffled down the lane. "Blue Sky Boys. Quiet harmonies. Slow. Know how hard it is to sing quiet and slow?" He started humming "When the Ransomed Get Home," the old gospel tune he used to perform with Saro, but Earl and Bill headed for the woods. "That's a warmer reception than I'm gonna get tonight," he said.

The truck was in the barn, but Cyrus had no key, so he scrounged a flat-head screwdriver from the bulldozer's toolbox and jammed it in the ignition of the Ford. He fiddled under the dash until the engine sputtered, then hammered the accelerator with his hand.

"What are you doing to the truck?"

Cyrus whacked the back of his head on the wheel. "Jesus, Jorge. You like to get the jump on people, don't you?"

"I work this property. I use this truck."

Cyrus pulled himself up into the seat. "I need it to go see my mother."

Jorge clapped his hand on Cyrus's shoulder.

"You are taking my truck."

"Let me tell you," Cyrus said, "Isaac's fixing to see you not only won't have a truck, you also won't have a job." He eased his foot off the clutch and backed from Jorge's grasp. "Unless you like caddying for a peck of Kansas City lawyers."

He drove beyond the vines, recalling his last trip north to the hospital with his father. Saro was there, her fret hand bruised by the IV, her body restrained by casts and cables. Two floors down, Ruth was medicated and confined. Ott and Cyrus met Isaac at the nurse's station, and the brothers stood without speaking while Ott consulted with doctors, men who kept their hands in the pockets of their white coats. Driving back, Ott did not speak until the arbors: "'The fathers have eaten a sour grape, and the children's teeth are set on edge.'"

"Jeremiah," Cyrus said.

"Jeremiah what?"

"It says in days to come people won't say such things. I know that much."

"God's will will be done," Ott said.

"God doesn't care one way or the other."

"I didn't say he did."

Saro recovered with small complaint, but her left leg mended shorter than her right. Ruth continued to suffer visions, and though she could not recall events that had landed her and Saro in the hospital, she surmised she was in part responsible, and grieved. Two years later, after Ott died, the church he had built of brick to outlast his passing burned, crumbled, and was abandoned by a congregation that scattered to churches led by preachers who, as far as townspeople knew, were untouched by scandal.

But there were degrees of caring. Cyrus cared for his mother, how she'd taught him hymns and taken quiet pride in his rebellion; still, he did not wish to see her in her present state. A common enough sentiment, he figured, caring for what was gone instead of what remained.

Turning onto the county road, he drove west. On the AM dial he pulled in country hacks singing twangy rock 'n' roll, a farm report, and talk radio belting out the bad-government blues. One caller bemoaned the lack of White House leadership. "Ain't nothing good ever come out of Arkansas," he said. Cyrus stuck with an announcer who droned on about hog futures. So busy was he with the radio that he'd passed a figure on the roadside before he thought to check the rearview mirror: jean jacket, round hips, long hair in need of a wash. She was limping. Cyrus braked hard, but by the time he stepped from the cab she had vanished. Ditch weed stood still; low limbs of oaks were unmoved. *Some woman*, Jorge had said. "What woman?" Cyrus said to the empty road. They came— and they went—by the dozens. He got back in the truck and after another mile turned north, driving into a landscape so altered that it confounded him: limestone hills blasted in two, wide lanes of excessively smooth limited-access highway, burnished fields slid-ing off to either side, faster and faster, until finally he reached the hospital.

A cheerless old gal at the front desk directed him to an eighth-floor room where the head of the bed was hinged up so far that Ruth sat as if startled from a dream. Flags outside the window lifted and dropped, pulleys clanging against the pole. "Mom?" Cyrus said, but her eyes were pebbles in a shallow well, her face drawn to one side.

"Ott's gonna rent out my room to Delphi," she said, slurring words.

Cyrus gripped the bed rail. "What?"

"Says Ott's down to Afton Street, playing music with those Mas-terson boys. They drink."

"Nobody's renting out your room, Mom. Who told you that?"

She tried to point, but her hand barely stirred the sheets. "Hog-eyed man. Cronies."

Cyrus peered into the far corner. Years back, if he did not go along with the visions, she would grow frightened, reckoning that she was alone in her world, and stuck outside of his, which meant there was no way she could keep him from harm. To join her in her fancies again was the only kindness Cyrus knew to give. "You know who I am, Mom?"

A nurse wheeled in a tray of food, but Ruth kept her gaze fixed on the door.

"They got you a meal here, huh, Mom?"

"You take the train?" Ruth said. "They said you'd be on the train through Apogee."

"That's dead track, Mom."

"Said you'd come."

Cyrus did not give a damn what they said. "I been gone so long, Mom, you went and turned beanpole on me."

"Said they was looking for you."

"Let's have a look here instead. Tapioca? You like that. That's . . . I guess that's creamed corn. They don't want to startle you with a burst of color, do they?"

"I let them eat the Jell-O," Ruth said.

Cyrus spooned up some pudding. "How about you take a crack at this before they get to it?"

Ruth squinched up her face.

"You like tapioca," Cyrus said, working the spoon between her teeth. "C'mon."

Ruth worried the gob in her mouth. She smiled—then spat the pudding at Cyrus. "I say I don't want it, son, I don't want it."

Here, then, was a scrap of hope. Cyrus wiped at her face and blanket with a napkin. "Which son am I?"

"You left a fiddle and run off with your sister's guitar. That's a real Harper thing to do."

"That's your fiddle. I left it for you."

"I burnt it in the coal stove," Ruth said. "Ott said it was the Dev-il's instrument."

"We don't have a coal stove."

"You run off with it too?"

"I didn't run off with anything. And she left the guitar."

"Give them what they want," Ruth said, and she closed her eyes. "When they come. They tell me they didn't take her. That so?" She was slurring now. Cyrus stayed put, wanting to hear her say his name. Without her knowledge of him, some part of his life was cut loose, but she lay silent until he tucked the blanket to her shoulders, then she began to sing to him a series of questions: "Who'll rock the cradle? Who'll sing the song? Who'll call you honey when I'm gone? That's a lullaby, Cyrus," she said, and opened her eyes. "No matter what. Women come before David. And his old harp."

"You know who I am."

"I didn't want to believe them."

❧

Cyrus rolled down the window, taking air. In the old songs singers penned sentimental verses in which wandering boys knelt by bedsides to be welcomed home, and no wonder, for how could you write *My mother might as well be dead because she isn't all here anyway?*

As he neared home hills and curves began to catch him off guard, and light over the back roads went sugary. He kept both hands on the wheel. Blue vistas flanked tar-paper houses; faded barns advertised caverns that claimed to have sheltered Jesse James. The smell of manure and rotting leaves came to him, then a sheriff's patrol car was angled into the ditch a mile after the blacktop met gravel. Pulling off, Cyrus called for Darby, but found only keys in the ignition and the scanner chattering.

A woodpecker throttled a tree as Cyrus floundered through blackberry brambles into a clearing; there, a primered school bus was parked, a soot-black chimney sticking from its roof like a witch's hat. Hillocks of two-liter bottles surrounded a mound of sand back in the trees. Cyrus circled the tamped ground, toeing aside a stuffed dog with kapok spilling from its backside. In a hanging cast-iron cauldron a pair of blue jeans floated.

"Darby?"

"What?"

Halfway down a wooded slope, he found Darby straddling a felled tree.

"What's going on?"

"Soon as I get my wind I'm gonna pay a call on a couple of losers. I've busted Mama once for peddling dope, and Daddy for shoplifting. His old man's some high-priced counsel out of Houston, so all they get's a tap on the wrist and a kiss on the head. She's home-schooling the kids, but they run naked as a jaybird's ass in whistling time, so you tell me what they're learning. See those bottles? They're gonna fill them with sand and build a house. In a pig's eye."

"Why're you down here?"

"See that bent limb? Those leaves?"

"I see mulberry. And pawpaw."

"You never was much for hunting."

"I never was much for cleaning what got hunted."

Darby staggered up, gripping his knee. When Cyrus moved to help, Darby waved him off.

"Shouldn't you maybe call for backup or something?"

"You watch too much TV."

"We never had TV."

"You all were entertainment enough, weren't you? C'mon with me."

When they reached a brushy hill, Darby told Cyrus to split off to the southeast. "Stay back, though. I don't want you in this."

"Aren't they just a couple of harmless hopheads?"

"Ain't nobody harmless," Darby said. Lumbering through leaves, he looked bloated and off balance in his uniform. Sun had left the hollow. Cyrus trudged up through deadfall until he heard below him children laughing and water spilling over rocks. Slate-blue threads of woodsmoke wove through the trees, and twenty yards down the slope hulked the rusted skeleton of a junked Model A. He leaned against a sapling, his head so heavy on the stalk of his neck that when a pale thing flashed at the edge of his sight he reckoned he was dreaming. A milky face appeared over the door of the Ford, and Randy bolted from the frame just as Darby yelled and a woman screamed from somewhere out of sight. Hard footsteps followed. Brandishing a stick, Randy scooted beneath a crimson canopy of dogwood. His pant leg was rolled up, his shin wrapped in bloodied gauze. Then he vanished. Late light filtered through a mottle of persimmon leaves, and Cyrus's arms seemed to glow. Strange woods, these: Headless things roamed, idiots disappeared like conjurers, and sisters went *poof* without a trace of smoke.

After Saro had disappeared, Ott and Ruth were so addled that Cyrus and Isaac had to give Sheriff Hoke Albers the necessary information: five feet five, 125 pounds. Long brown hair parted down the middle. Gray-blue eyes. A limp. Right upper incisor chipped and filed so that the tooth was uneven. A green copper bracelet on her left wrist. A brown suitcase missing from the closet. "Ask Willie Gilmore if he's seen her," Cyrus said.

"What about Gilmore?" Isaac said.

"You don't know."

"I don't if you don't tell me."

Albers raised his eyebrows, watching the brotherly tiff die out before it could get started. Then he said Saro would turn up. Besides, she could go where she pleased; she was free, white, nineteen. He did question Gilmore, though, who said she'd had notions to take off. Three weeks later, Albers was dead from a heart attack, his patrol car in a ditch, the roof lights flashing. Willie Gilmore moved on to Colorado Springs to serve his country.

Cyrus had not told Albers how Saro drew men like split persimmons draw bees, nor did he mention how she met them at Coffer's, where she pumped gas in a yellow bikini, which embarrassed Ott and Ruth no end. She was not amoral; she just couldn't be amused with one thing for too long. Once Saro had mastered a tune, even, she wanted to get to the next one. You could not put enough songs in front of her. She was the same with boys. As soon as she figured one out, he was history.

So she gained a reputation. She was well built and quick witted, and did not suffer fools, or rules. She thought she was thick in the thighs, though, and that her eyes were set too far apart, and that her crooked smile failed to conceal the chipped tooth. Nevertheless. "She's hard to look at," Darby had said once, and Cyrus took him to task. "Like looking at the sun is what I mean," Darby said.

So what had become of her? Inside the question was a question: What had become of him? Afternoons he'd go to the falls and play her guitar. Later, he found that singing in bars was pretty much the same. No one heard him; no one cared.

"Cyrus?" Darby hollered.

"Yeah?"

Beneath the dogwood branches where Randy had stood, cool air rose from a jagged hole no bigger than a car tire. Cyrus called into the darkness, but not even his own voice came back to him.

"I might could use me a little help down here," Darby said.

He sat beside a fire with his leg out straight. Aluminum cookware lay scattered around a split package of hot dogs and a cooler of beer. Another mound of two-liter bottles sat back in the brush. "They scattered. Them and the kiddies was having at a water pipe, I think. Family outing."

"You going after them?"

Darby glared at his knee. "They got to come back sometime."

"Randy Ellston was up there," Cyrus said. "He went down a hole. Like he thought I might chase him."

"He tries to play with the stoner kids. But they're as cruel as any others—peace, love, and understanding not withstanding."

"His leg was bunged up."

"He'll be all right."

Cyrus stared up at bright leaves stirring. "I saw Mom today."

"How is she?"

"A little crazy, I guess."

Darby pointed at the pile of soda pop bottles. "Crazier than that?"

"She's not well," Cyrus said. "But she ain't stupid." He tugged Darby to his feet. "You mean to leave your keys in the car?"

"Again? Some high school shit'll run off with it one of these days."

"Sounds like a stunt you'd have pulled."

Dusk was seeping into the hollow. The trees around them were black candles. "Yeah," Darby said, leaning against Cyrus as they climbed, "but, unlike these kids, I wasn't never mean."

Through a day and into a night of wind and rain Margaret slept, stirring just long enough on the Fury's back bench seat to note her ankle swollen as big as a grapefruit and her hand crusted with dried blood. When finally the skies cleared, she woke for good to red and yellow leaves pasted over the windshield, and the dinosaur—a flippered, bulbous thing—perched on the front seat back. A gift, or a curse? Peering out the side window, she expected to catch Randy lurking, but only the malt froth of risen water tumbled over the bluff and ran on toward the lake.

Her favorite dress bloodstained, her ankle disfigured, she was on her way to setting a record for the fastest trip to Nowhere. Her shooting hand hung useless, a swollen gash running from the Mount of Venus to the juncture of her love and life lines. Flecks of rusted metal were embedded in the wound. Still, she managed to hop to the stream with a cookset, limping back with a filled pot balanced in front of her. After coaxing a fire, she set the water atop two stones to boil, but one stone cracked and the pot spilled, dousing the flames. By the time she got water ready, her dress was sopping and the wound throbbed. Teeth clenched, she scrubbed her hand with a bar of soap until the white lather turned pink with blood, then rinsed it and held it to the fire to dry.

Back in the car she unfolded the state map. There. Independence.

Harry Truman's town. Her late husband, Nat, had said Truman once lived in a white Victorian house on a corner lot, a wrought-iron fence surrounding the yard. As a boy, he'd even seen Harry S. Truman, former president of the United States, fetch his morning paper off the porch. Harry had waved. Harry, Nat called him. Margaret didn't buy it. When she asked Nat what the *S* in Harry S. stood for, he said, "Samuel." Margaret had looked it up. The *S* was just an *S*. It stood for nothing.

What if Madeline lived in a house like Harry Truman's? What if she played in a yard guarded by a fence? That would be for the best. But likely Nat had been raised in a squat ranch with torn screens and broken sidewalks and a bare yard sloping to a stagnant ditch. That was his kind of place. She would find something better for Madeline. She didn't know how. She just would.

Studying the web of roads, she measured the miles again. After her release, Margaret had taken a cab to a friend's house to get her belongings, but the friend was gone, along with half of Margaret's things, so she started walking as if she might reach Madeline that very day. Then the next. The next. But no back road ran straight to Missouri, and she met with obstacles. Hail, lightning, wind, rain so hard it seemed to snatch hair from her head. Oiled aggregate so hot she thought her feet might blister. Bean farmers who stepped to their barbed wire fences and asked where all she thought she was headed. Dogs that rushed from porches, possums with their wise-guy grins. Once, she rounded a curve to find a panther sprawled outside a trailer. A man reclined against the cat, a felt hat over his eyes. "She's eaten," he said. What he meant was *Move on*.

"All right," Margaret said.

The man watched from under his hat brim. The cat bit at a blow-fly. "You might hear her come dark," he said. "She makes a racket to stand your hair on end."

Camped that night in a stand of pines, Margaret did hear the cat—the voice of a demon set on stealing souls, or children—and when she could take it no longer she pulled a breath into the box of her chest and loosed her own cry. To have such a crazed sound in her body pleased her, and the cat stopped. She thought of herself as something feral—an outlaw, or out-and-out liar—to anyone who might slow her down, and a false friend to the few who might ease her labored way. Her wild cry, though, each time it escaped, could not begin to silence all that bedeviled her.

On the night Timmy died green light flashed at the edge of drawn curtains. In the Green Rose Motel, everything was green—comforters, carpeting, dresser—but none of it matched. James Leroy was cutting a brick of heroin with baking soda, claiming that the more he cut it the more money they'd make. What did he know? Already he'd squandered cash on a scale and traded some heroin for cocaine, which he had cooked and shot up.

James Leroy had dialed up the pay-per-view, and a pornographic movie played on the TV. Margaret had told him it cost money they didn't have, but he said that when he wanted her opinion he would give it to her. She was too stoned to argue. Propped against the headboard, she watched Timmy bounce a tennis ball he'd found in a ditch beside the motel lot. Madeline was crying because Timmy wouldn't let her have a turn. At least neither of them noticed the television. On-screen a naked woman tied to a chair tried to loosen the ropes; a postman sat on a couch, his striped pants to his ankles. The ball bounced higher, higher, hovering before it fell. Green light from outside flashed on the scale. The woman in the chair tossed away her restraints and stood. Timmy's shoe was untied. Margaret went to fix it for him, but the ball hit the ceiling, then the TV, then careened, toppling the scale and spilling heroin to the pine-green carpet. James Leroy folded his hands in his lap; he looked very tired. "Goddammit," he said. He grabbed Timmy by the waist and carried him, kicking, to the bathroom. Margaret was on her knees; she had wanted to tie Timmy's shoe.

Now she folded the map and set it aside on the bench seat. *Dear Maddie,* she thought. *I will get to you and make things right. But it rained yesterday, and though I like rain sometimes, I could not make a move to get to you. This boy comes around now, and bothers me some. He puts me in mind of your brother. Except there is something not right about him. Like he does not have much boy left in him. Like he is part dead. I hope you forget what happened. I hope you have forgotten. This boy here carved me a little dinosaur. I will give it to you when I see you next.*

I should maybe say this about rain because it is what a mother should say. Rain will always stop. Do not let it bother you. Nor boys neither. I have said it before, and even if it does us no good, I will say it again. I love you.

She dumped out her duffel bag and put on her only clean dress— navy blue with burgundy peonies—then took the gun from its holster. Running her thumb over the SMITH & WESSON stamped on the barrel, she could not tell if the metal was damp or well oiled. A gun was hard to keep clean. Her father had been meticulous with his service revolver, but he had died young.

She tore a strip from an old T-shirt in her duffel and dropped the cylinder of the gun, emptying cartridges onto her skirt. With a stick, she forced the rag down the barrel, squeezing the cloth back through the breech and running it in and out of the chambers. One-handed, her work was sloppy, but she wiped each cartridge clean, then, holding down the trigger, eased the hammer in and out of the pin slot. As best she could tell, the movement was smooth. She slid the rounds back into their chambers, then yanked the laces from her worn tennis shoes and threaded them through the holster. Hiking up her dress, she cinched the weapon to her thigh. It hung fat and heavy. The man at the flea market had told her a more ladylike model might be her speed. "I ain't planning on being ladylike with it," she'd said. But now when she tried to draw it with her split hand, the pain was a cold rod up her arm; her left-handed grip was weak.

Off east a gust knocked down a swirl of leaves, through which a hooded figure came skulking. She managed to draw a bead on Randy as he pushed his bike to the edge of the cul-de-sac. "Don't remind me," she said. Her finger warmed the trigger. He set a bag of cans on the ground and slipped back into the woods.

By the time she'd cinched the dress with the whip, wrestled on a jean jacket, and tugged a work boot over her bad ankle, she was in tears. Blood beat like a board in her leg. She left her duffel in the car, stepping from tree to tree down overgrown lanes to the highway and cutting through fields until she found the railroad tracks. A sunken spur led her to the Apogee square. People clotted the curbsides behind painted sawhorses. Some craned their necks as if there were a fight, but the street was empty.

Margaret had to cradle her hand, while the pistol on her leg kept shifting her off course into passersby. They seemed to take her for not much more than another strange face drifting among strangers, a trickster quicksilvering with the crowd. But outside Dunstan's Drugs, one of her inadvertent tricks waited: Coffey. He jammed a wad of popcorn in his mouth. Drums sounded in the distance, and a squat woman grabbed his arm, pointing. The hearts-playing wife.

Margaret considered turning back. *No*, she thought. *He'll scare.*

"Coffey?" she said. "Coffey?"

"That girl there's talking to you."

Coffey toed a bottle cap into the gutter. His new boots were very clean. "Huh?" he said.

"That girl there."

"Pretty day, ain't it?" Margaret said.

The wife scowled at the sky as if expecting foul weather. Her dye job clashed with her red blouse. "Who are you?"

"I worked for Coffey once. A compadre, you might say. Right, Coffey?"

Coffey studied the street as if something interesting might turn up there.

"You worked for him, you worked for me," the wife said. She dug into Coffey's bag of corn. "I can't say I recall you."

"You still tear up the tables at hearts?"

"Once or twice maybe sometimes."

"Good day for a parade," Coffey said.

"Is that what this is? I just come to get me some items. I've been poorly."

"We like them Shriners," the wife said, packing her cheek. "Those itty-bitty cars are something to see. Who all'd you say you were?"

"Delilah," Coffey said, "is her name."

"Don't have to shout," the wife said. A hand on Coffey's forearm, she leaned toward Margaret. "I lose track of what girls we get down to the lake. They look the same after a time." She squinted at Margaret's scar. "You got a distinctive face, though, no offense."

Margaret touched the wife's hand. The pistol shifted toward her knees. "None taken," she said. Clenching her thighs, she grabbed a handful of corn, winked at Coffey, then turned toward the drugstore.

"No, I don't recall her at all," the wife said.

"Can't say I do either."

"You just said her name."

"I might could be wrong about that."

"Well," the wife said, "that's embarrassing."

As she entered the drugstore, a small-boned man in a lab coat nodded to her from the window. He had a face as pale as bacon grease and black hair oiled to his head. Faded boxes lined shelves, dust coated a soda fountain, and between each stool ran lengths of masking tape. Hands locked behind his back, the druggist attended again to the scenes beyond the glass. "Can I help you find something?" he said.

"Just looking."

"If there's something I can help you find you let me know."

Margaret pretended to study a box of gauze pads. "OK. Thank you."

"Folks steal me blind come parade time."

"Oh?"

"Folks steal anything ain't nailed down." The druggist craned his neck at the parade as it entered the square, dragging in blatting horns and slamming drums. Blindered horses flicked their heads, and a stagecoach with black velvet curtains passed. Margaret stuck the gauze under her dress.

"You come for the Homecoming?"

"No."

"I don't see sense in it. Once you're gone, it's best to stay that way. I say it's like this: The dead don't come back, and they're about as gone as gone can get, so they must know something, what with all the living they did. Course, some say the dead do come back, but me? I come out of Arkansas. I ain't gone back."

Eyeing a bottle of peroxide, she stuck a roll of tape, a box of Clairol, and an ACE bandage under her dress. "Coming from Arkansas count for being dead?"

"What say?"

"You Dunstan?"

"He's dead. I bought this dump from his son—who knew exactly what he was doing. Told me flat out I could beat that old Wal-Marts. Said people across the state come for the soda fountain alone, what with strolling down memory lane and all. Memory Lane. You wouldn't catch me on that road." The druggist got on tiptoe. "Yonder," he said.

Outside crept a cortege of antique convertibles. Women in tiaras and sashes on which the receding years had been stitched sat atop backseats. Most were thick in the hips and arms.

"Old homecoming queens," the druggist said with distaste. "I tell you, if folks come, they must just peek in the window. I had to shut the thing down."

At the back counter Margaret set down peroxide, a Milky Way bar, and a packet of peppermint Chiclets. Lab coat billowing, the druggist hot-stepped from the window to the register. "I had some kids work this kit and caboodle with me for a while, but good help's hard to come by." He peered at her hand. "What's ailing that there?"

"I hurt it."

"I ain't blind. You aim to fix it? Or you just gonna let it fall off and grow you a new one?"

"I got peroxide for it."

"Foot," he said. From the back shelves he fetched a cardboard carton. "Soak that in hot Epsom salts three times a day. Cures everything. A doctor won't say so, but it does."

"You got a smaller box?" Margaret said.

"I got what you see. You do as I say or you'll get a nasty red streak up your arm and have to see a doctor. That streak gets to your heart, well . . ." He tugged at an invisible noose. "Blood poison."

Margaret placed some bills on the counter. "I like to avoid doctors."

Outside, a voice counted off. The druggist pointed at twirlers in purple sequins. When trombones glissandoed into Henry Mancini noise, the twirlers tugged theatrically at long white gloves. "I'd try avoiding the law too," the druggist said.

"How's that?"

"I see everything goes on in that glass. You got you some twelve-count gauze pads, some ointment, some aspirins, and one or two other items I didn't quite catch."

"You're real observant," Margaret said. Her hand brushed the holster as she retrieved the things. The band outside was loud. She smoothed her dress, then set the wares beside the salts. "Times are hard."

"Don't tell me."

"Thank you."

He pushed her change across the counter. "Don't thank me neither. Just don't come back."

Margaret threaded her way into the crowd. When a siren whooped she stopped, clutching her bag to her chest. A red-haired officer tossed candies from his car, scattering children like perch. Fire trucks crept past, then mules and Model Ts. Knees to their chins, fezzed Shriners go-karted in formation. Cheerleaders carried a banner—PANTHERS: MONSTER MASH THE MUSTANGS—followed by tractors pulling floats: SEND THE MUSTANGS BACK TO THEIR MUMMIES; PANTHERS: GO PSYCHO ON THE MUSTANGS; NIGHTMARE ON MUSTANG STREET; and last, GODZILLA: MANGLE THE MUSTANGS. A rickety mutant lizard towered over a city of painted cardboard boxes and fleeing plastic horses. Its jaw spasmed while roars rattled speakers at the back of the float. Smoke dribbled from its maw. The cheering of the crowd disintegrated into laughter.

Randy scuttled along the curb with two overstuffed garbage bags strapped to his bike. He flapped his free arm like a bird with a bad wing, screeching at the dinosaur as if begging it to bear him skyward. Onlookers guffawed. A wagonload of football boys tailed the float, a few pointing. What a show.

"That boy don't know shit from apple butter," a man said.

At the corner the float's front tire struck the curb, and the wagon clipped Randy's shoulder, tearing him from his bike, cans spilling across the courthouse lawn as he slid beneath the paper skirt. The giant lizard rocked so hard its moorings snapped, and it creaked to the street in a heap of one-by-twos, chicken wire, and green tissue paper. The wagon went on. Silence settled over the crowd. The lizard head gnawed circles around Randy where he lay.

Without thinking, Margaret fetched the bike, but Randy stood and ran so hard at a cluster of onlookers they parted, granting him wide passage. Football boys on the wagon wolf-whistled as she pushed back through the onlookers.

"She that boy's mama?" a woman said.

"Naw," a man said. "That boy's mama's scattered to the wind."

Down a street of grand old houses gone to seed, Margaret found Randy rocking in a pile of leaves, his torn pant leg showing a patch of scraped shin. On every porch was a pumpkin, corn shock, or scarecrow, autumn touches on a day that had turned warm. She flipped down the kickstand and dumped out her bag on the walk. Randy hissed.

"Hush," she said, gripping his ankle. "I'm one-armed and crippled, and you still don't scare me." She had expected his leg to be soft, like Timmy's, but his calf was covered with dark hairs, the flesh pale yet firm as a man's. His eyes were on her as she doused the wound with peroxide and taped down gauze. "Done," she said. "Now get on before I steal your bike too." Without looking back he pedaled down the walk. A cold twinge of regret passed through her, as when something comes that you never can have, though it's what you want the most. "That's right," she said. "You just go on."

❧

Darkness fell before she could reach camp, so she bought a five-pound bag of ice for her ankle and rested between heat-pump units at the side of a new strip mall, a pizza joint its only tenant. To the west a hollow was heaped with busted cinder blocks and gypsum board scraps; beyond it, an arc of white stadium light drew night birds. A marching band began to play, the brassy tones muffled by a line of trees and sporadic traffic from the four-lane.

Margaret emptied out the bag from the drugstore, going over

her hand with peroxide and ointment before she swathed it tight, then she wrapped her foot, lacing the boot as snug as she could, and retied the holster. Hanging her head, she tried to catch her breath. A voice from a distant loudspeaker called out the number of a down, then another, another. *Homecoming*, Margaret thought, before the droning advance and retreat of high school boys lulled her into a fitful sleep.

She woke to a can clattering in the parking lot. The western sky was dark. A teenage girl yelled for someone to knock it off, and an engine revved. Margaret gathered her things and limped into the pizza place, where teenagers jabbered in vinyl booths and Top 40 blared from the ceiling. Through a doorway left of the back counter was a bar lined with high school boys in game-day jerseys, each with a pilsner glass and a sweating pitcher of beer. In a dim corner, Number Nine shouted at Number Sixty-three, who was hunched over a table game. "You gotta eat the ghosts," he said.

"I've played the game."

"There's four ghosts. You eat all four."

"I ain't blind."

"You don't eat them, they'll get you."

Margaret leaned against the doorjamb, but the bartender kept his gaze fixed on the TV over the mirror. "I could use some service here," she said.

The boys tensed as if caught by their mothers. Number Seventy-two—a mud-haired teen with a beard encircling his mouth—glanced back and elbowed Thirty-four. "I'd give her a little service," he said.

Thirty-four told Seventy-two to shut up, that he was drunk.

The bartender looked over his shoulder. "Be right with you."

"Go for it, Riggs," Seventy-two said.

Margaret shook her head. How tenuous a boy's existence—from boy to man to nothing at all. In the corner, Sixty-three kept englishing pixels of light. Nine smiled at Margaret. A 35-millimeter camera hung from his neck. "This old game," he said. "He still can't figure it out."

"I know how to play," Sixty-three said.

Nine did not stop smiling. "You do."

The barman met her at the counter. He had a gut and the aimless bearing of a former athlete. Yes, he said, the boys were underage and a little drunk and a lot obnoxious, but, by God, they were bound for State, sure as a goose shits, and when he'd played they were never bound for State, and it was Homecoming anyway, and they'd managed to skunk the Mustangs. Here they were caught up in the prime of life, and he meant to prime it further. Besides, he said, nobody was buying pizza.

"I'd take a pizza," Margaret said. "Unless you give up selling it."

"Oh, yes, ma'am. Or, no, I mean."

"Go, Riggs," a boy yelled from the bar. Seventy-two raised his glass to Margaret.

"Riggs?" she said. "I'd take a small pepperoni with mushroom. And a beer."

The man blushed to hear his name. "Oh. Yes, ma'am."

Margaret winked at the boys, which, as she suspected, spun them back around. Their faces were drained and indistinct. Even the stout ones looked worn down. Poor boys, with nothing to fight for. In some third-world country, they would be shoeless and armed. Here they lived in houses that smelled of fried pork and cigarette smoke. Windows painted shut, sills peeling, linoleum curling from the corners. Their fathers wept after four beers, their mothers' sofas were soiled at the arms. Anything worth defending these boys would rather damage.

By the time her pizza came Riggs had turned one beer into three, and these had numbed her enough that she felt determined to get up and go. The boys were stealing glances, giggling and slapping their knees. Riggs was nowhere to be found.

"Ma'am?"

Margaret jumped. Seventy-two was poking at her shoulder. He doubled over with laughter, his beer sloshing on the carpet. "You don't mind me calling you ma'am, do you, ma'am?"

"Depends," Margaret said. "You being polite? Or are you being an asshole?"

"Um, we got this friend," he said.

"You didn't answer my question."

He looked to the bar. His buddies were waving like stage mothers.

"They didn't ask the question," Margaret said. "I did."

"Right. What's the question again?"

"Are you saying ma'am to be polite? Or are you saying ma'am to be an asshole?"

"Oh, polite, ma'am. Polite. We're all of us very polite."

Margaret tried to take a bite of pizza, but the boy grabbed her arm. "See, we got this friend? He's very polite too. Very. That number thirty-four? We call him Okie. See?"

Margaret tried to stare the boy's hand off of her. "I see."

"Okie needs him a date to the Homecoming tomorrow night. So we thought we'd ask you."

"What's wrong with him that he can't get a date?"

"Wrong? Nothing's wrong. Ain't nothing wrong with any of us."

"You're all very polite. Junior-fucking-Jaycees."

Beer foam glistened in the boy's beard.

"You got you a name?"

"Oh, uh, Sawyer. They call me Sawblade. Or just plain Blade. Because I'm so sharp." He stepped back to steady himself.

"Well, Just Plain Blade, if your friend can get him a date, what're you asking for him for?"

"He's shy. Besides," Sawyer said, tapping his temple, "we put our heads together . . ." He swallowed, swayed. "Put our heads together. Saw you. At the parade. Thought you'd make a fine date."

"Oh?"

Sawyer draped his arm over her shoulder, pinning her to the counter. "Ma'am," he said. "I mean, you got that look."

"What look's that?"

"Yeah." He ran a damp finger across her scar. "That putting-out look. Ma'am."

"Get off me," Margaret said. She jabbed him with her elbow, and he staggered backward. Before he could reach again she was out the door, trailing the laughter of the boys behind her.

A paring of moon was lost in treetops by the time Margaret found the overgrown lane to her camp. Clutching the bag, she used her good hand to push back branches as she made her way through woods darker than night. Falling leaves whispered down around her, and small animals stirred deadfall. When a wild thing snorted not a body's length away, she sidestepped, but it snorted again, and coarse hair brushed her arm, the ground trembling like a drumskin. She limped away as fast as she could, but by the time she realized she'd fled nothing but deer, a crackling fire in the cul-de-sac had appeared. Atop a flat-black Camaro sat a case of beer; the football boys were gathered at the Plymouth. Sawyer had backed Randy against the open door while Sixty-three was on his knees, shaking a box of cartridges from Margaret's duffel. Nine took photographs. At every flash, Randy cried out. The one called Okie had his back to Margaret. He told them quit. He said he needed to get on home.

Boys. They turned into men. What if Timmy had turned into a man, one who brought only grief and pain? She'd had the thought too many times before.

Sawyer parried an ember-tipped stick at Randy's face. "You gonna make our yearbook, Skink," he said.

"C'mon, guys," Okie said. "Let's go."

Sixty-three stuck a pink pair of underwear on his head. "Panties."

"You wear panties, Skink?" Sawyer said.

Margaret set down her bag of drugstore items. "Leave that boy be."

The players turned. Sixty-three quieted the cartridges. Randy tried to run, but his hood was hooked fast in Sawyer's grip.

Nine took Margaret's picture. "How about you put that camera away," she said. "I ain't anything you need to see."

"Why, it's your sweetie, Okie," Sawyer said. "She's come to take you away from all this."

"Let's go, guys," Okie said.

An intuitive boy, Margaret thought. Intuitive men knew, sometimes, what she was thinking before she did; they were therefore not to be trusted. Margaret nodded at her clothes on the ground. "You boys go through your mamas' purses like that?"

"You ain't our mama," Sawyer said.

Randy bolted to the falls. A leer sliced Sawyer's face, his cheeks pink with chill and beer. He waved his stick but the ember had gone out. "I know what you want," he said.

Watching Margaret through a long lens, Nine took another picture.

"C'mon, Blade," Okie said. "Let's leave the lady alone."

Sixty-three sneaked the underwear off his head, leaving a rooster comb of hair. "Yeah, Blade. Maybe we should go."

"C'mon?" Sawyer said. "Go? That's a dream come true right there. Straight from these woods to do you right." He took three deliberate steps toward Margaret. "Besides, know what your daddies'll do if you come home drunk? They'll say, 'Just 'cause you run a little ball across cut grass don't make you no big shot. Don't give you no right to get drunk, you little shit.' That's what your daddies'll say."

"That's what *your* daddy'll say," Nine said.

Swaying, Sawyer regarded Margaret. "His daddy fell into turbines at the dam."

Nine looked over the top of his camera. "Shut up, Blade."

"Yeah," Sawyer said. "He's lucky. You too. I know what you want."

"Boys," Margaret said. Then Blade was heading for her, and Okie was yelling stop. Left-handed, Margaret undid the whip from her waist, flipped back the braided leather, and brought it forward, but the thing was unwieldy, and it plopped in a heap at Sawyer's feet.

A flash popped. Sawyer flung Margaret over his shoulder, but he stumbled and fell, dropping her hopping into the middle of the other three. "Wait," she said. But the boys had made no move. She put up her hand; blood was seeping through the bandage. "You all want to see something?" she said.

Sawyer staggered to his feet. "I want you on the ground."

"C'mon, Blade," Okie said. "Just shut up and leave the woman alone."

Margaret took off her jacket and tossed it behind her. The air filled with a damp static that might have been desire. Probably it was fear.

Sixty-three stood, the bag sliding from his hand. "Blade," he said. "Blade. C'mon, just leave the lady alone."

"Guys," Okie said, "I got to get home."

Nine fumbled in his pockets for a fresh roll of film. He was feeding it into his camera when she saw Sawyer coming. He was drunk and slow; she could have sidestepped him any other time, but her ankle gave, and he caught her by the waist. She pushed a bloody print onto his jersey as he tore at her dress. He stank of beer and woodsmoke. The three were yelling: stop, go, some sort of action. Margaret stretched her left hand to the holster strap and tugged. Working her fingers down the grip, she got it solid in her palm, then jammed the muzzle of the .38 so hard under Sawyer's chin it lifted his gaze skyward. Stars shone down through yellow leaves. Beyond them lay infinite blackness.

Cyrus showed up late, slipping past a line of men crowded at the ropes until a bouncer spun him around and sent him to the east door—someone there would let him in.

No one did. Security lights illuminated cars at the edge of the lot. RESERVED FOR BO'S BEAUTIES, a sign said. Cyrus knocked at a door that pulsed with galloping club music, then he waited, taking the bottle of pills from his pocket. He didn't care for pills—didn't know them, really—but these were free for the taking; the illicit drinks tonight might not be. He popped three white ones, dry. The music ceased, and he beat at the door. When finally a buzz-cut bouncer answered, Cyrus told him he had come to sing.

"To *what*?"

"Sing. Music." Cyrus lifted the guitar case. "Maybe you've heard of it."

"Not here I haven't. C'mon in." More rhythms commenced as Cyrus climbed to the top of a dark staircase. The bouncer pointed to a door. "Dressing room," he said. "You got to share. Newbern wants to talk sound, though. You kept him waiting. And Bo's pissed. I should tell you he docks you for being late."

They took another staircase to a freight elevator crammed with liquor boxes, then rose to a carpeted landing, paisley patterned and red as blood. Couples promenaded past doors on which brass numerals gleamed. The men wore jeans and boots, but the girls were clad in shimmering cloth and heels. Below the walkway railing men drank at tables and floor girls labored at couches. A blue spot illuminated the stage, where a dancer twirled one tit clockwise, the other counter.

Beyond the landing a spiral staircase corkscrewed to the top of the building; there the bouncer flung open a door. "Newbern. Singer's here. You still want to see him?"

"Hell, no, I don't *want* to see him."

The bouncer held the door and, bless him, smiled apologetically as Cyrus stepped into a dark room lit by boards and monitors. The floor was covered with albums, Coke cans, and CDs. A large window looked down on the stage. "I'll wait outside," the bouncer said.

"Shit," Newbern said. "One-man band come walking in my cripple cave, thinking he fed on cornbread and turnip greens."

A black man in a racing wheelchair was grinning at Cyrus—not unkindly, it seemed. A monitor cast a blue sheen on his skin. The legs of his jeans were pinned up with brass cattle tags. He took a long drink of Coca-Cola.

"How'd you get up here?" Cyrus said.

Newbern belched. "I am one magic Negro. Mr. Hoodoo Voodoo flew up these stairs. Hah. White man been carrying my ass for years. And you—Mr. Singer Songwriter—can quit staring at my legs. They ain't there."

"I see that."

Newbern threw back his head. "Ha. God knows what you see. I've heard your music. You are one sad-ass motherfucker, Cyrus Harper."

"You what?"

"Think I just listen to rap? Think I give up on music? I say leave rap to the white boys. This is one cripple Negro thinks we ought to think up more shitty music for you whiteys to steal."

"You can cut the crippled Negro crap," Cyrus said. "I just come to get the sound straight. That bouncer said Bo was mad. He didn't say you were crazy."

"Bo? Shit." Newbern peered out the window. "She's gonna shake them loose if she ain't careful." Left-handed, he tapped the keyboard. Stage lights went orange. "So. You gonna jump in front of a bunch of drunk-ass motherfuckers wanting booty and you worried about greasy old Bo? Worry about the man does your sound."

"It's just me and the guitar," Cyrus said.

"You go out there you gonna need you a big band and some girls."

"I mean the sound ain't hard to figure."

"Oh, is that right? Well. Willie Newbern can take it away; Willie Newbern can give it back. The Newbern gives, and the Newbern takes away. What I give might be feedback, and what I take might be your voice."

"Willie Newbern?"

"Yes, which is why I go by Newbern. I get scrawny old music whiteys like you thinking they want to go talk about Hambone Willie Newbern. I ain't related, and he's obscure, and when you cripple like me, you don't want somebody talking about a long-gone song like 'Roll and Tumble Blues.' You can just see them stewing the bad jokes."

"You play?"

Newbern held up his right hand. Half of it was missing, and what remained was covered in pale scar tissue. "Motorcycle accident. Old lady pulls out in front of me, sends me through a car dealership window. Drag my ass out from under a Mercury Topaz. So what. I played clubs but didn't have no fire for it. I'd have ended up giving music lessons in some strip mall teaching white boys to tommy-gun sixteen notes to the bar. That ain't any kind of music, and that ain't got nothing to do with the blues. Except for living it, and you don't want to live it. You want to play it. That's where you white boys get confused."

"How do you know my music?" Cyrus's vision seemed Vaselined, the dancer onstage tiny, as if viewed from the wrong end of a telescope. "That girl out there's done," he said.

"Oh. Thanks." Newbern killed the stage lights and took a swig of Coca-Cola. Flipping on the mike, he spoke in a voice that was half 1950s-TV father, half B-movie god, and all white. "Gentlemen—give a warm hand to Candy Sells and her fine flirtatious folderol. Where does she tuck those twenties? What secret spots will she share? Find out on Wondrous Wednesdays, when our lovely ladies lap-dance languorously for you, and the libations are, well, cheaper than usual. Now, let's give it up, give it up, give it up for Nikki Slick, and her salacious, salubrious, sinful—" Newbern flipped off the microphone. "Shit," he said. "How do I know your songs? I deejay. In the morning. Classic rock. All classic. All the motherfucking time. A few years back your mama was making rounds with your CD and come in the booth and give me one. Lord knows how she got past the desk."

"My mom?"

"Little sweet white-haired lady? I remember she said you was from around here, and I said there ain't nothing from around here, and she said that's where you're wrong, bud. Bud—she said it just like that. I get sick of classic rock all the livelong day, so I give you a listen. I didn't play you. We got playlists. Lord, do we got playlists. You ain't bad. Your songs are a little spare, and they from the wrong era, but I like that flat thing you do. Like you had one too many conversations with the dead. You don't get many takers for it, I bet."

"I can't be but what I am," Cyrus said.

"Shit. A man's everything but what he is. But, hey, you're welcome here no matter what you think you are." He extended his remaindered hand; it was damp and difficult to grasp.

"Thank you," Cyrus said.

"Thank you?"

"For not running my mom off."

"Any old lady ain't afraid of my ugly ass is all right. Hey, Schlep?" Newbern called. The bouncer opened the door. "Set this child up with mikes and monitors. He'll go after Leathery Lola. Just make sure he gets to spend some time with a drink. He's sweating like a whore in church."

On his way to the dressing room, Cyrus thought that, if Newbern was a truth-telling man, his mother had taken his CDs to stations she'd never listened to and handed them to deejays who'd never play the songs. She had shilled his music the way she and Ott had shilled their own years ago, which would have taken more courage than Cyrus knew she had.

"There you go," Schlep said, shoving open the door.

The dressing room was a bright cavern of young women in various states of undress. Some were slouched on metal folding chairs, others lined on stools at a counter scattered with paper towels, makeup, and cold cream jars. They watched Cyrus in the mirror. One blonde applied base to her breasts. Through the wall, music rumbled like a passing freight train.

"There's women here," Cyrus said to the bouncer.

"They ain't gonna hurt you."

A girl, naked from the waist up, stepped from behind a rack of costumes. "A lot you know, Schlep." The bouncer pointed pistol-like at her, then shut the door.

Cyrus feigned interest in the corners and hanging fixtures before his gaze fell on a brunette in a very untied velour housecoat, a hamburger in her hand, a paper box of fries on her knees. She waved at Cyrus with a mustard-smeared pinky. He wiped his forehead and bid the floor good evening.

"Where's that tie?" the girl at the rack said. "Why do men wear ties?"

"Jacket pocket, Annie," the girl with the burger said. Smiling at Cyrus, she pointed a french fry at a folding chair.

He stayed put, gripping the handle of the guitar case, and

gripping it harder when, from behind a trifold screen in the corner, a woman covered from head to ankles in something like black patent leather appeared. The rise of breasts and pubis, the long pan of belly, the jut of hip bones—all were evident beneath polished armor that creaked with each breath. She wore six-inch rubber platforms. Her hood revealed a bud of nose, a crab apple of mouth, and green eyes.

"Break out the leather, baby," said the woman applying base.

The bouncer returned with a tumbler so full of bourbon and ice Cyrus had to take the glass with both hands. "You're up after that one there," he said, and slipped back into the hall. The leather girl folded her arms across her chest as if to protest, but off in the theater, Newbern's fifties-TV-dad voice started up, and the dressing-room door swung open so hard it struck the wall. Cyrus turned to face an abundant girl, naked except for gold stiletto heels and a belt of spangled nylon over which were folded bills of notable denominations. She blushed from head to money belt—late, it seemed, for modesty. "Um," she said, "who are you?"

Cyrus tried not to look, but there she was. College age, maybe, younger than he would expect, or care to see, in such a place. A ragged pageboy sharpened her high cheekbones, and her toenails were japanned to a sheen, but in her face he saw shades of a girl who'd likely played dolls on some suburban deck overlooking a cornfield in the Midwest. When she caught Cyrus studying the Celtic cross tattooed below her navel, she smiled in a way that seemed so genuine he felt ashamed. "I'm supposed to sing," he said.

"Cool." She took hold of his arm as if to present him to the other women. "Did you know we have a singer?"

"Oh, we know," Annie said, stuffing her hair under a fedora.

In heels, the girl had to stoop to meet his eyes. "They call me Sade. Like sadomasochist? Or Sexy Sadie? That Beatles song? It was 'Maharishi' first, though, you know, after they got duped by that Yogi. You probably do know that already."

Music through the walls shifted—a manic poetaster flaying a perfectly good guitar. Sade cocked her head and started humming in a clear tone suited to glee clubs. "I like this part," she said. "You like this part?"

Cyrus admitted that he was not familiar with the part.

"Hey, Sade?" Annie said, tugging her tie into a Windsor. "Before you get too friendly, or freaky, or whatever it is you get, the singer's cutting into our take and taking our floor time."

Sade squeezed Cyrus's arm. Lifting a twenty from her belt, she dabbed at perspiration on her breasts. "I like the singer. Like, the singer should take what all he can get."

"Don't you at least want to get his name first?" Annie said.

"Cyrus," Cyrus said, louder than he intended. "Cyrus Harper."

The leather girl stomped past him into the hall. Sade watched her go. "She OK?"

"Her girl's sick," the blonde at the counter said. "Again." She jabbed her thumb stageward. "How the hell can she dance on those things?"

"She can dance on those things," Annie said, straightening her tie, "because she's got more talent in her pinkie than you've got in both your pendulous breasts."

"Screw you," the blonde said.

"No time for that now. I have to go get dominated."

❧

Cyrus clutched a fresh drink and the guitar. Onstage, Annie and the leather girl were going at it, their movements choreographed and cliché. Heavy metal grated like a poorly tuned engine as Annie mock-licked the platforms of the leather girl, who wielded a blacksnake whip. Then Annie's suit whirled off, revealing not a businessman but a G-stringed, fishnet-stockinged woman who stalked down the runway to do her own variety of business. Taking the uplifted heads of men between her breasts, she gathered bills like blossoms.

The job done, the G-string gone, Annie slipped behind her partner, tearing at flaps to reveal thighs, buttocks, breasts, pudendum. The leather girl threw one arm into the spotlight beam, and with the other twirled the whip, but when Annie reached to remove the hood, the leather girl flogged her lazily from the stage and knelt, spinning one breast clockwise, the other counter—a motif for the night—before she twirled offstage toward Cyrus, greenbacks folded and fanned between her fingers. The stage went dark. A bouncer carted an armload of costumes past Cyrus. "You got mikes and a monitor at the start of the runway," he said. "Don't go past them. They's hungry tonight. We got buses in from Rolla."

From on high Newbern requested that the gathered please welcome a particular pleasure for the evening, recording artist Cyrus Harper. Cyrus threw back the rest of his drink and strode to center stage, squinting against the hard light, hunting for Darby. The room went quiet. Tuning—stalling, in fact, for an appropriate song—Cyrus scraped his talc-dry tongue on his teeth. "Evening," he said. Feedback squawked. "Little less treble, please."

"We want titties," a man shouted.

"Check," Cyrus said, strumming a G chord. "Check. More guitar. Check."

"Titties!"

"Thank you, Newbern. Check. Check. OK." Cyrus peered into the dim. "Friend, if you weren't so god-awful ugly you could get your titties at home like most folks."

Tepid laughter washed through the crowd as Cyrus started in on a Johnny Cash tune. They'd at least know it, he thought, but if they did, they didn't care to hear it. A beer bottle bounced on the stage. Then flew other projectiles. Down in the theater bouncers began dragging offenders toward the lobby. Cyrus kept on until a shot glass struck his fret hand. Knuckles in his mouth, he hunched off-stage, the audience cheering his retreat.

Wearing voluminous pink frills, Sade stood beside the leather girl, who was unzipping her hood. "That was great," Sade said.

"No. It wasn't. But thanks."

"It'd be like you, Cyrus," the leather girl said, "to just up and leave, wouldn't it?" She tugged off her hood, black hair tumbling down her back, and forced a smile.

"Do you two, like, know each other?"

Impeccable posture. Excellent grades. A taste for modern jazz and classical music, both of which Cyrus despised for their complexity. Her body was her instrument, one she'd never let Cyrus play until the end of high school. On the back of her thigh a birthmark shaped like Portugal. But Cate O'Connor was heavier in the face now, and dark half-moons lay beneath her eyes.

"My God," Cyrus said. "What are you doing here?"

"I'd ask you the same, Cyrus, but right now I need to get home."

Bo mounted the steps behind Cate.

"You've got a daughter?" Cyrus said. "That's what I heard in—"

"Yes. And yes, I work here. If that's what you mean."

Bo squeezed Cate's shoulders. "Nobody seems to be doing any kind of work I can see. You're supposed to sing. And you two, you're supposed to dance. We have dancing. We have drinking. And now . . ." He rolled his eyes. "We have singing."

"I ain't a target," Cyrus said.

Bo ran his hands down Cate's arms. "I can't fire you, but if you don't sing, I don't pay."

"I need to check on May," Cate said.

"Hundreds of girls would kill to have your job, Cate."

"By all means, Bo, hire them before they hurt somebody." She pulled a shawl tight and turned, but Bo slapped her bare bottom. She stiffened, then moved on.

"Prime," Bo said to Cyrus. "So. How about you sing us another pretty song?"

Armed now with plastic cups, the customers scattered ice at Cyrus like bird shot. A young man in khaki pants climbed atop a table, and when the spotlight beam struck him, he waved to the cheering crowd and, mocking Cyrus, belted out a ribald version of "I Walk the Line." He swiveled his hips and fumbled with shirt buttons, while Cyrus picked—why not?—accompaniment. "I keep my pants up with a piece of twine," the drunk screeched. "Because you're mine, please pull the twine." Then he shoved his pants and boxers to his ankles.

Cyrus flatpicked "Shave and a Haircut" and at the "two bits" the drunk shook his hind end, the crowd beating the air with their fists. Of course. If they wanted bawdy lyrics, Cyrus could oblige them, thanks to Loman Kirby, with an endless raunchy repertoire.

The last time he and Saro had ever performed together, she had argued with Cyrus over tunes meant to please the baser humors. For a Fourth of July festival overlooking the Gasconade River, they'd worked up "Rock That Cradle Lucy" and a titleless waltz and "Bear Creek Sally Goodin," which required Black Mountain Rag tuning, a scordatura brought over by Scottish fiddlers. There was a cash prize for the fiddling portion of the contest. But it was hot, and Cyrus's pegs kept slipping. Saro's mended hip ached. She was on edge. Leaning against the truck, they waited to be called to the tent along the shaded fringe of the grounds.

"I don't want to do that 'Bear Creek,'" Saro said. "It takes too long for you to retune, and I have to keep the crowd up."

"What do you want to do, then?"

Passersby ambled the midway with their popcorn and paper cups of Coca-Cola. "Look at them," Saro said. "Death eating a soda cracker. I saw one with pee stains on his pants. His family just let him out like that, the poor old man. We're playing dead songs for people on Death's door. If they get up and dance they look like skeletons on strings."

"I like their dancing," Cyrus said. "They've been with each other so long they know where the other's fixing to step. Just think if we got like that with our singing."

Saro looked off toward the faded tents.

"What?"

"Nothing."

"Nothing? Or never mind?"

She began to sing a blue version of "Fly Around My Pretty Little Miss."

"Well, we ain't doing that," Cyrus said.

"Loman taught us it."

"He taught me. He thought your ears might break."

"Little does he know," she said, and she gave Cyrus her tooth-concealing grin.

"There's old people out there."

"It's old music, Cyrus."

"They didn't do that sort of thing in mixed company. They didn't use that word."

Saro shook her head. "People got to keep everything hid."

"There's rules," Cyrus said.

"You got it in your head how a thing should be. Don't you think every one of these people is here because somebody somewhere got fucked at least once?"

"Oh, please. We can't do a song with the word fuck in it."

"And I can't play second anymore. Not to you. Not to anybody. I'm tired of this."

Saro turned, and when Cyrus stepped toward her she ran for the carnival grounds. At a break in the contest, he went looking for her. He wasn't of much interest on his own; he knew that. A fiddler had been in demand way back when—called to a funeral, a Masons meeting, a barn dance—but Saro was right. The audience was dying. Soon they'd play for a tentful of ghosts.

"Kid," a barker called from behind his counter. He wore a stained green hat advertising a make of tractor. He was missing his front teeth. "Come win your honey something."

"You see some honey I don't?"

"They'll swarm you if you win one of these prizes."

"You haven't seen a girl go by, have you?" Cyrus said. "Blue dress? Long brown hair?"

"I see the girls. Ain't none of them notice me." The barker clutched theatrically at his heart. "Girls are the cause of man's misery. Play this game. Forget your misery."

"You just said girls'd swarm me if I won something."

"One man's misery," the barker said, "is another man's pleasure." He lifted a tray of prizes—Budweiser mirror, stuffed polar bear, lacquer box with a pinup decal on the lid, and a copper bracelet stamped with fiddles, guitars, and a serpentine lariat.

"What do I got to knock down for that?" Cyrus said.

"Four fuzzy little pussies," the barker said.

The object was to throw baseballs at cats on tracks. The cartoon felines were edged with pink polyester fibers that made them appear larger than they were—a trick to upset your aim. Cyrus hit two.

"A pussy is a dark-hearted thing," the barker said.

Cyrus slapped down a five. "Let me buy that bracelet."

"I just take tickets."

"That bracelet ain't worth but a nickel," Cyrus said.

The barker glanced up, then down, the midway; he tucked the five in his shirt pocket. "I like a man knows what he wants."

Cyrus found Saro with Willie Gilmore between the Whirligig and Haunted Manor. A loudspeaker played a loop of screams. "If it ain't the music man," he said, his hand below Saro's waist.

"Shut up, Willie," Saro said.

"You don't tell me when to shut up."

"I just did."

"I need to talk to my sister."

"You talk to me, Cyrus. Not him."

Willie stared at Saro. "Don't keep her too long now. She might spoil."

Whatever had incited Saro and Gilmore that day Cyrus ignored; he had his own agenda. Beside a moat stocked with plastic ducks, he told Saro they could perform what she wanted. But she said no, she was done. He gave her the bracelet. Then Gilmore nosed into the conversation. "Ah, it's got geetars on it," he said. "Ain't that sweet."

"Shut up, Willie," Saro said, and he did.

She held the bracelet, looking down on it a long while until she smiled to herself and slipped it on her wrist. "Thank you, Cyrus," she said, and agreed to perform. When their names were called, he switched a breakdown for "Bear Creek," and for the sake of propriety, Saro did not announce the title—"Trade My Name for a Piece of Tail." Still, a few old-timers in the bleachers grinned. No, they were not dead yet.

Within a month, the bracelet turned Saro's wrist green. Within another month, she was gone.

Two bouncers circled the drunk on the table as he shook his ass at the spotlight; one got hold of a calf and tugged, the other caught him on the way down, and together they dragged him away.

When the cheering died down, Cyrus said, "Ladies, let us pray our friend here's blessed above the neck because he sure ain't blessed below the belt." The men laughed, and Cyrus bowed, the floor seeming to slide from under him. Out in the dark, amber lights glowed like coal fires in weathered shacks. Cyrus was not sure where he was until an old man at the footlights grabbed his pant leg and said, "Son, can you do 'Great Speckled Bird'?"

Black-rimmed glasses at the tip of his nose, a pale halo of crazed hair, a bramble of eyebrows. "I know that song, yessir," Cyrus said.

The man shook a tuberous forefinger. "How 'bout you sing it then?"

"That's a sacred song. That's for church."

The geezer did a tour-guide sweep with his hand. Men in line at a barside ATM. Topless women at tables. He cackled and Cyrus kicked him away.

"Ladies, I expect you're at least as hip as Mitch Miller, so maybe you can handle a sing-along, which means, ladies, you sing when the chorus comes along. This here's to the tune of 'My Bonnie Lies over the Ocean.' Call it 'My Father was Hung.'" Someone whooped. "That's right. Not like our friend, Mr. Bud Pud."

> *My father was hung for a horse thief,*
> *My mother was burnt for a witch,*
> *My sister bides time in the whorehouse,*
> *And, me, I'm a son of a bitch.*
> *Oh! (Here's where you ladies come in, ladies.)*
> *All gone! All gone! The devil it matters to you and to you!*
> *All gone! All gone! But they left me some fucking to do!*

The song was long as a sea chantey. How had he come to this, hooting at busloads of men on a stage in south Missouri? How had Cate ended up in a tin warehouse, flaunting what Cyrus, years ago, had rarely glimpsed? The drunks picked up on the chorus. Cyrus didn't even need to sing, and he knew that in the morning he would be but a hallucination to them, as vague as their glimpses of flesh. Cyrus nodded at Sade, who watched from stage right. She was pretty. She was there. So too was the rest of the night.

The crown of Sawyer's head misted into a pink glister that settled on the game-day jerseys of the boys. His legs folded under him, torso quivering as if stomped upon until it went still. Someone whimpered. Maybe Margaret. The boys stood as still as rabbits in tall grass. She took them to have been raised hunters and fishers, reverence instilled in them for how simply life could be removed: a buck felled with one shot, greasy scrim passing over its eyes as the animal ceased kicking at fallen leaves; winged bobwhite flapping circles in milo only to be cupped warm in hand and taken with a snap of the neck; channel cat writhing on weathered dock boards until a one-by-two cracked its skull. Now here was one of their own. They watched him where he lay.

"He's all right." Margaret said.

"He's dead," Nine said.

"I had a boy died," Margaret said. "It's all over now. Killing boys. All over."

The three looked up as if she had just arrived. "You killed him," Nine said. There seemed some point he wished to debate.

"You bury what's over with. That's proper," Margaret said. No one moved. She expected them to scatter soon. "Go on now. That hole there. Go on."

A gust stirred yellow leaves, kicking them up between her and the boys.

"I said go on. Get him in there." Finally, Okie and Sixty-three took leaden steps toward the body, then paused to look at Margaret. The gun hung at her side, thin smoke curling from the muzzle. "That's right," she said. They hefted the body by the armpits and dragged it to the lip of the hole, its legs straightening from under it as they went.

"It's wet in there," Okie said.

"We wouldn't have let him hurt you," Nine said.

"You never know what you'll do," Margaret said, "until it's done. Now, let's get it done."

The two boys split apart, the body a bridge between them as it sagged toward the hole, and then dropped.

When the sloshing waters stilled, Margaret nodded for the boys to get into the hole. "Help him," she said. "Help your friend now." Sixty-three and Okie kept their gazes lowered as they scooted over the edge.

"Do what?" Nine said. "Help him do what?"

Margaret was gripping the gun so tightly her hand had gone numb. She leveled it at Nine's chest. "Drop your camera."

"It's the school's camera."

"Your pictures go in the fire there."

Nine dug in his pockets. Trembling, he tossed the capped rolls. A few flamed up. Others melted or careered off the firestones.

"Leave them lay," she said. "Get in."

Nine looked around him as if expecting counsel, but there was only darkness, emptying branches, water running on without him. He slid in beside his friends. "You don't have to do this, ma'am," he said. "We'll just bury him like you say. We won't tell. We won't know what happened."

"I don't know what happened," Okie said. "I don't know what's happening. I just said let's go home."

"I ain't gonna stop you from home," Margaret said. "Where's the keys? To that car?"

"Take the camera," Nine said. "If you need it take it."

She kicked it aside as it rolled to her.

"They're in the car, ma'am," Sixty-three said.

A plastic canister of film popped open in the fire, and Okie winced. "Any of you named Timmy?" Margaret said. "Timothy? Tim? Timmy?" She gripped the pistol with both hands, widened her stance.

"Ma'am?" Okie said.

"Yes."

"What's it matter what our names are?"

"It doesn't." From left to right, she dropped them. Chest, head, head. Over by the falls, Randy was flapping his arms and whining, and with the pistol she waved him back from the water. "You be still," she said through the ringing in her ears. He turned for the woods as she stepped to the edge of the hole. The boys lay tangled and silent, and she could not tell where one began and the other ended.

Dropping the cylinder, she pocketed the warm cartridges, re-loaded, and holstered the gun. Blood soaked her bandaged hand. Stepping to the falls she gathered an armload of flat chert stones and dropped them by the hole, which the contorted bodies had almost filled. Then she hacked at mounded earth, flinging it to cover what she'd done. She kept her bad hand to her breast. The fire began to fade, and too soon she reached a mud that was cold, slick, and stony. Chert sheared off in pieces, and by the time she had hidden the boys, packing the earth with her feet and knees, cold sweat was dripping from her face. Then she heard men. Camouflaged in shades of sum-mer, they came crashing through the brush, but she fled with her things into thick sumac above the falls before they reached the Fury. They clutched rifles. A few wore helmets. Most wore feed caps, including Captain Coffey, who tipped back his head and made a whip-poor-will call, drawing his comrades, mute, to the fire ring. "Major?" Coffey said.

A white-haired man tap-tapped his helmet on his knee.

"I know I heard shots," said one geezer. "They was a good many of them."

"Sir," the Major said.

"What say?"

"Sir."

"Oh. Right. Sir."

"The tongue is the strongest muscle in the body," the Major said. "But one must control one's tongue. The government can spy on us from the stars. Catch us crack a cold one at the sink. They can even snatch us up in the night." He shook his head. "So fan out, men. Private Grady says he heard shots."

A pink-cheeked boy, rabbit gun at the ready, wandered the encampment.

Grady tossed a stick into the fire. "What all do we need to fan out for?"

"Sir."

"Oh, that's right. Sir."

"Grady," Coffey said, "if it's the Armageddon, wouldn't you want to know who all's left?"

Grady tugged at his wattled neck. "No, Coffey, can't say I would."

"Sir," said the Major.

"Huh? Oh. But now, sir, what I do want to know is why someone's gone and filled that foxhole we all dug. I ruined me a good pair of boots digging that."

The boy toed the mound. "Something's went and got buried here," he said.

~⁊~

Margaret limped through the arbors all the way to the barn. The truck was gone, but she shouldered open the crib door to find the laborer asleep, moonlight across his body, empty wine bottle on his chest. The dogs at the foot of the cot lifted their heads. She rummaged through pants on a chair and came up with three pennies and a dime. When she snatched a packet of beans and a bag of tortillas from a shelf, Jorge sat up, knocking the bottle to the floor.

Margaret pointed the pistol. "Where's that truck?"

"Eve," he said. He lay back, drawing the covers to his neck. "Eve, Eve, Eve. That is, as you Americans say, for me to know and you to find out." He giggled, and the dogs groaned, looking from him to her to him.

Down through thick brush Margaret made her way to the lake. She stripped and stuffed her clothes into the duffel, balancing it atop a thick block of styrofoam washed ashore, then shoved off into darkness. She had expected clear passage across the lake, but by the time the horizon had gone gray, she was still sidestroking along a bluff. Finally she came to where frigid turquoise water flowed from a low cave. Working her makeshift barge onto an outcropping inside, she found just enough room to lie down and just enough light by which to unwrap the filthy bandage. Her palm was red and swollen to bursting. She doused it with peroxide and tried to forget about it.

From her duffel she pulled a pair of jeans and a work shirt, stirring a snake from a clump of sticks. It was reddish brown and banded, eyes like glass beads, and as it unraveled she couldn't bring herself to care. Something about the eyes meant a snake was poisonous. If this one bit her, men might find, in time, a naked woman bloating on a shelf in a cave on a lake in the state of Missouri. Buzzards would circle, unable to land.

The snake slid over her foot and rippled across the water. Though the walls around her sank into darkness, the lip of stone afforded a slim view of glimmering lake. Traffic began to hum on a distant bridge. As close as she was to Madeline she should have just taken it from those boys, but instead she had taken everything from them. Now that it was done, she had to admit that a warm and satisfying liquor had risen in her bones. Margaret's mother used to say do what you're good at, a way to justify labors that kept the house so clean Margaret was forced to watch TV on a bare basement floor, the better to preserve the nap of the living-room carpet. Margaret herself had found that worthwhile efforts did not come easy, if they ever came at all.

❧

After Timmy's death, they had driven all night and into the day, stopping only for gas and restrooms until, come afternoon, James Leroy pulled into a field blooming with faded tents. Margaret told him to just go on. "How about you, Maddie?" he said, but Madeline squeezed herself into a corner of the backseat, so he strode alone across the flat toward faint calliope wheezings, his mantis body distorted by falling sun and swirling lights. He returned at dusk with a stuffed iguana, a greasy bag of corn, and the whip. Madeline would not touch the iguana. No one ate the popcorn. The whip was for Margaret.

"This fat-assed barker I won it off of? She said when problems come along you whip them. That's a song or something."

At a roadside park Margaret set Coke cans along a fence. One by one she popped them with the tip of the braided leather.

"What you gonna do with a talent like that?" James Leroy said.

Margaret threaded the whip through her belt loops. "Take that barker's advice."

Late that night they ended up at an abandoned farmhouse well off the road, its fields overrun with wild hemp. A hand pump stood in the yard. Swifts chattered from the chimney. "Good a place as any," James Leroy said.

But Margaret would no longer be a fool. "No," she said.

"You gonna swing a suite at the Ritz?"

She cinched the carnival whip. "Might."

"We're on the run, honey."

"You are."

"You're an accomplice."

"No, I'm not."

"Go on, get in there," James Leroy said, and he gripped her by the forearm.

"Go on yourself," Margaret said. When he did as told she began to tremble.

Margaret locked the car doors and coaxed Madeline into telling her a story. The moon hung over a galvanized metal barn, and Maddie said the moon lived in the barn with the cow that jumped over it, but the moon and cow did not get along, what with all the jumping. The tale set Margaret to dozing until Maddie declared that the cow would no longer jump over the moon.

"Why's that, Maddie?"

"Just because the moon says jump doesn't mean the cow has to."

"You might be right," Margaret said.

In the glove box James Leroy kept a razor knife folded inside a map of the southern states—a mother-of-pearl-handled job he said his father had used to kill Krauts in World War II. Margaret doubted that. She slid the knife out and told Maddie to stay put.

A strip of loose barn roofing creaked in a breeze. She stepped with care through the damp grass and then, flipping open the blade, eased back the screen door. Moonlight through the windows glowed on a whitewashed pie safe, and roses stared from the torn wallpaper. Five spoons, handles bent, dippers charred, were arranged in a pentagram on a rickety dining table. The place stank of cats.

She found James Leroy asleep across a mattress on the floor in the next room, and for a long time she stood over him, watching the mullion shadows crisscrossed on his chest. Then he gripped her ankle. "Hey, baby," he said. Margaret swung the blade at his neck but caught his chin, and when he yanked her to the floor, the razor shut on her thumb. She flung it away, but James Leroy fetched it, jerked Margaret upright, and held the blade under her jawbone. When he began to slice, she went slack, and he cut her from ear to nose.

She lay still until the front screen slammed, then nabbed his keys from beside the mattress. In the yard, James Leroy was working the pump handle, cursing a trickle of water. Margaret ran for the car, and when she shouted for Madeline to stay put, blood got in her mouth. Halfway down the rutted drive she checked the rearview mirror to see James Leroy chasing them, one hand a brandished fist, the other cupped to his chin as if his head might topple.

At the sound of a boat engine outside the cave, Margaret pulled her knees to her chest and strained to track the crackle of two-way radio over the slap of waves. When a polished white V-hull idled into view, close enough for her to glimpse a Water Patrol seal, she pressed herself back against the wall. *Dear Maddie*, she thought, *I am trying* . . . Then the boat was given throttle, its wake splashing over the ledge on which she huddled. "I am . . . ," she said.

Mama, you say one see makes twenty hears. One night I wish I never saw, a boy says to me, "Say one word I'll see you dead." But you know words hide in my mouth, and I know words cut to the heart like sharpened knives. I keep this barlow sharp. To shave pin curls from wood. To see what I make of the here and gone. But what good is the here and gone to me or you, and Mama, you say let no kindness pass without me giving thanks, but my words hide, and what good are the things I give the girl not now a girl but was? And she was kind to me. She ran boys off. She brought me food. One time she watched me carve a pterosaur and called it something nice, so I made it for her. I couldn't keep her safe, but still she keeps watch on my coins. That boy had words for her, and she had words, and then she had a knife he took away. What good could come to say what I saw done? He cried for her. He sealed her underground. I do my best these days to tend to her, but thanks like that does only me some good. This other woman comes to find me now, and when she shoots the boys what run the field in light and run me down come dark I hear you say to let no kindness pass, but would you call a kindness what I saw? She waved that gun at me to say *Be still*. And I wish I had ways to say to her how all I want for now can no more be. Still.

"Everybody Know What Maggie Done"

The kitchen door swung open, letting in the aluminum glare of midday. Cyrus looked up through a welter of quilts on the linoleum, and Isaac looked down, the silence between them charged with years of rebuke. "What are you doing, Cyrus?"

"Sleeping."

Isaac began to tap a file folder against his leg. He lifted the edge of a quilt with his wing tip, then tamped it back in place.

"Trying to," Cyrus said.

"Ah."

Cyrus followed his brother's gaze to a ladder-back chair in the corner. Over the top rung hung a pair of sheer black panties, one pink rosebud centered on the lace waistband. "Those aren't mine."

"Not your size," Isaac said.

Cyrus nodded.

"She still here?"

Cyrus wrapped a quilt around his shoulders and scanned the kitchen: pants on floor by the icebox, boots at his side, shirt hanging over the counter.

Isaac smoothed his tie. "Well. You want to go on ahead and get dressed?"

"Let me get my bearings."

"I didn't know you had any."

Cyrus stood, knees and ankles popping, and steadied himself with one hand on the pastry table.

"You fixing to be sick?"

"No."

"Maybe she's a modern-day Cinderella or something," Isaac said. "Maybe you're supposed to hunt her down until you find who fits them."

Cyrus stepped into his pants.

"Longer I live, less I understand, though. I'm practically a dull-ard." Isaac cleared his throat. "Mom's dead. As of this morning."

Cyrus got his arms in his shirtsleeves, but a sharp pain from his lower back spread into his shoulders, and he faltered.

"We'll need to make arrangements. She gets buried out by Pop on our plot at Dooley. I've started squaring that away, but we do have some other things to talk about." He set the folder of papers on the pastry table.

"I thought I had bad timing."

"I know it's hard, Cyrus. Just take a look when you get a chance."

What, according to Isaac, was hard? Hearing of his mother's death, signing away land for a resort, maybe having Isaac as a remaining relative? "Right," Cyrus said. He thumbed through the pages in the folder, then flung them ceilingward.

Someone knocked at the door and Cate stuck her head in the kitchen, papers drifting down in front of her. "I'm sorry. Am I interrupting?"

"Not at all," Isaac said. "Please. Come in."

Cate took note of the scattered pages, the rumpled quilts, the underwear over the chairback. Finally, her gaze settled on Cyrus. "I just came by to apologize. For being rude last night. I saw Darby, and he said you were in a bad way, what with your mom." She looked again to the chair, then out the window above the kitchen sink.

"Yeah," Cyrus said. "Well."

"I just wanted to say sorry. I should go. You've got company and all."

Cyrus started working on his buttons. "It's just us," he said.

"Still—I should go."

But she was stopped short at the door by Darby, who stood in a muddied uniform, one clay-stained fist raised to knock, the other resting on the butt of his revolver.

Blood thumped through Cyrus's head. Darby set his hat on the counter. "I was just in the neighborhood. Sorry. Missed your show last night. Thought I'd best stop by. We got some bad business out at the edge of you all's property."

"Excuse me a second," Cyrus said. Around the corner and out of view of the kitchen, he leaned in the doorframe of his parents' bedroom, struggling for air. His mother's fiddle sat in its opened case on the bed. He did not recall playing it, and only flickerings of last night came to him: a feathered garter, a small mole on a belly, a Celtic cross bluer than a bruise, a bourbon in hand, the bourbon spilling, pea gravel on a burgundy car mat, shredded tones from a jukebox drifting over water while flowing hair caught the moonlight, and a black high-laced boot stomping a puncheon floor. Laughter started, stopped, and a woman spoke his name. What was real? What was yellow-laced nightmare edging his sleep? Hand to the wall, he shuffled back to the kitchen, where Isaac was on his knees, gathering his pages into the folder. Darby and Cate looked as sober as two front-row churchgoers. "Had Mom been playing her fiddle?"

"Isaac just told us," Cate said. "I'm sorry."

Darby let out a long breath. "God, what a day. I was just saying we got four dead boys down by those condos Isaac's building at the falls. Four football boys shot dead. Now your Mom."

Isaac tap-tapped his papers on the table. "Just what I need."

"I am sorry," Cate said to Cyrus.

He could not help but stare. She was lean legged and graceful in long black pants that cinched at her waist, and her hair was pulled back, a few wisps hanging strategically past her cheekbones. She had not changed much from those years ago when he could recall her laughing with his mother in the kitchen.

"I'm gonna leave these here," Isaac said, setting the folder on the counter. "We meet at the funeral home tomorrow at two to make arrangements. After that we'll need to see the lawyer."

Cate reached for Cyrus, holding him for so long he felt her warmth. "We'll talk," she said.

When they were gone, Darby pulled tobacco from his shirt pocket. "You OK?"

"Yeah. You?"

"I got me a mess. I used to let these football boys slide. You remember how it was. These ones was mean, one or two of them, but not so bad as to get stuffed in a hole."

"Somebody went and buried somebody?"

"Yeah," Darby said. "The big boy got dropped in the bottom with a hole out the top of his head. The other three were crammed on top; one took a bullet in the chest, other two caught one in the bucket each. Weirdest thing I've seen in a while. Rolls of film all melted or exposed, filthy woman's T-shirt in that Fury of your pop's, which someone's been living in. These militia jackasses we got around here found the whole deal, then took their sweet time telling me so they could go play vigilante. Hell, they don't know what they're after."

"Do you?"

Darby packed tobacco in his cheek. His hands were crusted with mud. "You remember Riggs? A year ahead of us?"

"Our quarterback with the lineman's brain?"

"He's got this pizza joint. Last night he was tanking the varsity up after their big win, and some kids there saw these boys with a woman. Riggs said as much. Story goes she was flirting. Or they were pestering. We got footprints the militia knuckleheads tracked over. I don't know. One of the boys' cars was down there. Old beater Chevy. Maybe they come across her. Or she hitched. I don't know why she didn't take the car. Must have got scared."

"Some woman killed four boys," Cyrus said.

"They'll pull the same shit as a man if you give them half a chance. Speaking of," he said, nodding to the chair. "Those drawers can't possibly flatter you at all."

"Why didn't you tell me about Cate? I didn't need to see that."

"Shit," Darby said. "There's a lot worse out there than that. I seen maybe half of it this morning."

❧

Throughout the day the scenes of the previous night troubled Cyrus's mind, so he kept moving. He picked up his mother's fiddle, put it back. Opened the guitar case, shut it. He rearranged family photographs on side tables, ran his hand over bedsheets, then stepped back to examine what he'd smoothed. He opened cabinets and closed them. Finally he walked with the dogs along the arbors until he came round to the bluff. He could not bear to look over the edge.

The day Saro fell he had gone to fetch groceries. No one else could. Ruth was not in her right mind and hadn't been for some time. Ott had gone to preach a revival in Carthage. Isaac was getting his MBA. Though Saro had said she was working at Coffer's, Cyrus saw her leave the Dree-Mee Freeze lot with Willie Gilmore, and he followed them back to the bluff. At the honeysuckle fence, Gilmore's Trans Am idled, a cement mixer hitched to it. Lately he had been putting up rock walls for lakeside homes. He had a way with concrete.

Cyrus pulled up at the edge of the woods and, from behind the wheel, watched Gilmore take a drag off a cigarette. Distorted guitar blasted from the open car windows, but Saro's laughter rose above it. Then Ruth shooed something off the Trans Am's hood, and Cyrus stepped out, coming round the front of the truck. Ruth wiped her hands on her apron and stepped to the driver-side window. "Know what I'll do?" she said.

Gilmore stubbed out his cigarette on the side mirror and turned down the volume. "Huh?"

Shutting the passenger door, Saro told Willie to just go on.

"I said, Know what I'll do?"

Gilmore glanced over at Cyrus. "What's that, Mrs. Harper?"

Ruth snatched a hank of Gilmore's hair and pulled a paring knife from her apron pocket. "I'll cut your piggy eyes right out of your head," she said.

Gilmore gripped her wrist and pushed her away so hard she stumbled. Backing out, he almost jackknifed the cement mixer, but managed to rattle his way out to the road, where a rust-colored gout of dust spilled after him.

"They won't have you," Ruth said to Saro.

Cyrus never understood why Saro had run to the bluff, and he never asked. Maybe she wanted to lead their mother there. Maybe she figured it was her last escape. Maybe she wasn't thinking. Or was. Branches, muddy ledges, and brush slowed a fall that would have killed her otherwise. The incident lay between them after Saro healed, leaving him to question whether he'd done all he could. He gave chase when Ruth grabbed Saro's sleeve and stabbed at the air around them. Then Saro slipped. She did not cry out.

He looked away from the lake and walked halfway back to where the waters ran to the falls, where those boys had gotten themselves killed. By a woman, maybe. His first thought had been of Saro, then of that woman limping along the road. *Some woman,*

Jorge had said. Rain beat leaves off of the black branches overhead and pasted them to the ground. He was soaked, shivering, but for a long time he watched his warm breath escaping into the cold woods around him.

ლ

That night on his way to Bo's he stopped at a liquor store and depleted his meager tip money from the night before on a pint of Early Times and a six of Black Label. Driving, he scanned the ditches and the darkness beyond. Someone was in these hills. And Saro had known the land so well it had swallowed her entire.

In the club lot he drank three beers and decided to wash down a few pale pills with the bourbon—enough maybe to smooth out his jagged edges, turn back waves of grief, dim any flickerings to come. Or not. He felt as though he needed to find Cate and apologize to her, but for what? She'd been an old girlfriend, which meant nothing except that she knew his past and therefore might spare some sympathy—pity, more likely.

Guitar case in hand, he crossed the parking spaces reserved for Bo's Beauties, passing a well-waxed German make of convertible just as two bare feet pressed against the inside of the windshield and stuck. Then came moaning suited to movies, and Cyrus hurried into the club. When he entered the dressing room, all chatter stopped. A bead of sweat was crawling his neck. Two girls stepped toward him on a breeze of scented oils. "Cate around?" he said.

The girls exchanged glances. An older woman at the mirror— too old, Cyrus thought, for this line of work—yanked a brush through her hair. "Called in sick."

"She OK?"

The woman snatched up a can of hair spray. "You be OK if you worked here?"

Cyrus set down the guitar. "I do work here."

"Well?"

"What's going on?" Cyrus said. The old woman leveled the can at her head, and he tried to fix on her reflection, but the mirror seemed to undulate. Her hair was a lacquered hive. She wore a man's pink oxford and no pants and blue eye makeup the shade of a tropical fish. Frown lines crimped the corners of her mouth. Surely she'd had her heyday in burlesque, a Tempest Storm or a Rose Lee. Now maybe she was a novelty act cooked up for the road. Cyrus leaned nonchalantly on a chair, but it scooted away with a honk.

"What's going on?" she said. "Same as anywhere, honey. People getting screwed right and left."

"Who am I after?"

The woman clucked. "Honey. All these pretty young things and you ain't decided yet?"

The light in the room was going wrong. His depth of field distorted. He needed to get some order to his thoughts, but the gobbling laughter of girls trailed him into the hall, where he was assaulted so hard with metallic sound—sheet metal torn loose in a cyclone—that he could not orient himself, and he stumbled. There onstage was Sade humping flame-washed air, hands reaching to her from the floor in Pentecostal gestures. She turned to him and—he was sure of this—bared her teeth, her hips chopping at the dangerous light. He closed his eyes and a yellowed image wavered: Saro, in fetal position on a limestone outcropping, a dribble of blood from her ear.

Cyrus hurried down stairs that led to a concrete hallway where a ratty broom leaned against an ice machine. He sat on the floor and, catching his breath, took the broom across his lap as if it might protect him. Bass notes beat down from above, and cubes rumbled in the bin. In times past a contraption that made ice would have been a miracle. A waxen cylinder that spun music, a box that carried voices, a bin that made ice—miracles. But the machine had been relegated to a hallway, nothing but a prop for a broom, and with the broom in Cyrus's hand not even that. Now music had him surrounded. Walls, relay towers, satellites. It shook fillings and hummed through fenders of cars, and he felt it pulsing in his chest. Or was that his heart?

He didn't stay to find out. From out of the freight elevator, broom still in hand, he ran smack into a bouncer, who shoved him at a brass-numbered door that swung open. A girl in a white G-string sawed her hips over the lap of a gap-toothed fool sunk into a velveteen easy chair. The girl glared sidelong at Cyrus. He held up the broom as if he were housekeeping. "Wrong room," he said.

The bouncer yanked him into the hall. "What's your deal, bud?"

"Newbern broke something. Something broke. It's broken. Where's he again?"

The bouncer pointed down the hall at a set of double doors and twirled his finger.

When Cyrus reached the crow's nest, Newbern was cuing a record.

"You seen Cate?" Cyrus said.

Newbern spun around. "Who in the hell is Cate?" Down on the stage a pale girl writhed from the darkness. Newbern peered at Cyrus. "Some old witch trade you for your guitar?"

"Something's not right," Cyrus said. He steadied himself with the broom. "I don't know. She dances."

"It's old rules here. You don't let no cripple Negro talk to a white woman. Not that I'd want to. They're dangerous. But management thinks I might just sprout legs and grow handsome." Newbern wheeled to a small refrigerator on the floor. "Co-Cola?"

"No."

"Right. You hit the strong stuff."

"Maybe not anymore. I don't think. No."

"You don't think," Newbern said. "Naw, I ain't seen no Cate."

"She does the leather thing."

Newbern cracked the can. "They all look the same to me. Now, you? Last night, you looked like something different. A target is what you looked like."

"They went for the bawdy songs."

"Bawdy? Shit. Whatever happened to double entendre? Your mama teach you to sing that way?"

"My mother's dead," Cyrus said. "As of this morning."

Newbern shook his head at the girl on the stage. He drank thoughtfully from his Coke.

"She taught us hymns sometimes," Cyrus said. "Or old songs on the sly."

"I am sorry," Newbern said. "No matter how old you get, it ain't worth nothing being a motherless child. My mama left me and my brother for Cleveland, Ohio—to find work. One night at Grammy's I dreamt Mama died in some warehouse, dreamt they locked her in like at that shirt company, and she died screaming my name. I told Grammy Mama was dead, so she let me hitch to Cleveland—fourteen years old, mind you. I find some falling-down house by that river chopped into rooms. This greasy puke runs the place says she took off with a man named Madox, headed for New York City. She's dead by now. That river burned later on."

"I'm sorry," Cyrus said.

"So. What nastiness you gonna start us off with tonight?"

"'My Pencil Won't Write No More'?"

Newbern sang: "'Now listen here, man, you ought to know.'"

"'You can't write for that woman,'" Cyrus said, "'you got to let her go.'"

Newbern killed the lights as the girl left the stage. "Jackasses won't know it."

"What do you mean white women are dangerous?" Cyrus said.

Newbern inspected Cyrus's reflection. "I don't mean just white women." He swept his half hand at the stage. "I mean people. Women end up included in that."

Out on the water, light changed from golden to amber. In time, Margaret curled again on the stone and slept, waking to fever and darkness and lights flitting like will-o'-the-wisps through woods across the lake. Dogs yelped on the far shore. Voices of men drifted over the wind-chopped waves to where she lay shivering, her body hot, the limestone slab freezing. Her hand had begun to split like the skin of a delicate fruit. She could neither stay on the shelf nor return to the main road, but no other options came to mind. So when the lake went quiet, she crawled naked into the water, shoving the styrofoam out in front of her and sidestroking into thick fog until she struck something, her duffel almost dumping into the drink.

A lantern rose above her, vaporous ribbons drifting through its light. At the stern of an aluminum johnboat an old man kept one hand on the throttle of an Evinrude and a paddle across his lap. In his flannel layers and checkered hunting cap he resembled a boy sent out to play in the snow. "You ain't a fish, are you?" he said.

"No."

"I've heard old boys catch a catfish and have it turn into a woman, but I ain't never heard of old boys snagging a woman to have her turn into a catfish. That your story?"

It pained Margaret to tread water. "No," she said.

"I don't discount nothing."

"You mind giving me a lift? It's a little chilly."

With the paddle he lifted from the water a Clorox jug knotted to a moss-gobbed cable. "I'm running trotlines."

"I'll ride along."

"I got room for fish."

Her breath billowed through brackish lamplight. The water thickened around her, and she fought to keep her head above the surface. "Where's shore?"

He poked the business end of the paddle over her head. "You got to swim a piece for shore."

"Please," she said, then tried to haul herself over the bow, but the old man shoved her back with the paddle.

"I got things to do, and ain't none of them include hauling some witch that might or might not turn into a fish just as soon as she gets into my boat."

"If I was a witch, why would I turn into a fish in your boat? Why wouldn't I be a fish that turns into a woman?"

"Because I'm a smarty britches," he said. "And you think you can trick me."

"Pull me in. I'll turn into a fish."

"You said you wouldn't do no such thing. I hear what you say."

Margaret grabbed the gunwale, but the old man chucked the paddle into her shoulder, a blow that seemed to split muscle clear to bone. She cried out, water pulling her under, where she conceived of trees bound with moss and sagging houses and a cemetery on a hill, the emptied graves remaining. She could drift into one with ease. Instead, she broke the surface, sputtering. The styrofoam floated at the edge of the lamplight's reach, and she swam for it. "You old fool," she said.

"Ain't fool enough to let some witch into my boat." He lifted the lantern and gave the Evinrude throttle. White bottles bobbed in the johnboat's wake.

She kicked her way through the darkness until she managed to crawl onto a gravel bank, oily water lapping at her waist. Footfalls crackled, and when a light crept over her, she did not bother to cover herself. "Fine," she said. "You got me."

A lantern hissed by her head.

"Get it over with."

Randy's eyes roamed her length, and for a moment she thought him the spirit of her own boy come to snatch her away. He took her duffel, killed the light, and dragged her to her feet. After a long blind stumble into the woods, he set her on a stone wall and relit the lamp, revealing at the edge of darkness the remains of a chimney. She was naked and her teeth were chattering, and Randy turned from her. She tried to dress but could not button her shirt or lace her boots, so she reached for him, and he spun around, wielding the lamp like a weapon. "C'mon," she said, pointing at her laces, her unfastened jeans. "Give me a hand."

Kneeling, he started at her boots, but by the time he fumbled with the button at her waist his breath came fast, and when he got to her shirt, his face was flushed, his Adam's apple pronounced. He smelled of mud. Margaret pushed him away so hard he struggled to keep his balance. "God knows what all you got in your head," she said.

He helped her with her coat, though, and carried her bag, and when he got too far ahead he lifted the lantern and waited. Margaret fell flat twice on a rise gone slick with leaves. He helped her the first time, but the next time as she reached for him, he dropped the duffel, killed the light, and ran. From the crest of the hill came voices. Fire flickered there. "You little shit," Margaret said. "You trapped me."

If it was a trap, it was an odd one. From the rim of a clearing, she saw a steaming cauldron and whites hanging on a line between two trees. A gray bus blocked the south edge of the muddied ground, but on the other side a man stuck a shovel into a heap of sand. He was long haired, lanky. A droopy beard made him seem forlorn. "You hear something?" he said.

"Quit screwing around, Rob." On her knees, a woman shook a two-liter bottle, a galvanized funnel blooming from its neck. Shadows contorted her features, but Margaret recognized the cheese buyer from the grocery store—Little Miss Mind Your Own Beeswax, Alice. Without looking, the man dumped the sand in the funnel. "It's wet," Alice said.

"You wanted it done."

"I said if we're gonna do it we better do it. I ain't living in a bus another winter."

He twisted his mustache.

"What?"

"I got that feeling."

Alice stacked a bottle like cordwood against a tree. "You're paranoid."

"I'm not that stoned."

Margaret needed to rest where she did not have to worry over what was to come. There was only one way to find out if this was such a place, so she stepped into the firelight.

Alice stood. The man jabbed his shovel into the ground. "See?" he said.

"Can you spare some fire? It's awful cold."

He spread his arms like a Passion-play Christ. "The fire is for all the woods."

Alice beat an empty bottle against her thigh.

"I'm Rob," the man said. "Rob Welch. This is Alice Ford. My wife."

Margaret staggered, dropping her bag, and Rob reached out to steady her.

"I know you," Alice said. "What's your name?"

Margaret could not recall what she'd said at the store. "Mind if I sit? I'm a bit puny."

Rob unfolded a lawn chair. "Please," he said.

"I know your name."

"Louisa," Margaret said, and she sat. Alice became a bent visage viewed through old glass and Margaret blinked hard to straighten her. "What's the bottles for?"

Alice wagged her head. "A house. Before DFS comes. You know how you don't build your house on sand? Rob here wants to build a house *out* of sand. He read it in some magazine."

"There's so much waste in this world," Rob said. "Don't you think, Louisa?"

"We've been fixing to build this house for two years now, Rob."

"Time is of the essence," Rob said. "Wouldn't you agree, Louisa?"

Margaret had seen enough domestic discord to know to keep her mouth shut. She needed to figure out if they'd heard dogs or seen lights. Or knew of the boys.

"That's the wrong context, Rob," Alice said.

"I know what I'm saying without you telling me. Alice."

Branches overhead shifted and creaked. "Far out for a house, ain't it?" Margaret said.

Rob pointed. "Road's right there."

"Oh. Yes."

Alice was listing like a rammed ship. "You always just creep through woods like this?"

"I like to get away."

"The world is full of evils, isn't it, Louisa? Radio. TV. Agricultural conglomerates. Life has been devalued. We didn't want that for our children. That's why we came to the country. So they would grow to be free."

"Your children?"

Rob nodded at two blanketed bundles on the far side of the fire.

"One boy. One girl. Six and three. Out here under the stars. Ours is an apostolic life."

"And just what is it we're apostles of, Rob?"

He set his hand on Margaret's shoulder, massaging it. "Your hair's wet, Louisa." He leaned over to study her face. Flecks of ash had lodged in his beard, and his eyes were bloodshot. Margaret had a notion that he was going to kiss her. "You're shivering."

A log shifted, swirling sparks to the wind. "I'm fine."

He pressed his forehead to hers. "She's burning up."

Alice scooped a shovelful of sand. "You're the one's got a fire needs put out."

"I'm serious, Alice."

"She's got a coat on. It's not that chilly."

"I am . . . ," Margaret said. "Fine." She stood to prove it, but stumbled, drifting past Rob's outstretched hand down through the clothes on the line.

"Christ," Alice said. "I just finished those."

Rob rested Margaret's head in his lap. "Alice, look at her hand. Louisa, can you hear me?"

"Louisa," Alice spat. "She said her name was Billie."

"I'm just cold," Margaret said to the firelit branches above her. "That's all."

A boy, Cyrus wandered bare, ruined woods where twilight shadows slashed the ground. Breeds of mountain harridan in gauzy dresses and blue panties leisured outside an Airstream, its latticed deck slanting from the door. One leaning on a charred fifty-five-gallon drum reached out as he passed, but he juked from her outstretched hand into the trailer, where, in the scorched musk of air, three men, a triumvirate of musicians, faced each other in wooden funeral chairs. At their feet lay a stringless zither, a lute, and a toy xylophone, its plastic cord curled like a piggy's tail. Scabs of lichen grew on their coveralls. Their bald-skin skulls were mottled with mildew. Ears a tattered fringe, desiccated lips drawn back, and the eyes—the eyes were gone. The girls, whistling like groundhogs, began crawling in over the low sills, and Cyrus stumbled back amid the men, even as their black stares accused him of neglecting to take a seat and make a little music.

Cyrus sat up, soaked and struggling for breath. He left the quilts on the kitchen floor and filled an ice-tea glass from the tap, then drank like he was thirsty. "That's how it starts," he said, recalling his readings in the library. Nightmares to picture shows to delirium tremens—which only one percent of juiceheads suffered. Not Cyrus. He had steered clear of drinking once before, and a few songs had come, but they were nothing he would have wanted to sing with Saro. He plucked the picture off the counter. Sunlight on the ribs of instruments. Shut sanctuary doors. Swirling leaves. Two clueless kids looking out from a time long past. He stowed the photograph in his shirt pocket and stepped outside.

Pressing his hands to his temples, he recalled how unsettled he'd been last night. He'd made a vague promise to himself to lay off the juice—and steer clear of his mother's pills. The better to keep the nights from getting weird. The better to focus on what was wandering these woods. The better to reacquaint himself with Cate.

By early afternoon, when he got out of the truck at Burrs Funeral Home, he had to stuff his hands in his pockets to conceal the tremors from Isaac and Mr. Hobb Burrs, who stood waiting on the porch at the crest of a plywood wheelchair ramp. Isaac tapped his watch at Cyrus. Burrs flicked a cigarette at the bushes. "Didn't think we'd ever see you again, young man," he said.

"Inevitable, isn't it, Mr. Burrs?"

"I am sorry to say that that is true."

In his office Burrs offered them each a chair. His walls were covered with framed Olan Mills photos of grandchildren and funeral home advertisements run from as far back as the turn of the century, when ambulance and undertaker were the same business, never mind the conflict of interest. With the fresh faces and silhouettes of black carriages, the room was a pine-paneled demo of cradle to grave. Burrs set his elbows on the desk. He was a block of a man with varnish-colored flesh and bulbous lips and a smile trained to convey sympathy. "Busy time for us," he said. "Busy time."

"Folks dropping right and left?" Cyrus said.

"Pardon me?"

"The town's old."

"Oh, no. I mean these murders. Four of our own. Haven't you heard?"

"Yes," Isaac said. "It was at the edge of our property."

"Isn't that interesting," Burrs said. "We have the boys here in back with your mother. The county morgue holds just two at a time, so when we get an accident on the highway, or a tragedy—though I can't say we've ever had one like this—the medical examiner works out of our modernized facility."

"Mr. Burrs," Isaac said, "I don't mean to rush, but we got another meeting shortly."

"Of course." Burrs pushed across his desk two notebooks containing marketing materials for sarcophagi. He explained interiors and extras as if he were selling a car. Isaac pointed at a coffin, a walnut thing resembling an old stereo cabinet, and Cyrus said fine. Burrs said they needed to coordinate the service and interment. "You'll need a preacher and a singer." He turned to Cyrus. "Didn't you sing at your father's service?"

"Yes."

"You sang at your sister's too."

"Our sister disappeared," Isaac said.

"Oh, yes."

"I ain't singing for this."

"May I recommend someone?"

"You bet," Isaac said, checking his watch.

"What are you in such an all-fired hurry to get us to?"

"The attorney. Remember?"

Cyrus pushed the notebooks back across the desk. "Mr. Burrs, as far as singers go, get some old Baptist gal with a voice that warbles like a sick bird. As for preachers, nix the lard-asses shouting damnation. Nobody here needs reminding."

Excusing himself, he headed the wrong way down the hall, but refused to turn back, so took the next hall, the next. He wouldn't sign a thing. He'd make do in bars, or move dirt. He did not want the money. He did need to know how to get out of the funeral home, though. The place was a fluorescent-lit funhouse, Muzak drizzling from the ceiling, each hall lined with unmarked doors. Finally he just opened one.

A mustached man in a lab coat stood behind a table on which four black vinyl bags resembled giant pupae. "Help you?" he said.

Coffins on stainless carts lined the far wall of a cavernous space; others had been hoisted to the rafters. Cyrus stared at the bags. "Is Ruth Harper here?"

The man nodded at a metal door.

"It's locked," Cyrus said.

"That's how they keep them."

The coffins above Cyrus were swaying. A breeze from the vents, maybe. "It's awful cold."

The mustached man unzipped a bag, the vinyl crackling. "Folks here don't mind," he said.

❧

He pulled to the honeysuckle gate just as camouflaged men emerged from the brush beside the road. Gripping the strained tethers of three beagles, two blueticks, and an English bull terrier, a bearded man tried to kick Earl and Bill back from the well-armed cluster. Cyrus got out of the truck.

"Better call your dogs, bud," the bearded man said. Under his mustache was the pink zigzag of a harelip scar. "I know my dogs; they'll take the hide off your sorry pups."

Hackles up, Earl dropped into a crouch; Bill kept stalking. "Earl?" Cyrus said. "Bill?"

Among the G.I. Joes were pubescent teenagers, unshaven couch jockeys, a skinny old coot, and a well-tanned white-hair with a helmet on his head and major's clusters on his shoulders. Two men carting automatic weaponry tried to draw a bead on Bill. In back of the group stood Mr. Coffer.

"What's the deal?" Cyrus said.

"We're minutemen, sir," said a teenager.

The Major wagged his head. "You don't need to sir *him*."

"You're what?"

"Minutemen," the Major said. "Patriots. We're hunting a woman that's killed four ballplayers, God rest their souls. Local, state, and federal law-enforcement agencies are just pawns in a bureaucracy of rampant minorityism. We want justice done."

"They say there might be a reward," the teenager said. "From the families."

Earl shifted on his haunches, stirring the tethered dogs into a frenzy. "If you don't get your dogs, buddy," the harelip said, "I'm gonna let mine fly and we're gonna see us some fur."

At the threatening pitch in the man's voice, Earl and Bill attacked. The harelip belly-flopped into the ditch while the other men high-kicked like Russian dancers. Earl went for a bluetick's ear. Bill shook a beagle like a rug before another gnawed him, squalling, into a retreat.

The harelip sputtered up, his hounds scrabbling off into the arbors. "Can't you control your dogs, buddy? A man ought to be able to handle his dogs."

"Yeah," Cyrus said. "These ain't my dogs."

He shut Earl and Bill on the porch, then trailed the men through the grapes to the barn. The bloodied bluetick was on his hind legs, scratching at Jorge's door.

"They got them a whiff," the harelip said.

The Major gripped Cyrus's biceps. "What all you got in that shed, boy?"

Cyrus peeled the Major's hand from his arm. "Nothing for you."

Then Jorge cracked the door. He was dressed in dingy briefs and rubbing his eyes—a man caught sleeping off a bender.

"What do you call that there?" the Major said.

"I call that Jorge. He calls himself that too."

"You *habla* any English, Jorge?"

"He *hablas*. He *hablas* better than you, even."

Jorge smiled expansively, his silver tooth catching the sun. "Thank you," he said to Cyrus.

The teenager pointed his rabbit gun. "That's a whale of a scar, sir."

"Yes," Jorge said. "I know where you can get one just like it."

The boy took two steps back.

Jorge turned to the Major. "My friend," he said, "the law has already been here, so I must tell you what I told them. If a woman were here, she would be in bed with me. Alas, there is no woman."

"You trying to be funny?" the Major said.

Jorge shrugged as if comedy were beneath him. "I have had the dogs in here. Maybe your dogs smell dog. The others that were here did."

"Marty?" the Major said.

"I trust my dogs before I trust a wetback," Marty said.

"Very wise," said Jorge. "We are known for our deceit. It is all the Indian blood."

"So how're you doing, Mr. Coffer?" Cyrus said.

Coffey shuffled his feet. "Oh, fair, fair enough. Sorry to hear about your mama."

"Yeah," Cyrus said. "Mr. Coffer, do you remember my sister? Saro? Used to work for you?"

"Well, sure, I remember. She was awful pretty. Fellas liked her too. She used to sing all out on the dock." Aware of his comrades' eyes on him, Coffey began to gaze at his boot tops. "I ain't given her much thought lately, no offense."

Cyrus nodded. "She always said you paid her about what you thought a woman was worth."

A few of the men chuckled. "Well, I always did try to be fair," Coffey said.

The armed retinue moved on, searching barn, arbors, bluff. The sky took on a burnished cast. In between the howling of dogs came the crackle of leaves and the creak of ammunition belts.

"So who is she," Cyrus said to Jorge, "this woman that was here?"

"It is rare to know who anyone is, is it not?"

"It's nigh on impossible if someone wants to be cryptic." Cyrus took the photograph from his pocket. He held it out for Jorge to see.

"I have heard of your sister. Fifteen years? Since she was gone?"

"More," Cyrus said.

"And you want me to tell you if that woman is her? I cannot say."

Cyrus pocketed the photo. There was no sense trusting a man who had no reason to trust him. "What do you think they'll do if they find someone?"

"If they do not know how to use those guns, they will kill each other. If they do know, maybe they will kill her."

The dogs' yelping had grown faint. "You just tell her I'm looking for her. If you see her."

"She will not show here again."

"Then I hope she gets away," Cyrus said.

"That is an American way of thinking."

"You can't deny what you are."

"That," Jorge said, "that is not so American."

❧

Cyrus drew the shades and hauled his sister's guitar and his mother's fiddle to the attic, then pulled up the ladder and dragged the trap across the hole. The glare of bare bulb on raw wood blurred the room into a poorly focused photogravure of washed-up wreckage. *Where am I in this picture?* he thought. Tucked among boxes were things his parents, then he and Saro, had abandoned. A Grafonola. The nine-tube Philco with the Bakelite dials. Seventy-eights and reissued 33⅓s. Player piano rolls. Silverfish-infested hymnals and collections of ballads from the turn of the century with overblown discourse accompanying:

> We talk glibly of the creative musician, but, however clever and inspired he may be, he cannot, magician-like, produce music out of nothing; and if he were to make the attempt he could only put himself back into the position of the primitive savage. All that he can do and, as a matter of fact, does, is to take the materials bequeathed to him by his predecessors, fashion it anew and in such manner that he can through it, and by means of it, express himself.

Cyrus tossed away the book and took out the fiddle. "What do you say," he said, "if all your predecessors are dead?" Dragging the bow across the strings, he shivered, the human squall unnerving him. Melodies lurked in his head—"Sourwood Mountain," "Humansville," "Kiss Me Waltz"—but he slid the fiddle to his chest and said, "How ya, how ya do it, Mr. Hog-Eye?" then set the instrument back in its case.

He sorted records: string band, jug band, hokum blues, country blues, ballads, ragtime, cornpone comedy. What had become of it? Microphones and amplifiers had pushed back crowds and lifted musicians to stages of scaffolding. Air-conditioning had drawn front-porch players inside—the end of intimacy and tunes passed through generations. But the audience was just as responsible for the demise of the old music. So were the performers. Any sharecropper, tie hacker, or miner could keen a tune, but they couldn't all own a Victrola or shell out for a radio. They could envy their neighbor's, though. They'd even buy a disc with no way to spin it. And if somewhere someone would pay, somewhere someone would play. Savvy musicians were more than willing to tap strings with broomstraws, act a rube, or rip through jazz riffs if that would draw a crowd. And it would. People coveted what they were not.

Cyrus slapped a 78 on the Philco. A hill family recorded in Memphis. He'd heard their story somewhere; it was kin to more than a few others. The father had seen a handbill calling for musicians. A farmer and sign painter, he was high spirited but prone to depressive fits. *This, this,* he said, shaking the ad at his wife, *this was their chance.* She sighed. The beans were canned, but more food needed to be put away before first frost. Besides, music was for her family, two children remaining out of four she'd borne—not bad odds back then. They were done with school by sixth grade. With the Great War long over, the boy had considered the service. Lately, men's eyes were on the girl, but not wanting to appear improper, she would turn away.

In a vacant warehouse, a secretary took their names and asked for their sheet music. They had none. In back, a harried man made them face a curtained booth from which poked four horns. Afternoon light poured down over them through streaks on the high windows. A fly-by-night deal, the mother figured.

"Closer to the horns, please," the man said, wiping his neck with a handkerchief.

The father played fiddle; the mother, autoharp; the boy, guitar; and the girl, a banjo ukulele, which she had taught herself to pick. The man pointed at a red light above the curtain. "It comes on," he said, "play. It goes off, keep playing, but if it comes on again, stop."

The light stopped them four times. The man cursed, and the father thought sure they would not get a contract. Then the man appeared from behind the curtain. The banjo uke was drowning everyone out. "Can't we just get rid of it?" he said.

The girl thought she might cry.

"No, sir," the father said. "We can't."

The man shooed the girl behind her father. The light went off, on. "You, you," the man said. "Right. Go stand over there." He pointed the girl to a spot eight feet behind her family.

As they played, she could not see their faces or fingers, just the backs of their heads bobbing like sorghum in a breeze, and she felt as though she were watching her family leave her for good.

Cyrus toed open a book of ballads on the floor. For that girl, a song was not the same after that. Maybe she had heard her mother sing lullabies, play-party ditties, ballads for the hearthside, but if she did not know every song signified a yearning, she found out soon enough. A ballad let a woman forget mornings wasted with a baby at her breast, days squandered hoeing cabbage, nights endured with a man while cold wind hissed through chinks in the logs. In a ballad a heroine could flee with an illicit love, harm a suitor, mother-in-law, or brat. And she could enjoy it. But:

> *Oh, what is yonder mountain, she said,*
> *All dreary with frost and with snow?*
> *Oh, yonder is the mountain of hell*
> *Where you and I must go.*

So they went. To love was to die. To yearn, to grieve. Every song was a song of yearning.

Cyrus put on a raucous dance tune, but as the needle hovered over the spinning black, a snippet of verse—something he could call his own for the first time in years—came to him.

> *Oh, sister, oh, sister, why have you returned*
> *Like frost that creeps o'er the leaves?*
> *I've come back to see to our mother's grave*
> *And to ask you if anyone grieves.*

Forget it, he thought. He was glad he had no way to commit his weak-minded words to paper. Besides, what did he grieve for? The smoky olive scent of his mother's hair when he was a boy and she'd held him? To know a person was as difficult as catching the words of a song in a windstorm. They fled as shadows. Better to pick up a fiddle and play tunes that required only fingers pressed to strings. If you couldn't figure out a life with words—and you couldn't—do away with them. Cyrus envied the woman who'd killed four boys, her freedom to sweep lives away like crumbs in a chair, and if—*if*—Saro could do such a thing, he envied her. She must never have grieved.

"Hey, you got that loud enough?"

Cyrus pulled back the trap. "You don't ever knock, do you, Darb?"

"You got doors unlocked and racket going to wake the dead. There's a killer loose, son."

"That racket," Cyrus said, "is Fiddlin' Bob Larkan and His Music Makers."

"Put it that way, then," Darby said, "maybe it ain't so unpleasant." File folder in hand, he climbed the ladder and pulled up a funeral chair. Everyone brought file folders to the house these days. "You look like you been shit at and hit. You all right?"

"I'm not drinking is how I am. Or else I'd offer you something."

"Is this not drinking for good? Or just not drinking for the time being?"

Cyrus shrugged. He fingered the bottle of pills in his pocket. "How's the hunt?"

"I got four dead boys still dead. I got a county gone apeshit, a slew of government acronyms in my business, and some bitch making me look like an idiot."

Cyrus glanced at Saro's guitar case. "You're for certain. She's a she."

Darby handed over the folder. Inside were three black-and-white photographs. "One of those boys was on the yearbook staff. I guess he appointed himself event photographer. These sort of came out."

Cyrus pointed to a hazy figure in the first image. "What's this?"

"That? I think that's Randy Ellston."

"What are they doing to him?"

"I told you they was mean," Darby said.

Cyrus flipped to the next photograph. In the background, a hooded figure, splinter thin, ran for the darkness; in the foreground was tangled hair and a blurred shoulder. The last photo showed the bottom half of a woman's face: fine bones and a scar from the flare of her nose to her ear. She was screaming, or laughing. "She caught the wrong end of a knife somewhere," Cyrus said.

"She either broke up their fun—or egged them on." Darby shook his head. "Hell, likely she's just some dick tease, and those boys bit off more than they could chew. Bullets in brains. Shit for brains—but nonetheless."

"Randy?"

"God knows. We're pretty sure she came through your grapes, though. Had us a little chat with your hired man. Folks said he was talking up some woman down at The Squeezebox the other night."

"He was."

"Cyrus, I'm awful sorry."

"What for?"

"You were thinking she was Saro. Not that you'd want her

to be, I guess, but I could tell by the look on your face the other day."

Cyrus handed back the folder. "How can you know she's not?"

"Those pictures don't favor her at all, I don't think. Besides, that'd be awful convenient. You and her coming back at the same time? I mean, life ain't a tidy little song, you know."

"Is that right? And I always thought it was."

"It is somebody knows the lay of the land—I'll give you that. Or I'd have found her by now."

Cyrus took the pills from his pocket. "It's a big world, Darb," he said. Steadying his hands, he pinched a capsule from the bottle, then put it back. "Like you say, it ain't particularly tidy."

"What're those all for?"

"Something to remember my mother by." It might have been the lack of liquor nagging him or Darby gawking or loneliness sifting off the rafters, but Cyrus felt a meanness coming on. Darby had a life. So did Cate. She fixed lunches, brushed hair, picked up barrettes. And here Cyrus was, holed up in an attic, a fugitive from bad habits and a ragged past. "I tried to find Cate last night," he said. "You haven't seen her, have you?"

"No. Why?"

"I figured she didn't much want to talk to me."

"You didn't care much for seeing her do what she does, did you? Sorry."

"Give her credit. She's still dancing. Where's she live these days?"

"Why you want to know?"

"Curious. Why don't you want to tell me?"

"You just got a lot on your mind. Nostalgia Lane's one rough ride."

"I ain't going anywhere."

"There's new houses on Tubb's Cove. Little yellow clapboard thing. White picket fence."

"An ironic one, I'd guess."

Darby tapped the folder on his knee. He stood to leave. "I wouldn't know," he said.

❧

Cyrus opened a book of ballads on his lap. "A Dark Road Is a Hard Road to Travel" ground round, the *sh-took, sh-took* of the Grafonola needle as unsettling as a hand scratching at a window screen. The killer was a woman; the woman bore a scar; Cate was a mother; she had a picket fence; Saro was gone, his mother dead, and no one in this life needed a reason to vanish, murder, or die.

Cyrus turned pages. But: John Lewis killed Naomi Wise because she carried his child and he desired, instead of Naomi, Martha Huzza. Tom Dula knifed Laura Foster and tossed her body in a river because she gave him a social disease. A ship's carpenter slit Polly's bosom with a short knife because she would not marry him; he dumped her in a grave that, as he put it, he'd worked on the best part of last night. Down in the willows a lover poisoned Rose Connelly with a bottle of wine; he stabbed her and rolled her into a river; even the murderer said it was a dreadful sight.

Those dead girls had fled as shadows, and for no good reason.

But: Lady Margot knifed Love Henry because he chose another woman. Mary Hamilton tossed her baby in the sea to gain the affection of a prince. A sister drowned a sister to steal a suitor. A Jewess penknifed a boy because his ball rolled into her yard. Lady Isabel shoved the Elf Knight off an ocean bluff when he tried to make her his seventh victim. She told him to avert his eyes while she undressed—her gowns, she said, were too dear to rot in the salt, salt sea. The brown girl stabbed Fair Ellender because Ellender insulted her. And what did the brown girl get for her trouble? Lord Thomas, who loved them both, lopped off her head and booted it against a wall. Then there was Frankie, good old American Frankie, who glimpsed her loving Albert, or Johnny, with a girl named Nelly Bly or Alice Wise or Lillie, Josie, Sadie, or Annie and shot him, whoever he was, once, twice, or three or four times. He had been her man. He had done her wrong.

No good reason? There were reasons. But they were not always very good.

D istorted faces peered down at Margaret, and a hand shook her by the shoulder. Madeline came to visit, and Timmy stood beside her at the end of the aisle until their faces melded with those of the hippie children, orange dirt on their cheeks and straw hair in tangles. Coarse powder had been sprinkled on her palm, and a damp cloth wrapped around her hand. Fever dreams plagued her and from beyond the bus came the howling of dogs. Margaret tried to rise from the sweat-soaked sheets, but her hand felt knifed to the mattress. An unmade bunk lay across the dim aisle. Dishes were piled in a sink, clothes scattered, and the bag that held the pistol was propped in the driver's seat at the front of the bus. She lifted a corner of blanket covering the window. Rob, Alice, and the children stood slack armed at the fire while camouflaged men tromped into camp.

"Let go of my babies," Alice yelled.

A white-haired man in full military gear gripped the children by their pajama collars.

"Please," Rob said. "Gentlemen."

The men Margaret had seen in the cul-de-sac had increased in number, semiautomatics, and camouflage, but they were still a motley group of geezers, gap-mouthed teens, and couch campers. Some wore leafy sassafras twigs in their hats. One codger lit a cigarette with a Zippo and blew smoke skyward. A beagle howled, and the other dogs countered with a sloppy chorus.

"Marty?" the white-haired man said. "You want to shut down your dogs?"

"They's onto something, Major," Marty said. "I feel it."

The Major glared across the fire.

"Sir, I mean," Marty said. He cluck-clucked, and the dogs sat, whining.

"Hell," the codger said, "they been onto something all day. You sure you don't mean they's *on* something?"

"Screw you, Grady," Marty said.

Grady chuckled puffs of smoke from his nose.

"Our purpose here, men," the Major said, "is to help, not harm."

"*That* explains the guns," Alice said.

A grim smile crossed the Major's face—the look of a man who thinks himself patient. He guided the children into Alice's arms. "I would hate for such innocence to meet with harm. In times like these it is the children who suffer."

"The only time it is here," Alice said, "is bedtime. And you're interrupting it."

"We are looking for a woman," the Major said. "She murdered four young men, solid citizens, high school football players."

Before Margaret could see if a look passed between Alice and Rob, a man stepped between the bus and the fire, and by his bathtub gut and swayback stance she knew him to be Coffey. The Franchi from his bedroom was tucked under his arm.

"You seen you a woman?" the Major said to Rob.

"Indeed, I have," Rob said. "Woman is the warmth of earth, the center of creation, the Hellespont of life. Woman lights the fire in my loins. And I can say with some pride that I have seen a few women—and seen them well. Would that I saw more."

The Major nodded. From the nearest man he hefted a rifle,

and swinging the stock, caught Rob so hard under his eye that he dropped like a soaked rag. The children split for the woods. Two men caught Alice up by the arms. "Men," the Major said. "Take a look. Coffey, go give that bus the once-over." He nodded for the two to set Alice down. "We'll be out of your hair real soon, ma'am." With a polished boot he toed away a two-liter bottle and poked at Rob's thigh. "Then maybe you can get back to your little home-improvement project."

The men slipped into the brush. Coffey picked beggar-lice from his hat.

"Coffey?" the Major said.

"What do I got to go check for? Marty's got the dogs."

"Oh, no," Marty said. "If they's somebody in that bus, I don't want my dogs killed. They's money to me."

The Major looked to the treetops, then hung his head. "One, Coffey, you're closest to the bus. Two, you've yet to fire that Franchi, so I'm thinking it don't work. Three, I gave you an order."

"Fine," Coffey said, chambering a shell. "Sir."

Coffey boarded the bus, but Margaret lay still as he hunched down the aisle toward her. "Who's there?" he whispered. Jabbing Margaret's thigh with the muzzle, he bent to see what he might have stirred. A blade of firelight cut across his face—one eye wide as a whipped mare's. "Speak up. Or I'll blast you in two sure as Christ's a Jew."

Margaret tried to swallow, but her throat was very dry. "Nobody. Nobody's here."

Coffey adjusted his grip on the gun. "I can't shake you."

"Same for me."

"I thought it might be you we's after."

"And you still want to track me?"

Coffey squared up his hat. "You'll go and tell, won't you?"

"What do you think I have to tell?"

"Anything you damn well please."

"Who'd believe me?"

"My wife."

"You should've thought of that."

He nodded at her hand. "You hurt?"

"Yes."

"The reward calls for you alive," he said. "So they can kill you with the courts. You run off with cash of mine; my wife thinks I drank it." He tucked the Franchi to his shoulder. "That's cause to kill you right now."

"You won't get your money back that way," Margaret said.

"I expect you got it on your person. They ain't much to spend it on out here."

"Before you go killing me?" she said. "Your safety's on."

He tipped the magazine up so it caught the light. "Ain't you a smarty britches," he said, then he left her where she lay.

The major asked Coffey what all he'd found.

"Nothing worth the trouble. Sir."

Warm wind lifted blankets from the bus windows, and the light revealed Rob curled around Margaret. When she sat up, he flopped toward Alice, who lay across the aisle under dingy sheets, an arm thrown over her eyes. Margaret was dressed in a bra and underwear. Unwrapping a gob of yellowed gauze from her hand, she found the flesh stained and the wound open like an exotic flower. Halfway up her forearm ran a red streak, but the swelling in her palm was down, her fever broken.

She peeked out the window. The children in their pajamas were beating at the cauldron, the girl with a stick, the boy with the handle of Margaret's whip. Then he brought the handle down on his sister's head. By the time Margaret wrapped herself in a sleeping bag and stepped from the bus, he had gone back to whacking the cauldron. The girl was wailing. "Quit it," Margaret told the boy.

He pointed at the sleeping bag. "That's mine," he said.

Margaret looked down. Stanley Steamers and Stutz Bearcats were printed on the grimy cloth.

The girl tottered, screaming, to the edge of the woods.

"You scare her. But you don't scare me."

"Give me that belt," Margaret said.

"It ain't a belt. It's a whip."

"Well, give it."

"My mom says you're dangerous. And you're a liar."

"Both are true," Margaret said. "Now give it. Please."

"I'm Gabriel," he said. He pointed at his sister, her finger jammed so deep in her mouth that her nose was aimed at a locust limb overhead. "That's Janis. I saw her get born. It was a mess."

"Yes," Margaret said. "Now, give me that and I'll show you how to use it."

Gabriel flopped the braided leather against the ground. "I know how to use it."

Feelings of maternal incompetence rose in Margaret. She could neither order her life nor direct the manners of children. "I'm gonna use it on you if you don't hand it over."

"It's just a cheap carnival thing."

"Give me the whip, Gabriel."

"Give it," Janis said, and she threw a rock that dropped just shy of her brother, who turned and chased her, shrieking, into the woods. Alice stepped off the bus, a sweatshirt over her robe, a crosshatch of sleep marks on her face.

"What're you doing to my babies?"

"Your boy's swinging my belt at his sister."

"I don't know who you are," Alice said, heading into the woods, "or what you're up to, but I want you packed and gone."

Getting gone was Margaret's intention, but she was winded and unsteady. She leaned against the bus. Gray primer, cracked windows, bald tires. She wondered if the engine worked. Climbing aboard, she dug from her duffel a dress and the pistol, which she placed on the driver's seat.

Rob sat up in bed. When Margaret let the sleeping bag drop, he did not look away.

"What were you doing in bed with me?" she said.

"Alice takes up a lot of space."

"Your Alice just said for me to pack up."

Rob took a dime bag and rolling papers from a metal cabinet under his bed and, head bowed, began to labor over a joint. "Don't know why she'd say that." He lit the stick and inhaled from the corner of his mouth, then studied his handiwork. The left side of his face was swollen. "Alice rolls too tight. She's wound tight. She rolls tight." He offered the joint to Margaret.

"I got to be getting on."

"Oh, Louisa, come here. What's happened to your bandage?"

"It went yellow on me."

"That's the medicine. C'mon, let's have a look. Don't be shy."

"You've looked about enough already."

Rob toked and sighed. "It's just skin. It's the body's largest organ."

"Uh-huh. So tell me. What happened to your face?"

"Nothing. Kids leave their stuff all over. I fell is all."

"One hell of a fall," Margaret said. She slipped the pistol into the bag and wrestled the dress over her head, zipping it as far as she could. What intentions were these two hiding? If they knew the truth, she would have to quiet them. He would be easy. "Organ or no organ," she said, backing toward him, "do you mind? I'm one-handed, here."

He set the roach on the sill and threw back the covers. "Yours is a lovely shade of skin," he said, his breath warm on her neck.

"Zip it," Margaret said, and he did. She turned to find him naked—sloping shoulders, a hairy paunch, and a thicker patch below. The blatant plainness of him was a comfort. He scratched his shin with the flat of his foot, then took her forearm, his thin fingers stained as yellow as her own. Layers of blue smoke shifted overhead as he traced a finger up her forearm. Hair rose on her neck. "That streak was to here last night," he said, tapping her biceps. "When that hits your heart—"

"I know," Margaret said, "I'm dead."

"You were hallucinating. Do you remember?"

"Should I?"

Rob cleared his throat. "You were very sick. You need to let me take care of you."

"Your wife's got other notions. Isn't that her I hear now?"

Rob dropped Margaret's hand. He pulled on a pair of pants just as Alice boarded the bus, burrs covering her sweatshirt, the whip coiled in her hand. "I said I want you out of here. And I said I want you building a house, not ogling some gal comes out of nowhere."

"She's sick, Alice."

"I'll say."

"Alice?" Rob said. "Remember?"

"Can it." Alice swapped her sweatshirt and robe for jeans and a flannel shirt. "We need food, Rob. Remember food? We eat it. If you want a wife when I get back, get her out of here." Excusing himself, Rob tailed Alice off the bus, whispering to her until finally she shouted, "All right already."

When Rob returned, he smiled and handed the whip to Margaret. From a cabinet over the sink he took down plastic bags of roots and leaves and corked apothecary bottles filled with dark tinctures.

"Where's your Alice gone?" Margaret said.

She had gone to town for groceries on her bike, he said. The task gave her a purpose when she was on a mad. Then he bagged up bottles, two pans, cups, and a mortar and pestle, and nodded for Margaret to follow him. Though she sensed a trap, she couldn't fathom what sort two hippie wannabes might set. Would Alice be prone to stop by a courthouse? Would two dropouts want a reward? Were they just like anyone else—people with something to hide and nothing to lose?

. "What is it your Alice needs to remember?" Margaret said.

"I'm sorry?"

"You told her to remember something."

"That we need to be understanding. We need to understand the needs of others."

They came into a clearing: a picnic table, a circle of charred stones, and a creek where Rob filled the pans. To the east and west were steep rises. One could be observed from above and never know. "Why're we down here?"

Rob set the pans on the fire ring and started a blaze. "The establishment wants Gabe in school, you know? They think we can't take care of our children, but it's the establishment that can't take care of its own. We love our kids. They don't. They want to take them and change how we live." He dumped the bag on the table and gestured for Margaret to sit. "We can hear them coming for us down here."

"If you love your kids so much," Margaret said, "you might want to get them some breakfast."

"Gabriel and Janis are learning how to be free."

"Hungry too, huh?"

Rob slammed the mortar on the table. "You sound like my father," he said. He began pounding roots, his movements petulant and overwrought. After he'd fetched the pans, he stood so close to Margaret she smelled hot aluminum. "Look," he said. "I know you know men came last night. They're hunting a woman that's killed some boys. There's a reward. We could use the money."

"I had a boy of my own," Margaret said. "And a girl. I didn't take care of them. I lost them."

Rob watched smoke rise into a canopy of hickory leaves. "There's two ways to think. If you stay we could lose our kids. If we turn you in we could lose them too."

"I'm not what you're looking for," Margaret said.

Rob nodded. "I told Alice as much. She's just jealous."

"You may not know what all she is." Margaret limped to the creek bank and disrobed, folding her dress and scrubbing her underthings in a clear pool. Though she felt Rob watching, she would not turn toward him as she waded into the water to bathe, and she ignored her reflection on the surface. She knew what was there. The hired man had said the scar on her face told a story. Sure. And the story came down to this: No matter how much help this simpering hophead might bring, no matter how much harm he might do, if he plotted to stop her, he and his wife would learn just what Margaret was capable of becoming.

Even after she'd smoothed her damp underwear beside the fire and slipped on her dress, Rob was still holding the steaming pans. "I guess what's on the table's for me," she said.

"Yes," he said, adjusting his grip on the pans. "I'll take care of you."

She set a cold hand on his arm. "You just try."

The cup after cup of grassy tea he coaxed her to drink made her vomit. A good sign, he said. He swabbed her hand with a yellow paste and wrapped it and swore the infection would be gone tomorrow. In the meantime, he would deal with Alice. Margaret said thank you, but when he tried to kiss her, she pushed him away, so he sulked off to the creek to wash the pans.

By the time they'd climbed to the top of the hill Alice was back, seated in a lawn chair on the far side of a roaring fire. Straddling a log, Gabe and Janis shared a can of pork and beans. Rob disappeared into the bus.

"He cure your ills?"

Margaret watched the children eating. "I doubt it."

"Good."

Stepping out and joining them at the fire, Rob asked about the trip to town.

"I had a flat. Got as far as Mack Reaves's."

"Where'd you get the beans?"

"Hot dogs too," Alice said. "Mack lives off that and canned soup. He ain't well. The old man's drinking himself to death."

"Why didn't you have him take you to town?"

"Why don't I ask where the hell you been so long?"

"You're drunk," Rob said.

"And stoned. I offered Mack some, but he prefers a drink." Alice lifted a paper bag at her feet. "Get you something to eat, Rob. There's plenty. For once."

Rob shook his head. Kneeling beside Alice, he whispered to her until finally she passed Margaret a steaming can of beans wrapped in a towel. "Enjoy it," she said. "That's all you get."

Margaret ate at the fireside opposite husband and wife as the wind snatched their hushed voices. They touched each other. They laughed. They seemed to have agreed on something—turn her in, let her go. No matter.

At the farthest reach of firelight the children began to play, the burble of their voices a reminder of her losses. Then the girl came to Margaret and, sucking on her finger, stared at the bandages. What awaited a child like this—all gold lashes and cornflower eyes—raised in a bus in the middle of nowhere? Margaret set aside her can. "You cold, sweetie? That wind's getting awful cold."

The girl took her finger from her mouth and asked Margaret why.

"Oh, I don't know much about weather. It just is."

Rob and Alice broke out a water pipe. Watching them, Gabriel pushed a truck through the dirt while Janis climbed into Margaret's lap.

"Careful of the hand, sweetie, OK?"

"Why?"

"Are you at that age when everything's a question? That ain't gonna change, you know."

"She wants a story," Gabe said.

A story. Margaret had rarely told stories to Madeline or Timmy; they'd made up their own. And she had wanted to forget her father, a gifted yarn spinner who had told her tales he'd learned from his mother, who'd gotten them in turn from her father. Margaret would lie on pink sheets and listen while a lamp glowed on the night table. Beneath its shade were porcelain flowers and a bench where a boy sat in breeches, ruffles, and buckled shoes, next to a girl with curls, petticoats, and a hoopskirt. Smiling, the girl strained to escape the boy's clutches, though he seemed only to want a kiss.

"A story," Margaret said. "Well. OK. I know one starts like this. Let's see. . . . Once there was this old boy named Jack."

She paused. The voice on her tongue was deceivingly homey and salted down with false good cheer—her father's voice—and it frightened her. "Anyway," Margaret said. "Old Jack wasn't none too swift. Kept to hisself in the woods of a kingdom."

The details brought back to Margaret childhood nights when she feared moths scratching the screen or a neighbor's chained dog barking or the way her father stared at the headboard as if he sought safe passage to an innocent land where some fool named Jack was always lucky. In this tale, Jack came upon a puddle in which seven butterflies had gathered. He swung a stick and killed them, and was so proud he hired a blacksmith to forge a belt buckle that said KILLED SEVEN WITH ONE WHACK. When by chance the King saw the buckle he asked if that was so. Jack said you bet, and he could do it again, so the King offered Jack a thousand dollars to kill something else. Jack said fine, so they rode the King's horse north to where woods were dark and weird birds sang and a wild boar terrorized the people.

"You know what a boar is?" Margaret asked Janis.

"It's someone tells stories," Gabriel said. He knelt beside his parents, who were busy at their pipe, but he was watching Margaret.

"It's a pig that eats children," Margaret said. "Like you, Gabe. But this one plowed up crops with its tusks. Chased folks from home. The King was so scared he dumped Jack in the woods and said good luck and rode lickety-split back to the castle."

Janis's eyes were wide, and her hair shone like the burnished bell of a trumpet. A mother could lose herself in such brilliance. "You OK, sweetie? Not too scary?" Janis snuggled deep into Margaret's lap.

The story was not scary at all. It was a tale of fortunate mishaps and was therefore unbelievable. Her father's version ran just long enough for Margaret to doze, each impossible situation tacked to the one that came before it. Margaret cut the tale short—she could not bear to cradle the girl for too long because she hated to hold what she could not have. Jack smelled the boar before he saw it. Its eyes were big as platters, its tusks sharp as knives. It chased Jack into a house where a roof had caved in, but Jack scrambled over the wall and locked it inside. The King's men roasted the boar in Jack's honor. When the King asked how Jack had managed the feat, Jack said he'd just grabbed that piggy by his tail and tossed him over the wall.

After that, the King offered a reward for each beast Jack could kill: a unicorn in the south, a fire-breathing dragon back east, a wildcat out west. Jack's ignorance was his fortune, his obliviousness his vision. The usual methods of men. The unicorn corkscrewed its horn into a tree that Jack had sidestepped. The dragon boiled himself in a river Jack had forded. When Jack fell from a branch onto a wildcat, the cat bounced him all the way to the castle, where the King's men shot her. By the time Margaret had given these accounts, Gabriel had pushed his truck around the fire ring to her feet. "So then Jack," Margaret said, "took his cash and lighted out for the territory, where he was called Little Man Jack, Killed Seven with One Whack."

Janis pointed. "Ack," she said.

"That's right," Margaret said. Then she saw Randy peeking from behind the locust tree.

"That's Randy," Gabriel said. "He burnt up his parents and didn't even get in trouble."

Rob passed the pipe to Alice. "They think that's what happened, Gabe. It's not nice to say what might not be true."

Alice held up a can of beans and whistled. "C'mon, Randy. C'mon, boy."

He skulked into camp until he was close enough to grab the can, but Alice pulled it away and held out the pipe instead. When Randy recoiled, she tossed the can after him.

"He's weird," Gabriel said.

"Gabe?" Rob said. "Bedtime. Janis? You too."

The girl slid from Margaret's lap. Alice proffered the pipe to her children, and they smoked until Rob said, "To bed," and the children giggled their way onto the bus.

"Kiddie dope, I know," Margaret said. "But I don't know as I've seen the likes of that."

"They sleep better," Alice said. "Besides, it ain't your beeswax, right, Rob?" Alice touched his swollen face. Rob said they should get to bed too. "You better head on, Louisa," Alice said, and she led her husband away from the fire. "We don't keep your kind."

Margaret's bag tumbled out the bus door, which Rob and Alice shut behind them. The wind was coming hard now, branches scraping against each other. *I've trapped them,* she thought, but at the edge of darkness Randy's eyes glimmered, and she made no move.

All night, to stave off sleep and its accompanying nightmares, Cyrus had thumbed through stacks of 78s and moldy murder ballads in the attic, then taken out his guitar and run through them, one after the other. Finally he strummed a lone A minor and let it drift away. He walked down to G, over to D. Chord by chord, he lifted notes from the past and sang words to the present about some woman with bloodstains on her sneakers and smoke drifting from her hand. She walked along a four-lane, searching for another man. Then he set his palm on the strings. He didn't know what had happened down by the falls, nor did he recognize the woman in his words as Saro. How could a woman kill? How could Saro vanish? It would be worth a song to find out. But who listened to ballads anymore? Saucer-eyed academics and illiterate third-world peasants who got their news from a cadre of songwriters—*narcocorridistas* in Mexico, say, penning celebratory tales of drug lords who paid for songs to enhance their questionable reputations.

But there had been a time. After Jesse James stood on a chair to straighten a picture frame and Bob Ford shot him, a poem running ten feet long was sung on the streets of Springfield. Jesse had a wife, the song said, three brave children, and Bob Ford was nothing but a dirty coward for shooting Jesse—alias Mr. Howard—and laying him in his grave. No more would ride the vengeful Southern sympathizer, marauder of the rich, answered prayer to the poor, a tipper of his hat to the ladies. If that had ever been. A blind woman keened the song from the Taney County courthouse steps, and passersby dropped coins into her cup, but when the old gal took her routine to Richmond, Missouri, she was kicked into the middle of the dusty street—Bob Ford's sister had happened by.

Cyrus packed up the guitar and fiddle and carted them down to the kitchen, which was awash in strong light. He had missed his gig at Bo's. He started to call information for Cate's number, but there was no dial tone. Isaac paid their mother's bills, and Isaac never forgot anything to do with money. The power was still on, though, and the well pump worked, so Cyrus cleaned up, changed his shirt, then drove the gravel road down to Tubb's Cove.

The other night, Darby had spilled his life story: troubles with the job, reelection no guarantee; Jackie hated to be back in Apogee; the kids were why they stayed married—the gripes of any man who lived in a good neighborhood with a good wife. But all he would tell Cyrus about Cate was that she'd left New York for Las Vegas. She was a mother now, but Cyrus couldn't fathom a husband.

He had offered to fill the bill one time, though, up on Mount Nebo where an abandoned Nazarene church leaned toward the ground. Bats had swirled from the steeple, flitting dark against distant lights across the lake, and Cyrus was buzzed on Little Kings cream ale that Cate had managed to buy in town—already she had the full body and head-thrown-back haughtiness of a woman who can get whatever she wants. Ott had died at the end of March. Beating his fist twice on the pulpit, shouting, "The glory of the Lord came down," he dropped to his knees as if to lead his congregation in prayer, then, his face ashen, toppled to the carpet. Saro had been gone for two years, and every time Cyrus spoke of his sister, Cate would say he needed to get on with it. They were graduating soon, heading in different directions. When he said they should get married, she laughed. That was what girls stuck in Apogee wanted to hear. "How could you even say that?" she said.

"I thought it might be nice."

"Nice? Jesus." She kissed him so hard he tried to squirm free, but she did not relent, and that night, in the bed of the truck, they made love—the only time. It was awkward and chilly and frantic, and overhead the wings of passing bats beat a powdery sound into the air. After that no more was said of marriage, not even in the few letters he sent to Cate on the Lower East Side.

~

Cyrus parked outside the yellow house. The property sloped to the lake, a black limestone bluff looming on the far side of the water. Surrounding the yard was the white picket fence, as if Cate had gone to the trouble to keep something in, or out.

He shut the gate behind him, stepping under an arched arbor of shriveled trumpet vines. Mums guarded the porch, pinched dead-heads littering the cypress mulch. *A bad idea to come here,* he thought, and turned back to the truck, but watery light had transformed the far side of the road into a rendering of a storybook wood, one inhabited by spindle-toothed trolls and child-eating hags. A sharp gust stirred branches, bringing down a wall of leaves. The day was coming apart. "Get a grip," he said, and he rang the bell until Cate flung open the door.

"Jesus, you scared me. I thought it was May."

"You what?"

Cate pushed open the screen. Her hair was matted on one side, and a sleep mask lay against the lapels of a blue velour robe. "I thought something was wrong. My girl. Mom watches her when I work."

"Oh. Right."

"Please," Cate said, waving him off. "Don't start. You want to come in or not?" She turned, and Cyrus followed her into the living room. "Go on and have a seat. I'll get us some coffee."

What had his face betrayed? Ashamed, he lifted an afghan off a pile of magazines on the couch. "You're reading high-falutin' these days." He held up an *Art in America*, hoping she might ignore his unsteady hand.

"I ran with some high-falutin' art types in New York," she said, "where I learned mostly that I didn't want to be like them." Ducking into the kitchen, Cate talked over the whine of a coffee grinder. "I can't dance all my life. Gravity's taking hold, not to mention the baby. I'm trying new things. Or thinking about them."

Cyrus started stacking magazines, but they slid away at his touch, so he paced the room. Mission chairs, Shaker table, Navajo blankets—or good enough reproductions. Dancing paid better than he'd reckoned. On the walls were framed photographs of May, and in the latest she looked to be about two, wearing a straw bonnet and clutching a hand-tinted daisy—a stagy shot only a mother could love. May had Cate's lips, and wide, pale eyes that would deepen in hue and candor. Over the TV was a picture of men and women in tights posed among drapery and Doric columns. Cate stood stage left, thin arms uplifted as if she were reaching for a line swinging past.

She entered the room carrying a tray crowded with two coffees, bowls of yogurt, granola, and sliced apples, then set the food in front of him as he cleared space on the couch. She'd run a brush through her hair and put on lipstick. "If you still take milk, you're out of luck. May goes through it like water. I've got blueberries if you want, but they're frozen." She plopped into a chair across from the coffee table. "Decent food's lacking in these parts."

"I'm not all that hungry."

Cate spooned up a bowl of fruit and yogurt and placed it in front of him. "You look like you haven't been hungry in a while."

"I see you're not digging in."

"Long night. Speaking of, where were you?"

"Why? Did old Bo miss me?"

"Oh, Bo's all right."

"If you don't mind getting your ass grabbed, I guess."

"You get used to it in this line of work."

Cyrus took up his mug, sloshing coffee across the tray.

"Still getting used to my line of work, huh?"

He swabbed the spill with a napkin.

"One thing about it," Cate said, "you become an observer of male behavior. You read men's thoughts before they think them. Like whether they're going to grab you or be disgusted or whether they just want someone close. Sitting here I have the benefit of knowing the old you. He was hardheaded and idealistic. And I liked him. But if you've come to sit in judgment, let me tell you, it's way too early in the day to deal with your thoughts on my matters."

"I just wanted to see you," Cyrus said, "when we both had all our clothes on."

She stared at him over the rim of her mug. Color rose in her face—embarrassment or anger? The coffeemaker in the kitchen burbled.

"Your daughter's beautiful," he said.

Cate took a deep breath. "I wouldn't trade her. I'd trade the father, but he's hard to track. I wouldn't get much for him anyway. No, I wouldn't give her up for anything."

No husband, no father. The thought cheered Cyrus. "Somebody saying you should?"

"Mom thinks she ought to take her." Cate sat back, crossing and uncrossing her legs. Small bruises glistened on her shins. "I came back so May could be with family. With people who'll love her no matter what. But my options are limited. Same as for you. I didn't want to come home and start some dance studio. One, I didn't have the money; two, there's not much call for it; three, it would have depressed me. I can make a lot of cash at Bo's real quick, so I do what I do because I can. And because of May. I know I can't keep doing it because of her too."

Now that Cate sat before him, he wanted to know her again, to understand how things had turned out. Still, he feared any question he asked might be construed as criticism, so he studied a liquor ad on the back of a magazine, an image of a coach vanishing down a foggy cobbled street, and wished he were on board.

Cate put down her mug and picked it up. "New York was a real grind, you know, and the dancers were mean. There was too much competition for too few parts, and I was in debt. This girl I ran with talked me into coming to Vegas. Said that's where the money was." Cate nodded to the photograph of dancers on the wall. "I was the fat one. New York fat anyway. I smoked a ton of cigarettes to get down to that. Vegas was a little more forgiving. In some circles they don't mind tits and hips. Anyway. Just after I started at one of the casinos I was up in this hotel suite—some rich man's party. The room was all windows. Past my reflection in the glass I could see that desert, and the wind was kicking up dust out on the horizon. I thought the town would get buried sooner or later. I just hoped I wouldn't get buried with it."

"But you made it OK," Cyrus said.

"I made it," Cate said. "Guys hung around the dancers. Lots of guys. Lots of money. What they figured they couldn't get they wanted most. Some girls made a little on the side, even out in the parking lots. I met a guy. He bought me things." She glanced at Cyrus. "Your coffee's getting cold."

Cyrus moved the soaked napkin away from his mug. "Little late in the day."

Cate went to the kitchen and came back with a bottle of bourbon and a tumbler of ice, which she set on the table in front of him.

Shadows were scraping across the room, sharpening the features of her face. Already the yellow light through the changing leaves had turned sepia, and the liquid in the bottle glinted. "I've quit," he said. "I mean, I'm quitting. Drinking."

"I thought Darby was kidding."

Cyrus turned the label of the bottle to the wall. "I made a fool of myself the other morning."

Cate grinned. "I don't know anything about it. You know, girls at the club never talk."

"There's not anything to know."

"I'm teasing, Cyrus. I was actually kind of glad that if I had to be embarrassed, you got to be embarrassed too."

"I'm just . . ." A cube of ice shifted in the glass. Cyrus cleared his throat and clasped his hands. "When you say things, what sort of things? I mean, what'd he buy you?"

"Oh," Cate said. "A car, for one, a BMW convertible, which I still drive, if you can believe that. Jewelry, dishes, furniture—most of what's here. Finally he said I should quit dancing and move in with him. He was a dermatologist in Orange County. House in Laguna Beach. Pool. Maids. Six cars and a five-car garage. I was tired. I'd gone to Vegas thinking I wouldn't do topless. I'd stay with the *art*. I started supplementing casino shows with strip club work. Things are changing there. Those headdress-and-high-heel extravaganzas are few and far between, and besides, you know how many shows you can do with your top on? I think I did maybe one." Cate shuddered. "Lip-synching to Madonna."

"So why'd you keep doing it?"

"Lip-synching to Madonna?"

Cyrus smiled grimly at his hands. The ice shifted again. He could feel Cate staring, encouraging the silence to bear down on him. A chill slid over his bones, even as sweat began to bead on his upper lip. Outside, light in the leaves was catching fire. He would have to go to visitation soon, but he wanted to stay right where he was. "Could I get some water?" he said, but before Cate could get up to fetch it, he stood, concentrating on each step back into a narrow kitchen where everything was in order, from knives sunk to their hilts in a butcher block to child scrawlings taped in rows to the stainless door of the refrigerator.

Washing back a rising nausea with a swallow of tap water, he took the bottle of pills from his shirt pocket and worried it in his hand. On an oak branch over the shore a brilliant cardinal sprang up and down above an idling Water Patrol boat, the officer's face hidden beneath a hat brim. "What's Water Patrol doing over on this arm?"

"Looking for that woman, I expect. She's outsmarting them."

"I think it'd be something to find her," Cyrus said. "Talk to her."

In the next room, Cate began sorting CDs, the clicking of cases like the gears of a bad clock. "Why on God's green earth would you want to talk to her? It's awful. Those stupid boys, the poor parents, the kids at school. Imagine the sadness that got made when she went and did what she did. It'll hang on the town for years."

The patrolman drifted past the breakfast room windows. Cyrus tucked the pills back in his pocket. "I haven't written a song in a while."

"You think she'd make a good songwriting partner?"

Cate was out of sight beyond the frame of the doorway. "She'd make a good subject," he said, filling his glass again.

"Darby says you think she's Saro. You're done with all that, right?"

"You make it sound like a bad hobby," Cyrus said. "Like macramé or something. She disappeared, for Christ's sake."

"No," Cate said. "She went full speed until she hit something, sank, and left you all treading water. Did you forget those guys across the lake? Nights at the Nightingale banging a piano so old men would buy her drinks? Gilmore had her peddle dope from Coffer's dock. It killed your father, and your mother went more on the fritz and your brother didn't come back for years, and when he did, he started clearing things away and covering them up. Cyrus, she ended up a wedge between us."

"She wasn't peddling anything."

"You're not really listening to me, are you?"

Cyrus stepped to the doorway and found Cate kneeling in front of the stereo. "Darby showed me pictures one of those dead boys took."

"So then you know she's not Saro."

He propped himself against the jamb as she fed a CD into the player. Low sunlight through the window caught the red in her hair. He wanted to touch her, but with her in that rich blue robe and the wind bringing down the woods and night lurking in the hills, he could also stand a drink.

"I'm not sure which would be crazier," Cate said, "wanting to find her because you think she's your sister, or wanting to find her so you can write songs about her." She pressed play. "I bought this in San Clemente. It's very good, but very sad."

A slow riff in G started. Cyrus could not meet her gaze. "Turn it off," he said.

"I wouldn't go looking for songs, Cyrus. You're weighted down with them. Mother, father, that old man—Loman."

"Turn it off," Cyrus said.

"'I'm waiting on the years,'" Cate said. "That's what you sing in the chorus."

"I know the song."

Cate tossed him the case, which he fumbled to the floor. "You're not worried about not writing a song. You're worried about writing one. You can't lie when you sing. I know you, remember? You're afraid to move on from old troubles and get to the new ones."

Cyrus gestured with his water glass. "That song's not me. The singer's not the song."

"It's of you," Cate said. "And if you're serious, God forbid, about wanting to hunt a woman that's killed four boys, you won't find Saro, and you won't find anything you don't already know."

"I'm out of words," Cyrus said.

Cate flipped off the stereo. "You know, I think I expected you to come by and look down your nose at what I'm up to. That's my own insecurity. I'm tired, I guess, and I've got worries, but you've got yours too. You probably want kind words and affection. Who doesn't?"

"I just wonder where we've gone."

"As far as I know, Cyrus, when something goes, it goes. I'll tell you more about that, and what's going on with me, but you need to get ready for visitation tonight, don't you? I know I do. Now's probably not the time."

"You came back, though," Cyrus said. He toed the case out between them. "You went to California, started a life with a dermatologist. You had his baby, then you came back."

Cate stood and smoothed her robe. "I didn't have *his* baby. That's why I came back."

Cyrus spun the ice in his glass. Her shadow cut across him. "Well," he said.

⤎ ⤏

Mama, you say wood from a tree what calls down fire will draw to you your heart's desire, so I carve lightninged cottonwood to see what lies inside for me until dark comes. Sometimes I rest. Sometimes I can't help see not things that are, but were: I see that boy no more a boy. I see him sing so hard he leaned against the girl like shadows do to kiss in cars, and they both sang where folks sat down to hear, but when I stepped up close to see their songs I never heard but felt the air thrum round me like a passing train. He sang for her long after she was gone. He walks these woods, but Mama, no one finds all of the beads come off a broken strand. The one who took those boys runs through these woods for what I wish I knew. Old Knobhead and his crew want her with them, but let them hunt. Townfolk say I don't know my backside from page eight, but I can cut and sand until her skin persimmon shines. And I can draw her heart to see what it can want. With me.

"The Girl I Left Behind Me"

They arrived early, gathering in a tasteful anteroom reserved for grieving relatives—brass lamps on dimmers, walls a neutral shade, pastoral watercolors matted and framed. The hog-eyed man pushed aside a pea green velvet curtain dividing the room from the dead and placed his derby over his heart. "Gentlemen," he said. "Please."

His comrades doffed homburgs, porkpies, derbies, and fedoras. Oh, the dignity of a hat, and the distinction of horehound and charcoal suits tailored years ago in clothiers on town squares across the country. Nevertheless. A few hog-eyed men had unbuttoned waistcoats to free their bellies, and each had worn a sheen into the elbows of his jacket. Their spats were dusty, watch chains tarnished, handkerchiefs frayed, and their ties too wide and too short to be called stylish.

They followed each other past rows of empty wooden folding chairs, then lined up on either side of double doors at the back of the room. "Gentlemen," the hog-eyed man said, "let us take a moment to think on Ruth as she was among the living, not as she is among the dead."

"How's she among the dead?" a fedora said.

"How are most all the dead," the hog-eyed man said, "but full of regret?"

"So then we wait for him to show?"

"For him to see. He will show."

"What if he don't see?" said a porkpie. "We'll be dead then, won't we?"

"With the insidiousness of technology," the hog-eyed man said, "it is likely we shall live forever. Museum pieces, field recordings, seventy-eights in a government library, diodes and chips and crystals of sand compacted into diamonds of sound. So long as someone re-calls, we endure, and so long as someone flees that which is fated, we will fetch that certain someone."

"If it's in a museum, it's gone," a homburg said. "If it's on the folk festival stage, it's dead."

"All we need be," the hog-eyed man said, "is a glint of motif in some little ditty. We can live on in 'Sally, Will Your Dog Bite' if we must."

"I don't get why we don't just tail that Isaac. He looks like an easier nut to crack."

"He has devoted his life to other pursuits. If we managed to show ourselves to him, he would be puzzled, or terrified, and our reason for being would be squandered. Now. Let us move on."

As they filed past the organ in its alcove, a porkpie slipped onto the bench, pulling stops and flipping effects. He had once hunched over a Wurlitzer Model 190 in a silent-movie house in San Fran-cisco. At the start of each show, he rose with the organ from the floor, and the audience gaped as if a god had materialized. Now he whirled out a version of "Frankie and Albert" he had picked up more than a century ago in a brothel in the West Bottoms of Kansas City, just down from a foul-smelling abattoir:

> *Frankie peeked into the window*
> *And seen to her alarm*
> *Albert wasn't using his finger.*

He was using his goddamn arm.
He was her man, but he done her wrong.

The syphilitic tremor in his hands infused the tune with a boogie-woogie beat, and his colleagues stepped to the rhythm, a few pausing to devour blossoms from the arrangements, until, at Ruth's coffin, the hog-eyed man drew his derby across his throat. "Gentlemen, please. This is not a whorehouse. It's a funeral home. A home is not a house."

The porkpie slinked off the bench. "Flowers're nice."

"Tasty," another said.

At the end of the line one gestured with his fedora, a pheasant feather waving from the satin band. "She looks peaceful enough. But they ought to close her eyes."

"Eyes go with her dress," said a grim homburg. "Brings them out."

"You don't want a corpse's eyes brought out, do you?"

"No," the hog-eyed man said. "You do not."

"Her hair ain't right neither. I never once saw her hair like that."

"Don't you dandies carry combs?" Ruth said to the ceiling.

Gasping, the hog-eyed man's colleagues stumbled back toward the rows of chairs. "We," said the grim-faced homburg, "we don't have no hair to speak of."

"Nor brains," Ruth said. "That's yet to stop you."

"Ah, Ruth," the hog-eyed man said. "Someone must be thinking on you. Your youngest, perhaps?"

"If I'm gonna have to deal with the likes of you all, I wish he'd stop."

"Ruth. We have come to pay our respects."

"I'm carrying on fine, thank you."

The hog-eyed men crept back toward the coffin. A few hid their faces behind their hats. "Ruth is not wholly wrong," the hog-eyed man said. "She will carry on. She is in our sphere right now, but—" He spread his arms in a gesture of futility.

"I made those recordings," Ruth said. "I wrote songs."

"Those red and green forty-fives, the songs Ott took credit for? Ruth, the lot on which the SoCo label once operated is now a Quickie Mart. I don't expect re-releases to be forthcoming. And though it is true that the song ends long after the singer, if the song ends, well—"

"I don't need songs. There's people to remember me."

"Memories fade. Or fail. We remember people the way we want until we don't quite remember them at all. And those closest to you? They die. It is no marvel to remember, but it is appalling how we forget." He gestured at the blooms in the corner of Ruth's coffin-lid, the white satin band that said MOTHER. "Life is all hope and flowers, but a graveyard is a stony crop of misses. Mistakes, miscues, misunderstandings, mis—"

"Clever," Ruth said. "But I know you. I know your phony accent. I know every last one of you. Bunch of black-eyed roustabouts. I even know your sad story."

"I doubt that," the hog-eyed man said. "We do try to keep it even from ourselves."

"I know some muggy afternoon you stepped off a flatboat, and the captain paid you what you thought was pretty good, and—"

"Most of us worked steamboats, Ruth. Or started out in medicine shows. Besides—"

"And you took you a little stroll downtown, as the poet says, and bought you a suit and a hat to match. Thought clothes would impress the ladies because the ladies—given your vast stores of knowledge—were either sweet things or whores."

"Ruth—"

"Never smelled river mud again. Never stuck your feet in water.

You denied your very nature. Turned your back on your past. Found married tail to your liking because you never had to make a sacrifice that way, then you moved on before she, or the husband, killed you. You ain't complete ninnies. But you fool yourselves into thinking you love life. What you love's a frolic, a nasty song, a good old drunken barn-burning."

"A problem, Ruth?" the hog-eyed man said. "Loving what we choose?"

"When blind loving brings others grief, it is. Let me tell you. You got to where you could spot the house. Picket fence, irises out front, bushes trimmed, lawn raked. But maybe there was a thing or two wrong—a loose gutter, a torn screen—something that hinted her husband had been gone awhile. You'd lurk at the fence trying not to eat the flowers when she'd pop out to her garden."

The hog-eyed man glanced back at the doors. "Hush, Ruth."

"You can't tell me how to be now. I'm dead, remember? Somehow you'd sweet-talk your way into the kitchen. Oh, what a lovely house, what a pretty dress, what bright roses on that wallpaper, did you choose that yourself, I'm sure you did because it's so lovely. She'd laugh, and you'd say, no, I mean it, it's delightful. You'd finagle peach cobbler and a glass of tea if you didn't swing a meal your first time up. What a darling cook she was, you'd say. She'd never heard so many compliments, or, if she had, it'd been so long she'd forgotten.

"By the time the light climbed those paper roses and katydids scraped the screens, you'd volunteered how you'd been all around the world, down to Cape Girardeau and parts of Arkansas. You never said all you saw was mudbanks and levees and whorehouse parlors. All around the world, you said. So to prove hers was a good life too, she showed you upstairs."

"Ruth—"

"You waltzed right into her bedroom and squealed over hospital corners, blue bottles on the sill, metal bedstead painted cream—to brighten the room, she told you. Then you ruined her sheets and got her to squeal too, both of you sifting your sorry bunch of sand."

"Let's not be crass, Ruth."

"It's your deal. But the regret liked to kill her. If the husband found out—and you could fix it he would—it liked to kill him too."

A few of the gathered toyed with their hatbands. Others toed the carpeting. "Fair enough, Ruth. Yes, regret trails us like a loose thread. We got caught in songs, and songs got caught up in us. Who better, then, to show you how to avoid a life of regret? Who better to prevent mistakes that keep you from life's calling? Of course, for you it is too late. As for your daughter, she would have made a fine singer with that strange boy of yours."

"When do I see her?"

"Not our bailiwick, Ruth. But there was a time we recruited all manner of beings to help save you, and her. Music fills the ether, and the ether is full of spirits—winged things, ghosts, misanthropes— populating the rim of heaven and the bald of hell. You might have made a worthy fiddler, a scribbler of songs, but you swept music to the darkest corners of your heart. So in the end there was no saving to be done. Yes, we denied our earthly nature, Ruth, but you denied us yours. We are no longer roustabouts of freight, but roustabouts of souls."

The doors at the far end of the room swung open, and Cyrus strode down the aisle, the hog-eyed men creeping in close to him when he stepped to the coffin. "Aw, that can't be you," he said. He glanced to either side, and then, with a tremulous hand, tried to fix his mother's hair. He shook his head, closed her eyes, and walked out.

"Give it time," the hog-eyed man said. "Unlike dear Ruth, we have all the time in the world."

Outside the funeral home Cyrus stumbled through mourners come to witness the slain boys laid out in a single room. He passed TV vans and tanned broadcasters and a line of long-necked curious folk who attend such spectacles so that they may say, *Yes, I was there.* He had come early to sit alone with his mother's body, and though there were only pungent flowers and cloying organ music and a windowless room with curtains on the walls, he had felt crowded at the coffin. So he'd fled.

But now a stranger brandished a microphone and demanded to know if he felt safe with a killer at large. To the east a wing of darkness stretched over the post office. The newsgirl's face seemed very close, her eyeteeth very long. A psalm was in order, something along the lines of, "'Oh, that I had wings like a dove! For then I would fly away and be at rest.'" Then a chill gust shoved him down the walk.

After his visit with Cate, he'd gone home to change into his funeral suit and found the electricity disconnected—no phone, no heat, no light. The well pump wouldn't run, so he'd washed up at the hand pump outside. While knotting his tie in the dim kitchen, he had flipped through the folder on the counter: shalls, therefores, subject tos, a line for his signature. He would end up as cut off as that woman in the woods.

"C'mon, Cyrus," he said, his words thrown down in the wind. "It's just you now. Let's keep it together."

He tripped, catching himself against a well-lit window. Water-man's Liquors. Candy-colored neon and amber life. Why not? Cate herself had set out a bottle. *Take*, she might have said. *Drink*. So he bought a pint of bourbon and hurried past the abandoned store-fronts of Woolworth's, Netter's Dresses, Eldridge Auto. The Apogee Bank was a pawnshop, the windows crammed with rifles, cameras, blenders. Hanging from its scroll by a length of fishing line was a Gibson L-5, the center seam of the archtop split: Loman's guitar, the one Saro had found lacking, the one that tweaker had sold. Cyrus thought of the tapes he'd made with Saro scattered in a ditch at Lo-man's place. Falling leaves would be burying them.

By the time he had managed to crack open the bottle, he found himself standing in Dunstan's Drugs. The soda fountain was dis-mantled, the peanut machine missing. A white-coated druggist was watching from behind the back counter. Cyrus slipped the pint into his jacket pocket. "I need a comb," he said. "Maybe a brush."

"You in town for those boys' funeral?"

"No."

"I am doing one whoopdinger of a business. Folks forget tooth-paste, panty hose, shampoo. I guess they ain't found the Wal-Marts yet. I myself use Brylcreem. Oh, sure, you got your mousse, your gels and your whatnot, but I tell you, I got the flyaway hair."

"You got combs?"

The druggist pointed with a pencil. "Know what I hear? I hear that woman lured those boys into the woods with promises of sexual gratification. I believe it. I believe every word."

"Brushes?"

"Left-hand bin. Now, I don't always cotton to what people say in this town, but I got reason to believe. She come in trying to woo me before she took care of those boys." The druggist looked as though he'd stepped out of 1962, and his black hair was hardly Brylcreemed—it was greased, a zipper of scalp running up the left side of his head.

"Is that right?" Cyrus said.

"That *is* right. She tried to steal hair color off me. And twelve-count gauze pads. I caught her, and that's when she made me an offer I could refuse. She'd cut her hand, so I said she'd have to get that amputated if she didn't buy Epsom salts. I'm a businessman, first and foremost."

Cyrus set a pack of combs on the counter. "Epsom salts," he said.

"Pulls that infection right out."

Cyrus offered up the pint. "You catch her name? Where she's headed?"

The druggist squinched up his nose. "That stuff'll eat out your internal organs, and it's a crime to drink in here, but don't you worry. Punks come in, try to steal me blind. Ain't a officer of the law lift a pinkie to help me yet. So I don't intend to lift a pinkie to help them. No, sir, I ain't telling you nothing neither. She'd come kill me if I told."

"So tell me this," Cyrus said, pocketing the bottle. "What'd she look like?"

"Look like? Real shifty eyed. And just as mean as snakes."

ᑖ

Cyrus pushed through the line of mourners still flowing out the doors. Not one gawker was here to see his mother, but a few of his father's former congregants were inside, and they whispered as Cyrus made his way down the aisle and set to work.

"What're you doing?"

Cyrus turned. Behind Isaac, Burrs was feigning interest in a potted fern.

"Are you drunk?" Isaac said.

Cyrus pointed the comb at Burrs. "She never wore her hair like this."

"I had him get someone to do her hair," Isaac said.

Burrs took cigarettes from his breast pocket and studied the packaging.

"Did you switch coffins too? We never agreed on this white Cadillac of a thing. I thought I had the wrong room."

"I handled the extra cost," Isaac said. "I knew you couldn't."

"You've handled some utilities too."

"Nobody lives there anymore, Cyrus."

Cyrus aimed the comb at his brother's head. "All that hair spray must have shellacked your brain."

Isaac slapped the comb to the floor. "This is serious."

"No. This is." He tackled Isaac into the first row. Old women grabbed handbags and old men grabbed women, turning over chairs in their flight. Cyrus staggered up, panting, but Isaac stayed seated on the floor, straightening his yellow tie. In the back of the room stood Cate and Darby. Burrs patted himself down for matches.

Cyrus smoothed the lapels of his jacket, took a deep breath, nodded, and walked out a side door. He'd seated himself at the top step of the post office when Cate appeared, watching him from the sidewalk below. Leaves skipped past her, and she held down her dark skirt with both hands. Cyrus set the bottle at his feet. "How come you're not at work?"

"I told you I'd be here. Remember?" She climbed the steps, and taking the bottle, held it up to the streetlight. "I thought you'd quit."

"I was. I am."

"Then I guess you won't need this." She tossed the pint into the bushes and sat beside him. "It's rough," she said, straightening her skirt. "But it's rough for Isaac too."

"You don't need to tell me."

"Who does, then? You know, Cyrus, Isaac couldn't play or sing, and if I remember right he wasn't much thought of until he got to selling. Your mother shared secrets with you. She gave you songs. Isaac watched after her. No offense, but you were gone."

"He wants me to sign off so he can build a resort. That's why he took care of her."

"C'mon," Cate said. "Blood isn't that simple. Besides, what's the big deal if he builds a resort?"

"It's home."

"It's not your home. It's not Isaac's either."

"I don't want to give up on the place."

Cate rested her hand on his knee. "Saro, you mean. I should have gone easy on you this afternoon. I'm sorry. When you played it was like nothing could get to you, and your voices together could make me cry. But Saro never cared for music, Cyrus. So who knows? Maybe you're right. Maybe she did find her way out. Just like we all said we'd do." Cate leaned her head on his shoulder. For a long while he did not move.

"Listen," he finally said. "And don't laugh at what I'm gonna say."

"All right."

"Some nights I'll do an old song. One with parts that switch off or one with a solo run in it, and I'll catch myself stepping to the side of the mike so she can come in. It's like she's right there."

Cate set his hands in her lap. "Within an hour of our first date, remember? You took me across the dam for pizza? Within an hour I knew two things about you. You believed in music, and you believed in ghosts."

"So then you know sometimes I think she's dead."

Down the walk, a streetlight went out. A wind-spun can clattered at the curb and rolled off into the darkness. Cate put her arms around him and pulled him to her. "What's this?" she said. She took from his jacket pocket the bottle of pills.

"They're just in case."

She shook some into her palm, separating them by size, shape, color. "Good God, Cyrus, in case of what?"

"Why?" he said. "You know these things?"

Cate capped the bottle and stood. She smiled. "Fat dancers take ups to cut weight. Downers to get to sleep. We have aches, pains, bad feet. A good many of us are crazy too."

"You look all right to me."

"God knows what you see," she said. She pulled him off the step and turned toward the wind, her hair strung out and wild. "C'mon. You need some rest. I'll follow you home."

Margaret woke tangled in her sleeping bag beneath the oily carriage of the bus. Polished tree limbs clacked above the encampment. The ground beyond was pale with snow, the iced-over cauldron glossy. "Hands up," Gabriel said, sleet popping off his nylon jacket. In one hand was the box of hair color, in the other the pistol, but the two-plus pounds of steel were heavy, and he struggled to aim at his sister as she hopped from one foot to the other in a yellow summer dress. Then came a rusted creaking, and a report so loud Margaret flinched. A branch crashed to the road. "Bang," Gabriel said.

Crawling from under the bus, Margaret told Gabriel to give it. He turned his gaze on her and handed over the hair color. "The gun," Margaret said.

Janis balanced flamingo-like on one leg. "Give it, give it."

Margaret lunged, and the gun fired. Gabriel fell back, staring at treetops, and Janis began to bawl. Margaret grabbed the pistol from the boy. He scuttled, whimpering, into the cold ashes. "Ain't a toy, is it?" Margaret said.

She found Rob and Alice in bed beneath a haze of dope smoke, their backs to the fogged-over rear window. They looked from a hole in the cabinets to a hole in the ceiling. "Oh, man," Rob said. "That's gonna leak."

"Give me the keys and get out. Both of you."

Alice began to laugh.

"The bus was just here, you know?" Rob said. "I mean, I don't even think it's got a battery." He pointed at Margaret's hand. "Hair color?"

Howling, Alice slapped her thighs.

Margaret raised the pistol. "Shut up," she said.

"Oh, go ahead," Alice said, and she stuck her chin out, offering a target.

From her coat pocket Margaret took three fifties and tossed them onto the bed. "Buy those two some winter clothes, some food."

Snowmelt dripped from the hole in the ceiling to the bills on the bed.

"Ah, she gives to the poor, Rob. How noble. What do you think? Bonnie Parker? Belle Starr? How shall we remember her when she's dead and gone from us?"

Rob pulled the blankets to his neck, and when Alice made to speak, Margaret stepped to the bedside and stuck the muzzle in her mouth. "Bite. I said bite down. Good. Is that enough to shut you up? Because I ain't noble. And I ain't dead." Margaret cupped Alice's chin and, with great care, removed the pistol. Then she closed Alice's mouth, patted her lips with two fingers, and turned down the aisle.

"Yet," Alice said, but Margaret had stepped off the bus. Janis ran for the woods. The boy began to pedal a rusty tricycle around the cauldron until the front wheel sank in a soft patch and he toppled. Mouth full of mud, he got to his knees, crying.

Timmy had not cried. The medical examiner's report would indicate that the subject, a male Caucasian, five years of age, had suffered repeated trauma to the head. A nineteen-year-old employee of a Rent-A-Center had discovered his body beneath a stack of pallets in a dumpster behind the store. At Margaret's trial the prosecutor had repeated these details with zeal. And this: Timmy's skull had been cracked against the porcelain bowl of the toilet.

Margaret plowed on across the slick ditch and crossed fields ringed with cedar and blackjack oak. She skirted a cemetery with a ragged blue tent flapping along the fence line. At a fork in a gravel road, weathered signs pointed to family cabins or trailers or Coffer's. Sleet changed back to snow. Soon men would be able to track her with ease, so she retreated into the woods, where ravines steered her off course. Branches dropped in front of her and behind, and she changed direction over and over until she came to a heap of quarried limestone, moss-covered chunks like the imploded walls of an ancient temple. A falling bough missed her as she skirted the rocks, but when she heard voices on the wind she scrambled into a pillbox hole and unholstered the pistol. Snow was falling hard now, melting in beads on the gun, and by the time four men in county-issue khaki scanned the glade, it had blown across her tracks.

"Who wants to check it out?"

"Why don't you, Sheriff? You're the one gets all the credit."

"And the blame," the sheriff said. Hitching up his holster, he started toward the heap of limestone, a freckle-faced Howdy Doody with a solid layer of fat and a hitch in his step—some old football injury, she figured. Margaret drew down on him as he teetered from rock to rock. Then, quick as a dropped meal sack, he fell from sight.

"Y'all right, Chief?"

"Goddamn knee."

The men scrambled up the pile. Margaret pressed herself into the stone.

"What's wrong with your knee?"

"Nothing. See? I got it."

"You plan on hopping all the way back to the road?"

"Hopping, my ass. This is a modified perambulation."

As soon as the men had kicked their way back into the woods, Margaret took off for Coffer's, intent on finding a car. The carport was empty, though, so she climbed over the windowsill of the cabin farthest from the lake. She would warm up, dry out, wait. The room was furnished with two twin beds stripped to plastic mattress covers, a stainless kitchenette, and an Adirondack chair facing a stone fireplace. It stank of soured hickory smoke and dusty vinyl, but the wall heater came on when she tried it, and she huddled there until blood tingled in her fingers, then she filled a pot from the tap and set beans from the hired man to boil—there was no time for them to soak. She took the .38 from the holster. Mud had crumbled into the cylinder, and the pin slot was gritty. She tried wiping the gun down with a towel, but it needed solvent and brushes.

After a long shower she risked a light over the mirror so that she could work the colorant through her hair. She realized her error after the color was set: not blond, but a silver-blue crown common to dotty women at church potlucks and chamber bake sales. From the mirror stared her mother. Then the light went out. The heater shut down. The beans stopped boiling. She ate cold tortillas while snow hurled itself to no avail against the panes.

Cate lay next to him in his childhood bed, but still he was cold, the pillowcase clammy. His skin twitched, synapses gone haywire. An incessant ticking kept on at the window, and he saw june bugs, drawn maybe by the luminescence of Cate, whom Cyrus tried to hold on to before he was dragged into the nightmare flickerings of a picture show.

A dark and stormy night. No shots rang out. Hail tore across the sky, along with cattle and shredded clothing and car doors and lengths of straw that could screw their way into telegraph poles. Cyrus crouched beside a dirt road—wagon rutted, washed out, hell to travel. He had lost track of a woman but expected to find her back east, hiding in a torn gown that was too dear to toss in the salt-salt sea.

He made it as far as a city of red brick and rusted steel. Beyond a limestone cathedral a clarion rang, accompanied by grunts of encouragement: *Uh-huh, that's right, tell 'em, tell 'em,* and he ran to a bridge lit from above and thought, *This could be a bad fall.* Lengths of shattered railroad ties stuck up halfway across the bridge, but in the distance she was singing.

Below, brown water roiled and dark forms floated—Huck's father and the *Walter Scott*'s stowaways destined for swamp gas on a slow stretch of Delta. Pigeons drafted on winds below the bridge, their shadows skimming the water. A barge churned into view and at the stern she stood, all bones, strumming on a banjo uke—*chinka, chinka, chinka, chinka, chink*—as she sang:

> *Haul out the rubber-tire carriage,*
> *Drive out the six-horse hack.*
> *You're goin' down to the graveyard,*
> *But you're bringing nothing back.*

The barge slipped into darkness. The ukulele ceased. Somehow she dropped behind him, her bone legs wrapping round his thighs, and whispered, *Baby, I'll follow you down.*

Cyrus sat up, grappling for air. He could see his breath. He was deteriorating into vapor.

"What? What?" Cate said.

"Nothing. Dream."

"You're soaked."

Her hair was fanned across the pillow. She lay atop the covers, wearing her skirt and blouse. His jacket hung over the foot of the bedstead with his tie and white oxford. He wore dirty jeans and a T-shirt. "Go to sleep," he said, and she closed her eyes.

In the kitchen, the folder was open on the counter, which he gripped to stay upright. He stuck a jelly-jar glass under the tap, but there was no way to pump water, so he rummaged in a closet, found an old coat of his father's, and headed outside.

Sleet assaulted a sheet of ice and a layer of snow that crackled as he crept past the arbors; the crust of earth might give way at any moment. When the dogs rushed from the barn, circling him like thieves, his steps became a high-wire act. A branch cracked, another fell. Cyrus thought of femurs splitting lengthwise, then his knees turned to sawdust. The dogs leapt over him where he lay, an air of malice about them, and he waved them back as a dark man stepped from the barn. Cyrus had seen him before in the Greyhound station in Barstow, where seats in the lobby did not invite a traveler to take his rest. The man had mumbled with incoherent malevolence in front of the lockers, but here he was now. *Mayday, Mayday*. He wore a straw cowboy hat and a thick denim coat. A blue Samsonite lay at his feet. He was well suited for the shoulders of interstate on-ramps. When he offered Cyrus a letter shut with bloodred sealing wax, or blood itself, Cyrus thought, *No one knows I'm here.*

The dark man spoke, but before his accusation crossed the air, Cyrus knew. He had said as much himself: "They flee as shadows." The man's eyes glinted beneath the brim of his hat. His left bicuspid was made of polished steel.

Cyrus stood, and when the man shook the letter, he closed his eyes: Ott Harper lay facedown behind a lectern, his Bible an arm's length away, his body convulsing like a science fair frog. Ruth stood nearby, her dress hoisted above her calves. She was dancing.

Stop it, Cyrus thought he was saying, and the dark man grabbed him by the shoulders. The letter was in fact three tarnished keys. "For the shed," Jorge said. "The truck."

"What?"

"I am leaving. I will have to miss your mother's funeral."

"You don't know my mind," Cyrus said, and his body began to quake.

Jorge stepped back. "Maybe a small drink is in order? To mark my departure? No?"

"Yes," Cyrus said.

In the shed Jorge opened the suitcase. A jug of burgundy and a bottle of vodka lay snug between folded shirts. He set two glasses at the edge of the sink and pointed the bottle at the window. "It is freezing." Steadying himself in the doorway, Cyrus was afraid to look. "I will pour you a double," Jorge said.

With both hands Cyrus took the glass, working the drink from chin to cheek to lips before he collapsed in a chair by the table. His hand convulsed on the formica. Jorge poured again. "You're leaving," Cyrus managed to say.

"I told you last night. When you were working on the bulldozer."

Cyrus took a long drink. "I'm sorry?"

"If you had not wakened me you would have been funny. You dropped many tools. But the machine is running now. It has not worked for some time."

"I don't know."

Jorge poured wine for himself. "It comes back when you are ready for it."

"Yes," Cyrus said. He was afraid of that. "Where you going?"

"Isaac tells me that soon there will be nothing left for me to tend, yet he wishes to retain me as a gardener for his resort. He did not ask me if I care for flowers, which I do not."

Cyrus scrounged enough courage to look outside. The land had burned white, the sill of the shed layered with ash. "Bad day to go," he said.

"It is apple-picking time out west. A few orchards have housing. And water. When Isaac turned you off, it seems he did the same to me."

Cyrus gripped the glass so tightly it spun across the table. "You need a ride somewhere?"

Jorge checkmated the glass back to Cyrus. "Maybe I could drive us to town? And you can take the truck from there?"

"Sure," Cyrus said. "Yes."

Jorge loaded his case in back and hung his hat from the gun rack. The dogs piled into the bed—all slicing tail and slavering tongue—as Cyrus stepped into the cab. Jorge drove with grave caution, slowing round a bend at Dooley long enough for Cyrus to study a backhoe, its shovel silvered with use, and a royal blue tent reserved for his mother's interment.

Gravel turned to blacktop. Over the salted patches, Jorge relaxed his grip on the wheel. "You are still wanting that woman?"

"What?"

"Last night in the barn you wished to find her. I thought you were going to take the dozer and tear down trees—the better to see with." Jorge downshifted. "You seemed to think she had something to do with your music."

A vein in Jorge's temple was pulsing. Cyrus's heartbeat kept time with it.

The dogs stationed themselves on either side of the cab, their ears and tongues flapping, and Jorge smiled at the rearview mirror. "I will tell you some of my grandmother's nonsense," he said. "Outside our village, at harvest, we cut corn and tied it in sheaves. This is why I am such a hard worker, yes? We sang and worked. My mother remembers the words. Women recall such foolishness, but I can only say that once, as a boy, my grandmother put me into her lap. She had been working fields, and smelled of sweat. There were dark hairs on her chin, and when I cried she shook me and asked, 'Do you know why they sing?'

"I did not. So she told me. A woman can always tell. When we were still tribes, there was a son of a chief. On the last harvest day this son worked the fields, but he went down to the river to fetch water and was never heard from again. An enemy tribe. A wildcat. Who knows? People walked the fields, calling. Calls became cries, cries became chants. These were the songs we sang in my village. Maybe they still do. I left those lands. I found a way into school, and you see what good it did. Still, I do not wish to return home."

Cyrus swiped at condensation on the window. Tall grasses in the ditch were trembling filaments of glass. "Is this some answer I was asking for?"

"You know I have seen that woman. She is a fool. Like me. Like you. But for five years I knew your mother. A few times I heard her sing, and I would ask after the song. 'An old one,' she would say, or, 'An old one. I made it.' Then she would say, 'So much for that.' You see? A song goes to the wind and fails to call anything back. That is why there are so many songs."

Near the edge of town was a roadblock: fluorescent cones and three cars—two county, one state. Jorge lifted a finger off the wheel. "That is funny, yes?" A deputy stepped from the ditch, and Jorge slowed, but the officer scanned the barking dogs and the suitcase, then waved them on. "Besides," Jorge said, "who wants to sing when a song only makes us mourn what is lost?"

Who indeed, Cyrus thought. But a song taken by the wind might be whirled away to return stronger and clearer than it was before. He maybe could believe that much.

"I begin here," Jorge said, pulling into a service station along the four-lane.

Cyrus tapped his fist against the door. "I'm not crazy."

"Crazy?" Jorge said. "No. A wetback walking through an ice storm in the Ozarks to go pick apples in a desert—that is crazy."

Jorge slid from the cab. Land beyond the windshield was wrapped in shredded gauze. Cyrus wasn't sure he could drive. "You could freeze to death out there."

"I considered your mother a friend," Jorge said, lifting his case from the truck bed. "But I am not so fond of loss I wish to prolong it." He headed out across the lot, the dogs scrabbling over the tailgate after him, and though Cyrus called to them, they did not come back. Jorge sidestepped down to the four-lane until he, along with the dogs, was gone.

Cyrus put the truck in gear. "I can't even keep me a couple of dogs," he said.

❧

He arrived at the funeral home smelling of bay rum shaving soap and wintergreen toothpaste. Cate was gone by the time he'd returned to the house, and it had taken his entire morning to get ready. Four variegated pills had yet to calm his nerves, but his tie was knotted, his gray jacket lint-picked, and now, sitting straight-backed in the anteroom designated for family, he resembled a poster boy for a 1950s barbershop ad: LOOK YOUR BEST. VISIT YOUR BARBER EVERY TEN DAYS.

Isaac hurried to the front row, tailed by his wife, Beverly, and Derrick, who was maybe ten, puffy and shambling, his head a mouse brown, spiked, gelatinous mess. The Harper legacy. When Cyrus nodded to them, Isaac took a deep breath and came back, laying his arm across his brother's shoulder. "Two things," he said. "Sorry about the heat, and lights. Bev says come stay with us if you need to. It's OK. Also, I had the lawyers redraw the papers. You get a cut of twenty-year profits. And you won't have to raise a finger. It'll all work out. I promise." He patted Cyrus twice, then took his seat beside Beverly, who turned to give Cyrus a closed-mouth smile, a lock of frosted hair caught between her lips—a small gesture for which he was grateful. And for this as well: She blocked his view of the open coffin, which Cyrus had volunteered to help bear at the close of the service because Burrs had not managed to field a six-man boneyard team. All day the sky had coated roads in sleet and rain, then freezing rain and snow, and Cyrus feared he might end up the lone pallbearer, dragging the coffin along the slick crust.

The final notes of "Just a Closer Walk with Thee" faded from the ceiling speakers, and a huge-breasted woman in a plain black dress stepped to the lectern, her girth ratcheted down with a girdle. The organist commenced a prelude, heavy on vibrato, and the woman began to tear through the hymn called "In the Garden." A milliner's nightmare of black feathers on her head stirred as if it might take wing. Cyrus twisted the pill cap, but the bottle popped from his grasp, rolling two rows in front of him, and by the time he'd retrieved it, the song was done, and a preacher—one Ruben J. Stark—stood at the lectern. His Adam's apple protruded over a brown tie. "Praise Jesus," he said, then he rustled the onionskin pages of a white calfskin-bound Bible.

"Amen," said a man in the next room.

Cyrus sighed so heavily that Derrick turned, his flinty eyes creeping up at the corners. Isaac torqued the boy's head back to the front.

"Neighbors," Stark said. "Friends." He checked his notes, shifting one sheet atop another. "Ruth Aileen Harper." Ale-een. Already, he'd mispronounced her name, which did not rhyme with *ailing* but was a one-legged woman's moniker. "Ruth Aileen Harper was born February 27, 1928, in Stobbs, Oklahoma, the daughter of Alpert Bosef Garland, a sign painter and farmer, and Dillie Bond Garland, a homemaker. The youngest of seven children, she graduated from high school in 1946, whereupon she worked as a switchboard operator in Tulsa. She sang in a country-and-western band, and played fiddle. In July of 1955, she married the Reverend Arthur 'Ott' Harper, who founded the Baptist Church of New Light and Free Grace. She is survived by two sons—Isaac Harper of Apogee, and Cyrus Harper of San Francisco, California; a daughter-in-law, Beverly Harper of Apogee; and a grandson, Derrick, also of Apogee. A daughter, Saro Harper, cannot be accounted for at this time."

Who among the gathered had tried? Wherever Cyrus had sung, from Eureka to Santa Cruz on down to San Diego, he saw girls who resembled Saro enough to give him pause. He'd kept up the hunt until shadowed alleys, murky undersides of piers, and rusted-out cars began to draw his gaze. Although he'd tried to account for her—hadn't he?—some things were not meant to be seen. Even before she'd disappeared he had realized this. One afternoon he'd come home early from school and found Willie Gilmore and Saro together in her bedroom. Willie's khakis hung over a chair. Saro's clothes lay on the floor. Cyrus stood as still as he could, convincing himself this was not his sister. He had become deft at seeing things that were not as they appeared. He stepped out on the porch, where his mother was watching the lake. The hog-eyed man, she said, was at the edge of the bluff. She pointed toward a stand of scrub cedar. Yes was all Cyrus could think of to say.

Which was more than he would give for this chicken-necked preacher squawking facts of a life that hadn't amounted to much and a big-assed Baptist gal crying hymns that could be heard on any given Sunday in any church set in thick chickweed beside a gravel road. Thunder stomped across the roof and Stark smiled. "Our scripture today comes to us from the book of *Matthew*," he said. He proceeded to read too long from the parable of the lord who granted talents to his servants—five to one, two to another, and one to him of least ability—a confounding tale to Cyrus until he learned that a talent was not an aptitude but rather some six thousand drachma.

"And so," said Ruben Stark, "'for unto every one that hath shall be given, and he shall have abundance: But from him that hath not shall be taken away even that which he hath. And cast ye the unprofitable servant into the outer darkness.'"

Ah. The outer darkness. Was old Stark insinuating that Ruth had squandered her days because she had never glorified the Lord with special music at New Light and Free Grace? Never mind how Ott Harper had not wanted his congregation to witness the spiritual sensuality of his wife when she sang, which had drawn him to her in the first place. Or that Ruth had quit the Devil's music the year Elvis appeared on Hank Snow's segment of the Grand Ole Opry, singing "Blue Moon of Kentucky" and "That's All Right" only to be told he should stick to driving a truck for Crown Electric. Elvis boohooed all the way back to Memphis. But he didn't quit. Ruth did. Who, then, had squandered days? Where was the glory?

Cyrus stuck his face in his hands. He began to laugh. It sounded a lot like crying.

"Some of you know I got me a auto parts store over to Rocky Heights," Stark said. "Well, one day I was down to Wal-Mart, and there's Ruth Harper with her hired man selling grapes and such from the back of a old truck. Now, late August, friends, it's hot, and I just wanted to get on home, but Ruth Harper calls to me, and when a soul calls, I answer. 'Preacher,' she says, and she holds up a bunch of grapes just so. 'The vines with a tender grape give a good smell.' Now, I know Solomon's song, but I didn't know how she come to know I was a preacher. So I asked her. She says, 'Preacher, ain't no class of man dresses any shabbier than a preacher.'

"'Fair enough,' I says to Ruth, but then I says, 'To live a life of Christ you must give up worldly ways.' I myself donate a portion of store proceeds to assist the Lord in His good works. But Ruth says to me, 'You want to live a Christian life, preacher? Don't preach.' Now you all here know of Ruth's troubles better than me. Trouble at home. Trouble in mind. Trouble gets portioned out unequally, don't it? I says, 'Sister, you ain't give up the Christian life. You just spoke God's word.'

"'Preacher,' she says, 'even the Devil can quote a mean scripture.' Then she laughed like the joke was on me. But Ruth was a kind soul. A forgiving soul. I come to find she'd been saved. She even bagged up with the grapes I purchased some Peaches and Cream corn and Big Boy tomatoes at no extra charge to me, but, friends, I am here to tell you that if you think a kind nature, a quick wit, or forgiving manners are enough to get you into the kingdom of heaven you are sorely mistaken. The joke, such as it is, is on you. But there's no joke on me, or Ruth, because we have been washed in the blood of the lamb."

"Amen," said the amener.

"You see," Stark said, "I asked Ruth if she'd been saved, and she looked me straight on and says, 'I'm as saved as you are, preacher.'"

Cyrus took his hands from his face.

"I am here to tell you, friends, that whosoever is not written into the book of life shall be cast into the lake of fire. Sinners, are you saved? You may quote scripture. You may grow sweet tomatoes or trim fine vines, but if you do not know the Lord Jesus Christ as your personal savior you will not be admitted into the kingdom of heaven. . . ."

Cyrus's eyes felt gritty. He pushed himself up by the chairback in front of him. The room rocked off its axis and the floor came up hard to meet him, but not before he called out for Stark to sit down and shut up. Then the crow-topped gal was warbling "Put Your Hand in the Nail-Scarred Hand." Derrick stared back as Cyrus crawled into a chair. Mourners began filing past the coffin. Cate passed, and Cyrus lifted a hand, the gesture of a man drowning, but Darby blocked her view, his arm flush against her back.

The family was given time alone with the body, but Cyrus opted to step outside the back entrance, where a hearse, limo, and van idled. Ice weighed so heavily on the trees that all across town branches cracked like rifles fired in celebration. Under an awning five men made room for Cyrus. They were thick armed and windburned. A few had long hair, tangled beards, silver rings on more than one finger. Skullcaps, leather vests, and calf-high boots suited them better than their ill-fitting Sunday best. Cyrus had no idea how they knew his mother. Maybe they were ringers in the funeral trade, hired guns at corpse hauling.

Double doors behind them wheezed, and out stepped a man in a chocolate brown suit. His pink face was bristly, his black eyes watchful. He swept a derby before him as the coffin rolled like a grocery cart onto the landing. Roses atop the box went bright as embers, then Weber Burrs, grandson of the home's director, pulled the cart to a halt. Once a stringy kid with mathematical gifts, he now resembled all the other Burrses: varnished and smoke worn. A yellow carnation was pinned to his lapel. He was not wearing a hat. "Cyrus," he said, and the doors clicked shut behind him.

"Web," Cyrus said, clearing his throat. "Sorry. For a second there I thought you were someone else."

"Nobody but Burrs got stomach for this business."

"Well. How you doing?"

"Busy." He peered out from under the awning. "Lousy day for a funeral."

"Most are."

Weber shrugged. He asked the gathered to form two lines and grab the bars at either side of the coffin. A turnip-shaped pallbearer grunted, but to Cyrus the burden felt far too light. At the hearse they guided the box onto rollers and locked it in place. Flowers were tossed in after it like brush.

From the backseat of the van Cyrus watched Weber step to the edge of the lot with Hobb and another man, who threw back his head, laughing, before he looked Cyrus's way. He spun a derby in his hands, which seemed to be arthritically gnarled, or split.

"Look at my hands," the man next to Cyrus said.

No, Cyrus thought.

"Hey, bud. Looky here."

Maybe if he made no sudden movements, his mind would play no tricks. He turned as slowly as he could. A beard concealed the man's pocked complexion. His earlobe was missing a snip of flesh as if it had been tagged. He shook his hands. "They're all swole up. Caught a mess of channel cat on trotlines. Took half my morning cleaning them. They say their whiskers are poison. Ain't that something?"

"Yes," Cyrus said.

"That's an allergic reaction to your suit, Riley," said the turnip-shaped man up front. "What's that thing made of anyway?"

Riley tugged at the knot in his tie. "That might could be, Del. Last funeral I swelled up like a drowned man."

After Weber climbed behind the wheel, the cortege—hearse, limousine, van, cars—took side streets, fishtailing around electric lines bowed beneath snapped limbs. Power was out at the edge of town, and though candles flickered in a few windows, the houses looked abandoned. When the cortege paused at the highway, a sugar maple branch fell toward the limousine but stopped short on a long cord of bark. Cyrus watched Isaac gawking skyward from the rear window of the limo, until the car squirted away.

"I wouldn't mind seeing that old boy get crushed," Riley said.

Weber checked the mirror. "Riley."

"I wouldn't."

"That's his brother you're sitting next to."

The pallbearers turned as if a snake had been uncovered in their midst.

"Hell," Riley said, "he can't help that. You're Cyrus, right? You know everybody? That's Del up there. Niles and Stutz in front of us, and Pie—as in cherry—beside me."

The men grunted hey.

"Your mother used to let us hunt your land. She'd give me grapes to make jelly. I didn't know all that about her being in a band. I saw her holding a fiddle not too long ago out on the porch, but she went and told me she couldn't play it. Naw, she was nothing if not all right. But that brother of yours? Know what he did?"

"No," Cyrus said.

"Son of a bitch outbid me and my daddy for my granddaddy's land. Granddaddy didn't keep no will. That acreage sits right next to mine, and now old Isaac's fixing to stick condos on it. Know what he says when I pitch a bitch at a commission meeting? Says it'll raise property values. Well, whoop-de-doo—and taxes too." Riley leaned toward Cyrus. "But you ain't from around here anymore, are you? You ain't fixing to screw me over."

"No," Cyrus said.

"You ought to come on out to our fish fry. You look like you could stand you some eats."

"Fish fry," Cyrus said.

"For the families of those dead boys. Pay their funeral expenses and whatnot. They was good ballplayers." Riley whacked the seat in front of him. "They gonna catch that old gal?"

The men agreed she would be apprehended soon.

"I don't know," Riley said.

"She's gotta pop out sometime," Del said.

"That one old boy's dogs ain't found her."

"Ray's dogs wouldn't know their own shit if they smelled it."

"How about Alis Townes, then?"

"Townes wasn't no woman, Riley. Besides, he was just about raised on bark and berries."

"Townes plugged some old gal with a twenty-two and took her rings," Riley said to Cyrus. "Hid out in caves after that, and some folks put him up in their barns. Anything to help the little guy. But right about the time the law was all in, he got so hungry he tried to lift some Slim Jims and Cheetos from a bait shop, and the counter guy shot him. Townes was none too bright, though. You never know about a woman."

The closer they got to Dooley, the quieter the men got. No cars met them until they hit a straight stretch, and in the distance bulbous headlamps shimmered into gusts of angling snow. An old Packard had pulled to the shoulder, and a thick-necked hulk stood by the front fender, head bowed, gray porkpie clenched to his heart. As the van passed, a hog-eyed man grinned up at Cyrus, who shut his eyes and did not open them until the cortege reached Dooley.

Weber popped the hatch of the hearse. "Gentlemen," he said, and the men took their places to bear the coffin. Gusts tacked their pants to their legs as they carried the load toward the tent. Beside a barbed-wire fence at the edge of the cemetery two men in coveralls leaned against a backhoe—one was white haired and weathered, the other fair and black headed. When the pallbearers set the coffin atop the scaffolding under the tent, the young man sidearmed a stone into the neighboring field, scattering cattle. The old man walked away.

Weber directed Cyrus to one of four velvet-covered chairs beside the coffin. Isaac took a seat next to him, and his family followed. Mourners' steps cracked the snow crust. Stark sandwiched an open Bible in his hands and recited a psalm, but the wind shredded the words, straining the tent at its stays. He prayed for lives lost and gained, for Cyrus, for Isaac and family. He asked that a song be in their hearts when they left these plots of death.

Isaac gripped the back of Cyrus's neck, pulling him so they were cheek to cheek. "My brother," he said. He handed Cyrus a rose from the coffin-top and stumbled down the snowy lane to where Stark was receiving mourners.

"Cyrus?"

Cate was staring down at him.

"Shouldn't you have a coat?"

"Where's Darb?"

"He had to get back to work. Do you want a ride?"

"I'll walk."

She pulled her coat tight at the collar. "It's seven miles to town."

"You didn't leave a note this morning. I got back and thought maybe you hadn't been there at all."

"There wasn't any paper."

Not true. A gum wrapper, envelope, the folder on the counter. "I can walk," he said. "I know shortcuts."

"Cyrus." A skirl of wind was broken by the report of a branch breaking. Snow would cover all paths. "You scared me this morning. You were screaming."

"I'm fine."

"There's no heat at your house," she said, but she did not offer up her place. Instead, she leaned against him, crushing the rose.

"I want to see you," Cyrus said. "I need to see you."

"OK. We'll talk soon, OK?"

Over her shoulder, Cyrus saw the men at the backhoe waiting. "Yes," he said.

She stuck the rose in his breast pocket and left him, as did the cortege, its taillights fading into the white.

"Fella? We gotta break this down." The workman shook snow off a chair cover. A thin gray mustache seemed painted on his upper lip. He patted the coffin—the better for Cyrus to get his drift—so Cyrus wandered out among the headstones: Kirbys and Vernons, Garretts, Barnards, Cunninghams. They had lived the music Cyrus loved. They had rolled up rugs, dragged back furniture, turned a moist-eyed portrait of Christ to the wall lest He witness the goings-on. Sometimes they charged a dime a head to pay for a band: a greasy fiddler and a doughy blind guitarist, even a banjo man or mandolinist, depending on who could get down the road or clear of his wife.

The band would start with "Chicken Reel," maybe, but the dancers would be buttoned up and shy. By early morning, though, after they'd run through the alphabet, from "Annie Poke" to "Zack from Tackus," even the windows would sweat. Outside, a few drunken men might draw knives, or blood. Inside, they might steal a kiss from the girls, and the girls, whose fathers would rather see them dead than squirming like minks on a griddle, would make

cinder-sifting motions. Then that blind guitarist would brush aside
the fiddler and holler:

> *Cheat your partner, swing Miss Lucey.*
> *Up with her petticoat, out with your ducey.*

Cyrus's mother had witnessed the last of such gatherings as a girl.
The old songs linked him to her, to his sister, to this place, but all that
was going or gone. Now the music buzzed inside him like a rattle-
snake rattle in a fiddle when the bow is sawn across the strings. No
matter what, you could not split that sound from the instrument.

The backhoe roared, the old man working the controls while the
boy leaned on a shovel. Cyrus ran toward them.

"Would I what?" the old man said.

"My mother. I can bury her. I used to work these things."

"I don't think that's your best idea, son."

"I can pick an egg out of a rock pile," Cyrus said. "Please."

The old man fingered his mustache, then shook his head at the
sky and tugged Cyrus up into the cab. "Just brush the dirt from
there to there. R. J.'ll do the rest."

Cyrus flipped the bucket and a red clod tumbled to the concrete
lid of the mausoleum. Already, snow covered the box in which was
a box in which was his mother's body. Knobbed levers trembled
with the idling engine. Dirt in a hole. Easy. Cyrus flipped the bucket
again. "I'm sorry," was all he could say.

The old man lifted Cyrus's hands from the controls. "Gets to me
every time too," he said.

Cyrus climbed down and walked away, letting the two men finish, making of the grave a mound covered with mums in paper
urns. They offered him a ride, but he said thanks, no, and they
drove away.

On the distant hillside where the Ellston place had stood, a hooded figure appeared, angular and lurching as if it might break apart before it reached the graveyard. "Mama?" Cyrus said to the raised earth at his feet. "If you give them a tune, you said, and play hard, they let you be."

Nearer and nearer the figure drew. Cradling an object under its clothes, it passed between strands of fence and Chaplin-stepped around headstones. Then Randy was standing at the graveside. He eyed the rose in Cyrus's soaked jacket. "Sure," Cyrus said. "Take it."

Randy pointed the bloom at the mound of mums.

"You remember," Cyrus said. "My mama. She gave you grapes. You used to give her fish." Cyrus tapped at the object in Randy's jacket; Randy stepped back. "C'mon," Cyrus said. "You know me."

Glancing over his shoulder, Randy pulled a length of pale wood from his sweatshirt and passed it to Cyrus. She was naked and sanded smooth. Locks of hair curved over her shoulders to the dip of her back, and the curves went on, sacral dimples to buttocks to slow descent of thigh. Cyrus turned her over—arched eyes, thin nose, scar on her cheek. Gravity had begun to flatten her breasts, and her belly rose to a hillock of hair. She clutched a pistol to her hip, one leg lifted as if to test a pool of water. Cyrus handed her back to Randy. "You see what all's in these woods, don't you?"

Randy pressed a finger to his lips.

"Where'd she go?" Cyrus said.

Randy lifted Cyrus's chin—the better to see his words.

"I said, Where'd she go? My sister."

Randy pointed at the grave, and Cyrus said, "Take all the flowers you want." Grabbing up two paper urns, Randy hurried out across the cemetery, but at a headless angel he looked back for a moment, and again before he crossed the road, ducking into the woods. What in these hills did Randy want with flowers?

Cyrus flipped up the collar of his jacket and followed him deep into hardwood stands, but dusk began to come down thick, and he made out men pushing eastward through the glazed brush. They wore hats. They pointed rifles at the ground. When finally they had passed out of sight, Cyrus turned back toward town.

When darkness settled and the snow ceased, she slipped out
the way she'd come, stalking from the cabin to the water
and stutter-stepping up an icy ramp to the boathouse. She
found a trailer that cradled an antique V-hull, its teakwood staves
so avidly polished she could make out her distorted reflection. From
the bow of the boat a cable ran to a rusted winch, which she cranked,
backing the trailer down the ramp until it jerked to a stop just shy
of the lake.

Light cut across Margaret's face. "They drain the water out."
Coffey's wife clutched a flashlight under her arm and a shotgun to
her hip. "I said they drain out the water. For the power."

"Power?" Margaret said.

"Electricity? Maybe you've heard of it?"

"Yes."

The wife crouched to keep from sliding down the ramp. "You
trying to steal my husband's boat?"

"I'm not stealing it."

"I see you're not. I said you trying to."

"I'm just looking."

"Sister, a child lies better than that. Now, get away from that
boat."

Thick fog was curling off the lake. Margaret wanted to disap-
pear into it.

"Look here," the wife said, slipping on the ramp. "First thing, that cable won't reach. Second thing, Coffey—my so-called husband—has winterized the engine."

"I know Coffey."

"You think I'm brain-dead? I know who you know, and I know who you are. Color your hair any way you want, that scar's a distinguishing characteristic. By the by, what all you done to your hair don't suit you."

"Yours ain't much to speak of either."

The wife cackled. "If you're fixing to go tit for tat, I've had nigh on a half century of practice folks call marriage. Now get away from that boat."

Margaret took a small step down the ramp. "I don't want to fall."

"I'd say you've done damage enough to your well-being. They got a sizable reward on you. How it's come to be you know my husband I got no idea. I don't know as I want to know."

Margaret peered up past the retaining wall. "Where is Coffey?"

"You concern yourself with me," the wife said. One leg skated out from under her, but she snatched it back.

"I brought cans down here to sell," Margaret said. "He attacked me. Violated me in your bedroom and gave me money not to tell. That's how I know him."

The hearts-playing wife sucked at a tooth, struck dumb, it seemed, by the accusation. Margaret was sorry she'd spoken. The old gal was not much more than a step-and-fetch-it for fish-stinking, whiskey-sweating men who grabbed off gobs of boot mud with the bath towels.

"Ha," the wife said. "You expect me to believe that? He ain't attacked me in years."

"Well," Margaret said, "I can't say I'd recommend it."

The wife began to slide into the water. "I can't recall if it's something I'd recommend either."

"Ma'am?" Margaret said, but the old gal was already ankle deep in lake.

"That son of a bitch." She gave a grim smile. "I'm guessing those football boys maybe gave you a pretty rough go of things too?" She shook her head. "Men. Bah. Pen of hogs'd be more agreeable. C'mon. He's got other boats. Paddleboats, Evinrudes, a half-swamped pontoon. Reach me out of this potty pond and I'll fetch you one." She held out the shotgun to Margaret. "Here. It ain't loaded. He keeps hiding the shells from me."

She led Margaret down a catwalk to a dock listing so far to port that a few slips had nosed into the water, taking their craft with them. Boards underfoot were slick with a greasy frost.

"All this work to do," the wife said, "and where is he? Playing army. Chasing you."

As promised there were johnboats, paddleboats, a moss-bogged pontoon linked to a buoy by a rusted cable. They did not look like they'd float, let alone move. The wife tugged a dented Grumman to the end of the dock and gestured for Margaret to get in. The resort name was stenciled in yellow below the gunwale.

Taking a seat at the stern, she kept her duffel in her lap and her feet in the air. "It's sinking."

The old woman handed her a scoop cut from a Clorox jug. "Better bail."

Margaret dumped an oily bilge into the lake while the wife yanked at the starter cord of an Evinrude. The engine barely coughed. She yanked again and again, starting up a string of curses until the thing sputtered to life. Over the racket she explained throttle, choke, and rudder, then, tossing in the towrope, shoved the boat from the dock with her heel.

Fog slid between Margaret and the shore. "Which way?"

The old woman waved her light, the beam shining over the snow crust until it went out. When Margaret twisted the throttle, the bow lifted, and she zigzagged over open water, struggling to trace the black outline of shore. She saw no lights, no boats, and she began to imagine she was free. Then her speed began to wax and wane. She cranked the throttle. The engine missed, stuttered, and started again until finally it stopped altogether, leaving her drifting soundlessly into a narrow cove. Snow plopped from overhanging branches into the water. From the far shore came voices.

"Gimme a hit a that."

"If ya wanna drinkie, ya gotta say sir."

"Hell with that; it's cold. Lemme have another drink. Hey, you hear that?"

The boat struck gravel shallows, and Margaret jumped out, shoving it back to deep water. Lights cut across the trees as she turned for the woods.

"I said I heard me a boat engine. I don't know why nobody don't trust my ears. They's old ears, but they's good ears."

Margaret went from tree to tree while the men clamored across the gravel.

"Looky there. What's that?"

Lights swung out over the cove. A command was given to fire, and enfilade commenced, smacking at aluminum or chipping into water or hissing through branches above Margaret.

"Hey, hold it. Hold it."

"Hold it? I give orders here, Coffey."

"That's my boat you're shooting at. We got somebody in a boat of mine."

"Well, if they's somebody in that boat, Sir Coffey, I'd say that somebody's dead."

The woods went quiet. Margaret heard the men running back the way they'd come.

⁓⁓⁓

Cyrus was stiff and muddy, but he managed to smooth his hair and straighten the lapels of his funeral jacket before he entered the club. Newbern had quit or been fired. No one knew for sure. Cate could not be found. And Bo had scheduled a special show—Persephone Plenty, the alliterative porn star with 40 EEEs (tax write-offs, a bouncer claimed)—so the girls were pissed. Plenty would cut into their floor time. As would Cyrus.

Stage right, he waited. Sade's well-lit body spun offstage, trailing a ham-armed bouncer who plucked up cast-off apparel like daisies. When the spotlight sliced at the back curtain, men loosed a primitive garble that evolved into a unified chant: "Plen-tee, Plentee." At the opposite wing stood Bo, halved for a moment in the sickle edge of the beam. He wore high-heeled boots and a suit as shiny as snakeskin, and he kept his slick arm lashed to the headliner, whose awesome augmentations—as Newbern might have assonanced had he been there—were strapped into a saloon-girl corset.

From on high a stranger announced Cyrus as Wakoda County's own. The microphones had been set at the runway's end, where he would be surrounded by men expecting other talents. He glanced back, questioning the wisdom of this new arrangement, but Bo slapped his knee and Ms. Plenty threw back her head, baring her throat to the creeping scythe of light. She had a well-developed sense of humor.

"Evening," Cyrus said, shading his eyes.

Ice clicked and men cleared their throats. At tables, beside the patrons' sweating drinks, there sat hats—derbies, porkpies, homburgs, varietals of John B. Stetsons. Where had they stowed their stilettos and pearl-handled derringers? Where had all the hat checks gone? From the audience, a hog-eyed man said, "Grant us a delicious little song."

Cyrus gripped his guitar and tore into the tale of a lost lamb, missing for several Sundays but sought by a shepherd who had abandoned his fold. He stumbled through dark and cold. All seemed lost. Half Holiness hymn, half bluesy rocker, the sacred song was one he thought sure would drive these pigs from the middle of his middling life. Cyrus stomped the stage on two and four, turning the tune into a rocking little dirge. Where had he gleaned it? His mother? A crackly field recording? No matter. Saro's high-lonesome coiled around his, her presence so palpable that he stepped back from the mike to make a place for her, working a nasty down-strum that buzzed the low E against the frets. *One and two and three and* . . . a slow train pulling from the station, its cars carting gamblers, drinkers, harlots. Boxes in black crepe. The coffin of Jimmie Rodgers, maybe.

Onward the shepherd searched, and Cyrus sang louder and louder, sending the herder down stony paths edged with thorns. His feet grew bruised, torn, but he trod his way into the final couplet, counting the cost until he'd found the one he'd lost. Then the flog box shook off its last mortal chord. "Thank you," Cyrus said.

A few hog-eyed men applauded, but others tugged their fobs, studying the time. What did they want from him? What more could he give these figments of a song he had in mind but their own song? Light fell from above, and Cyrus saw Cate lean over the

railing, her locks falling past her shoulders. Then she sank into
shadow.

> *Sally is a hot one, a hot one, a hot one.*
> *Sally is a hot one, takes it in her hand.*
> *Sally is a hot one, a hot one, a hot one.*
> *The cheeks of her ass go slam, slam, slam.*

The hog-eyed men snorted in feral abandon as Cyrus ran again
through the chorus, straining to keep them jolly, but when he
looked out again only one hog-eyed man remained. He flourished
his derby before him as if to say, *You are but one of us; you are but
shadow.* Busloads of boys began hurling plastic cups. "Plenty," they
yelled. *Less is more,* Cyrus thought. *More or less.* He tacked a few
grace notes to the end of the tune and fled.

Beams on high, pedal down, he gripped the cold wheel of the
truck as if it might steer him elsewhere. The woods flapped by like
ragged hanks of celluloid. He saw his hand closing his mother's
eyes, Saro gripping an apron string, a portrait of Christ glistening on a cross, piano keys pounding of their own accord. He could
not drive fast enough to leave these visions behind, but still he
sped on, until just outside Dooley he saw—almost too late—Randy
leap the ditch, lantern and mums flying as the truck skidded
around him to a stop. The brittle figure lay quiet in the road. "Get
up," Cyrus said. The truck engine idled. A screech owl called.
"Look," Cyrus said, and he threw open the door, but Randy was on
his feet now, abandoning his things and running for the woods.
Cyrus lit the lantern and followed.

He tracked the sound of stirring brush beneath a moon that cast
little light, working his way farther and farther from the road, skirt-
ing a sinkhole from which greenish water bubbled, then walking a
makeshift chert dam across a creek, his wing tips slick on the stones.

Off to the south, a boat engine hummed upchannel, but just ahead, leaves whispered and sticks cracked on the long rise ahead, and these Cyrus tailed into a stand of cedars, until a stob tripped him face first into the snow. Yards away, cut boughs lay over a stone that had been pushed back from a hole in a bluff.

Lifting the lantern, he saw the stone was not a proper stone but was a crudely trowled mass of moss-covered aggregate. He stooped inside the hole and made a long slow crawl down a mud lane, past shallows stirred by pale fish, until he came into a high-ceilinged vault. Names and dates and assertions of love forever had been candle-smoked or scrimshawed into swollen calcite. There were scrawls from settlers now buried in Dooley, save one—JESSE JAMES, 1872, a prank, likely. Cyrus pumped fuel into the lantern, moving along a sinuous lane that opened again and again into small rooms. Marbled walls began to shed their graffiti until the stone turned white. In one wide passage, water trickling over a ledge had carried its sediment through the ages to form a laced Niagara of gleaming dolomite. Behind the curtain lay a crude stairway, which he followed into a tunnel that forced him to slither, pushing the lantern out before him. Finally he stood, soaked and chilled, in a chamber as spacious as a Victorian parlor. From a dark pool sprouted flowerlike objects crafted from fans, clock faces, and snipped pie tins. There were whirligigs speared on rebar and tomato stakes and dinosaur carvings stuck into jagged nooks—a post-apocalyptic garden. Gathered at the base of a low stone column were coffee cans brimming with coins, and atop the stone lay other flowers—some plastic, some fresh from his mother's grave. Amid the blossoms were bones. The remains of a species long run from these hills, Cyrus thought, or some extinct creature Randy had discovered. Cyrus came closer, closer. Glistening, pumpkin colored, well tended. A human skeleton cleaned of sinew, fabric, and rot.

For years he'd glimpsed his sister's straight hair on hippie wannabes wandering Telegraph and the Haight. He had seen her arched brow that said, *Impress me,* heard her doubting laugh, witnessed the coy cock of her hip. He had not glimpsed her chipped tooth, though, or her verdigris bracelet, and in his nightmares she came to him shrouded in old-time clothing, her voice disembodied as all voices are. If Cyrus had veiled the truth, though, the veil, as Saint Matthew would have it, was rent in twain. The ghost was gone.

Randy coughed, and Cyrus turned to him. He had been brought here to reckon with a story sung in countless variations throughout the centuries: Boy kills girl. He picked up a bouquet from his mother's service and set it beside the skull, then Randy unburdened him of the lantern and took his hand. They were deaf to the present. They were struck mute. Cyrus let Randy lead him from the grave.

C ome morning, the ice-shredded branches offered little cover, so Margaret hid in buckbrush along the periphery of a two-story stone house. Masonry had crumbled and a corner of roof sagged, but the place drew visitors—teenagers, mostly—who crept from the northeast rim of woods to the porch, fidgeting until they gained admittance. Occasionally someone stepped outside to smoke. No one seemed to leave.

With the sun out and the snow melting, the day was not without pleasure. A south wind flapped plastic sheeting over the windows. From behind the walls came ragtime piano, laughter, loud talk. Then a man stepped out on the back stoop. He was gripping a .44, its absurdly long muzzle angled away from his rubber boots as he relieved himself. Then he strode down to Margaret's hiding place and stared, his pupils wide, one eye steady, the other focused on some distant point in the woods. "I thought you was Hiley," he said, his shoulders twitching underneath his shirt. "Hey, hey. You ain't Hiley."

Margaret unsnapped the holster in her duffel. "No," she said.

"Hiley says to watch for agents. You ain't a agent, are you?"

"Agent of what?"

"I don't know. *Agent* agent."

"You got a car?"

"Ha. You got to walk in. Ain't you walked in to see us?"

"Sure," Margaret said. "I walked all this way just to see you."

"Well, I'm waiting for Hiley. You come too."

Margaret figured inside and warm was better than outside and cold, though she was well aware she had figured wrong before. She threw her duffel over her shoulder and tailed him toward the house.

"My name's Gerald," he said. "Who're you?"

Down on the lake a johnboat trolled; Margaret could make out the checkered earflaps of the man at the stern.

"Call me Polly," she said. "Like Pollyanna."

Gerald jumped the porch railing and kicked off his boots beside the door, adding them to a row of shoes arranged by size and color. He told her she would need to do the same.

"They're not that muddy," Margaret said.

"Hey, hey, but the ground's all dirty, you know? It's made of dirt."

She could not argue with that so did as she was told. When Gerald shouldered open the door, the air inside seemed weighted with a grainy resin, and the room stank of starter fluid and cat piss. It appeared Gerald's compulsiveness was limited to dirt. Scattered across the old-gold shag were compact discs and cassette tapes, Hostess cupcake wrappers, pork rinds, and crushed beer cans. Hip-hop thumped from a portable stereo atop a player piano in the corner.

For a disconcerting length of time Gerald stared at Margaret's head. Then he pointed to a barber's chair, in which a teenage boy reclined, his breathing as labored as a dying dog's. Another boy lay in a nest of hair clippings on the floor, his gaze fixed on a TV/VCR combo in the fireplace that played a movie involving two women, a man in a corset, and velvet pillows. "I cut hair," Gerald said. "I could fix yours, maybe. Unless that's your real color."

"Verily," said the boy on the floor.

From out of sight came a girl's voice. "Walleye?"

Gerald grimaced. "They call me that," he said to Margaret. "Yeah, Shelia?"

"I just wanted to know you were, like, still there."

The girl was propped in the arched doorway to the next room, the sleeves of her blouse rolled to her biceps. A thread of spittle swung from her lips as she toppled, mumbling, to the carpet. "I should have smoked, Walleye. Last time I drooled was my eighteenth birthday. New York smack. Man."

Gerald shook his head. "Walleye," he said to himself. Pressing his forefinger to Shelia's wrist, he checked his watch. "Hiley says you got to keep the customers alive. He says if you kill the customers they don't come back."

The stench from the kitchen at the back of the house seemed strong enough to singe nostrils. Margaret recalled paneled innards of a mobile home rotting in a cornfield, a torn screen, a pale arm thrown over the cushion of a cracked naugahyde couch. "You make crank here," she said.

"Ain't that why you come?"

"These kids are smack happy," Margaret said.

"Smack's shot. Hiley's gone to get supplies so we can cook."

They did not have a business plan per se, Gerald explained, but they did have a house, where someday anyone could visit any room and do any drug he wanted. "Progressive psychedelia," Hiley called it, a term he'd made up himself. Progressive psychedelia was inspired by church suppers wherein members went from house to house to eat. Hiley had been raised Methodist. For now the two offered more rooms than drugs, but they had a kitchen, and as long as they could keep smokers out they could cook. Hiley smurfed of late because high school kids were not deft thieves. "You can't get good help these days is what Hiley says. You want you a cupcake?"

"No," Margaret said. "Thank you."

Gerald liked the cakes, especially chocolate, which had more icing than the strawberry. "Hey, where's my manners? Can I take your bag?"

"No."

He introduced her to the boys—Jack in the chair, Davy on the floor. Neither seemed capable of exchanging pleasantries.

"Do you have a bathroom?"

"Can I cut your hair? Hey, hey, I cut hair."

"So I hear. Where's your bathroom?"

Upstairs, all eight doors were shut and etherous fumes mingled with scents of ages past: florid powders and stringent tonics, a faint formaldehyde stink. Margaret thought of liver spots, and of wheelchairs behind lace curtains. Dust coated the hardwood floor. Wallpaper pansies were shredded to the wainscot.

In the first room, a brown sheet nailed over the window cast tintype light over three beds. A girl lay on a bare mattress, her arms over her eyes, her breathing shallow. On another mattress a smooth-skinned boy with fat cheeks was curled tight. His socks were filthy. They resembled children put to bed sick.

Behind the next door a silent stag movie played on the wall of a closet-sized room lined with eight-millimeter film cans. Four naked women splashed in a river, fluttering eyelashes and dancing in a circle until a title card appeared: THEY FLIRT! A horned devil with phony Vandyke whiskers parted willow boughs. HE WATCHES! The devil leapt to the bank, scattering women, his arrowhead tail bobbing as he snatched one by the hair. SHE STRUGGLES! He dragged her into a meadow of black-eyed Susans.

As if in accompaniment, a tune commenced on the piano downstairs. "'The Ragtime Nightingale,'" Gerald shouted. The abducted woman hoisted herself atop the devil; on the floor beneath the flickering beam of light, a young man knelt with his pants to his ankles. "Oh," Margaret said. The boy grabbed for his belt as she shut the door.

The bathroom at the end of the hall was no more than a rust-stained toilet bowl and a claw-footed tub speckled with bird droppings, but the light through the broken window was true. She took the pistol from her duffel, dropping the cylinder to check the chambers, then aimed the gun at a mirror screwed to the door. The muzzle was steady between her reflected eyes. "Whatever," she said. She jammed the gun down the back of her pants and smoothed her coat hem over it.

When she came downstairs, Gerald dragged Jack from the chair to the hearth. "Hey, hey, Polly," he said, rolling a stainless steel cart next to the barber's chair. "Everything OK?" On a white towel were two pairs of scissors, a box of hair color, and a jar of Barbicide, long black combs pickling in the blue juice.

From the hearth, Jack giggled. "Verily," he said. Davy was sorting obliviously through compact discs. In the doorway where Shelia had collapsed the boy from the screening room upstairs appeared, flannel shirtsleeves unbuttoned, a rodeo buckle low on his waist. He watched Margaret through fallen black bangs.

Gerald flipped a striped chair cloth, scattering hair, then bowed like a courtier.

"Just spare me the movies," Margaret said.

"You bet. I told the guys we got a lady in the house, and they said OK, no movies, didn't you guys?"

"Verily."

Margaret climbed into the chair, the pistol digging at her back. "What's with the verily?"

"Elizabethan porn," the boy in the doorway said.

"That's Mose," Gerald said. "Mose knows." He slipped a paper collar around Margaret's neck and cinched the chair cloth. "Look what I found," he said, opening a cart drawer.

Margaret recognized pinks and drunk pills and a cheap brown scat. "No. Thanks."

"You won't get nothing stronger around here."

She shook her head. "Way back you could buy heroin over the counter. For aspirin you had to get a prescription."

"Irony," Mose said.

Margaret tried to get a look at the boy as he stepped behind her to the fireplace, but Gerald had a firm hand on her head.

"Mose knows," he said. "So how do you want this?"

"Buzz it down."

"But your hair's pretty. Even blue, it's pretty." He tapped the box of colorant. "Aubergine?"

"I don't need pretty."

He shrugged and began snipping her locks to the skull. When he went to fetch a pair of clippers, Mose whispered something in his ear.

"Mose knows," Gerald said, buzzing Margaret's hair off in rows. "Mose knows."

"What is it that Mose knows?"

Gerald shut off his clippers.

"I know the news says you got a scar," Mose said. With the heel of his boot, he rolled Jack away from the hearth. "And I know you got you a scar."

Gerald pressed the point of his scissors to Margaret's neck.

"Walleye?" Mose said. "You think you might want to try that gun you got?"

"Walleye," Gerald said, shaking his head on the way to the kitchen. "Shit."

Margaret stayed put. "Sorry to have interrupted you," she said.

Mose licked his lips. They were cracked.

"It's a crime to have a scar?"

"You just killed some people I knew is all."

"I didn't kill your friends."

"They weren't my friends," Mose said. "I just got nothing better to do."

"Hey, here it is," Gerald said, waving the pistol. "Shelia had it in the kitchen." He pressed the muzzle to Margaret's temple. "We're gonna get us that reward, huh, Mose?"

Jack flipped over on his back. "Verily," he said.

Neither efficient nor savvy in their methods of detainment, they took her coat but left the chair cloth. They patted up her legs but not down her back, then duct-taped her wrists but bound them in front of her so that she could have poked one in the nose if she'd wanted.

Mose's lower lip had begun to bleed. "Where's your gun, lady?"

"I don't have a gun."

"Sure," he said, and he pressed a strip of tape over her mouth.

They pushed her through the rank kitchen, which was strewn with food scraps, pseudoephedrine boxes, and lighter fluid canisters, and on outside, where the wind whipped the chair cloth over her face. When Mose tore it away, it tumbled down the back steps into tall grass. Down on the lake, the helmsman was tooling his johnboat in smaller and smaller circles. Mose kicked loose a two-by-four latched over the cellar door, which Gerald opened with painstaking drama. The stink of rotting onions rose when Mose shoved her down the stairs. "Hey, hey," Gerald said. "Sorry, you know?" And the two-by-four slid into place.

Blue morning lay atop Tubb's Cove, and a heron lazied through briny mist rising from the water. Heartened by the lamp glowing in the front window of Cate's house, Cyrus hurried to the porch, but before he could scrape his funeral shoes on the steps, she opened the door. Gripping the neck of her robe, she said his name, then scanned the mud-caked lapels of his suit. "Cyrus," she said again. From inside a small voice called out for Mama.

She glanced back to the kitchen. "What, May?"

"Mama, show?"

"Show what, May?"

Laughter. "Mama?"

"Cyrus. OK. Just wait here."

But Cyrus followed her to the kitchen, where he saw over Cate's shoulder a girl with pale eyes and black ringlets locked in a high chair. She twisted a spoon to reveal three milk-soaked Os defying gravity.

"I see, May," Cate said.

Across from the girl—in a white T-shirt, county-sanctioned trousers, and brown socks—sat Darby. A pair of crutches leaned on the chairback, and before him were set a bowl of cereal and a cup of coffee. He straightened his spoon on the table as Cate backed to the counter. Cyrus examined mud on his shoes. The coffeemaker sighed. "I see I've made a mess," he said. "Sorry."

"See-ee?" May said. The Os were still holding their own.

"I do see," Cyrus said. "That's a neat trick. What do you think, Darb?"

"Yeah," Darby said.

Cyrus smiled to himself. "That man there's got two places to lay his head, May. Ain't that something?"

May gave a squeal of delight.

"Cyrus," Cate said.

"So." But he had no right to speak. He had been wrong. Not wronged.

"Sigh-us," May said. The girl could not keep her happy feet still.

"Your mother and I, May, used to be somewhat of an item. But there was this old singer named Charlie Poole? If he were alive, May, he'd say that sort of thing might happen again when—" Cyrus began to croon:

> *The grocerman puts sand in the sugar,*
> *milkman makes milk out of chalk,*
> *boys stay home with their mothers,*
> *women forget how to talk—*

May beat her spoon on the tray. She was the first avid audience he'd had in some time.

"Charlie Poole got a phone call in 1931 to come to California and play backup for a Western movie, May. Went on a thirteen-week bender, celebrating, then passed at his sister's in Spray, North Carolina. Thirty-nine years old. Cost 265 dollars to bury him. His sister had to foot the bill."

May stared into her cereal. So much for his audience.

"Cyrus," Cate said. "Look, I was glad to see you. I am glad to see you. But Darby's been here other nights long before you showed up. He and Jackie are separated. Given Darby's work, and mine, we've kept this quiet. You know how the town is. I'll admit I felt something when I saw you, but it was just that twinge a person gets when the past appears. It's like a breeze. You feel it, it's good, it's gone. Besides, you've got a life elsewhere." She glanced at Darby, who was watching May spackle her mouth with yogurt. "You probably even still have a chance."

"I was just stopping by."

"Do you hear me, Cyrus? *Can* you hear me?"

From the drainer he took a coffee cup and tried to pour for himself; Cate took over.

"So why were you so all-fired to get me to that club, Sheriff?"

Darby wiped May's mouth with his napkin. "Best of intentions, I swear," he said. "But. Road to hell's—" He glanced at May. "Sorry."

"It embarrassed me when you found me at Bo's," Cate said. "Not because I'm ashamed of what I'm doing. Not because things aren't how they're supposed to be. But because things didn't work out like I'd planned. But then you make other plans."

"She put on a pretty good mad about it," Darby said. "She was right to. I was wrong."

"Right," Cyrus said. He set his cup on the counter, looking from Darby to May to Cate. "I'm out of the past."

She would not meet his gaze.

"Speaking of, Darb," Cyrus said. "What's become of the Gilmores?"

"Gilmores? Down on Dead Horse? I don't know. Your brother fixed them. Bought up their cabins and dozed them down. Those folks all got scattered to the wind."

Like bad seeds, Cyrus thought. *Like shadows.* "Willie?"

"Willie? Aw, Willie's long dead."

"He is."

"Yeah. Air Force booted him. He ended up shoveling cans for

some scrap metal outfit down in Arkansas. Got pretty well baked one time, then crawled up in a crusher and fell asleep."

Cyrus considered the news. He deemed it good.

"Why do you want to know about Willie?" Cate said.

"How things should be—how things should be is how they end," Cyrus said. "Short and painless, if possible. I was thinking maybe that's how it was for Saro. Now who can say?"

"Cyrus," Cate said, but already he was at the front door. The sun had crested the hills beyond the lake, turning the living room into a sanctuary of light. Cate called to him again, but she did not give chase.

"Bye-bye," May said, beating the rhythm of the word on her tray. "Bye-bye."

❧

When he parked beside the honeysuckle fence, the sun was high. From his breast pocket he fished the pill bottle and shook it, then considered a sealed fifth of tonsil polish on the seat beside him. He saw no reason to buy into delirium tremens. It was the mercuric buildup of memories that did a man in. After all, Ezekiel saw the wheel. Daniel read the *me-ne, me-ne, te-kel, upharsin* on the wall. Cyrus had borne witness while Cate shared her table with the county sheriff; he had stood over bones in a flower garden gone to rust and heard tell of Willie Gilmore crushed and cracked apart. The past, in time, crashed down on the present and, clotted with debris, washed back from the future. Leaving what?

One morning the brown suitcase had gone missing from the hall closet, and Saro's bedroom window screen lay in the grass. Though she had spoken of San Francisco, it was more than likely she was in trouble, so it may not have mattered where she was bound. Before she could leave, though, Gilmore caught up with her, they argued, and a knife was drawn. Then he sealed her in the cave. If Randy was a witness he could not tell. He would not. But he could care for the bones, frail emblems of a life unfinished. He could watch over its remains, which in turn could watch over his carvings, his rusted creations, his coins.

Cyrus pocketed the pills and tugged the guitar in its case across his lap. Though he had labored for years to keep his sister among the living, making the hollow box boom and ring against the silence that threatened him, he had not saved her, and now he couldn't even swing $265 worth of 1931 currency to bury her. She deserved to live. He deserved to take her place. The guitar, after all, was hers.

He left it in the truck and headed up the walk. A manila envelope addressed by Mr. Viswanathan leaned on the porch step, and inside was an overnight letter from Cyrus's former publicist, notifying him that his erstwhile label had been purchased by a New Age outfit in Los Angeles interested in diversifying its offerings. They intended to re-release his first album; they'd inquired about a second. Brat Splat had requested that Cyrus open for him on tour. Contracts awaited his signature. "So," Cyrus said. "What'll it be? 'Whalescape Number Seven'? 'Autumn Memoir'? 'Two-Chord Progression on a Good Piano'?" He tossed the envelopes to the wind, but jammed the letter in his pocket, pushing wide the screen door to find the porch swing creaking.

The hog-eyed man sat with his hands in his lap. Mud had stained his spats. "Good news?"

"You ain't real."

The hog-eyed man shrugged. "So I've been told."

"I see now."

The hog-eyed man tipped back his derby. "Oh?"

"Saro."

"Hmm. How maudlin. I gather you are obsessing on those songs where women perish at the hands of men? Dutchie fairy tales? Morose musings off the moors? Among the oldest in that category, one

Jellon Grame kills Lillie Flower in Silver Wood because she's to bear his child. Young Benjie stabs Margorie when she wants another love. Lord Barnard slays his wife after he catches her in bed with Little Musgrave. A dismal death. If I recall—'he cut her paps from off her breast/great pity it was to see.' So much blood, so little motivation."

"I wish you'd let my family be."

From the woods came birdsong: *drink-your-TEA, drink-your-TEA.* "Ah, a towhee," the hog-eyed man said. "I should tell you your mother never would be social with us—an error in judgment, akin to one on which you seem bent. You do nurture some odd notions: infatuation with corny parlor songs; idealization of mother, women, home; a quaint fear of change."

"Maybe my notions are changing."

"Allow me to push them in a fruitful direction."

"I won't scare."

"Ah. You misread me. The day Saro fell, Cyrus, we simply wished to speak with your mother. To encourage her in her music, which, unbeknownst to you, she had been mulling over. Our visit went awry." The hog-eyed man shrugged. "But the outcome was the same. In good time at least."

"You mean death."

"I prefer to speak of life, though there is nothing wrong with death. In truth, one's departure should be more pleasing than one's arrival. Regret trails me like a comet's tail because I shall always live within a song. Of course, everyone knows that in death, sickness and sorrow and trouble depart forever. *Ars moriendi,* say the ancients. The art of death, which is, in a roundabout way, an art of life. But you wish to forsake this art, you with your right and wrong, your good and evil, your inability to exist between ideals no one can live up to, including you. Cyrus, take us. We are wholly American, which means we are not wholly anything."

"You're roustabouts," Cyrus said. "Shoulder-bone boys."

"Do you fear the word, Cyrus? Flat-out malign it? It is an ugly word." The hog-eyed man shook his head. "And no doubt it is fraught with malicious exclusion. But its very exclusivity has the potential for inclusive generation. We have become, you see, every disenfranchised group that had to howl to enter the realm of American song. We adapt, of course, depending on the tune. We deny our past in order to survive. I myself took elocution lessons from an ex-Quaker woman living above a jewelry store on—what street? Well, it was Cincinnati, and I could smell the river from her window. It made me lonesome, but I did manage to lift a diamond stickpin from downstairs, which I lost rolling bones in Louisville. Drinking, gambling, carrying on, we took our share of single girls and married girls alike, and if it was a big deal then, what does it matter now?"

"You got to be true to yourself."

The hog-eyed man removed his derby and peered inside as if a speech were taped there. "Truth . . . is messy. The blood and semen of truth is an elaborate form of lying. There is a time for truth, as well as a time for lies, which, by concealing the truth, contain the truth. Of course there is also a time to get, to lose, to work—your father's book elaborates."

"'Every man should eat and drink,'" Cyrus said, "'and enjoy the good of all labor, it—'"

"Yes. Labors I first enjoyed began as soon as I was free, but I started rousting in—1867? Time means little to me. My most dignified employer included the Lee line, but I worked as well on the Tennessee Star, the Kate Adams, the Cairo Queen. Our women were on their own the whole month we were gone, and when the boat neared the levee the captain would blow a sob of steam. Our women heard, and put their kid men out on the street. Mine was no exception. She had been taking care of him—so to speak—with my money. But when I caught her with him, well . . ." The hog-eyed man chuckled to himself.

"You killed them," Cyrus said.

"Her weapon. The Frank Wesson double shot pocket pistol with extension dirk knife. Walnut grips, thirty-two caliber. Two octagonal barrels. It was meant for women with a certain incandescent allure. In my haste to flee I abandoned my clothes, so purchased the finest suit I could. I found the current of life ran both ways, all was fair, there were two sides to every coin, et cetera. Life, Cyrus, is a bilateral activity. When we unloaded cotton bales, a good five hundred pounds, we shouldered them. The steward would shout, 'Move, move,' but, Lord, all that weight to haul up a plank in low water and down in high. The secret was to rock it. We staggered, but hid our pain in a sand-sifting dance. And we sang. We were a creative force to be reckoned with. We stole balladry, queer snippets from damp islands and snowy woods, but those verses were not our life. Love, loss, and lasciviousness; coke, dope, liquor; wisdom, stupidity, and prayer—these we used to twist hoedowns and forge spirituals into ragtime, jazz, country and country blues and blues, and, yes, rock and rap. Yet you adore little musical stories so overwrought they might have been penned by newspapermen. What became of your fascination with weird strains? Your love of fiddle? Your melodies and lines?"

"You mean what happened to my music."

"You don't know what yours is. You are too afraid to enter a song because the song is"—the hog-eyed man thumped his chest—"right here."

"That's a saccharine view."

"The heart can be a foul place. Fair and foul and everything in between. Four chambers. Two and two, and the blood rocks: *thump-thump* out of what never was—in your case, old players possessed by song and a loving sister whose voice lifted yours. You waste your powers by fashioning seemly memories. A grave weakness. Please don't be weak, or else you'll see more of us than you ever wanted."

"That's already the case."

The hog-eyed man nodded. "I am locked in a shifting melody, Cyrus. For all eternity I will rattle the bars of a stave. Consider my history. Please." He stood, rolling the derby up his arm so that it landed square on his head. Along the bluff a line of hog-eyed men stood waiting. A homburg waved the bottle Cyrus had left in the truck. "Now, will you be inviting us in for tea?"

"No," Cyrus said.

"So be it. But do know that we can get to you anytime, any way we please." He pulled the screen door shut behind him, then waved his cronies into the woods, a vanishing so quiet and smooth they might have been vapor.

❧

From the attic Cyrus carted the Grafonola into the sunlit yard, cranking up "Get Along Home, Cindy," a sprightly tune as performed by Pope's Arkansas Mountaineers. Not a Pope in the group, just Chisms, McKinneys, and one Sparrow hired by J. P. Pope and son to promote their store in Searcy, Arkansas—early celebrity marketing. Accompanied by their song, Cyrus hauled out records and ballad books, shape-note hymnals, sheet music—a yellowed print of "Ophelia Rag" on top—and booklets shilled by medicine men and radio players, *Hamlin's Wizard Oil New Book of Songs* and *Songs That Tell a Story* among them. To the stacks he added playbills and photos of him and Saro working crowds in dusty gymnasiums. He set the fiddle apart from the relics and took it from its case. The needle on the record said *stuck, stuck.*

Shades began to gather beneath the silver maple—crashers and stags, sloe-eyed cusses with knives in their boots, mule-toothed uncles come to give their nieces a leer. Bad company, every one. Slope-shouldered gals stood to sift sand when Cyrus put his fingers to the strings. He could conjure for them the Ozarkian variations Loman had taught him; he could saw them off a chune: "All I've Got Is Done and Gone," "Arkansas Traveler," "Big Sweet Taters in Sandy Land," "Bile Dem Cabbage Down," "Billy in the Low Ground," "Coming Through the Rye." The music meditated on forces to which one was always subject—desire, time, fear, thirst, hunger, pleasure, and pain: "Cripple Creek," "Devil's Dream," "Dry and Dusty," "Eating Goober Peas," "Everybody Know What Maggie Done," "Fire on the Mountain," "The Girl I Left Behind Me." College professors in their wisdom had proclaimed once to a struggling folklorist that titles of such tunes were of no historical, anthropological, or cultural value. They were floating and impermanent and subject to too many variations.

"And what are we?" Cyrus said to the shadows. He shut the fiddle in its case. From the kitchen he took his brother's contract, signed it, and nailed it to the silver maple as if it were a proclamation. The end of this place would be brought to order. He stripped and scrubbed himself clean at the well pump. Dressing in his father's clothes, he transferred the pill bottle and the letter to a coat pocket. Clouds were stacking in the southwest, promising more snow, maybe rain. Cyrus stalked off to the barn.

The dozer started on the third crank, and the controls moved easy. All those years of labor in the East Bay were good for something, yet still it took him nine hours to bring down the house and barn. He snapped the dead power line and dragged it away. He tapped the blade along eaves and shoved corners until the roof collapsed. Bit by bit he coaxed splintered heaps over the bluff, and when that was done, he turned the dozer on the vines, the cedar posts of arbors cracking, copper wires whipping at his head. The land became an avalanche of stone and clay and twisted limbs until only the musical relics and the instruments remained. A ray of sunlight on the lake chipped at the waves, then sank into bare hard-woods on the horizon. Cyrus bore down with the dozer, striking the stacks; a few items fluttered over his head, while on the wind he heard his father say, "'I have forsaken mine house, I have left mine heritage, I have given—'"

"Jeremiah," Cyrus said. "A jeremiad."

"'Many pastors have destroyed my vineyard; they have trodden my portion underfoot, they have made my pleasant portion a desolate wilderness.'"

"No, sir," Cyrus said. "I don't preach." He gunned the engine and killed it.

Swiping her bound hands at cobwebs, Margaret stutter-stepped until she'd grown used to what light leaked through the grated window wells. They had stored her in a cellar of whitewashed stone, littered with bushel baskets and five-gallon buckets. Shelves were lined with dusty Ball jars of beans, pickles, peaches, and wine bottles sealed with paraffin. Taking a seat on a bucket beside the canned goods, she pulled the tape from her mouth and bit through the binding on her hand.

Darkness congealed around her, while upstairs the piano banged out a melody reminiscent of sawdust-strewn dance floors and cuspidors. Another movie started up, its lascivious bass line lurking beneath the old-time tune. Margaret ate green beans from a jar. She twisted the wax seal off a wine bottle and shoved down the cork, but the wine was bitter. For a long time she did nothing but turn the cylinder of the gun, its clicking a cold comfort. Then someone hollered: "What'd I say about lights? You'll have every boat on the lake at our door. Kill that racket too."

The rag ceased. Feigned groans did not.

"Hey, hey, Hiley. How'd it go?"

"Fine, no thanks to you."

"Hiley, hey, can we use the special phone? That one you keep in your car?"

"Why? You got you a hot date?"

"Hey, no, we caught that woman? In the cellar?"

"What woman in the cellar?"

"The one that's killed those boys. Mose says it's her."

"Gerald," Hiley said, "Mose is so doped he don't know his ass from a hole in the ground. Ain't that right, Mose?"

Mose did not say whether that was right or not.

"But it is right," Gerald said.

"Good God, Gerald, you are no doubt a product of the Wakoda County R-1 Public School District. Didn't I say turn that shit off? Ain't nobody on God's green earth screws like that." The movie stopped. "Gerald, if you call the sheriff's department, then—deaf, dumb, and blind as they are—they will see this, and you and me and the baby-makes-three outfit will get hauled off, along with what all you got down cellar. Got it? Good. Now, we got work to do."

"Hey, hey, Hiley?"

"What?"

"You want to see her?"

"She got two arms?"

"Yeah."

"Two legs?"

"Yeah."

"Tits?"

"Well, yeah."

"One head, two eyes, essential appendages, most of her teeth?"

"I guess."

"Why would I want to see her, then?"

"She's got a scar."

"Don't we all," Hiley said.

Pots banged. Objects scraped the floor. As night wore on, meager moonlight blued the ground beyond the window wells. Rap songs about cop killing, or cops killing, began. Then Hiley called for silence. "What in hell's out there? Gerald, didn't I say kill the lights?"

"It's probably just somebody wants to buy. Talk about *me* getting paranoid."

But something rustled in the tall grass beyond the window well. Margaret lifted the pistol just as the two-by-four over the door slid from its latch.

"What's that in the kitchen?" Hiley yelled. "That's a fire. We got fire. Who left the burner going? No, don't throw that on it. Are you stupid?"

"Hey, hey, don't call me stupid."

A low *whump* sounded upstairs. Hiley commenced a high-pitched strand of expletives while oily smoke curled down through the slats above her. Then the cellar door groaned, revealing starlit sky, at which Margaret pointed the gun. Randy handed down her boots. "Goddamn," she said.

At the edge of the woods she told him wait, but when she turned back for her coat and bag, flames shot out the kitchen, thick smoke distorting a moon that shone on tweakers and scatheads scurrying away. Randy grabbed her hand, guiding her over rocky knobs and trails. As they climbed a rise, a clotted explosion echoed, and Margaret turned around to see the fiery hindside of the house light up the clearing in the distance. "Get me out of here," she said.

They cut southwest through a cemetery of broken angels and weathered obelisks, then across a gravel road, and by the time he tugged her into deep woods she could hardly catch her breath. He kept on, though, until they ducked through cedars along a bluff and he put his back to a stone and shoved it from a hole. Randy slipped into the passage, and Margaret thought, *One darkness is the same as any other.*

The darkness of the cave, though, was complete. A breeze rushed through it, the air warmer than outside, as he led her blind down gritty steps, through low-ceilinged rooms and narrow passages that seemed to swell into resonant, dripping chambers. She sank in mud until the legs of her jeans were soaked to her thighs. When the ceiling closed in, she had to slither. "I want you to know I never trusted nobody like this," she said. "So don't screw this up."

He led her into frigid water, but when he tried to push her down, she balked until her forehead smacked an overhang. "How about some light?" she said, wading with him into a swift stream. The gravel bed shifted and she slipped and went under, gripping the pistol above the surface. He hauled her by her wrist onto a sandy bank and there he got a lantern going. Water trickling down high walls had deposited swollen falls of milky stone, and stalactites and stalagmites had met to form columns. Upstream, water boiled from the earth and a crescent of damp crystals glimmered. From the ceiling hung a scaly bark of bats. "Cozy," Margaret said.

He dropped a woolen blanket on her shoulders and set beside her an apple and a tin of sardines. Then he placed a piece of carved wood in her hands. "Good God," she said. "You got an eyeful of me, didn't you?"

He patted the likeness—hers to keep.

"I need my things. My bag. My coat. I'll freeze."

He snatched up the lantern and backed into the water.

"Where you going?"

From midstream, he shouted something, a mush of sound she strained to comprehend. Green light shattered over the current and was gone. "You'll be back?" she said. "Great."

୭

She ate the sardines and fumbled around for the apple, which she could not find. Water rushed by, taking days, weeks, centuries, even. Who could tell in the sheer dark of a cavernous grave? Only her mind, it seemed, survived, and it wandered away from her into the past. She missed Madeline and Timmy. She missed the shadowed bark of sycamore in late sun. Clean sheets. River-mud breezes. She longed for the first sip from an iced bottle of beer. Margaret even missed her mother, wherever she was. She was missing life, which she had failed. Better to sleep, then. But how to know when she woke? *This is death,* she thought. *Or is this a dream of death?*

Downstream, a light appeared, trembling over tumorous karst, distended walls, white water. "You," the old man said. He straightened his hunting cap, set the lantern at his feet, then let the johnboat hang in the current. "You said you wouldn't turn into no fish, so how'd you swim up here?"

"I said I'd turn into a fish if you let me in your boat."

"They's folks hunting you, you know that?"

"Yes."

He scratched at the briny bristles along his jaw. "I used to creep up this way when I was a boy. Bunch of old river rats come here to get clear of wives or law or long days passing. Taught me to play poker. Wasn't allowed in my house, cards wasn't."

"You played cards here?"

"Naw. Down by the bank where it's all got drowned. You can't get in until they drain the water. Then they go plug it back up and fill this place again with lake—if you can call it that. I don't. Big Potty Pond, I call it. My boyhood got washed away under gallons of human filth. People. The longer you know them, the better you like dogs."

"When's the water come back?"

"April. May. You be dead you stay here that long. Unless you eat bat. You might well be dead soon as you come to light. Folks just love hunting witch."

"You're full of good news."

"Old as I am I'm full of something, and it ain't news. I been all around this world, and I seen strange fruit. People manage all manner of cruelty, and that gives us all manner of unburied. I don't let them in my boat. Used to be you could swim this river, but you go try it now."

"I did," Margaret said.

"You don't know nothing about it. But they was a time, oh, they was a time I'd be down at the mouth of this cave, and that sun was just as sweet as morning molasses. Those old boys'd pass a bottle, and I was a stripling getting dealt a fat hand. But then one of those old boys'd say, 'Yonder.' Out on the river you'd see tie hackers bobbing on a raft of hardwoods they was fixing to sell just so trains could build cities big and dirty. How them river rats would grieve. Hard times was on, the end was near, and they was sure they'd seen God riding naked on Time's shoulders. Now every last one has got the green quilt laid over him."

He pointed upstream. "They told me if I drank from that spring three times in three minutes I'd be cursed to come back to its waters forever." He lifted the lantern. "I suppose you're wanting a ride."

"No," Margaret said.

"If you so much as step in my boat, it'll sink. They say it's your soul weighs you down." He tied his earflaps and shut off the trolling motor. Current spun the bow downstream, and the boat drifted away from her, until finally she lay down in darkness, her face against the cold sand. Then Randy was sitting beside her. His lantern sputtered, but his clothes were dry.

"How long've you been here?"

He stuffed her wooden likeness down in the duffel bag and got the strap over his shoulder.

"Where's my coat?" she said. "I could freeze to death." She unholstered her pistol but could not determine its condition.

He killed the lamp and dragged her to her feet. Before she could ask why, they were wading the fast current, stones and silt shifting at each step until up the tunnel the water grew still and shallow. Ahead, a faint light shone.

Rain returned with the darkness. He packed up clothes and the fiddle in its case and, with Saro's guitar at his side, maneuvered the truck down rutted resort roads gone slick with mud until he found the drive to Loman's, overgrown with locust, blackhaw, and cedar. It would be a long, thorny walk. He swept his flashlight beam over beer cans and condom wrappers. Up on the knob a piano was playing a melody so muffled by rain that Cyrus did not recognize it until he stepped into the clearing. "Climax Rag." Loman's house was burnt half away, the grass littered with splintered wood, melted gobs of tile, and shoe soles. A gaunt man was hunched beside a glowing fireplace, and the light cast his shadow on the player piano against the far wall. Cyrus slipped past an open cellar door, but the man called out to him. He held in his left hand a large battery with wires running from the posts to a dim bulb. The contraption resembled a bomb. In his right hand he gripped a broken hoe, its blade sharp and clean. "Hey, hey, Hiley. I knew you'd come back."

Gerald. The tweaker. His neck muscles were twitching.

"Wait. You ain't Hiley. Hiley's gonna kill me. I lost his gun."

Cyrus eyed the glinting hoe. "I've just come to look for something. I'll get gone soon."

"Hey, hey, I know you."

"There were tapes in the house," Cyrus said. "Where'd they go?"

"I do know you."

But Cyrus ran for the woods. Scooting down a ravine, he shone his light on rusted sheet metal, a washing machine drum, bald tires. He tore at hanks of leaves until he uncovered a busted reel-to-reel spool, loose tape snaking under the loam. Gerald's light crept over him, making the mud walls of the ditch glisten. "That music was ours," Cyrus said. He unearthed a bleach jug, a rolling pin, a coil of lead solder. He found a liquor bottle, but it was empty.

Gerald leapt down behind Cyrus.

A mound of canning jars covered five damp cassettes. Cyrus jammed them into his coat pocket, turning just in time to see Gerald bring down the hoe like a hatchet. The blade cut at his shoulder and knocked him backward into the dump. "Climax Rag" ended.

"Hey," Gerald said, scrambling up the steep. "You called Hiley an asshole."

❧

With his light out and his good hand on the tapes in his pocket, he locked himself in the truck. The key trembled into the ignition, which he cranked twice before he could let go. Peering beyond the reach of the high beams, he thought he saw Gerald skulking between cedars. "All yours now," Cyrus said, and he fishtailed along in first gear until he reached a gravel road. Steering and shifting was labor enough for him to break out in a sweat, but he kept patting at his pocket, making certain he still had the tapes; there, he would find her voice.

He parked on an overgrown farm lane west of Dooley, and by the dome light tried to determine the damage done to his shoulder. His shirt collar was sticky with blood, the jacket shredded at the neck, but the wound itself was small, just enough to shake off his stupor and roust him to action, the pain dulling into nothing more than another inconvenience as he carted the guitar through the woods to the cave and shoved the stone from the hole.

Deep in the limestone chamber, he studied the stacks of coffee cans overflowing with quarters. He noted again the rusted flora on the bank, carved creatures in damp nooks, and the flowers hauled off graves, he figured, as memorial. Cyrus uncased the guitar and knelt by the remains for so long he lost sight of them, then he began to tune. "I kept at it," he said. His voice sounded thin to him in this hole; it could shatter at the next word. "It ain't mine. I'm sorry, but I'm done. You take it." He set the guitar in its case and stared until the belly of the instrument grew hazy, the curved outline of purfling indistinct. When from across the way a spirit came rising out of the waters, vaporous and fleeting and not of this world, Cyrus swiped his sleeve at his damp eyes to see a woman wrapped in a blanket, her shorn hair like frost. "Saro," he said, but she scanned the cans and coins, then fixed her eyes on the altar.

"Your handiwork?"

"My sister."

Randy lit a lantern, and greenish light swelled in the chamber.

"His doing?"

"He wouldn't hurt a fly on a biscuit. He wouldn't mean to, anyway."

"Most people don't mean to. He pulled a knife on me when I met him."

"A barlow? Did you think he'd whittle you to death?"

"Ain't you smart," she said.

Cyrus steadied himself on the edge of the case. "I'm just dead and too dumb to fall over."

"You say so. What's that there?"

"Kitty. My sister painted her."

"Busking," the woman said. "You got any money?"

"No. We wanted it, though—so we could get away. She did. I didn't. I've been wishing maybe you were her."

"That doesn't sound like your best idea." She drew from under her blanket a pistol—blue steel, .38 caliber, a walnut grip—and waved it at the guitar. "That worth anything?"

Shifting lamplight altered the fine bones of her face into shadowed clefts and hard angles. She bore no resemblance to his memory of Saro, and for this he pitied her; then pity turned to blame. The woman peered down at him as if he were snagged under swift currents and she knew better than to reach out. "Used to be," he said.

"You got a car?"

"Yeah. On the side of the road. In Nebraska."

"Give me your coat."

"Is that a whip?"

"My boyfriend won it. The day before I tried to kill him."

"Bad deal."

"He took something of mine. Now, give me your coat."

Cyrus tried to wrest his arm from the sleeve. "See. I don't know your story. You killed four boys. What else? Where you headed? Where do you begin, and where do you end?"

She snatched the coat and told Randy to start gathering coins.

"He can't hear you. He reads lips some. He might get your drift if you shout."

"So that boy *is* deaf."

"He ain't a boy. He's my age."

She picked up a can, gesturing for Randy to do the same. "What's wrong with your neck?"

"I stuck it where I shouldn't have."

"That can get to be a habit." She eyed the wilted bouquets, the bones. "My story's the same as anybody's. Yours." She glanced at Randy, who was cradling cans, a duffel, and the lantern. "His." She pointed the pistol at the ceiling, then leveled it at Cyrus's head. "And every other sorry ass you run across. I lost something. I want it back." She thumbed the hammer until it clicked. "But what's the odds we get what we want?"

"In a story? A song? We get what's coming."

"That's life," she said, and she pulled the trigger.

"Gets damp underground," Cyrus said. "You got to keep your powder dry."

"Maybe that's the empty chamber. Maybe now you can go sing how merciful I am."

"That's right," Cyrus said, but already she was pushing Randy ahead of her into the passage. Already she was gone. He had neglected to ask her name.

Against her better judgment she let him lead her over rain-slick deadfall, white cattle stirring from the brush and scattering as she and Randy crossed a cropped pasture to a brick ranch house, smoke drifting down from the chimney. An efficient home of modest means, the residents sensible yet sympathetic. But when Margaret heard a car idling at the end of the driveway, she made Randy kill the light and take the coins, then pointed him into the woods.

A Ford Galaxie was parked crooked in the road, headlights on and wipers squawking. Randy came stumbling to her from across the ditch, spilling coins, and she told him to get in. A white-haired old man dozed over the wheel. Drawing the pistol, she tried to drag him out one-handed by his collar, but he was a long, strong bulk, and he grabbed at her shoulders as if to climb her. She loosed her bile-curdling cat's cry, stopping him just long enough for her to swing the pistol at his head and knock him to the gravel. When high beams from an oncoming truck caught her, she loosed her cry once more and got in the car.

"Get me somewhere," she said.

Randy pointed her down old farm roads, some so washed out she all but had to stop, others so narrow that scrub screeched against the fenders. Radio towers flashed to the north, igniting low clouds.

When they hit highway, he shrugged, so she opted to head for the lights, keeping the car just below posted limits as they crept through towns where, always, one cruiser idled along brick storefronts. Randy began to whine. "Hush," she said. He scooted next to her, resting his head on her shoulder. He was warm and small, and she could not bear to push him away, but when he rested his hand on her thigh, she leaned forward and dug in a coat pocket—a trick to back him off. She found a large bottle of pills and some muddy cassettes. After she popped a tape into the player, though, he settled back in beside her.

From the speakers an old man said, "Do it how you want. I do it slow."

"Let's just try it this way," a girl said.

A chair honked. A boy spoke: "I'm not running through the intro again. I got it down."

"Start where we quit," said the girl, then she counted off. Guitar and fiddle began. The boy and girl traded lines, singing how when the ransomed got home to a land fair and—

"It's too fast," the boy said.

The girl counted off again. The blending voices made Margaret think of tin trucks rusting in muddy yards and rose petals pressed between pages of a Bible; guttering candles, muffled laughter, yellowed postcards of gristmills on a dusty floor. She could barely stand to listen. Then the fiddle faltered. There were footsteps; a door slammed. "Christ," the boy said.

"Every woman's wrong until she cries," the old man said. "Then she's right."

Randy rested his head on Margaret's shoulder once more. Ahead, I-70 appeared, and she pulled to the ditch beneath the overpass. "OK," she said. "Get out."

He lifted his head, and she took him by the shoulders so they were face-to-face. "You got to get out now. Look, I know your kind—and this ain't your story. I'm just some bad luck you come into." She pressed a twenty into his palm and gestured him off the seat. Whimpering, he slid away and out to the ditch. "It don't cover the coins, I know. It's just I got farther to go. I'm sorry," she said, then she slammed the door and locked it. Still, he stood peering in the window, hands pressed to the glass. "No," she shouted, then pointed southeast, from where they'd come. "That's your way." She threw the Galaxie into gear and pressed the pedal, but he gave chase, screaming and flapping his arms. *His kind,* Margaret thought, wiping her eyes with the heel of her hand. He was her kind. His story was hers. He went where he could, how he could. She wrenched the rearview mirror from her line of sight and turned onto the westbound ramp.

Cyrus pushed the stone into place and covered it with cedar boughs. Loman's tapes and his mother's pills were gone, the guitar left behind in the chamber, but he had a few clothes, a fiddle, and a run-down pickup that could get him somewhere down the road. His shoulder throbbed as he pulled from the farm lane, and he had trouble downshifting when he came upon Mack Reaves's Galaxie, its high beams angling across a field of white Charolais. When Cyrus drew near, he saw the woman beside the car. She lifted her face to the falling rain and cried out, a sound to crack plaster and bust laths, and not until she had pulled away did he step from the cab, watching the taillights blink at the next hill and vanish.

Mack lay facedown in rising ditchwater, his left eye swollen, rain washing clean a sickle-shaped cut across his cheek. Wrestling him over his good shoulder, Cyrus staggered under the weight, dumped him on the seat of the truck, and drove him home. Behind curtains a lamp glowed as if someone were waiting up, and the front door was unlocked. Beer cans littered the floor. In the kitchen a TV played the brassy theme from a cop show rerun while Cyrus laid Mack on a braided rug. The old man began to babble at shadows cast from worn furniture and bric-a-brac—dewy figurines, embroidered pillows, framed photographs of Mack and Delphi in which, even early on, they seemed mismatched. Young Delphi had dark eyes ready for a joke, high cheekbones, and swept brown hair, but old Mack with his heavy slouch and hair gone white kept his gaze fixed beyond the camera. In later photos their ages converged, though, and their mien said, *Love? I don't know why I ever cared.*

Cyrus spread an afghan over him. A siren sounded from the kitchen TV. Someday Mack's death would render each object in the house meaningless: the chubby boy tooting a fife, the cuckoo clock that said the time was always 3:17, the milk-glass ashtrays. For years, Cyrus had feared the aftermath of grief. Now here he was, watching a thin hook of blood hardening on a weathered face. A body responded to trauma and healed itself. He fetched a beer from the refrigerator and held it to Mack's cheek. A long night was coming, and a short life. He tucked a pillow under the old man's head.

⚮

Waking to a broth-colored light, he struggled to sit up. There seemed to be something wrong with his shoulder. Two birds flashed across the sun and dipped toward the Wakoda County courthouse, but when he tried to track them, the chrome strip in the center of the truck hood glinted, and he shaded his eyes.

The street was empty. The courthouse dwarfed a statue of a doughboy, his back to the western front. No Civil War figure here: Few residents could have afforded a slave, and the square itself had been cobbled together by those opting to commemorate a carnage closer to their hearts. Now every last one had fled as shadows.

"'*He* fleeth,'" Cyrus said, but he could not recall the entire passage. A tree continues after it's felled, its root pursuing a scent of water, but rivers dry up, and seas, and a man lies down and dies. Then there came a question: "'If a man die, shall he live again?'" What was the answer?

Taking the fiddle case by the handle, Cyrus crossed the square to the pawnshop, but the door was locked. In the window rifles were arranged by barrel length—bolt-action Remingtons, Savage 99s, .22 Magnums, and a replica of a Winchester Model 94, the Gun That Won the West. On a remnant of shag carpet lay handguns—grips to the center, barrels like sun rays—and at the center of them all was a nickel-plated .44 with imitation stag grips, the weapon one Frankie Lee had drawn from under a silk kimono after catching her pimp, Albert, in flagrante delicto. The black L-5 dangled like strange fruit above the weaponry.

A long shadow crossed him, and he turned to see the hog-eyed man step to the corner, a brown-bagged bottle under his arm. Cyrus shut his eyes and opened them to birds flitting over the street and bursting into the expanse. *American Bandstand* flashed on across a row of televisions in the pawn. "C'mon," he said, and he knocked until the bolt of the door clicked. Inside, a bearded man in a cowboy hat and tie-dyed T-shirt pinched a lit cigarette off the counter.

Cyrus opened the fiddle case between them. "What can I get for it?"

The cowboy jabbed his thumb at the wall. Seven fiddles dangled like fish on a stringer. On the televisions Dick Clark stuck his mike at a peroxided singer.

"It's a good fiddle."

"Only ones buy fiddles is city women. Put them on their mantels. Embellish a country decor. They read about it in the magazines."

The bottle-blond imp windmilled his arm at an unplugged Telecaster. He insisted his heart went *bang-bang-bang* when he saw his sweet little *thang-thang-thang*.

"Look," Cyrus said. He steadied his hands to rosin the bow, then got the chin rest to his shoulder, but the pain was too much. He slid the fiddle to his chest, managing a few bars of "Pig Ankle Blues" until he had to stop.

"You do it better justice than them old ladies," the cowboy said.

"This is worth more than that cracked Gibson in the window there."

The cowboy set down his cigarette. "Let's see. Detail work's a little vague. Purfling's good and clean, though."

Cyrus clipped the bow in its case. "I didn't call it a Stradivarius. I said it's a good fiddle."

"Rib's been repaired," the cowboy said.

"My grandfather drank. He dropped it."

"Heirlooms." The cowboy shook his head, but began flipping through a compendium of antique catalogs. "There was maybe some sort of sticker inside? It fall out?"

"It's a good century old."

Smoke curled from under the felt brim of the man's hat. "This says either a Kraut, or else maybe a gook fiddle."

"Well," Cyrus said, "gooks like fiddle."

"Two dollars is what it might have went for in the Monkey Ward's."

"In eighteen-ninety," Cyrus said. "It's worth nigh on two thousand now. That fingerboard's ebony. That's a clean scroll."

"All the more reason I can't sell it. I tell you, guitarists these days are thicker than fiddlers in hell. Somebody'll come in and buy that L-5. I myself would be more than happy to give it to you for two thousand."

"I knew the man owned that guitar."

"Well."

Blue haze began to creep along the ceiling, shrouding the pulsing TVs where boys in baggy pants monkey-jumped across platforms and girls writhed as if caught up in some primitive ritual. Clutching the case to his chest, Cyrus quit the shop and stepped into the square.

Long cars slid past as if on tracks, their passengers giving Cyrus the eye. Outside a boarded-up window, a little girl clutching a red rose pointed in his direction; the man beside her was hooked to an oxygen tank and paring his fingernails with a short knife; he paid no mind. *Move,* Cyrus thought, then a horn blared and the grille of a Buick grinned. Cyrus realized he was sitting cross-legged in the street. Over by the doughboy, the hog-eyed man tipped back his derby with the bottle.

"That's his," someone said.

The fiddle case dropped in his lap. Black birds were coagulating in the sky over the railroad tracks, their song an atonal fury he did not recognize.

Somewhere between Kansas City and Omaha, Margaret pulled off at a motel across the highway from an expanse of swift water. She turned off the engine but leaned on the wheel awhile, trying to make sense of a muddy-looking line on the front of the building and the dingy white planks below it.

A bell rang when she stepped into the lobby; a laugh track blared from a back room. Sidestepping a TV tray, an old man came out to meet her, his mouth still working at his supper. She set the coins on the counter and asked for a single room.

"I ain't got the magic-finger beds. If that's what them quarters're for."

Margaret said the quarters were how she wanted to pay.

He put his hand to his liver-spotted head. "I can use them for the boats, I guess."

"I'm sorry?"

He set a form and pen on the counter. "Casino boats. They're all the rage. From the looks of it, I can waste quarters until the boats ain't all the rage no more."

"I haven't counted it."

"It'll give me something different to do tonight. We can settle up come morning."

She pushed the form to him, and he examined it at arm's length.

"Well, Miss Margaret Bowman," he said, handing her a key, "you have you a pleasant sleep."

Before he could shuffle back to his TV show, she asked about the muddy line on the front of the building.

"That? That's where the river got to. Not something I wanted to wade through, but I did. Your room's clean; I just ain't got around to painting outside."

Margaret jiggled the key.

"Hundred-year floodplain. Unless you plan on sticking around another century or so you got nothing to worry about. At least that's what they told me."

Her room smelled of ammonia and new carpet. She emptied out the coat pockets on the desk and found a letter, which she had to read twice before she realized it was meant for that fool in the cave. He had been remembered well by some officious sort out west; good fortune was his for the taking. Who would listen? She tore the page in two and set the blank half beside the motel pen.

After a shower, she put on her ruined dress, took a seat, and addressed the page:

> *Dear Maddie,*
>
> *I expect once things get set wrong, you can't get them back right. I am sorry for that.*
>
> *I saw you this evening. I climbed up in that empty house across the street and watched for you. Somebody's working on it, fixing it up nice, starting fresh. I don't know why I expected different, but houses in your neighborhood are big and pretty, like dolls could stay there, and your grandparents' house has curved roofs, a round tower, and an iron fence to keep in the marigolds. I dreamed of houses like that when I was a girl. You had you ghosty*

sheets in a tree and jack-o'-lanterns on the porch rail. I lost track of time. I judged wrong your place.

All day I waited. What was one more day? At dusk, a woman in a ball cap and ponytail brought a werewolf, a clown, and a rabbit to your porch. Your granddaddy came to the door in a tie—he had a big bowl of candy, and you stepped from behind him. You were a princess in pink cheesecloth and blue satin shoes. The girl I knew is gone from me. The werewolf took you by the hand, and you smiled. I am not sorry for what it took, or for what all I took to see you. Some things you lose can for a while make you happy.

When you came back up the other side of the street, I was out on the walk. I said hello, but it was the mother that was with you said hello back. I wanted to touch you, you were that close. Maybe you saw me but did not know what you were seeing. Why would you want to? There cannot be a mother on earth wants her child unhappy. If so, I guess she is not much of a mother. But what is it I am? Not your burden, but someday you can answer what it is you are. I say—a beautiful thing. It is hard to believe I made you.

I have a wooden dinosaur and a doll that looks like me, and these are for you. A boy made them. You remember this, even though I have said it before, and even though it does us no good now. I love you.

> *Your mother,*
> *Maggie Bowman*

Margaret weighted down the page with the effigy of herself. Her likeness stood unmoved. Scar curved in a knowing grin. Breasts heavy, belly slack, thighs braided with muscle. But its stance was delicate, mincing. She knew it to be mocking her.

Stepping outside, she looked across the highway. Up a weedy berm lay the train rails, moonlight glinting on worn steel. The old man was shaking a rug in the lilac-tinted light that shone from the lobby.

"Always something else to do, ain't there?" he said.

"Yes."

"A blessing." He dropped the rug by the door and snatched a broom from the wall. "A curse." Gusts stirred the branches of cottonwoods along the river, their winter tags rattling, and a dry leaf tumbled past the old man. He batted at it with the broom. "Missouri River," he said, turning to the banks. "It don't get the credit it deserves."

"Pardon me?"

"Mississippi this, Mississippi that. It's the Mississippi runs into the Missouri, not vice versa, and that makes for nigh on four thousand miles of fast water. Third longest river in the world. Take what I say, you got a good quarter of U.S. runs down that channel, chunk of Canada too." He stepped off the walk and started sweeping. "What a mess."

The flood line along the motel wall came to the old man's chest. Sand, milky silts, slick glacial stones, dead dogs, fish heads, bottle caps, television tubes, rusted fifty-five-gallon drums, and bodies thoughtlessly interred—the lost and long gone came together here, then tumbled past. "Maps got it all wrong, huh?" Margaret said.

He tossed a paper cup into a mop bucket by the door. "Depends who makes the maps. Trace the source. Forge passage. Try to tame the thing." He picked up a coin and put it in his pocket. "Dam it, wing-dike it, levee it. It overruns. They go to map it, it shifts. Once upon a time it could take a whole town out in the night, leave Main Street on a snag or down a chute. Still can. There's limitations to what you do. And what you know." Head down, the old man seemed intent on sweeping the entire reach of asphalt, until a train engine blasted its horn twice and drew his gaze north down the main line. "True story," he said. "One night this old boy comes through with a crew, says he's following the river. I ask what for, and he says—without cracking a smile, mind you—'I write books.' Like that's an answer. So I says, 'Ain't that something. You know, I read books.'"

The southbound's headlamp swelled and shimmered like a dying star. Margaret looked down the line to where a signal glowed green, and beyond it, waiting off the block, a northbound engine thrummed.

"Oh, I might watch a show or two," he said. "But come witching hour there ain't much to do but read, so I can tell you this for true— that old boy didn't learn much worth putting between covers. You can't follow that river, not so to know it. Forty-odd tributaries from here on up, crooked creeks, dribs and drabs. You'll get to where you never know how to go."

He was working in circles, broomstraw hushing the dirt in closer and closer to some point he had in mind.

"You know a lot," Margaret said. "About this river at least."

"Well. It comes for you in the night, you tend to think on it some."

The southbound rumbled past, blocking her view of shifting currents. Coal cars loaded with ancient compressed matter scraped off the skin of earth and shipped east so homes would stay well lit and warm all winter long.

"That Clark," the old man said. "That Lewis. They followed it. Mapped it. Saw the end of civilization, and the beginning, and neither one could tell you which was which. 'Ocian in view! O! The joy.' That's what Clark wrote when they got to where they were going. Then they turned tail and came back. Lewis tried to shoot out his heart, had to settle for his head. Books say he killed himself, but books can't tell you why."

"My father killed himself out west," Margaret said. "El Segundo." Coal car, coal car. She tried counting them, but the old man peering over his broom handle distracted her.

"I guess joy's where all you find it," he said.

"My mother headed up the coast. Portland. Seattle. She tailed what men would have her."

Coal car. Coal car. The old man mounded up dirt with the broom. "I got a daughter," he said. "Calls on Christmas, every birthday. And that is more than I deserve."

The shivering river appeared again. Down the line the northbound sounded its horn, and the signal went red.

"So. That what you gonna do? Tail the river? Find your joy? Go see your mama while you're at it?" Twice the old man stepped around what he'd made, then, angling the broom, he swatted the dust to the wind, spinning it into devils that wasted away into the darkness. The lobby door swung shut behind him.

Margaret jumped when the horn blasted again. Onto open line crept the engine, its headlamp steady. Soon it would reach her. Soon it would pass. "Not tonight," she said.

C yrus set the fiddle case on the bar and held tight to the handle.
Above the long mirror three moth-trap fixtures illuminated
a flat-faced goon and a veiny fellow in a Dekalb feed cap. A
woman was giving them the what for. Stuffed into a blue sequined
dress, she leaned over her drink, her long dark hair hiding her
face.

On the corner jukebox, a man said, *There goes my only pos-
session.*

"Pretty Boy Floyd," Flat-Face said.

"Baby Face Nelson," said the plowboy.

They cracked themselves up.

There goes my reason for living, said the man on the jukebox.

The woman peered through the dim to get the joke. Grinning,
she aimed a shimmy at Cyrus, her dress flashing like a fish. It occurred to him she was very fat.

"OK, chief," the waitress said. "You gonna play us a pretty song
or what?"

The case seemed to be sliding away from Cyrus.

There goes my everything, said the jukebox man.

"So what is it you need, chief?"

"There's a question," Cyrus said.

Before rows of sulfurous yellow bottles, a red-haired man was wringing his hands in an apron. "He doesn't know what he wants yet," the waitress said, and she vanished.

A napkin fluttered down beside the case, and a bourbon on the rocks was set square in the middle of it. The bartender shook his head.

"Where you been?" the mermaid said, jabbing her finger toward Cyrus. "You said you'd keep me somewheres safe because I'm so pretty." She hefted her thick leg, pointing to a calf-high make of hook-and-eye footwear only a granny could love. "You complimented my shoes." Cyrus looked into the glass. The liquor was the color of gravel shallows in which he might drown.

"What?"

Then the two men were standing on either side of him.

"I've never seen that woman before in my life."

"Buddy," said the plowboy. "We don't mind talking, but shouting's another thing entirely."

"Is this your library?"

"OK, buddy."

There goes my reason for living, said the man in the jukebox.

"Does he not know another song?"

"They rigged the box," the mermaid said, "to get even with Red for not having nothing but old music."

"That song's not old," Cyrus said.

Red appeared from the darkness, stretching a bar towel into a garrote.

"It doesn't bother Red, though. Does it, Red?"

Red made the towel go *snap.*

"C'mon, Red. C'mon, boys. You don't kick a strange dog."

The two grabbed Cyrus by his arms. "The guitar," he said.

"Buddy, that's a fiddle."

"That's right," Cyrus said, but he was standing on a dark sidewalk, hugging the case to his chest. Small creatures gathered under

lamplight. A scissortail hulk of yellow feathers hopped past a headless soldier who scratched a scabbard at the concrete, daring Cyrus
to cross the line.

Down the street were skeletal wraiths, mouths bloodied, Wal-Mart
bags swollen and disfigured. Shadows shifted under ragged awnings,
so he stuck to the curbside until he reached the square, where dimin-
ished fifths and ninths pulsed and a palm slapped hambone on a
sill. From an upper-story window drifted a girl's voice: "Oh, she looked
so fair in the midnight air . . ."

Cyrus fumbled for his keys and eased the truck through hordes
of children flowing by. At the corner leading out of town the hog-
eyed man leaned against a stop sign, and as Cyrus drove past, he
tipped his derby and jigged once around the post. Stretching out his
arms à la Jolson, he began to sing.

The steep hills and bare ridges would soon give way to easy grids
of farm and town. Snapping on the radio, Cyrus dialed in bursts of
chatter advertising diet pills that changed lives and sports news that
was revolutionary. What songs he caught extolled lost love and
found life, but never death itself. Radio had gotten us beyond that.
Then a country-fried guitarist started in on a bent string and feedback harangue that wormed its way into an orgiastic fade-out, a
cliché of rock music that signified the player knew no good way out
of the song. Then the radio said, "Cyrus? Cyrus Harper? You on
my waves, man?" Beyond the railroad berm west of Apogee flickered radio towers. It occurred to him that Newbern had hijacked a
station.

"Yes."

"Ah, man, I *know* you're on the waves. You drifting along to the
corporate playlist of yet another clean, clear channel, where it is all
classic rock, all the motherfucking time.

"So, tell the Newbern. You hear things? You see things? You live
life in the dark you bound to bump into strange rooms. Now, those

men in the little hats? Half their notions come straight off the Chau-
tauqua circuit. Knowledge like that is syphilis—you pick it up, it
goes to your head, it blinds you. Then what you gonna do?

"What you gonna do is listen up. You fill a hole to make a whole.
I mean, look at the nature of human nature. It's in those fiddle tunes
you got: 'Belly to Belly,' 'Big Ass Rag,' 'Big Prick Coming to Town,'
'Frigging on the Floor,' 'Fucking in the Kitchen'—you catch my
drift?—'Josie Shuck Her Panties Down,' 'Keep Your Pecker Clean,'
'Mama Don't 'Low No Diddlin' Here.' That list plows right on
down the alphabet. So what is it on the fiddler's mind? The singer's?
The dancer's?"

"Don't ask me," Cyrus said.

"Ah, man, that's the procreative urge. Nothing shameful in it.
Makers make, and everybody want to make their image over and
over again. But what we make? The easy mind says death, but boo-
fucking-hoo on you, because all we make is less and less of us and
more and more of something else. Oh, it's watered down, but less is
more, and more is less, more or less. That's why a poor boy sad to
see his act come to a grinding halt. Shit. That's why you so sad.

"Uh-oh. Mr. Station Bossman got his greasy hands flat on the
glass. Thinks I need to get back on that prescribed playlist, which is
oh so good for what ails you. You betcha, boss. You betcha.

"But, Cyrus, take your good buddy, Loman. Mr. Kirby. You
shocked? They ain't a musician around here don't know his name.
They ain't a black man did not know his daddy. You ever wonder
where Loman picked up his strange strains? I was just two when a
tractor flipped over on my daddy, but Granddaddy, he took up
slack, and it was old Loman's daddy hired him for odd jobs—paint
a barn, weld a hitch, you know, just enough to keep a body living.

"Now, my granddaddy would take my daddy Herbert and
Loman himself when they was just striplings out to the north flats
and let them come with him into the Good Lord Saloon. Bar on the

first floor, gambling on the second, and sporting, so to speak, on the third. One colored boy. One white. Scandalous. That place was jumpin' with colored fiddlers and piano players.

"Now, you go add this to that. Loman's daddy used to play fiddle. Picnics, mostly. Fiddled for an old mule-pulled merry-go-round while a friend of his played straws. Later, he'd let a bunch of Osage that never got no oil and come up looking for work every year camp on his land, and, lo and behold, even those Injuns knew a fiddle tune or two. They'd play, and Loman's daddy'd play, and Loman heard. Breakdowns, schottisches, jigs, hornpipes, old rags floating across that big-ass river. Redskin, blackskin, whiteskin—they might bang drums different, but they all saw off a chunk of song.

"But let's be real. Most old-time fiddlers didn't know squat. Maybe 'Chinky Pin,' 'Durang's Hornpipe,' 'Arkansas Traveler,' 'Girl I Left Behind Me.' Toss in a call or two, you got a dance. People back then just dying for entertainment. But you? You got you a mess. And what you gonna do? Limp around and say, 'And am I born to die?' You bet your punkin' seed ass, you are. And what you know about that?"

The signal fluttered and the road stretched out, a yellow double line breaking apart. The half tank of gas might get him to Kansas City. "All I care to," Cyrus said.

"Nothing," Newbern said. "Nothing is right. Half of me is alive, and the other half's been incinerated. Newbern smoke rose to give the ozone hole a poke. Ha. So let me tell you about death if you so hot for it. You gonna step into a room of light? Wear a crown of gold? Say hideeho to Mama and Papa and sister Saro, wherever it is you think she may be? Get you a home in Beulah land outshines the sun? You know what I seen when Death come for me and I went flying through the plate glass of that car dealership? I seen the very clean underside of a Mercury Topaz—tailpipe, muffler, oil pan. You expect profundity and permanence? Sweetness and light?

Permanence is over the waves, man, and you just bob-bob-bobbing along."

"Over the waves," Cyrus said.

"Yeah. You catch my drift."

"Over the Waves." A waltz popular even into the 1970s and common at contests. People thought Strauss had written it, but it was penned by a pureblood Otomi Indian named Juventino Rosas. A boy, he'd played fiddle in his father's string band in Mexico City, busking for pesos. When Rosas's brother, the band's guitarist, was killed in a lovers' quarrel, Rosas got a job as a bell ringer in a church. At age fifteen he was first violinist in a touring opera—not much call for that in the villages of Central Mexico. He joined the army as a bandsman but quit to try composing. He wrote waltzes, including "Sobres las Olas." Mexican orchestras picked it up. It got the senoritas on the dance floor. But, hoping to forget the demise of a lousy love affair, Rosas joined up with a zarzuela company sailing for Havana, and with them he mastered folk opera and minstrel. Happy tunes. Then he died of a fever at twenty-six.

Somehow New Orleans jazzmen and country fiddlers picked up the tune. Henry Ford's Old Time Dance Orchestra. Bill Boyd and His Cowboy Ramblers. Jimmy Wilson's Catfish Band. Bob Wills. Somebody tacked words to it—a hit for Mario Lanza in 1951. No one knew how it slipped from Mexico into mountain fiddles. The song was a virus.

"The waves," Newbern said, "go on. Tune them in on some old Atwater Kent in the parlor of your long dark house. You turn that bone knob, Cyrus. It's cold, but it'll warm to your touch." Newbern began to laugh, and the signal ceased as if stifled by a tunnel. For a while there was only static. Then from a public radio affiliate came a requiem by Paganini.

Beyond the reach of headlights a flat horizon was broken by fence line stands of Osage orange. Celestial bodies lay low and thick, and sliding down among them was a shooting star, particulate matter no bigger than a grain of sand, its light the violent energy created when it met the atmosphere and burned into nothing.

☙

Cyrus hit Kansas City three hours before midnight. He passed cut-rate hotels, offices where bail bondsmen hunched over gunmetal desks, and a department store window in which mannequins in tweeds and woolens sulked on plastic blocks of ice. Crossing Twelfth, he thought to check out Vine and wait for some baby and a bottle of wine, as Leiber and Stoller had recommended, but by the look of the boarded-up buildings, the fate of this place was the same as that of any other middle-American city. A celebrated corner would likely be nothing but a weedy lot of brown glass and bullet casings.

He turned west, paralleling railroad tracks. On a hill to his left rose a column of stone, and below it hulked the abandoned behemoth of Union Station. The town was a last stop for wandering musicians. Fats Waller died in a Pullman of the Santa Fe Chief five minutes after arriving from Los Angeles. Patsy Cline went down in a plane crash with Hawkshaw Hawkins, Cowboy Copas, and Randy Hughes on their way back to Nashville after a benefit performance. At the end of a week's worth of concerts, Ira Louvin and his new wife got 150 miles east before they perished in a head-on collision.

One little ditty, though, departed from the old, inevitable fate. A bandleader named Bergantine had penned a tune that sat in the desk drawer of one Louis Blasco at Jenkins Music on Walnut Street. After Blasco pressed his wife, a colleague who dabbled in comic poems, to try her hand at song lyrics, Betty Peterson put some words to the Bergantine piece, calling it "My Happiness." Jon and Sondra Steele recorded it in 1948; it sold a cool two million. Five years later, a truck driver walked into the Memphis Recording Service at Sun

Studio and paid $3.98 to tape himself singing the song, a gift for his mama. My, my.

Down a side street running toward the tracks, a few brick warehouses had been converted into art galleries. A crowd had gathered outside one, so Cyrus parked at the curb and rolled down the window. A sheet banner was stretched above two men singing from the bed of a pickup—THE KEMPS, it said. One was giving a Martin hell, while both in raucous harmony asked the crowd, "How long has that evening train been gone?" Two women in broom skirts were dancing among sideburned art types who slouched in monochromatic clusters beside a keg on the sidewalk. There were flannel shirts and leather pants, ties and chinos. A few revelers wore sequined eye masks or latex grotesquery—fanged, popeyed, bloodied.

Tucking the fiddle case under his arm, Cyrus stepped from the truck, but at the edge of the audience, he stopped short. Beyond a high chain-link fence was a crumbling freight house where hog-eyed men sat waiting in a line.

The guitarist lifted a painted pickle jar. "Folks," he said, "this here's Kitty, and she's awful hungry, and, Lord, when she gets hungry, she gets sullen and silent." Then the two men ripped into the most common question sung in old American music: "Who's gonna shoe your pretty little feet?" They followed with a jugband tune, a graveyard song, a shape-note hymn. The guitarist was a middling flat-picker with gentle sass in his voice, his partner a fair-haired tenor who sloshed a cup of beer in one hand and with the other slapped juba on the pocket of his seersucker pants. Their musicianship was ragged, a frayed remnant of an American past where drinking and death, God and gore, cocaine and cohabitation, murder, mayhem, and malice were the norm. It was not so different from the American present. A girl handed Cyrus a beer just as the guitarist announced a short break.

He swung the fiddle case onto the tailgate. "You all for real?"

The two smiled with polite Midwestern caution. "We're just playing around," the guitarist said. "I mean, I paint. We're old art students."

"I work in a bank," the tenor said.

"Mind if I sit in?"

The tenor jingled pocket change. "I was gonna get another beer."

"Here. Have mine. I ain't touched it."

"We've just done this once at a party," the guitarist said, and he pulled Cyrus up off the street. "But we were pretty drunk."

Cyrus introduced himself, then lifted the fiddle from its case. "You both Kemps?"

Neither of them was. They'd abbreviated the name of a wealthy banker in town, one mule-toothed patron of the arts, and taken it as theirs.

"Ladies and gentlemen," the guitarist said. "We got us a change in plans. Please welcome, live to our truck, Cyrus Harper."

The hog-eyed man edged along the crowd, his derby tipped back on his head. The others were crowding the chain-link fence like refugees. Someone whistled. Cyrus could not quite get the fiddle to his shoulder.

"Just do what you do," he said, letting the box slip to his ribs. "I'll find my way."

The two dug into an arrangement of "Will You Miss Me When I'm Gone," a tune lifted by A. P. Carter from the Reverend George Beebee and H. E. McAfee. Drawing out the chorus, the singers tugged the *will* and the *you* on a long thread of sound, insisting on *miss me, miss me, miss me, miss me* until the song begged for an answer. Cyrus could saw off a melody or harmony easy, but he beat time on his calf with the bow, letting his silence last. After this, maybe he would ask the guitarist to strum up a circle of fifths, then Cyrus could wring out a rag hauled up from currents of the Mississippi and carted over to Sedalia on the Katy. If he could not call forth the entire tune or title, he'd make something up.

Still there was the question of the song. And the hog-eyed man lurking in shadows along Baltimore Street dared him to address it. Cyrus set the bow to the strings. Over the patched roof of the freight house, stars were dimmed by the city. He listened. He waited for a good place to come in.

Mama, you say the past ain't nothing but a pail of ash, but Mama? My heart hurts from what I say by now has passed. And gone.

Acknowledgments

Thank you—

For kicks in the pants, slaps upside the head, pats on the back, and/or all-around editorial push-and-shove:

Erin McGraw, Margot Livesey, Claire Messud, Padgett Powell, Kerry Madden, Tim O'Brien, Elwood Reid, Alice McDermott, Francine Prose, Leah Stewart, Greg Williamson, Daniel Anderson, Paul Harris Boardman, Andrew Hudgins, William Gay, Kevin Wilson

For the recommendation that I "try faith" after I threw my type-writer into a panel door of my rental house: Barry Hannah

For my deposit in full: University of the South Rental Housing

For a free desk with a view, cold drinks, warm conversation, and full-time employment: Wyatt Prunty

For a cheap room, a borrowed dog, mechanical advice, three chords, and brotherly love: Mark Stephens

For unconditional belief and support: Carl and Judy Stephens

For wisdom, clarity, open-mindedness, a light touch, and a cool hand: Liz Van Hoose

For kindness, hustle, smarts, a gambler's heart, and a penchant for the ghosty: Michelle Brower

For missionary zeal, peaceful workdays, and the hand of literary resurrection: Cheri Peters

For open arms, laughter, and friendship:
The staff of the Sewanee Writers' Conference

For love, respect, forbearance, countless first reads, the long haul, and faith: Jennie Hanna

For a change of plans and the blessing of distraction: Walker Stephens, Garrett Stephens